LITHIUM WAVES

A
LITHIUM SPRINGS
NOVEL

CARMEL RHODES

Copyright © 2017 by Carmel Rhodes

ISBN-13: 978-1977791993
ISBN-10: 1977791999

All rights reserved. No part of this publication may be reproduced, distributed, or transmitted in any form or by any means, including photocopying, recording, or other electronic or mechanical methods, without the prior written permission of the publisher, except in the case of brief quotations embodied in critical reviews and certain other noncommercial uses permitted by copyright law.

This is a work of fiction. Names, characters, businesses, places, events and incidents are either the products of the author's imagination or used in a fictitious manner. Any resemblance to actual persons, living or dead, or actual events is purely coincidental.

Proofreading: Shanesmommy
Editing: Kristen- Your Editing Lounge
Cover Design: Designs by Kirsty-Anne Still
Interior Formatting: Champagne Book Design

SHOUT OUTS

To my husband. Thank you for reminding me of my gravity. Also, thank you for dealing with my insanity throughout this process. Thank you for keeping the pantry stocked with hot chips, coffee and pepperoni. Also, thanks for not commenting on the amount of wine (and vodka) I consumed while writing this story. I love you. Always. Forever.

Shanesmommy. Thank you for loving Ryder and Jamie as much as I do. Thank you for knowing them better than I do. I wouldn't have been able to do this without you.

Diana and Kelly. My book pushers. Thank you for keeping it real. Thank you for believing in these characters and for encouraging me always.

Erica and Brittany. Squad. Thank you for keeping me sane and helping me laugh. Thank you for talking me off all the ledges. Thank you for your honesty. Thank you for reading this in every stage, and for understanding the vision.

My Ride or Dies: Jeanette, Helen, Michelle (x2), Niki, Melisa, Alexis, Suzan, Lori, Cindy, Linda, Loretta. (Sorry if I forgot anyone!)—Thank you for reading, giving feedback, supporting.

Boot Camp: Paula, Nikki, and everyone else. Thank you for teaching me how to be a better writer.

The Lithium Army. I wouldn't have had the courage to do any of this without you. It's really kind of amazing to have found my tribe so early on.

Readers. Thank you for taking this journey with me. I promise I won't let you down.

For Rosemary and her babies.

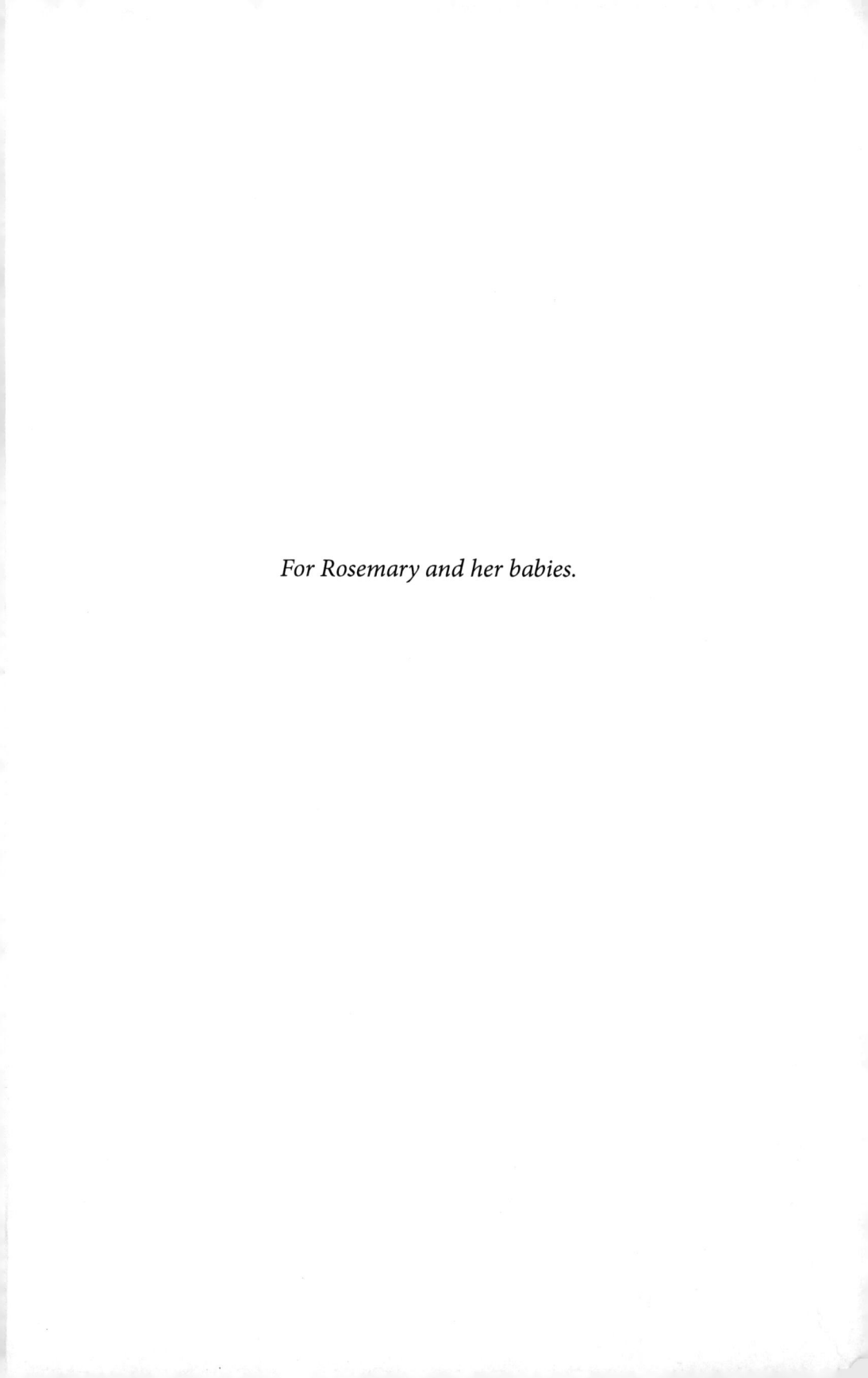

We return to each other in waves.
This is how water loves.
—Nayyirah Waheed

ONE

Lithium

Jamie

Life was suffering; at least that's what the Buddhists believed. It was a philosophy James Michele Manning understood all too well. Jamie spent the first half of her life craving the conditional love of her parents, and the second half rebelling against them.

Nothing she did was good enough, including graduating from the University of Southern California with honors. It didn't matter if she was at the top of her class because, as her father put it, broadcast journalism was a dying art. *"In fifty years when all the baby boomers are gone,"* he'd say, *"no one will look to the television for the news. The internet is the wave of the future."* The internet, where he made his millions.

Well, her father could go fuck himself. Her mother too. She gave up seeking their validation last fall when they abandoned her when she needed them most. Jamie was on a downward spiral. She indulged in the suffering of life, in drinking, in partying, and in casual sex. She relished the numbness alcohol provided, but recently, that life left her unfulfilled.

Party girl Jamie died months ago. Most days, she was happy that girl was gone, but there were days, like today, when she missed it. Then, as fate would have it, Lo called. Lorena Davis was her party friend. They met at a bar the year before and hit it off instantly. She had a front row seat for Jamie's, 'Britney circa 2007', meltdown, but she never judged. So, when Lo asked her to come to the edge of Seattle to see some local band perform, Jamie agreed.

That's how she found herself falling down The Rabbit Hole—literally.

The Rabbit Hole was a dive bar on the outskirts of town. Its claim to fame was a weekly skee-ball tournament, eight-dollar fish bowls, and live music.

Jamie sat at the long oak bar, nursing a cold beer. The only thing on her mind was getting shit-faced, but as usual, Lo was late.

Checking her watch, Jamie sighed, "Fuck it." She wanted to wait for her friend before she started taking shots, but Lo was twenty minutes late and she was bored. Jamie being bored in a bar was a Molotov cocktail of trouble.

She signaled for the bartender; a tall, curvy woman with bright green streaks in her brown hair. Her breasts spilled out of her black tank, and the itty-bitty shorts she wore made her ass look spectacular. Jamie made a mental note to ask her trainer about squats the next time they met.

"Hey," the punk rock Victoria Secret Model greeted, sashaying her way over.

"Is this band any good?" Jamie asked, shamelessly using her arms to press her boobs together. The move, coupled with the low-cut, black bodysuit that was painted on her body, made her small breasts look fuller.

The woman's brown eyes lit up as she leaned over the bar, her tits on full display, "Lithium Springs?"

Jamie nodded to her chest. *Eyes up James,* she scolded herself. Fuck if she knew the name of the band, fuck if she cared. She was only there for the drinks.

"They're amazing."

"There aren't very many people here," Jamie said, glancing over her shoulder at the fourteen or so people milling about.

The hot bartender opened her mouth to speak, only no words came out. Instead, her face turned a bright shade of pink, and her eyes darted over Jamie's left shoulder. "Hey Ry," she whispered in a breathy voice.

A long, tattooed arm brushed up against Jamie's. Honey colored eyes peered down at her. The energy between Jamie and the owner of the arm was electric. The hair on the back of her neck prickled when the man, *Ry*, settled into the space between her and the stool to her left.

He was close, too close, considering they were the only two people sitting at the bar. Too close, considering it had been a month since she'd gotten laid. Too close, considering she was just checking out the woman behind the bar.

Tilting her head, Jamie snuck a better look at the man who smelled like sunshine and sex—her favorite combination. He was gorgeous, tall and lean with wavy, blond hair that fell just above his shoulders. His eyes were hazel, his skin sun-kissed, and most importantly, he was covered in tattoos.

"I thought it wasn't the size of the boat but the motion in the ocean?" he asked. His voice was like hot fudge, slow, thick, and sinfully good. He eyed her, waiting for her to speak. His gaze held so much intensity it caused her cheeks to heat. She was fucking blushing, and James Michele Manning didn't blush.

"That's a lie created and perpetuated by dudes with small dicks," she smirked. Her tongue swept over her top and bottom lip, and Ry's eyes shifted down to her mouth. *Good,* she was desperate to take back control. This man, with his tattoos and steady gaze, unnerved her. Jamie wasn't a damsel in distress and she didn't do vulnerable.

Ry laughed, a deep belly laugh. The sound sent a rush of moisture between her legs. "You're probably right." He chuckled again, ignoring the stool behind him, leaning into her. "What's your name?" His gaze dropped from her lips, down the length of her body, and back up again. He was eye fucking her, and discretion was not in his vocabulary.

"You know," Jamie said, angling away from him, "there are plenty of empty chairs. You don't have to hover over me." His closeness diminished her ability to make rational decisions, and nothing about the way this man made her feel was rational.

"I kinda like hovering over you," he murmured, closing the space she created.

He was trouble. Jamie could see it dancing behind his hazel eyes, and fuck if she didn't want him, but unfortunately, she gave up trouble for lent. "Look, you're hot and everything, but this isn't happening," she waved between them, "so enjoy the show."

Jamie slid her phone out of her back pocket, and fired off a text to Lo.

Jamie: I'm at the bar. Hurry your ass up!!!!!!

"Tiff, babe," the blond hottie called the bartender in a voice that made her thighs clench.

Breathe James, he's just a man. Just skin and bones, breathe.

"What's up Ry?" the woman asked in a voice that made her sound like a baby. Jamie had to fight to keep from rolling her eyes; she never understood why women did that. It was annoying and men couldn't possibly like that shit.

"A shot of fireball for me and one of those fruity, Swedish fish ones for my little, Kitty Cat here."

Tiff nodded, looking from Jamie to the man, then back again. "Sure thing," she murmured, her face awash with disappointment. Jamie wanted the bartender. The bartender wanted Ry. Ry wanted Jamie. They were all screwed.

"Kitty Cat? Do I even want to know?"

He grinned a mischievous grin, one that had her clenching her thighs. "You look like you have a pretty pussy."

Yep, he was trouble.

Jamie was a lot of things, and modest wasn't one of them, but even she had to pick her jaw up off the bar after that. "You are so lame," she huffed incredulously, all but throwing her phone down. "I'm embarrassed for you. There's no way that has *ever* gotten you laid."

"Get your mind out of the gutter, Kitty Cat," he said finally sitting on the damn stool. "I was talking about a pet."

Jamie snorted, narrowing her eyes at him. "Ry, is it?"

"Ryder" he nodded, entirely too pleased with himself.

"Well, Ryder, you're full of shit."

Tiff set their shots on the counter, looking to Ryder expectantly. "Let me know if you guys need anything else."

He nodded but never took his eyes off Jamie. "I'm full of shit?" he asked with a raised brow.

"Yes, filled to the brim."

"Well, Kitty Cat, if you play your cards right, you might have the pleasure of being full of me," he smirked, staring at her denim clad thighs, "and for the record, I bet she's pretty too."

Jamie picked up the whiskey and knocked it back without flinching. "You'll never know." Her voice was surprisingly strong considering the way she felt inside. She wanted him just as badly as he wanted her, but she was going to fight the attraction like hell because she could tell by spending five minutes with him, Ryder had the potential to fuck up her life. Jamie then lifted the Swedish fish shot and gulped it down before hopping off the stool. "Thanks for the drinks."

He grabbed her hand, "At least tell me your name."

"You gotta earn that, Ry," she purred, winking playfully at him.

Jamie did her best to keep her composure. Part of her wanted to fuck him right there on the bar and another wanted to kick him in the nuts. She had slept with plenty of assholes in her time, but never one who made her feel like Ryder. Never one who set her world on fire.

Don't even think about it James.

Lo needed to get there fast before Jamie found herself covered in Ryder's sin.

TWO

Electric

Jamie

Jamie stared at her reflection in the dirty bathroom mirror. Her blonde hair was pulled into a high ponytail, her skin was flushed, and her pupils were so dilated that her emerald green eyes looked black.

The Ryder effect.

The cocky bastard had her hiding out in the ladies' room for the past ten minutes. Old Jamie wasn't the type to duck and run, she confronted things head on. Then again, old Jamie would have been face down and ass up within twenty minutes of meeting a guy like Ryder.

Old Jamie was kind of a mess.

New Jamie, on the other hand, was responsible and career-oriented. She wasn't interested in random hookups at dive bars. That's what she told her reflection anyway, over and over and over again.

Sighing, she considered calling Lo again when the bathroom door burst open and the five-foot-three fire-cracker, sauntered in.

"I'm sorry," Lo said, her high-pitched voice as full of energy as the woman herself. "My dickhead boss wanted me to swing past the office and get some business cards. Can you believe it? Like a bunch of dudes in a punk band are going to keep track of a damn business card." Lo worked as a PA to one of Seattle's top record execs. They were there that night on a scouting mission.

"I can't believe I let you talk me into this," Jamie huffed, rubbing her tattooed finger across her lips. It was her little secret, a white ink semi-colon, a physical reminder to breathe.

"Whatever, party pooper," Lo rolled her eyes. "And why are you hiding out in the ladies' room anyway? I looked for you for ten minutes."

Jamie had no sympathy for Lo. She had waited for her for nearly an hour. "Some dude started hitting on me, so here we are."

"Was he hot?" Lo asked, because of course, what he looked like was really all that mattered.

The women locked arms and headed back out into the main bar and Jamie's anxiety began to wane. With Lo there, she would be less likely to buy whatever it was Ryder was selling.

"I guess, in like a tattooed surfer kind of way."

"Is there any other kind of way?" Lo questioned.

On the hotness scale, tattooed surfer was up there with brooding rock star, but Jamie would never admit it. "I think I'm over random hookups."

"Don't tell me James Manning is looking to settle down?"

Jamie frowned, settling down wasn't something she liked to think about. In her world marriage was a contract, a business arrangement used for the purpose of closing deals and forging new allies. Kensie, her roommate and best friend since diapers, was the only person in their group with parents who actually liked each other. The Roth's were unicorns.

"No," Jamie shook her head, "fuck that. I'm just bored. I need to shake things up, try something new. Maybe switch teams for a while. The bartender was hot."

Lo chuckled, pulling her toward the sounds of a guitar strumming in the main bar. "Hot surfer dude or sexy bartender?"

"I don't know," Jamie whined, "neither."

Both.

"Boring," Lo snoozed. "One night, come out of retirement for one night."

Jamie rolled her head from side to side, mulling over Lo's words. Jamie made so much progress distancing herself from the wild child she used to be, she deserved to have a little fun. She scanned the bar for her surfer, gasping when her eyes swept across the stage. "Holy shit."

"What?"

"That's him," she said, tilting her chin. Ryder stood center stage, a microphone clutched in his hand and a guitar strapped around his shoulders.

"The lead singer of Lithium-fucking-Springs is your surfer?" Lo's voice held a tinge of jealousy, but Jamie was only half listening. Ryder, was both surfer and rock star. The hotness meter was about to explode.

"What's a Lithium Springs?" Jamie mumbled.

Lo snapped two manicured fingers in her friend's face. "The band, James, the one we're here to see? You know for a reporter, you sure don't seem too concerned with details."

Jamie tore her gaze from the stage long enough to flip Lo the middle finger. *This was her fault.*

"You already know Ryder," she yelled over the music. "That's Javi on bass." Javi was equally as handsome as Ryder and his light-brown skin equally tatted, but there was a playfulness about him. "And that," Lo, pointed to the drummer, "is CT."

Jamie stared at the man behind the drums. There was something dark about him, a sadness she recognized. It was like she was looking in the mirror all over again. "How are they all this gorgeous?"

"Right?" Lo agreed, "and they rock."

Jamie wasn't normally into grunge, but there was something about Lithium Springs. Maybe it was the hot as sin lead singer, or maybe it was because this was her first night out in months. Either way, she was drawn to them. Jamie's legs pushed forward until she reached the base of the stage. She stared at the three men in awe, captivated like everyone else in the room.

Tiff appeared behind them, carrying a tray with two shots of whiskey and two of the Swedish fish. "These are from Ryder," she said. "He told me to tell you that if you need anything else to let me know."

Jamie and Lo lifted the drinks off the tray. Turning towards the stage, Jamie mouthed a *thank you* to the lead singer. Ryder winked, never missing a beat.

"I take it that's her, the hot bartender?" Lo grinned.

"Yup," Jamie said, draining the red shot.

Lo raised her glass. "Lucky bitch."

Music infiltrated Jamie's bones as the set rolled on. Watching Ryder play was the greatest foreplay she could have ever imagined. She wanted him, wanted to feel his fingers plucking at her nipples the way they plucked at his guitar. She wanted to feel the vibrations of his voice while his head was buried between her legs. She told herself she wanted him because he was hot, and because he could sing, opting to ignore the butterflies she felt whenever he looked at her.

And he never stopped staring.

Ryder's gaze never seemed to strayed too far from Jamie. Every time she moved, his eyes followed. He watched her, as if spellbound, while everyone else was fixated on him.

Though the crowd was modest, everyone in attendance felt the energy in the air as the three men on stage bared their souls. They were witnessing greatness. Lithium Springs was destined for more than dive bars in Seattle. It wasn't a matter of if they would make it, but a matter of when. They had that thing, the *it factor*, the spark. They were ordained by some higher power; instruments of the gods, and Jamie felt their blessing in her veins.

She was playing with fire, but that didn't stop her fingers from sliding down her collarbone, over her damp skin and between her breasts. Her green eyes drifted up to the stage and she smiled, happy to find him still watching. Ryder quirked a brow as he strummed his guitar and sang about sex and drugs. Jamie slipped her index finger beneath the lace fabric of her shirt, flashing him her breast before quickly covering up again.

Ry's eyes widened in shock, and he stumbled through the next few lines of the song. The drummer took over, banging out a solo that sent the crowd into a frenzy. Ryder chuckled, shaking his head in apparent amusement. She was affecting him the same way he affected her.

"Thanks for dragging my ass out tonight," Jamie yelled, throwing her arms around Lorena's neck.

"Anytime," Lo grinned, "let's go get another drink."

Jamie agreed and they walked over to the bar. Lo ordered another round of drinks as they slipped onto a pair of barstools. "Have you made up your mind yet?" Lo asked.

"About what?"

Lo tipped her head in Tiffany's direction. "Which one you want."

Instead of answering, Jamie opted to avoid the question. "I can't feel my lips." She was doing it again, being reckless and self-destructive, but she was powerless to stop it. She knew what she wanted, it was the same thing she always wanted, the forbidden. Ryder was lithium and she was desperate for a dose.

"That means it's working," Tiffany grinned. She sat a glass in front of each woman before swaying to the other end of the bar. Jamie eyed her ass as she went.

"Was she flirting with you?"

"I doubt it," Jamie lamented. "She seems pretty enamored with Ry."

"And he seems pretty enamored with you."

"I showed him my tits," she confessed, and Lo giggled. "Another drink is probably a terrible idea." Probably? Try definitely. So far tonight, Jamie eye fucked the bartender and flashed the lead singer of the band. More alcohol would eviscerate what was left of her critical thinking skills.

"Man the fuck up, you only live once," Lo chided.

Jamie had been fully prepared to give Lo shit for YOLO'ing her, but before she could speak her stool spun around, and she found herself face to face with Ryder. "Yeah, Kitty Cat, man up." He pried her legs open, creating a home between her knees. A wave of goosebumps broke out across her damp skin.

"I think I owe you one." Jamie handed him the shot and he swallowed its contents in one gulp. Leaning over her, Ryder sat the glass on the bar. His body covered hers. His shirt was wet, drenched with sweat, and visions of their damp bodies colliding in a dark room bombarded Jamie's brain. The feel of his weight on her made her thighs quake.

"How'd you like the show?" he asked, his hand coming to rest on her hip. "I know I enjoyed it." Hazel eyes focused on the swell of her breast. His gaze was so hot, she feared her shirt would burst into flames.

"You gonna introduce us to your girl, Ry?" Javi asked, pushing his shoulder as he walked by. He took a seat in the vacant stool next to Lo, and CT, the drummer, grabbed the seat next to him.

Ryder quirked his brow, waiting for Jamie to tell them her name, but she was stubborn, and more than a little freaked out by them referring to her as *his girl*. Extending her hand, Jamie chirped, "I'm Kitty Cat."

They exchanged pleasantries as Ryder thumbed circles around her lower back. The five of them chatted for a bit, and not once did Ryder let go of her.

She was surrounded by him.

The fucking butterflies in her stomach went into hyper drive.

"I want you," Ry murmured against her soft skin.

Jamie pushed him back—but not away. "People in hell want ice water."

It was strange, not because he was a stranger, which he was, but because being with him felt as natural as the sun on her skin and the wind in her hair. He reminded her that even after everything that happened last fall, she could still feel. And she fucking hated it; this vulnerability, feeling things like warmth and protection. It was unsettling. In Jamie's twenty-four years on the planet, all she ever knew was sorrow, but twenty minutes with this man and she felt safe.

"We killed that shit," Javi yelled leaning over the bar. He was playful, like he saw the world through rose colored lenses, just like Kensie, her roommate.

"I just wish there was more than thirty people here," CT added, signaling for a round of drinks.

"Nah," Ryder disagreed, and kissed Jamie's shoulder, eliciting a blush. *Again with the fucking blushing.* "All that stuff will come when the time is right. You can't rush the climb."

"Did you just quote Miley Cyrus, motherfucker?" Javi asked. Everyone within earshot erupted into fits of laughter.

"It's a good song," he defended. "No, fuck that, it's a great song." He looked down at Jamie, tipping her chin up with his thumb, "what do you think?"

"About the song or the sentiment?" she asked. She agreed with the sentiment, life was about the journey, living in the moment, and being present. She chanted that shit daily. The song, however, was trash. Ryder's hazel eyes penetrated her green. He was staring into the abyss of her soul and Jamie worried he could see her drowning. "Why do you keep looking at me like that?" she asked, shifting uncomfortably.

"Like what?"

"Like that," she said pointing at him, "you're doing it again."

"I'm just trying to figure out why you're so sad."

"What makes you think I'm sad?" She leaned into his touch. She *was* sad, but she thought she was doing a better job of hiding it.

"Because I can see you," he replied, resting his forehead onto hers. The act was intimate, as if they were alone in a quiet room, not in the middle of the bar with their friends sitting two feet away. It was as if he'd always known her.

"I didn't realize I was invisible to everyone else."

"I didn't mean it like that smart ass, I'm just wondering what your trying to bury under all this whiskey."

"I think I liked you better when you were talking about my vagina," she snorted, pulling back from his embrace. If he knew how fucked up she really was, he'd run.

Ryder grabbed her by the waist and pulled her ass to the edge of the stool, "Are you going to let me see it?"

Jamie shrugged, the jury was still out. She wanted him, but she didn't want the complications. She didn't want the feelings. Something in her gut told her sex with this man would never be casual, and casual was all Jamie could handle.

"I can buy you dinner first, if that's what you want," he added with a grin.

What did she want?

That was the million-dollar question. Ryder was hard and masculine, but he brought out a vulnerability in her she fought her whole life to suppress. Jamie was the strong one, she didn't know any other way to be.

Tiffany, on the other hand, was soft and sensual. With her it would be fun. Light and easy, just the way Jamie liked it.

Hard or soft?
Pink or blue?
Easy or complicated?

"Are you ready to go?" Lo asked, interrupting her inner monologue.

Jamie nodded eagerly. Thankful to her friend for reminding her of a third option: getting the fuck out of there. "Yes, please," she said attempting to pry Ryder's hands from her hips.

"Don't leave." It wasn't a question. Ryder wasn't asking her to stay, he demanded it. "I know you want me, too. I can feel your body trembling with anticipation. Why are you fighting it so hard?"

"I can't ditch my friend." It was a weak excuse; one Jamie knew wouldn't hold up as soon as it left her lips.

"My boys will take care of her. Javi, make sure Kitty Cat's friend gets home safely."

"Sure thing, homie," Javi smirked, draping his arm around Lorena.

"But—"

"I'll be fine, Kitty Cat," Lorena assured.

Jamie narrowed her eyes at the traitorous jackass, silently calling her a bitch in every language she knew.

Puta.

Teef.

Hündin.

Tik.

"Good. Now, that's settled," Ryder said, forcing Jamie to look back at him. "I'll ask you again. What do you want?"

Jamie inhaled, and exhaled slowly, tilting her head towards the bartender. "I want her."

"Tiff?" Ryder asked, confused. Jamie nodded, running her hand down his hard chest. His body was a thing of beauty. "But, what's in it for me?"

Jamie swirled her tongue around his Adam's apple. "If you get me her, I'll let you pet my Kitty Cat."

THREE

Wrap It Up

RYDER

Ryder was having an out-of-body experience.

One minute he was standing at the bar, dry humping his latest obsession and the next minute, he looked on as a Ryder-shaped shell made the impossible, possible. He was a lucky motherfucker.

Luck.

If you asked Ryder ten years ago if he considered himself lucky, he would have laughed in your face. When you grew up where he grew up, with the father he had, there was no such thing as luck. There was only life, death, and music. But there he was, standing between the legs of the sexiest woman he ever laid eyes on, after performing on stage with his two best friends, negotiating the terms of a threesome.

Yeah, he was a lucky bastard.

Kitty Cat had balls bigger than most men he knew, sitting there, writhing underneath him, asking him to help her get some pussy.

Ryder groaned into her neck. The skin there was warm and

sticky from dancing. He wondered how warm and sticky she'd be when his dick was buried deep inside her body. "How did I get so fucking lucky?"

"You're about to get even luckier," she said in a voice so needy it was like she was talking directly to his cock. Every move this woman made affected him. She exuded sex; wore it like a second skin. Unlike Tiff, and so many of the other bitches he came across, and *came across*, Kitty Cat didn't have to try to be sexy, she just was. There was something in the way she carried herself. She wasn't timid or unsure, a little sad maybe, but mostly there was courage.

His little kitten was brave. His intuition confirmed the moment she flashed him. Ryder saw a lot of shit in his life, so much shit that nothing surprised him anymore, but nothing prepared him for the sight of her perky pink nipples staring up at him on stage. Thank fuck for CT. He hoped to God the drummer didn't see what had him flustered, but he was grateful to him for sensing his fuck up and improvising.

Reluctantly, Ry tore his mouth from the blonde's neck, "Tiff, babe."

"What's up?" she asked walking over to them, her hips swinging as she moved. It was annoying how hard she tried to entice them. She didn't care which member of the band she fucked, she just wanted to be fucked. There was no denying she was hot, but her desperation was a turn off. Still, Kitty Cat wanted her, and he wanted Kitty Cat, and fucking Tiff wouldn't be the worst thing he'd done for a girl.

"When's your next break?"

"I…uh," she stammered, looking at him in confusion. He never actually said much to her past his drink order. He prayed his previous indifference wouldn't come back to bite him on the ass now. "I don't know, why?"

"My little kitten wants to play and I can't seem to tell her no." He smiled a smile that was guaranteed to make her panties melt. Kitty Cat snorted into his chest. She saw right through the bullshit grin on his face.

"Play?"

"With you," he clarified, spanking the giggling blonde hard on the ass. "You asked for this, remember?" he whispered. She rolled her eyes, but it shut her up.

Realization washed over Tiffany's face, as she looked from the blonde to Ryder and back again. "It's not busy. I think Lira will be okay by herself for a little bit."

Thank fuck, he groaned internally. Ryder needed to be inside Kitty Cat, and now that Tiff was down, all that was left were the logistics, "Dave's office?" he suggested. Dave was the owner of the bar, and he was cool; the guys used his office as a makeshift dressing room, but Ryder wasn't so sure how cool he'd be with him fucking two women on his sofa.

"He left about an hour ago. What he doesn't know won't hurt him."

"Excellent." Ryder lifted the blonde off her stool, and Tiff whispered something to Lira, the other bartender, before ducking under the bar.

"Take care of my friend, Javi," Kitty Cat called as Ryder laced his fingers with hers, and dragged her forward. She reached for Tiffany's hand. The three of them looked like they were field trip buddies.

"Where the fuck are y'all going?" CT asked incredulously. He looked to Javi for backup, but the bass player was too busy with Lo's tongue to notice or care.

"To the back for a bit," he tossed over his shoulder, pulling the train forward.

"With both of them?"

Ryder raised a brow towards Kitty Cat. He wanted her to know it wasn't too late to back out, hell, he preferred it. Tiff was hot, he'd enjoy fucking her if he had too, but he wanted the blonde and the thought of sharing her with anyone made him a little nauseated.

Her eyes traveled the length of Tiff's body, and she nodded, chewing on her lip, "With both of us."

This girl was going to make him blow his load before he even got his dick wet.

"Can I watch?" CT asked amused. He knew Ry better than anyone, and he already knew the answer, but for whatever reason he and Javi, loved fucking with him. There wasn't anything he could do about Tiff, but CT? Over his dead body.

"Fuck. You. Asshole." He punctuated each word guiding the pair of giggling girls through the bar behind him. Their hands explored each other's bodies as they made their way through the dimly lit room. The bar was dead, but every eye in the place was on the three of them. Their mission was about as transparent as Scotch tape.

Ignoring the stares, Ryder tugged the train along until they reached Dave's office. The room was dark and damp. Humidity from the main bar and their combined lust permeated the air. A cheap plywood desk sat in the middle of the room, one of those Target or Wal-Mart specials, and a metal folding chair was tucked neatly behind it.

The girls stumbled backwards, falling on the old brown sofa that was pushed up against the back wall. Ryder locked the door and watched with hooded eyes as Kitty Cat straddled the bartender. Her hands kneaded Tiff's chest, but her eyes were locked on his. She stared at him as if he were a predator, and in that moment, he was. Kitty Cat, with her smart mouth and plump little ass, was his prey, and Ryder had a nasty habit of playing with his food.

He swaggered over to the couch in four long steps, his gaze never wavering. It was as if their souls collided. He never felt more alive in his life, even the high of being on stage didn't compare to how he felt when Kitty Cat looked at him like that. The girl had the power to destroy him. Oh, but what a beautiful tragedy it would be.

Kitty Cat's lips quivered as he towered over her. "I've wanted to kiss you all fucking night," he said, pulling her up off Tiff's lap and onto her feet.

"No kissing, not the lips on my face anyway," she added with a grin.

Tiffany came up behind him, and wrapped her arms around his torso while Kitty Cat moved to unbutton his pants. It was cute, they thought they were in charge. *Tsk-tsk,* he scolded, "I'm the conductor of this train. Kitty Cat, since you wanted to play, take her clothes off."

His little kitten didn't hesitate, pushing Tiffany on the couch, she yanked the tiny, black tank top over her head. Tiff's double D's spilled out and Cat lapped at her nipples, licking, and sucking and biting.

Ryder was six-two, lean with curly blond hair and he played guitar. He turned down more pussy than most bastards would see in a lifetime, but watching Kitty Cat in action was a thing of beauty. The word hadn't been invented for how hard he was. That's what she did to him, the sight of her on her knees reduced him to a fucking teenager. It was so bad he had to rub his dick through his jeans just to take the edge off.

Cat licked her way down Tiff's body, dipping her tongue into her navel before tugging the elastic band of her shorts down with her teeth.

That's what did it.

That's what broke him.

Ryder was on his feet and behind them in a flash. His hand fisted in Kitty Cat's hair, wrapping the long blonde ponytail around his wrist, and jerking her back so that her body contorted into the perfect arch. She looked up at him with lust-filled eyes, awaiting his next move.

Lifting her to her feet, Ryder yanked her back to his front, and snaked his arms around her waist. He unbuttoned her pants, letting the loose-fitting jeans fall to the floor with a soft thud. His hand was like a magnet, drawn to her pussy. So warm. So wet. She dripped with need. Her arousal scented the air, making his mouth water and his dick throb. "We can kiss these, right?" he asked, nipping at her neck.

"God, yes," she moaned. The sound was the sweetest melody he'd ever heard. Yanking at the snaps nestled between her thighs, he practically tore the lace from her body.

"Hey," Kitty Cat gasped, "I like this shirt."

Fuck the shirt and anything else standing in the way of his dick in her pussy. He needed to see every inch of her body, to memorize it.

Ryder wanted Kitty Cat to be burned in his brain like the lyrics of his favorite song or the chords to Alice Coopers, *Schools Out*.

Her chest heaved up and down. Her perky tits weren't as big as Tiff's but they were as close to flawless as he'd ever seen. Plump and round, with little pink buds standing at attention. Her stomach was soft, flat with a scar that ran horizontally across her mid-section. He explored the raised skin. Everything about her made sense. Even her imperfections belonged.

Ryder trailed kisses down her shoulder blades and across her back before sinking to his knees behind her, grinning like an idiot when he saw the two-tiny diamond dermal piercings in the dimples of her lower back. "Fuck, this is sexy Kitty Cat," he groaned, placing a kiss on each one before peeling off her panties. "On your knees, Tiff, tell me what she tastes like."

Tiffany's tongue darted out and with slow, soft strokes she lapped at Kitty Cat's core. "Like water," Tiff moaned, continuing her assault, her voice muffled, "but sweeter."

His little kitten purred and stretched, her skin turned an adorable shade of pink. A thin layer of sweat coated her body as Tiff pushed her closer and closer towards the promised land. It was the most erotic thing he'd ever witnessed. Her legs began to tremble as the orgasm built in her core, but Ryder wasn't going to let her off the hook that easy. "I didn't say you could come," he growled. He stood and pulled Tiffany up with him. He was punishing her for denying his kiss, and for including Tiffany in a moment that should have been reserved for him. "You don't get to come until I say so," he grunted, grabbing a hold of Tiff's chin and pulling her head to his. He licked into Tiffany's mouth savoring the sweet, slightly musky taste of the blonde. It wasn't the same as a kiss from Kitty Cat, but it would do.

"Lay down on the couch," he murmured against her lips. The bartender did as she was told. Ry turned, running his fingers down Cat's stomach, "I wanna watch you eat pussy too." Grinning, she licked her lips, nodding like a lunatic. "Enjoy this while it lasts because this will be the last time anyone but me gets to have your mouth on them, understood?"

Kitty Cat narrowed her eyes at him, but didn't argue. Instead, she crawled on top of Tiffany and pushed her legs open as wide as she could get them, and trailed kisses up one side of her thigh and down the other. Kitty Cat's ass was on full display as she lost herself between Tiff's legs. Ryder leaned up against the desk, watching as she ate Tiffany's pussy like a fucking pro. His cock was begging for attention. He held out for as long as he could, but the rock in his pants was becoming unbearable. Unzipping, Ryder pulled his dick out, and stroked his shaft slowly. The shiny metal of his Prince Albert piercing glinted in the dark room.

Her skin looked so goddamn smooth and soft, Ryder couldn't wait another minute to get inside her. The desire to bury his cock in her wetness was too strong. He was trying to be patient, trying to let her have her fun, but he needed to fuck her. He quickly shed his clothes, grabbed a condom from his wallet, and sheathed up.

Stalking over to them, Ryder knelt on the couch behind Kitty Cat, smacking her hard on the ass. She turned and glared at him, her lips glistening with Tiffany's arousal. "Did I tell you to stop?" he barked, positioning his dick at her entrance. He could see the snarky rebuttal on the tip of her tongue but before she could speak he rammed into her, burying himself to the hilt.

"What is that?" she gasped, pleasure etched across her face. He pulled back out, slowly, letting his piercing massage her inner walls.

"That, Kitty Cat, is your new best friend."

"Fuck," she groaned into Tiffany's pussy as he drove into her from behind. She clenched around him, squeezing his dick like a vice. She felt too good, he knew the moment he penetrated her that he would never tire of her. Ryder could spend the rest of his life touching her, fucking her, eating her, and he'd die a happy man. Kitty Cat's body tensed, her pussy constricted around his cock. Another orgasm loomed. She would never be able to fake it with him. Then again, Kitty Cat struck Ryder as the type of woman who wouldn't hesitate to tell him if he wasn't fucking her right.

Thrusting in and out of her once more, he paused. "Not yet."

"We should have left you at the bar," she panted, annoyance lacing her tone.

He spanked her again, before pulling Tiffany's legs down. Cat crawled up her body, her knees on either side of her head. "Turn around. Face me," he demanded.

He drove into Tiffany, mercilessly, never once breaking eye contact with Cat. It was carnal the way he fucked one woman with his cock and the other with his gaze. The physical connection with Tiffany was temporary. She was drenched. It felt fucking amazing to slide in and out of her warmth, but what really got him off was Kitty Cat. Watching her grind on Tiff's face, her eyes locked on his. The little devil was stealing his soul and Ryder didn't even put up a fight.

Tiff began to tense up, reminding him of her presence, "rub her clit," he ordered, angling her body so his piercing grazed her g-spot. He needed her to come, he needed her spent so he could have Kitty Cat to himself. Tiff yelled out in pleasure, her body shook violently as he pounded into her core.

Once Tiff's orgasm waned Ryder sprung to his feet, lifting Cat up, carrying her over to the wall. He slammed into her forcefully, filling her completely. "Fuck, Ry," she panted, clawing at his back. He was deep and at that angle, his piercing had to be driving her insane. "Please let me come," she begged, dragging her nails across his flesh. She drew blood but fuck if he cared, she could mark him as much as she wanted because the way her pussy felt stretched around his dick was worth the pain.

"Tell. Me. Your. Name," he grunted between thrusts.

She shook her head. "You. Haven't. Earned. That."

He fucked her with everything he had. He was trying to break her, break her physically, so no other man would ever compare, and mentally, so she'd let him in.

"I want you," he growled, inches above her lips. God he wanted to kiss her.

"You have me."

"I'm not talking about this," Ry said flicking her clit. He pumped into her hard, and she screamed out as she came all over his dick. Watching her come, feeling her juices drip down his shaft was enough to send him over the edge. He lost control, ramming into her wildly, spilling his seed into the condom. "I want this," he huffed, raising his hand over her heart.

Kitty Cat shook her head, bringing it to rest on his shoulder. "You haven't earned that either."

FOUR

Hell of a Life

RYDER

Ryder focused on the brown spot staining the ceiling in his bedroom. The room was spinning and his tongue was dry. The pounding at his temples was so intense it felt like a bullet was firmly lodged in his brain.

A fucking hangover.

His first, ever. Years of late nights and hard partying and Ryder never once woke up with more than a mild headache. He used to brag about that shit, saying it was the only thing his father ever gave him, but too many shots and a handful of bad decisions later, he found himself lying in bed praying to whoever would listen.

What the fuck was he thinking?

He'd asked himself that question at least a hundred times in the twenty minutes since he pried his eyes open, and he still couldn't come up with a decent answer. The *what* paled in comparison to the *who*.

Three hours.

That's how long it took for the gorgeous blonde with the sad green eyes to settle under his skin. From the moment Ryder spotted her sitting at the bar, he was a goner.

His friends always teased him, saying he was obsessed with the idea of love, but his terrible taste in women kept him jumping from one toxic relationship to the next. It was true, Ryder couldn't deny it. He was drawn to broken things—like him—but when his last relationship ended in a temporary restraining order against his ex, he swore off the idea of monogamy once and for all.

'Music over bitches' was the motto he and his band mates had adopted and since then, his life was much less dramatic. Ryder lived by those words, and he thought he would die by them. Pouring all his time and energy into the band worked. They were finally starting to make a name for themselves. Everything was falling into place.

Then last night. Last-fucking-night, when Kitty Cat swept into his life like a goddamned wrecking ball, everything changed. The way her muscles clenched around his dick was beyond sex. When Ryder stared into the depths of her green eyes and watched her fall apart in his arms, he felt whole.

Ryder thought it was luck, getting to fuck her and Tiff at the same time, but he should have known better. He was cursed, the only man on earth to walk away from a threesome unfulfilled. He had left for five fucking minutes to throw away the condom and take a leak, and when he got back, she'd vanished. He didn't know her name, her number, or any way to get in contact with her. He bought all her drinks, so he couldn't even ask Tiff for the name on her tab. Ryder didn't know anything about her, other than what her pussy tasted like. She was just gone, and as soon as he realized she wasn't coming back, he sat at the bar and drank himself into a near coma. He didn't remember coming home, much less how he got there.

Ryder sat up, bracing himself. Once the room stopped spinning, he swung his legs over the side of his bed and forced himself to his feet. His bladder was threatening to explode and pissing the bed would only serve to remind him how much of a tool he was being. Stumbling out into the hallway, the sounds of laughter alerted him that he was the last to wake. He headed for the bathroom, took the most satisfying piss in the history of pissing, then washed his hands. "Shit," he groaned, staring at his reflection in the mirror. Blond hair was stuck to the side of his face, and his eyes were bloodshot.

Pulling his hair into a bun on the top of his head, he ran a wash cloth under the warm stream of water and did his best to wipe the crust from his eyes and mouth. He still felt like death, but hopefully he looked a little better.

"Look at this dirty-dick motherfucker," Javi teased as Ryder walked into the living room. His band mates, roommates, and best friends were sitting in a haze of thick white smoke, watching *ESPN*. He plopped down beside Javi on the couch as CT eyed him from the brown leather recliner to the left.

"Fuck you," Ry grunted, reaching for the blunt. Wake and bake, the best cure for nausea there was. Inhaling deeply, smoke filled his lungs. "What time is it?" he asked.

"Almost two," CT answered.

"I've got to get ready for work," Ryder grumbled, taking another puff.

Javi held his hand out for Ryder to pass the blunt. "You going to make it through your shift, bro? 'Cause you look like shit."

"I feel like shit," he admitted, stretching his hands over his head. His body creaked with every move he made. He was getting too old for this shit.

"What the fuck happened to your back?" CT asked, pushing him around to get a better look at the angry scratches.

Ryder chuckled recalling exactly how he earned those claw marks. "Last night was fucking insane."

"Dude," Javi grinned, "how does your sensitive ass always end up getting all the pussy?"

"It's 'cause he's the lead singer," CT added. "Javi, pass the blunt."

"Last time I checked, you assholes weren't hurting for any."

The three of them were young, talented, and spent as much time in the gym working on their bodies as they did in the garage working on their music. Ryder may have been the lead singer, but in truth, they all pulled their fair share of pussy.

Being them didn't suck.

"Yeah, but a threesome with Tiff and the hot blonde chick? That's some real rock star shit right there," Javi exhaled, passing the blunt back to CT.

"You didn't happen to get her friend's number, did you?" Ry asked, nearly forgetting he tasked Javi with taking care of Lo.

Was Lo her first name or last?

"Nah, we just made out a little while we waited for her Uber. Why?"

"I didn't get Kitty Cat's name or number or anything," he said, taking another deep pull from the weed filled cigar.

"So?" Javi said.

Ryder sighed, he knew where this conversation was headed and he didn't have the energy to listen to them talk shit. "I should get ready for work."

"¡Ay Dios mío! Tell me you didn't?" Javi asked, his Mexican-American roots peeking through.

Ryder stood, rubbing the back of his neck. "I don't know what you're talking about." Fuck them. So, what, he liked her. Why was that such a bad fucking thing?

"You did, didn't you? Can you believe this?" Javi asked, turning to CT.

"I don't have time for this shit, I've gotta get ready."

"*You* would fall in love off a threesome," CT chuckled. He laughed so hard he started coughing.

"I'm not in love. I just…there's something about her."

"You're fucking hopeless."

"Fuck you both," he grunted, stomping up the stairs. He wasn't in love, he just wanted more.

The whooshing and swooshing sound of the dishwasher taunted Ryder as he walked through the kitchen at Cibo, the upscale Italian restaurant where he occasionally bussed tables. Music was Ryder's life, but it didn't pay the bills. Before getting the job at the restaurant, he worked at a call center, and before that, a coffee shop, and before that, a retail pet store. His job before the pet store wasn't exactly legal.

Eight long months and he was quite possibly the world's worst busser, but it wasn't like he'd been hired for his bussing skills anyway. Ryder, like most of the staff, was hired strictly based on his appearance. The owners, a husband and wife in their mid-sixties, collected beautiful employees like other people collected baseball cards. That was the point, the gimmick. The food was shit, the service was worse, but the front-end staff all looked like they belonged on the cover of a magazine. They were the reason Cibo managed a little over three hundred reservations a day.

Setting a tub of dirty plates on the belt, Ryder leaned back against the counter with a huff. His head was pounding, and the heat from the kitchen wasn't helping his dizziness. He should have just called out, but even though Lithium Springs played their best show to date the night before, rent was still due on the first. CT and Javi covered his ass last month and he couldn't ask them to do it again. Once they split the little bit of money they made from the door, Ryder barely had enough to put gas in his bike and buy himself a Super Value Meal.

"You look like shit," Oscar, Head Dishwasher, and resident smart ass said.

"Why the fuck does everyone keep telling me that? I know. I had a long fucking night," Ryder snapped, tugging at the neck of his black t-shirt.

"I forgot the show was last night, how was it?" Oscar asked, running a tray through the machine.

"It was cool. I'm hurting today, though."

"You know what they say, don't you?"

"What?"

Oscar pulled a silver flask from his back pocket. "You gotta bite the hairy dog, cabrón."

"I think you mean, bite the hair of the dog that bit you," Ryder corrected, eyeing the flask. The thought of drinking right now made him want to vomit, but he took it anyway, figuring there was no way he could feel any worse. Ryder tipped back the flask. The liquid burned going down. "What the fuck is this? Rocket fuel?" he choked.

"Moonshine. I made it myself," Oscar said proudly.

Sweat dotted Ryder's brow. Between the moonshine and the steam from the dishwasher he felt like he was trapped in a fucking sauna. "You're trying to kill me, dude."

Oscar grinned, "It will put some hair on your balls, pretty boy."

"My balls are plenty hairy, just ask your wife," Ryder quipped, taking another swig from the flask before handing it back. "Thanks man. I should get back out there."

"Don't mention it. Oh, and Ry?"

"Huh?"

"Tell your mom I'll be over around seven."

"Fuck you, Oscar." Ryder snatched an empty tub from the other end of the belt and pushed his way back out onto the restaurant floor. Another table got up to leave and Ryder went to work clearing the few remaining dishes.

Although he'd never admit it, Oscar's hairy dog moonshine was working for his hangover. Too bad it couldn't solve his Kitty Cat problem.

How could he find someone without a name or a phone number?

Ryder racked his brain, wiping down the table, lost in thought. *What was it about that girl? Were his friends right? Was he hopeless? It was stupid. He didn't even know her. Why was she so special?*

A firm squeeze to Ryder's ass caused him to jump in surprise. "Uh hi," he said, turning to see two middle aged women grinning at him.

"A little something for all your hard work," the blonder, of the two said. She was tall and fit, with a face that was botoxed to hell. Her friend didn't fare much better. The only difference was her hair was a slightly darker shade of blonde.

Arching a brow at the women, Ryder reached into his back pocket and pulled out a piece of paper with a hundred-dollar bill folded inside. He eyed it for a minute, then glanced back at them. "I wasn't your server," he said, handing the bill back to them.

The darker haired woman shook her head. "Don't be silly, this was the best lunch we've had in ages. My numbers on the paper," she winked. "Call me if you're interested in doing some *private* catering."

"Private," he smiled the lopsided grin he knew made women melt. Fuck it, he'd done worse things for money and the first of the month was rapidly approaching, "I'll do that. You ladies be sure to come back soon, okay?"

"You can count on it," the blonder one purred, running her hand down his chest. They turned and sauntered out of the restaurant. Ryder rolled his eyes, pocketing the bill and tossing the number in his tub of dirty dishes.

"So gross," Travis, one of the bartenders grimaced.

"Dude," Ryder snorted. Most people didn't go as far as to touch him, but he did get his fair share of phone numbers and tips, even though he only cleaned tables and never actually helped customers.

"Tell me about it. You see that guy over at the bar?"

Ryder nodded. There was a man in a suit talking to Amanda, the other bartender and Travis' girlfriend.

"He's been hitting on my girl for the past hour. I almost spit in his last drink, so she made me take a break."

"You know you don't have anything to worry about, man," Ryder said, not to make him feel better, but because it was true. Ryder tried to fuck Amanda his first week working at Cibo. Despite his best efforts, she turned him down. She was in love with Trav.

"You got any weed on you? I need something to take the edge off."

"Nah, man, sorry," Ryder shook his head. "Oscar has some moonshine, though."

Trav gave Ry a slap on the back. "Good looking out, bro. I'd hate to have to knock that guy's teeth out."

"Yeah, well, I should get back to work." Ryder shrugged. He didn't have much sympathy for the bastard, at least Travis had a girl. Ryder didn't even have a goddamn name.

FIVE

Bloodstream

Jamie

It had been a week since the incident at The Rabbit Hole.

The incident.

That's what Jamie referred to it as; it sounded better than the truth. It sounded better than relapsing. The drinking wasn't the problem, although it didn't help. Her problem was in the act itself, in the rebellion. Jamie made temporary homes out of random encounters with strangers to soothe the ache she felt inside. She did it for as long as she could remember. She convinced herself she'd grow out of it one day. She thought all the shit that happened last fall would have served as a wakeup call, but six months later and she was still fucking up. No matter how long she meditated or how many affirmations she chanted, hidden beneath the peace and light was darkness and chaos.

Chaos.

She courted it, then ran, seeking shelter from the tornado she gladly welcomed into her bed—and make no mistake, Ryder was a tornado. He blew into her life and knocked down the carefully crafted house of cards she had built over the last six months. The crazy part was she longed for the torment. There was something in the way he looked at her, like he saw the sadness in her heart. Most people didn't notice, and the ones who did ignored it, but not Ryder. He was drawn to it. Jamie didn't need that kind of complication in her world. She knew better than to wish for something she would never be able to have, but even so she couldn't deny the emptiness he left behind.

Empty.

Emotionally, Jamie long since accepted the omnipresent hollow feeling in her chest. She embraced it, donned it like an invisible cloak. It use to keep her protected, but *the incident* left her exposed. Ryder fucked her hard, ripping the pleasure from her body, but having him inside her branded her in a way she hadn't expected. He gave her the most intense orgasm of her life, but it wasn't the sex that scared her away, it was the affection.

"*I want you,*" he had said it more than once that night. It sounded good in the moment, but when the lust and alcohol induced fog lifted, he would see she was incapable of giving him what he all but demanded—her heart.

So, she did the one thing both old Jamie and new Jamie agreed on; she ran. It was better that way. Ryder would forget about her and move on to someone who didn't need to seek out happiness in the bottom of a shot glass and in the arms of random strangers.

A hand fluttered in Jamie's face. "Jam? Hey, Jam? Earth to Jamie."

Jamie shook off the regrets and smiled at the stunning brunette standing in front of her. Kensington Roth was Jamie's best friend and roommate. They'd known each other since birth; their mothers were friends when they were children and their grandmothers before that. They were so attached that when Kensie followed her boyfriend to school at USC, Jamie went too. James was the realist and Kensington was the dreamer. Jamie looked at the world for what it was and Kensie looked at it for what it could be.

"Good morning to you too," she quipped. "Also, I'm a grown ass woman. Why do you and Chris insist on calling me Jam?" Jamie hated the childhood nickname. Most of their family and friends stopped using the moniker around the time she grew boobs, but her brother and best friend wouldn't let it die.

"Jamie, it's seven A.M. Is the language really necessary?" Trey, Kensie's boyfriend, asked coming up behind Kensie and wrapping his arms around her terry cloth clad waist.

"Sorry, Trey I didn't realize you gave birth to me," Jamie said, sarcasm dripped from her words.

Trey Knight was a grade A douche bag. Much to Jamie's dismay, Kensie was falling for him. Her friend was a big believer in fairytales. She even saved his name in her phone as *Prince Charming*, but Jamie was convinced he was a toad.

"Will you two stop," Kensie huffed. "A. You will always be Jam to me, and B. What's the matter with you lately? You've been walking around like you're patient zero or some sh…stuff."

Jamie rolled her eyes at Kensie's self-censoring. "I just need my daily caffeine ration," she explained, jerking her thumb at the gurgling coffee pot behind her.

"Not just this morning. You've been like this all week." That was Kensie for you. She lived her life in a bubble, oblivious to her own bad decisions, but had an annoyingly accurate intuition when it came to Jamie's fuck ups.

"Work stuff," Jamie shrugged, turning to grab a mug so her friend couldn't see the lies hiding behind her eyes. It wasn't like she was keeping *the incident* a secret. It was just Kensie wasn't around much and when she was, so was Trey. Jamie didn't want to discuss the weather with that man, let alone her sex life.

"Work stuff has you doing all of this?" Kensie asked, motioning to the full jar of cookies, plate of muffins, and loaf of bread sitting on the counter.

"I like to bake," Jamie dismissed, taking a sip of her coffee.

"When you're stressed," Kensie amended. "I haven't seen this many baked goods since—"

"I'm fine." Add her spiral to the list of things she wasn't comfortable talking about with Trey present. She didn't like talking about it at all. It was in the past and Jamie was living in the present.

Kensie shook her head, taking a step towards her best friend. "Look, all I'm saying is if you need to talk, I'm here."

"I know."

"Are you sure you're okay?"

"Baby," Trey interjected, "she said she was fine. Drop it."

Kensie stared at her boyfriend, like she wanted to tell him to back off, but she refrained. It was the one-time Jamie didn't mind this new subdued version of her bestie. Jamie wasn't sure if Trey noticed her discomfort or if he was just bored with the line of questioning, but she was grateful either way. She'd sooner die than admit that to him, but she was.

"Shouldn't you be getting dressed?" Jamie added, mostly to change the subject, but also because Ken was still wearing her damn robe.

Kensie groaned. "Yes, Cruella is on a rampage so I need to get to the office before she does."

"Cruella?" Trey asked raising a brow.

The girls answered at the same time.

"Her boss."

"My boss."

"Jinx!" They said in unison again, exploding into a fit of giggles. It felt good to laugh. It was the first real laugh Jamie had all week. She could do this. She would forget all about the guitarist with the hazel eyes and get her life back on track.

"Seriously Jam," Kensie said, wrapping her arms around Jamie's waist. Her big brown eyes bled sincerity. "If you need to talk, you know where I live."

"I'm fine. I promise."

It was a lie and they both knew it, but for whatever reason, Kensie let it go. "I'm going to get dressed," she said, giving Jamie a squeeze before retreating into her bedroom.

Jamie sighed, and pulled her phone from the pocket of her slacks and scrolled through the day's headlines, determined to get her head back in the game. It was quiet on the news front, a house fire—no casualties—a community picnic, and a school board meeting. Jamie was halfway through the story about the house fire when Trey cleared his throat. "That smells good."

She looked up from the article and smiled tightly. Her instincts told her he was an asshole, but if Kensie was happy, Jamie could at least try to be nice. "I made extra if you want."

"Thanks." Jamie leered at Trey as he made his coffee, too much cream and too much sugar. God, everything about him made her want to puke. "You don't like me very much, do you?" he asked.

A noise that was a mix between a groan and a snort escaped her throat before she could stop it. She wanted to say, *no shit Sherlock*, but went with, "I don't even know you," instead.

"Then why the hostility?"

Jamie huffed, tossing her phone on the counter. "Must we?"

Trey bobbed his head up and down. "We must."

"I'm closer to Kensie than I am my own family. She's more than a friend, she's my sister and I'm protective of her. She's been hurt before. I don't want to see it happen again, and if I'm being honest, I'm a little jealous. I never get to see her anymore and when I do, you're here, too. You're *always* here."

"I get it," Trey held his hand up in surrender. "I'm not trying to take her from you, but I love her too."

Jamie's eyes widened in shock. She was not expecting that. "You what?"

"I'm in love with her."

"Have you told her this?"

"Not yet. It's too soon, right?"

Way too fucking soon.

Jamie looked at the man, really looked at him for the first time. Trey was handsome, in a privileged, asshole sort of way; a little overbearing, but he would never hurt Kensie.

"Talk to her. Ken wears her heart on her sleeve. I wouldn't be surprised if she felt the same."

"Thanks Jamie," he grinned.

"Don't mention it." She smiled weakly, making a mental note to add, *be nice to the asshole*, to her list of daily affirmations.

Jamie slid into her desk at the news station moments before Tina, her production manager, walked in. Tina Lin was a force to be reckoned with in the Seattle news scene. She'd been in the business longer than Jamie had been alive. At the peak of her career she was a co-anchor on a popular national morning show in New York, and she'd still be there if she hadn't moved back to Seattle to care for her ailing mother.

Tina was the reason Jamie took the grunt job at WSEA-9 over an anchor position at a smaller station. She wanted to work with the best, and Tina was the best.

"Good morning," she greeted, signaling the start of the programming meeting. The small Asian woman was reserved, but her presence was commanding. When Tina spoke, people listened.

A low murmur rumbled through the crowd in response. There were about forty people on the news team, including anchors, reporters, cameramen and production. Tina held daily programming meetings with the news staff to go over the top stories, and dole out assignments.

"As some of you may know, Sarah went into labor last night," Tina began. The room went quiet, so quiet all Jamie could hear was the sound of her own heart threatening to claw its way out of her chest. Sarah wasn't supposed to give birth for another two months. "Not to worry, she and her husband welcomed a healthy baby girl into the world." The relief in the room was palpable. "Yes, it's very exciting, but the surprise has left us in a bit of a lurch. We were in the process of finding her replacement and we'll need someone to fill in for her this afternoon for *The Local Spotlight*."

The Local Spotlight was Sarah's other baby. She created it to give local restaurants, artists, and influencer's a platform to promote their craft. The fifteen-minute spot ran every Saturday and Sunday after the six o'clock broadcast.

Jamie scooted down in her seat, trying to make herself invisible. *The Local Spotlight* had solid ratings, but Jamie was hoping to transition into more serious reporting and being stuck with the weekly gig, if even for a few months, would set her plan back. A lot went into researching and casting talent. She'd much rather spend her time covering government, crime, or injustice.

"Jamie," Tina said, looking right at her. *Be thankful. Be mindful. Be kind. Be thankful. Be mindful. Be kind.* Jamie chanted. "I want you to fill in for Sarah."

Shit.

Fucking motherfucking bullshit.

"Sure thing, Tina," Jamie said faintly.

"Good. You'll need to film this weekend's spot this afternoon, a hometown band," Tina glanced down at her notes, "Lithium Springs. Sean set it up."

"I went to school with their manager," Sean explained. "They're really good, have you ever heard of them?"

"Lithium Springs?" Jamie repeated, swallowing past the lump in her throat.

"Yes."

Jamie nodded slowly, sure her face was an unnatural shade of green. Of course, it was them because karma was a messy bitch who lived for drama.

Jamie spent the next hour staring at her computer screen. She should have been researching or meditating or chanting affirmations, but instead, she was having a nervous breakdown. She was on the path to nirvana and with one monumental lapse in judgment, Buddha drop kicked her ass all the way back to the beginning. She deserved this. It was Buddhism 101: do stupid, reckless shit, and said stupid reckless shit will come to your job, and fuck up your life.

Her worlds were about to collide. New Jamie was professional, responsible, and a team player. New Jamie was assigned this story and new Jamie didn't flake, but fuck if old Jamie wasn't shaking in her Jimmy Choo's at the thought of seeing the hazel eyed man who haunted her dreams.

"Why me?" She groaned, dropping her head on her desk. She peaked at the time on the bottom, right-hand corner of the computer screen. Her call time was in thirty minutes and she had nothing. How the fuck was she supposed to conduct an interview with no questions to ask?

This wasn't like her. Jamie didn't run from her problems—sure, she'd bury them under a mountain of whiskey—but shit-faced or not, she didn't run. This was her job and Jamie prided herself in excelling at her job. "Get it together James. It's a fifteen-minute interview. It will be over before you know it."

Be thankful.
Be mindful.
Be kind.
You can do this, she thought.

She'd made it through hell last fall; this interview would be a breeze. She was overreacting. Ryder was hot, young, and talented. He probably hooked up with random women all the time. The chance of him remembering her was slim. Plus, work Jamie looked totally different than party Jamie.

She was fine.

This was all going to be fine.

Rubbing her tattooed finger against her bottom lip, Jamie inhaled and exhaled deeply, mustering every ounce of courage she possessed before typing 'Lithium Springs' into the search engine. Images of the guys popped up along with their social media links and articles about the battle of the bands win. Twenty minutes later she compiled a list of ten questions to ask. It wasn't her most original or thought provoking work, but at least she was somewhat prepared.

Checking her reflection in the mirror, Jamie applied a thick layer of blush in a vain attempt to disguise herself and headed out into the newsroom. Reuben was already on stage setting up his equipment when she walked in. There were three stools opposite Jamie's chair and instruments sat stage right. "Hey Jamie," Reuben greeted as she walked onto the set. Her hands were so clammy sweat seeped onto her notecards.

"Hey," Jamie smiled weakly, doing her best to put on a brave face.

"What's wrong kiddo?" Reuben asked.

"Nothing." *I'm just about to interview one-third of the drunken threesome I had last weekend and I'm freaking the fuck out.*

The cameraman regarded her cautiously." Look," he sighed, "I know this isn't the type of stuff you want to be doing, but you've gotta pay your dues. You're great at this. You're quick on your feet and your instincts are strong. They'll take notice. You've only been out of school for what, a year and a half? Your time will come."

"Thanks Rube," she said, patting him on the back. He was right, she had to play her role, and she was good on her feet. She could do this.

The sound of the door flinging open down the corridor caused her mouth to dry. Laughter drifted onto the closed set and Jamie braced herself for the impact. Sean and a tall, light-brown haired man dressed in khaki Dockers and a white, button-down shirt came into view first. Next was CT and Javi. They wrestled playfully, the drummer pulling the bassist down into a headlock. So light and carefree, a sharp contrast to the man behind them. Ryder's head was down, blond hair pulled back into a bun, hands stuffed into the pockets of his jeans, and a scowl stretched across his impossibly handsome face. He was even hotter than she remembered, tall and lean, with black ink peeking out from under the sleeve of his dark gray t-shirt.

Heat traveled through Jamie's body as she fought to suppress the desire dripping between her legs. CT spotted her first. They locked eyes and he froze, releasing the bassist.

"Walk much douche bag?" Ryder grunted, pushing him forward.

"Take the stick out of your ass and look," CT nodded in Jamie's direction.

Taking a deep breath, Jamie forced a smile onto her face. She focused on Sean. She couldn't crack now. She'd come this far and it was too late to back down.

Don't look.

James, don't look.

Fuck.

She looked. Ryder's hazels found her green. His mouth tipped up into a devastatingly gorgeous grin, one that said, *gotcha.*

Shit.

Shit.

Shit.

It was official, she had zero self-control.

"Grant, guys, this is our cameraman, Reuben," Sean introduced, oblivious to the interaction happening behind him. Reuben, however, was more perceptive, raising a questioning brow towards her. Jamie shook it off, silently assuring him it was nothing. Judging by the look he gave her, he didn't believe her. Sean continued with the introductions. He pulled her forward, his hand lingering on the small of her back. "This is Jamie. She's going to do the interview."

"Jamie, huh?" Ryder snorted, his grin long gone. He narrowed in on the place where Sean's hand and her body met. In the span of ten seconds the atmosphere on the stage went from casual to intense as awkward silence filled the air.

"Hi," Jamie said, stepping out of Sean's embrace. She plastered on a plastic smile, and extended her hand. "It's really nice to meet you all."

Jamie prayed for the ground to open up and swallow her whole, while Sean explained how the segment would go. It was simple, a short question and answer session, then the guys would perform. Grant listened intently, while Ryder stood, brooding. The other two idiots thought it was the funniest thing they'd ever witnessed.

"Alright, I'll leave you guys to it," Sean said, excusing himself. The twelve o'clock broadcast would be starting soon and he needed to head back to the newsroom.

Everyone took their seats as Reuben counted them down and work Jamie took control. "Hi, I'm Jamie Manning, in for Sarah Lawson, and you're watching WSEA-9's *The Local Spotlight*. This week in studio, I'm joined by Lithium Springs, an up and coming band who recently began a residency at local pub, The Rabbit Hole. Welcome," she said, turning to the band. "Why don't you guys introduce yourselves."

The camera panned to the three men, and the bass player was the first to speak, "I'm Javi, I play bass."

"I'm the drummer, CT." He waved awkwardly to the camera before his eyes bounced back to Jamie.

Ryder rolled his eyes, mumbling out his name and position as lead singer and guitarist. Javi and CT looked at him sideways. His arms were crossed over his chest and his scowl from earlier returned. Apparently, he wasn't okay with pretending.

"Lithium Springs, that's an interesting name. Where did it come from?" Jamie asked, choosing to ignore the pouting singer.

"Lithium has the atomic number three, and there are three of us. It's a highly reactive element, when combined with water it's explosive, like our music," CT explained, miming an explosion with his hands.

Jamie continued to ask the questions she had prepared, feeling more like a robot, and not paying any attention to the answers they gave as she tried to convince herself that she was unaffected by Ryder's proximity.

"How long have you guys been playing together?"

CT answered again. "About five, or six years now. It started as something to do to stay out of trouble and it kind of evolved."

"Where did you meet?"

"My older brother and Ryder were friends in school and I was always tagging along. We both had a passion for music, but it wasn't until Ry met CT a few years later that everything just clicked."

"And how did you two meet?" Jamie asked Ryder directly, other than his name, he hadn't spoken a word.

"In juvie," he said roughly.

Jamie opened her mouth to continue but Grant yelled from the sideline, "Hold on, maybe don't mention the prison thing."

"Why not?" Ryder huffed.

"You can't tell a bunch of middle aged people you met in jail. It's bad for your brand."

"But it's the truth," Ryder argued, "and it's exactly our brand."

Grant pinched the bridge of his nose. "I thought the point of this was to get more people to the show?"

"They should know what the fuck they're in for." Ryder stared at Grant impassively. CT and Javi remained silent. Rueben cracked his knuckles. Jamie should have known Karma wasn't going to take it easy on her. If she didn't get this footage, it would be the first missed episode since the introduction of *The Local Spotlight*. Not only would Jamie be letting herself down, but she'd be letting down Tina and Sarah as well.

"Look, I know you guys think this is lame, but trust me, marketing yourselves to a wider audience is the smart thing to do, especially if you're serious about this," Grant reasoned.

Ryder turned to CT. "Can you please explain to your brother that we aren't interested in selling out?"

Jamie shifted in her seat, debating on if she should interject. Ryder was being pissy because of her, but Grant was right, almost no one showed up opening night. They needed to market themselves better. "It isn't about selling out," she began, "it's about making yourselves visible to a wider audience. Your music speaks for itself. You guys are talented, charismatic, and authentic. It will translate, I promise."

"Fuck this," Ryder seethed, jumping to his feet. "I'm out."

"Ry," CT said, trying unsuccessfully to grab a hold of his arm, "slow down, dude."

Jamie fought the urge to follow him, her subconscious need to soothe him. She told herself this was work, and her wanting to help wasn't personal. It wasn't her heart telling her to go to him, she was simply trying to finish the job.

"We got it," Javi called over his shoulder as he and CT chased Ryder out the door.

Jamie, Reuben, and Grant, sat in silence, unsure of what to do next.

"I'm sorry about Ry," Grant said after a few minutes passed.

"It's fine." She smiled up at the man who resembled an un-tattooed version of CT.

"No, it's not. We're wasting your time. I'm sure you've got more important things to do."

"It's kind of my job," she shrugged.

Silence fell upon them again. So much time passed, Jamie wondered if they were ever coming back. She began rehearsing how she was going to tell Tina about this mess, when the sound of Grant's voice filled the air once more. "I don't mean to be forward, but would you like to maybe grab some dinner or something, sometime?"

Jamie looked at him in confusion, unable to process what was happening. "Are you asking me out?" she asked looking at Grant, then to Reuben for confirmation. The cameraman rolled his eyes, unimpressed by the whole thing.

"I think I am," Grant grinned.

Before she could answer, before she could even process what was happening, she was pulled from her stool. "Fuck off Grant," Ryder growled, leading her by the elbow.

The look in Grant's eyes was one of pure confusion. He took a step forward, reaching for Jamie's other hand.

"Give them a minute, bro," CT said, pushing his brother back onto the chair. The two men locked eyes, some unspoken conversation passed between them, then Grant backed down.

"You okay, Jamie?" Reuben asked.

"It's fine. Just give us five minutes," she said as Ryder dragged her off set. He walked, with her stumbling behind him, until they reached the parking lot.

His anger was palpable. "Are you fucking that douche bag, Sean?"

Cars whizzed past, a cool breeze blew Jamie's hair in every direction. "That's none of your business," she huffed, tucking wayward strands behind her ears.

"Are. You. Fucking. Him?" Ryder repeated.

"This is so unprofessional," she shook her head in disbelief. "I could get into deep shit for this."

"Is he your boyfriend or something? Is that why you ran? Why you refused to tell me your name?"

"Why do you care? We had sex, that's it. Get the fuck over it."

Ryder was on her in an instant, his lips inches from hers. "Come on Kitty Cat, you and I both know this is more than just sex."

"Sean is not my boyfriend. I don't do the boyfriend thing. Are you happy now?" She exhaled, dropping her gaze. His intensity was overwhelming.

"Have lunch with me?" he asked, lifting her chin.

"I just want to finish this interview so I can go home," Jamie sighed, doing her best to ignore his intoxicating scent. It was a mix of soap, Ryder, and fresh air. He smelled of freedom, and of the ocean, her happy place.

"Tell me you don't feel it, this thing between us. Tell me I don't affect you the same way you affect me and I'll back off."

Of course, she was affected by him. She felt his possession bone deep. It would take an exorcism to expel him from her body.

Ryder was a bad idea, but then again, when did Jamie ever do anything good?

"What I feel for you is purely sexual. You're like some sort of a sex god, but I told you, I don't do the boyfriend thing."

The corner of his mouth tipped up into a crooked grin. "Sex god?"

"Shut up," Jamie said pushing him backward.

Cocky son of a bitch.

"Where do you think you're going?" Ryder caught her wrist, wrapping her arms around his waist. He looked down at her with a combination of lust and adoration. It was affection, and way too much of it. It made her uncomfortable, and she dropped her gaze once more.

"Let me take you to lunch."

"You don't even know me. I could be a serial killer," she said to the ground.

"You could be, or you could just be a really cool girl I'd like to get to know."

"Ry—"

"I'm not taking no for an answer Kitty Cat."

"Fine," Jamie groaned, burying her head in his chest.

"And if you're a good little kitten, I'll let you have this, too," he muttered, grinding his hips into hers.

Reuben stuck his head out the side door of the station, yelling, "Times up."

"Coming!" she yelled back, disentangling her limbs from Ryder's.

"You will be," he whispered, smacking her ass as she jogged back towards the door.

SIX

Irresistible

RYDER

There were two types of women in the world: ones who drank expensive cocktails at restaurants that boasted local and organic produce, and ones who took their whiskey neat and ate pussy like porn stars. Jamie Manning was firmly and resolutely in the second category.

That's not to say she wasn't accustomed to the finer things in life, it was just she didn't give a fuck about them. If Ryder had to guess, he'd say she'd been to her fair share of Michelin Star establishments. It wasn't just her custom white Range Rover, the one she let him drive to the diner, but also in the way she carried herself. There was an air about her, not ostentatious, but different, like she came from money.

Over the years, Ryder had gotten good at spotting wealth. His best friend, CT, had a trust fund with more money than most people would ever see in a lifetime, but like Jamie, he didn't flaunt it. It was subtle. There were little clues, like the way CT pronounced croissants with a French inflection. He wasn't pretentious, he just grew up vacationing in France. Same with Jamie, she wasn't a girl who was into labels. She had them, but to her they were just clothes.

Jamie Manning was a puzzle. Last week, he all but convinced himself he had imagined her. Hell, if it weren't for the claw marks she left on his back, Ryder would have thought he was crazy. Just when he had given up hope of ever seeing her again, BAM, there she was. Ryder didn't want to do the interview. He bitched about it the entire drive to the station, but thank fuck his bandmates didn't listen to him. Now, not only did he have a name, he had a lunch date.

Ryder considered taking her to Cibo, the Italian restaurant where he worked, but it didn't feel right. Not with Jamie. Not when she so clearly gave more of a fuck about what was going on in the Middle East than she did about fine dining. That's why he drove her fancy car to the old diner on Seventh Street.

The diner was quiet at that time of day; too late for the lunch rush and too early for the dinner crowd. The jukebox hummed an obscure country song as Ryder led the blonde back to his favorite booth. The seats were a hard, shiny, red plastic that felt more like plywood than cushion, and an ever-present layer of syrup coated the table tops. The place wasn't famous or well known, but they had great food and even better service.

"What are you doing?" Jamie asked as Ryder slid into the booth beside her.

"What's it look like I'm doing?" Ryder dropped his arm around her neck and her body melted into his side. He wondered if she even realized she did it. Jamie spent all her time fighting their attraction but her body always gave her away.

"Most people sit opposite each other," she quipped, arching her tawny brow. She was amused and a little embarrassed, yet when his shoulder brushed hers, she smiled and rolled her eyes playfully. For the first time, Ryder got a glimpse of the real her, not Kitty Cat, the wild child he fucked in Dave's office and not reporter Jamie Manning, the consummate professional.

Just Jamie.

He liked Jamie.

"If I sat all the way over there," Ryder murmured into her ear, "I wouldn't be able to do this." His hand slid from her knee up between her legs and cupped her warmth. He thumbed open the button on her gray slacks, and Jamie wiggled underneath him, gnawing her bottom lip. "You like that, Kitty Cat?" he breathed against her neck. His fingers dipped inside her panties. Soft and smooth, and so fucking wet.

"Mmm," she purred and his dick took notice. This girl was going to be the death of him.

"Napoleon?" the familiar female voice caused Ryder to jump. He pulled his hand from in between Jamie's legs and smiled up at their waitress, an older blonde woman, the one who gave birth to him.

"Hey Ma," he smiled, discreetly adjusting his boner. In his defense, she wasn't supposed to be there. She never worked on Fridays.

Jamie's eyes widened in embarrassment. "Mom?" she shrieked, pushing his arm from around her shoulder. Her face was as red as a tomato. It was the cutest fucking thing he'd ever seen.

"Why didn't you tell me you were coming?" his mother asked. "And who's this?"

Annette Ryder was what some people referred to as a helicopter mom, even now, when her son was twenty-six years old, she hovered.

"Mom, this is Jamie. Jamie, this is my mom, Annette."

"Nice to meet you," his mom extended her hand to the still pink Jamie. "You look familiar. Do you eat here often?"

"Oh…umm… no ma'am," Jamie stammered. "I…um…do you watch WSEA-9?"

She was nervous, a side of Jamie he'd never seen. He'd seen her annoyed, and he'd seen her naked, but seeing her nervous was by far his favorite. Scratch that—naked was Ryder's favorite—nervous was a close second, though.

"Ahh," recognition washed over Annette's face, "you did a story about the Easter egg hunts. A little girl peed on you."

"That's me," Jamie nodded.

Irony was spending a week obsessing over a missed connection when all Ryder had to do was turn on Channel 9 News.

"Pretty and smart," Annette beamed.

Ryder hadn't planned on this meeting, but he was glad it was going well. His mother was the most important woman in his life, and Kitty Cat, whether she liked it or not, wasn't going anywhere, anytime soon.

"She's alright," Ryder teased.

"Is that why you forced me to have lunch with you? Because I'm *alright*?" Jamie retorted. And just like that, nervous Jamie was gone and in her place, was the take-no-shit version he had quickly grown accustomed to. Actually, *this* was his favorite Jamie. Strong, beautiful, brave.

Annette's head fell back, her body shook with laughter. "I like her."

"Me too," Ryder said, eyeing the girl with the sarcastic smirk on her face.

"What do you kids want to drink?"

"I'll just have water, please, Ma'am."

"Annette, not Ma'am, okay?" Kitty Cat nodded her agreement then Annette pointed her pencil at her son. "You're usual?"

"Please."

His mother nodded. "I'll be right back. Try to keep your hands out of her pants while I'm gone."

Jamie's face was red again. "I'm going to kill you, *Napoleon*."

"Can you just pretend you didn't hear that?" Ryder didn't think bringing Kitty Cat to the diner all the way through. He'd inadvertently revealed his deepest, darkest secret, *Napoleon*.

"It's…interesting," she laughed. Her blonde hair fell over her shoulders, messy and imperfect, a stark contrast from the woman who interviewed him.

"She wanted me to have a strong name," Ryder defended.

"So she chose a dictator?" Jamie barely finished the sentence before the dam broke. She laughed so loud and for so long a cute little snort escaped her throat, which only caused her to laugh harder.

"You know what, fuck you," Ryder grinned despite himself. Her happiness, even at his expense, was infectious. The way the corners of her eyes crinkled, the sound of her high-pitched giggle, all of it, every part of Jamie's joy fed his muse. It was like she was singing directly to his heart.

His fucking heart.

Yeah, he was totally fucked.

"It's okay," she panted, dabbing at the tears leaking from her eyes. "My parents named me James, after my grandfather. I was supposed to be a boy. They thought I was one, up until they handed me, vagina and all, to my mother in the delivery room. They were so shocked, they just went with it."

"James is hot. Napoleon makes it sound like I have a small dick."

"But you don't," Jamie breathed, running her tongue across her lips. The air between them went from playful to sexual, *Napoleon* and *James* long forgotten.

"No, I don't," he whispered. Ryder wanted to kiss her. It was like she was taunting him, rubbing in the fact she kept that part of herself closed off.

"Okay, kids," Annette returned, her presence easing the tension, "one water and one Shirley Temple, extra cherries."

Jamie eyed his drink with amusement.

"What?" he plucked a cherry from the top of the glass and popped it into his mouth without an ounce of shame. He was a grown man with hair on his balls, so what he liked Shirley Temples?

"Nothing, it's just, I haven't had one of those since I was a little girl."

He stared at her, the look on his face said, *I like Shirley Temples and I'll still make you come like a freight train.*

Needless to say, Kitty Cat let it go.

"You kids ready to order?"

"I'm not that hungry," Jamie shrugged, glancing over the menu. "I'll just have the house salad."

"Sounds good—"

"Oh, and maybe the bacon cheeseburger, and the chili cheese fries and," Jamie looked up from the menu, "how's the pie?"

"Napoleon's favorite. I'll bring over a couple of slices," Annette promised, chuckling to herself.

If Ryder wasn't already obsessed with this girl, her order would have solidified it. She was keeping him on his toes, that was for damn sure.

"What?" Jamie asked, innocently.

"Open your mouth," he demanded plucking another cherry from his glass. Kitty Cat looked like she wanted to protest but obliged. He ran the cherry across her bottom lip, watching with hooded eyes as her tongue darted out to collect his offering. Juice dripped down her chin and he leaned in, licking up the mess, his tongue stopping just below her mouth.

Jamie exhaled, her breath sweet, warm. "That tastes amazing."

And because Ryder was a fucking masochist, he asked, "What's the deal with you and Sean?"

Kitty Cat rolled her eyes, "Way to fuck up the moment, Napoleon."

"He touched you."

"We had sex, once, at Christmas, and now he spends half his time flirting with me and the other half hazing me," she explained, switching her water for his Shirley Temple.

Kitty Cat had a past. He'd assumed as much and he didn't give a fuck about who she'd been with before, but the thought of her being with anyone now made Ryder's blood boil.

"And Grant?"

Confusion twisted on Jamie's face. "Your manager?"

"Yes, you were flirting with him." Ryder was acting like a jealous dick head. He knew it, but he couldn't help himself.

"I wasn't flirting, it's called being professional. You should try it instead of storming out of the room like a fucking child."

"I didn't like it."

"I already told you—"

"I know," Ryder put his hands up in surrender, "you don't do the boyfriend thing."

"I'm focused on my career."

"I get it, I do. The band eats up a lot of my free time. Most girls I meet can't handle that, they get jealous and clingy. I told myself I was done with relationships, but I can't just ignore this thing between us. It's weird and inconvenient but it's fucking real, so what are we going to do about it?" Ryder put his cards on the table, and he hoped like hell Jamie wasn't about to knock them back off.

"Ignore it and hope it goes away?" she suggested. It wasn't exactly what he wanted to hear, but she wasn't telling him to kick rocks either.

"No, Kitty Cat, we can't."

"What do you want?"

"I want you," Ryder stated simply, because he did. "I want to watch bad movies and go bowling or whatever people do on dates. I want you to tell me about your day, and I want to fuck you over and over again. I want to live inside that pretty little pussy of yours, Kitty Cat. "

"Sounds an awful lot like a relationship to me."

"We don't have to call it anything. We can go at your speed."

Jamie inhaled and exhaled, swiping a finger across her bottom lip.

"I know you're freaking out, but don't," he assured her. "I'm not asking you to marry me or anything. I just want to get to know you better."

"I don't—"

"Just say yes." Ryder pinned her greens with his hazels and she melted under his gaze. Jamie had big balls and her soul burned bright red, but with Ryder she was soft and pink.

Wrinkling her nose, the corners of Jamie's mouth turned down into a frown. "I'm not your girlfriend, and I can't promise to be any good at anything aside from the sex stuff but… I'm not fucking anyone else at the moment, so why not?"

Ryder grinned. "That was the most romantic thing anyone has ever said to me."

"Kiss my ass," Jamie rolled her eyes, taking a sip of his Shirley Temple.

"I plan to do more than kiss it."

Ryder's hand flexed around the soft, leather covering of the steering wheel. "This is a great fucking car," he said pulling the Rover onto his street.

"Thanks. It was a graduation gift," Kitty Cat muttered. She watched, enchanted, as a group of school kids with oversized bookbags ran down the sidewalk.

"Feels like I'm cheating on my Harley."

"Don't tell me you're one of *those* guys," she groaned, shooting him a sideways glance.

"One of what guys?"

"A gearhead." She spit the words out as if they were unwelcome in her mouth. Flashes of Jamie kneeling in front of him flooded Ryder's brain and he wondered, if she would spit him out too or would she swallow?

Shaking off the x-rated thoughts, he answered her question. "No, that would be Javi. I just really fucking love my bike."

Jamie's attention shifted back to the children. Her eyes shined with an emotion Ryder hadn't seen on her beautiful face. It felt intimate, real, like another flash of the authentic Jamie.

"You live here?" she asked looking up at the blue house. It was the standard reaction when people found out where they lived. Lithium Springs moved into the single-family home, in the modest, working-class neighborhood when they decided to get serious about their art. When they weren't working, or getting stoned, they were making music.

"Yeah, for a little over a year now." Ryder shrugged, killing the engine.

"I was expecting something a little more," Jamie looked towards the sky, searching for the right word, "murdery."

"Murdery?" He laughed. Ryder thought he heard everything about their living situation, including the theories that they were in some sort of gay, polyamorous relationship, but this was the first time he'd heard the term, *murdery*.

Opening the passenger's side door, Jamie grinned, "Yes, murdery, but this is better."

Grabbing the leftover food from the backseat, Ryder led Kitty Cat up the steps and into the house. They were greeted by the omnipresent haze of weed smoke and the sound of his band mates arguing over whether Oregon had what it took to make it to the *Final Four*.

Neil Young's face stared back at them from the framed poster hanging in the entryway.

There was a coat rack in the corner, though they never actually used it to hang coats, and an old *Welcome* mat that was so worn it simply read *come*.

"Smells loud in here," Jamie said wrinkling her nose.

"You'll get used to it." If Ryder had his way, she'd never fucking leave again. "I'm going to take the food to the kitchen. My room's up the stairs, first door on the left."

Jamie chewed on her finger as her eyes dipped down his body. Lust charged the space between them. Sex was the only language Jamie understood, and Ryder fully intended to drive his point home.

"Is that you Ry?" CT yelled from the living room.

Ryder groaned. He'd hoped they would be able to sneak past his roommates. "No, it's Santa Clause. Who the fuck else would it be?"

"Why so serious? Did your girl blow you off again?" Javi asked.

Jamie answered for him. "No, she didn't. At least not yet," she added with a wink.

It was quiet for a beat, the silence quickly followed by his high as fuck roommates running out into the entryway. "Kitty Cat," Javi panted wrapping her into a bear hug. "Thank God! He's been a real bitch since you ditched him."

Jamie laughed and it was like a shot of adrenaline right into Ryder's veins. The sound was loud, obnoxious and devoid of any fucks. Some men would have been bothered by Javi letting that little admission slip, but not Ryder. He wasn't a hyper masculine jerk, and he wanted Kitty Cat to know he was serious. He didn't want to play games, not with her.

"Where did you guys go?" CT asked.

Ry held up the bag of leftovers. "To the diner." Ryder and CT locked eyes. Shock was written all over the drummer's face. Ryder had one rule, *no bitches in the sanctuary*. He may have been a lovesick douche ninety-nine percent of the time, but he never brought girls to the diner. He went there to celebrate, to get away, to recharge. The fact that he took Jamie there after spending a total of six hours with her was out of character, at best. At worst, he was pussy whipped. In his defense, it was a pretty pussy.

"You didn't bring us anything?" Javi pouted, oblivious to the silent conversation going on over his head.

"It's okay, Son," CT said patting Javi on the back, "we can order pizza."

Javi grinned a toothy grin. "Thanks, Dad."

Ryder rolled his eyes at his friends. They were the only family he had outside of his mother. They were more like brothers, really. Ryder was the sensitive one, CT was the impulsive one, and Javi was the funny one.

"The game is about to start. You guys want to watch or do you have plans?" Javi wiggled his brows suggestively.

"We have plans."

"What game?"

Ryder arched his brow at Jamie. All he wanted was to be inside her, but apparently, she had other ideas. "Kitty Cat," he began.

"Chill out man," Javi threw his arm over her shoulder as he steered Jamie towards the living room. "We know where she works now."

Ryder sighed, stomping his way to the kitchen. Everything with Jamie was so damn hot and cold. She wanted him, then she didn't, then she did again. She was driving him insane.

"What's up with you and this girl?" CT asked, following him to the kitchen.

"What do you mean?" Ryder put the food in the fridge. He knew what the fuck CT meant, but he hoped he would at least wait to start the interrogation until half-time.

"Don't play dumb asshole. You falling in love with a girl five minutes after meeting her is nothing new, but taking her to the diner? That's beyond, dude."

Ryder dropped his palms onto the counter, leaning on it for support. The fading yellow walls of the kitchen were closing in on him. He opened his mouth to make up an excuse, but only truth came. "She's different."

CT's eyes darted to the ceiling, a groan emanated from his throat. "You said that about Misha, and Amber, and who was that girl you met in Portland, Brit, or Bree, Beth?"

"Bianca," Ryder huffed, "and it's not like that."

"Right," CT chuckled. He opened the fridge and swiped the pie out of the bag.

Ryder glared at him.

Picking the slice of pie up with his hands, CT shrugged. "Munchies, bro."

SEVEN

Unravel Me

Jamie

Jamie inhaled, allowing the smoke to fill her lungs and set her at ease. After a week of berating herself for *the incident*, then the entire morning stressing over having to do the interview, she resolved to let whatever was happening between her and Ryder happen. While she had no illusions about how this thing would end, she was living in the moment, and fighting it was only adding unnecessary anxiety.

The couch shifted next to her, and she opened her eyes in time to see Ryder lift her legs across his lap. "Hi," he breathed, kissing her nose sweetly. The golden flecks in his eyes shined with an emotion that tied her insides in knots.

"Hi," she replied, bringing her tattooed finger to her lip. *Her tell.* Jamie could deny her attraction to him until she was blue in the face, but her words meant nothing if her body wouldn't listen.

Ryder's scent invaded her nostrils, it was clean and manly, and the feel of his hand tracing circles on her thighs made her quiver with anticipation. Jamie craved his touch, and she hated herself for it. She wasn't this girl, this needy person who snuggled on the couch, stealing glances at her beau. She was James fucking Manning, a no-nonsense, ball buster who didn't need anyone.

So why did she need him?

"Do we really have to watch this game?" he asked, pulling her finger from her mouth, bringing it to his. He kissed it once, then again, and then a third time. She could see the longing in his eyes. He wanted to kiss her, he was practically begging for it, but that was one line Jamie wasn't ready to cross. Her body was fair game, but her heart was kept under lock.

Basketball wasn't Jamie's thing, she couldn't care less about Oregon State, and the only madness she recognized in March was Daylight Savings Time, because having to wake up an hour earlier was her personal definition of insanity. Even so, she was stalling. Sex she could handle. Meaningless sex was an art she'd mastered. It was the after that frightened her.

Ryder was unlike any other man she'd been with. He didn't pretend and he wasn't afraid to show affection; not in front of his friends, not even in front of his mother. Jamie signed up for a casual fling, but the entire day reeked of monogamy. She was starting to feel like a "g-word," and that was a truth she couldn't ignore. She contemplated running again, but Ryder was persistent in his pursuit of her. He'd probably just show up at the station and cause another scene in the parking lot. Running was pointless, and for the first time in her life, she didn't want to.

The game started, and the four of them settled into a comfortable silence, punctuated by the occasional profanity thrown at the screen. Jamie stayed firmly rooted at Ryder's side, her legs intertwined with his. His eyes were focused on the screen, but his hands continued to explore her body, rubbing, and caressing her through her business casual attire. Every touch, every stolen kiss to her temple, behind her ear, her neck, combined to turn her into a quivering mess.

"Are you okay?" Ryder asked, whispering on her neck. His warm breath on her throat did things to her body she didn't even know was possible. He regarded her for a minute, then smiled devilishly. He knew the effect he was having on her and the bastard was enjoying it.

"I think I'm ready to go upstairs now," Jamie purred, turning so she could look him in the eye. Her unspoken message, *fuck me, please.*

"Is that so?" His gaze focused in on her lips. Ryder laced one of his hands in her hair, pulling her mouth to his slowly. The intention was clear in his eyes, "Still not on the lips?" he asked, rubbing his nose to hers.

Jamie didn't answer right away, she also didn't turn her head. She trusted him not to force her. She trusted that he would respect her boundaries, but the fucked-up thing was she wished he wouldn't. It would make it easier to resist him in the end, because even with all Jamie's trust in Ryder, she couldn't trust herself.

"Still not on the lips," she breathed.

"Hey lovebirds," CT said, pulling them from the moment. "What do you want on your pizza?"

It was half-time.

Ryder looked at Jamie expectantly, waiting for her to choose. Inside she was screaming, *who gives a shit about pizza, just fuck me,* but went with, "It's up to you, I'm still kind of full from the diner," instead.

Ryder nodded, and turned to his friend, "Hawaiian then."

"On second thought," she cringed, "maybe I better choose. Pineapple doesn't belong on pizza. It's disgusting, I'm thoroughly disgusted. I can't believe I let you have sex with me."

"I told you, dude, pineapple isn't a real pizza topping," Javi said.

"I've seen you eat baked beans straight from a can, motherfucker. You can't judge me for liking pineapple pizza. And you," Ryder growled turning his attention back to Jamie, "if I remember correctly you begged me to let you come."

"Only after you begged me to let you fuck me."

"Ooohhh," CT and Javi jeered, simultaneously.

"And now you call me sex god," the smug bastard countered.

"Ooohhh." The guys fell over themselves with laughter.

Being in their little house was odd, but what was worse was how comfortable Jamie felt there. Like she belonged. Jamie never felt like she belonged anywhere, but amazingly, she fit right in with the band of gorgeous misfits.

It was an illusion of course, a fantasy she indulged. The guys were only nice to her because of Ryder and he was only nice because, well, she wasn't sure what he wanted yet, but Jamie decided to cross that bridge when she came to it. She'd be the one standing on the other side with a match, watching it burn.

Jamie's eyes widened, "That was… I didn't…" she stammered.

"I…I…I," Ryder teased pulling her back on his lap, turning her body so she was straddling him. He palmed her ass, daring her to keep going.

Jamie rubbed her finger against her lip, "Whatever, pineapple pizza is still trash."

"I work at an Italian restaurant, and we put pineapples on pizzas all the time."

"That's not an Italian thing. I bet some stoner came up with it," CT argued, and Jamie nodded her agreement. No one seemed to care that she was practically riding, Ryder, so she went with it.

"No, dude, it was probably invented by someone who had a surplus of expiring pineapple chunks," Javi reasoned.

"I know a way to settle this." Jamie reached over to the table and grabbed her phone. "Let me introduce you to my good friend, Google."

"Boo," Ryder grunted, taking the phone from her hand, "that's cheating."

Her initial instinct was to lunge at him. Her phone was like a vital organ; she needed it to survive. Deciding against violence, she asked, "How?"

"Because half the fun is in the debate, smartphones ruin that."

"Here we go," CT said with a roll of his eyes.

"Dude," Javi groaned, "I thought you wanted her to like you?"

"What?" Jamie looked around the room. She wasn't sure what they were talking about. She was still reeling from the knowledge that this seemingly perfect man liked fruit on his pizza.

"He's anti-technology," CT explained. "He still has a flip phone."

"What?!" Jamie asked incredulously, shuffling off his lap. "A fucking flip phone? They still make those?" She hadn't seen a flip phone since middle school. She knew there had to be a catch. He couldn't be this hot, and this talented, and this sweet, without something being amiss. Jamie thought it was Napoleon. She was wrong.

Ryder reached into his pocket, pulled out the little silver phone, and waved it in the air. "Smart phones are a waste of money. This does everything I need it to do."

"Now, I really can't believe I let you fuck me," Jamie said plucking the phone from his hand. "This thing belongs in a museum. Does it even have a camera?"

"Yes, smart ass."

"But how do you stay connected, social media, the internet, GPS? I use my phone for everything."

"I don't do social media."

Jamie gasped, taking personal offense to that last revelation. She wasn't as active online as she once was, blame the social media clause of her contract with WSEA-9, but still. "Who the fuck *are* you? Are you a serial killer? Is he a serial killer?"

"Shit," Javi chuckled, "maybe that's it."

Ryder took the phone and tossed it on the table, then lifted Jamie back onto his lap. "I just don't see the point. I'm more for authentic interactions, not typing "lol" over things that are mildly amusing at best."

"You *are* a serial killer," she groaned.

"Okay, okay," CT exclaimed, jumping to his feet, "according to Wikipedia the first person to bastardize pizza with pineapples was some Canadian chef. So, it looks like Javi is probably right."

"I knew it," Javi grinned falling back into the couch, "I fucking knew it."

Ryder's lips jutted out in a pout that rivaled *Derek Zoolander*. "You can all go to hell."

"I'll go anywhere as long as there's Wifi, Napoleon," Jamie smiled, rubbing her nose against his.

"And I'll go anywhere as long as you're there," he murmured, returning her Eskimo kiss.

"Stop," she whispered, "you're being weird again."

An hour and three large pizzas later, the game Jamie insisted they watch was now going into overtime, and she was squirming in her seat. When she suggested they stay downstairs it was because she needed time to sort through her conflicting emotions, but who could think after spending two hours with Ryder's hands and mouth exploring nearly every inch of her body.

"I have a confession to make," Jamie said nipping at his earlobe. In her twenty-four years on this planet Jamie had never been the touchy-feely type, but she couldn't help herself around the guitarist.

He angled his head, giving her better access, his eyes focused on the screen. "Hmm?"

"I liked the bastard pizza," she whispered, kissing, then biting his jaw.

That earned her a slow, sexy grin. "Trust me Kitty Cat, I'll never steer you astray."

"It's not you that I'm worried about."

"Why do you say that?"

"Nothing," she mouthed.

Jamie regretted the words as soon as they left her lips. They were having fun. It was nice, normal, and she couldn't help but think she just Jamie'd it up. She allowed herself to get too comfortable in his space, with his friends. She was stupid for pretending this wouldn't end in ashes.

Ryder studied her. "Tell me what's going on up there, Kitty Cat."

"Nothing. Now I'm the one being weird. Watch the end of the game. Forget I said anything."

"You want to head upstairs?" he asked, pulling her finger from her mouth. She didn't even realize she'd been gnawing on it. This man was turning her inside out, exposing her bones, seeing right through to her skeleton.

"Yes, but not to talk."

"James," he said, his voice pleading. He wanted her to let him in.

It was a fair request, but it was one she couldn't accommodate. So Jamie did what Jamie did best, self-destruct. "I could just leave," she suggested. She didn't come to the other side of town to talk about her feelings, she came for sex.

Ryder's jaw ticked in annoyance. Wordlessly reaching for her hand, he pulled her to her feet. He was pissed at her for shutting down, and she was pissed at him for pushing. They were two live grenades, ready to explode, in more ways than one.

"You're leaving now?" Javi asked, as they walked past. "There's only a few minutes left in the game."

"Let me know how it ends," Ryder grunted.

Nervous energy flooded her body as she stumbled behind him, up the stairs and into his bedroom. Jamie swallowed against the mixture of lust and trepidation caught in her throat as the door slammed shut behind them. She was anxious—for the sex—for the argument. Tension billowed into the air like a thick fog on a spring morning. It was kind of their thing, the push and the pull, the fighting and the fucking, she was quickly becoming addicted to it, to him.

Jamie stepped into the room, ignoring the heated gaze on her back. It was different than she expected, warm and inviting, a sharp contrast to the frat vibe of the rest of the house. The lighting was dim, the walls covered in artwork, and the dresser housed a display of succulents.

"Why all the cactuses?" she asked, her ire temporarily forgotten.

"Because they are the survivors of the plant world. They're found in the harshest environments, under the most barren conditions and yet they thrive. They're fighters."

Ryder's room, like him, was the perfect mix of masculine and feminine. It was decorated in deep, rich colors, with leather and wooden accents, but the plants and the art, gave way to his sensitive side. He was the type of man to fuck a woman within an inch of her life, then hold her, and tell her it would be alright. He was sunshine and rain, and Lucifer and Gabriel, all wrapped up into one tattooed package.

"Is this your mom?" she asked stopping in front of an oil painting of a blonde woman in a waitress uniform. She was hauntingly beautiful, sad with a quiet strength. Jamie only met her briefly, but the resemblance was uncanny.

"Yeah," Ryder answered coming up behind her. He snaked his arms around her waist, his erection poking her in the back. He either wasn't mad anymore, or he planned on taking his anger out on her body. Jamie was good with both options.

"Did you do this?" she asked, tipping her chin towards the canvas.

"I did them all," he murmured into her ear. His smell, a mix of Ryder and weed, overwhelmed her. His body was warm and hard, and set her skin ablaze. Jamie's attraction to him was unnatural. He was the modern Renaissance man: he sang, played the guitar, painted, and fucked her until she saw stars.

"The more you know," she said more to herself than to him.

"I'd like to know you, and why you said what you said downstairs."

"And I'd like you to fuck me," she countered, stomping all over that self-destruct button.

Ryder's grip tightened on her hips. "Jamie," he warned.

"No, I'm not your girlfriend. I don't need you to fix me. I just want to get laid." Jamie lifted her shirt over her head. Her green eyes met his hazel and her voice dropped down to a whisper. "This is all I can give you. Do you want it or not?"

Ryder ran his fingers through his wavy blond hair. He searched her face, looking for some sort of understanding, and she searched his, imploring him to have patience. They stood in silence for so long, she considered putting her shirt back on.

Just as she was about to admit defeat, he barked, "Pants too."

Dropping the shirt, Jamie peeled off her slacks, then reached behind herself to unclasp her bra. The straps slid down her arms in slow motion, and the bra fell to the top of the pile of her other clothes. Next, Jamie hooked her thumbs under the strings of her bikini briefs and stepped out of those too.

She stood bared to him, feeling a strange mix of pride and insecurity as he stared at her with lust filled eyes. Her hand ghosted up her stomach, hovering over her scar. She hated it. A painful reminder that she'd been broken and stitched back together, but they forgot a piece. She'd never truly be whole again.

Ryder walked around to her front, running a hand across her torso. His rough fingertips brushed her scar and Jamie took an involuntary step back. "Come here," he commanded, and the look on his face told her not to argue. She did as she was told, her body again reacting without consent from her brain. "Stop running," he growled into her neck.

"I can't make any promises. I'm…I," Jamie struggled for the words, "I'm just not accustomed to someone wanting more from me than—"

"This?" he asked slipping a finger into her sex. She nodded, dropping her head to his shoulder. He pushed the long digit in and out of her body, swirling it around and around. "This is mine now," he said, adding a second finger. "And this," he pulled his fingers, slick with her arousal, from her core then slid them between her ass cheeks, and rubbed her there. He made his intention clear, not penetrating, but applying a slight pressure. She jumped at the sensation of his finger exploring the tight ring. Jamie had anal before but didn't care for it. With Ryder, though, she might be up for trying again. "And this, too" he continued, placing his other hand over her heart.

Jamie inhaled, and exhaled, chanting her affirmations. She tried not to freak out and go all crazy Jamie.

"I'm not going to push, but I'm not going to play games or bullshit you either. I'm all in and I don't give a fuck if it's too soon to say that shit, it's how I feel."

"Okay," she nodded.

If Jamie weren't as emotionally stunted as she was, she probably would have echoed his sentiments. She felt the pull, but unlike Ryder, she resisted. Commitment was for dreamers, and Jamie didn't have the luxury of living with her head in the clouds.

Ryder gripped Jamie by the waist and spun her around. His fingertips trailed down her spine, leaving goosebumps in their wake. "I love these," he said, brushing his thumbs across her Venus piercing. "Do you have anymore?"

She shook her head, grateful for the change of subject, "No, but I thought about getting my nipples done. Did it hurt?" she asked.

His hands continued their exploration down to her butt. "Like a bitch, but worth it." He massaged her, pushing and pulling her ass, applying just enough pressure to make her core clench.

"What about the other one?" The mention of it made her shudder. He was right, his Prince Albert was her new favorite thing.

Ryder smirked darkly and instead of answering he barked, "Get on your knees, Kitty Cat."

Jamie dropped to the ground. She unbuttoned his jeans and dragged them down his thighs. His erection sprang free, and she stared, head to head, with the most beautiful cock she'd ever seen. She knew he was big, she felt it last time, but seeing it up close was breathtaking.

Sex god was fitting. She couldn't take her eyes off it. The tip was wide and smooth, with two silver balls sticking out at the top and through the head. The shaft was long and thick and veined. There was a smattering of sandy hair at the base. He was well groomed, not completely shaven, but maintained.

Jamie pressed a kiss to the silver ball, swirling her tongue around the metal. The reporter in her wanted to ask a million questions, but they could wait; there was a more pressing matter she needed to address. "How do I?" she asked looking up at him, licking her lips.

"Just like you would if I didn't have a piercing."

"But what if it gets stuck, you know, on my tonsils or something?"

Ry chuckled, "You watch too many movies Kitty Cat, and besides, this is a bar," he explained, running the metal across her lips. "Maybe if I was wearing a ring that might be a legit concern, but with this you'll be fine, just take your time. Get used to how it feels in your mouth, and I promise to make sure you get plenty of practice."

Jamie ran her tongue up the underside of his shaft before wrapping her lips around the tip and sucking. Working around the metal was different, not difficult, but new. She flicked the silver beads gently with her tongue, peeking up to gauge his reaction. Ryder's head fell back and his eyes closed. Jamie smiled to herself, making a mental note that he liked it.

She went slow at first, like he suggested, only taking him partially into her mouth, but once she was accustomed to the feel of it she pushed him in a little further, coating him with her saliva. Jamie's jaw dropped and she swallowed more of him, sucking him down to the root. Spittle seeped out of the sides of her mouth as he touched places in her throat she didn't know existed.

Fingers threaded in her hair, and Jamie's head flew back roughly, "Get up." His voice was disjointed, gruff, almost pained.

"Was it okay?" she asked, scrambling to her feet.

"Too fucking good." Ryder pushed her down on the bed, and finished undressing before climbing next to her. His mattress whined in protest. "I want to taste you too," he explained, pulling her on top of him. "Turn around, and sit on my face." In every other aspect of their relation-date-ship-thingy, Ry let Jamie take the lead, but in the bed room he was in charge. The assertiveness in his voice alone was enough to make Jamie dissolve into a puddle of need.

Jamie got into position, hovering over his mouth, and leaned down so she could keep sucking him off as his tongue, warm and wet, danced lazily around her opening. Ryder took his time, worshiping every inch of her, kissing and licking and sucking.

She moaned around his cock. A delicious tingle started at her toes and traveled throughout her body.

"Keep sucking," he hummed against her flesh. The vibrations caused her to squeeze her thighs together, trapping his head between her legs. It didn't deter Ryder at all, he devoured her, fucking her with his tongue. He swirled around and around and in and out, pushing her closer and closer.

She'd gotten comfortable with the piercing and was finding her rhythm sucking him into her mouth, allowing the spit to dribble down his shaft.

"Oh god," she yelled, grinding down on his face. His teeth grazed her clit, and she was lost in sensation. She'd given up all pretense of blowing him and instead focused on keeping herself upright.

"Come on, Kitty Cat, I want you to come in my mouth."

He sucked her clit, and she came so hard it felt like she was having a seizure. Ryder rolled her onto her back and climbed on top of her, his erection probing her entrance. He kissed her neck, holding her tightly as he rubbed the head of his cock through her folds. He was warm and smooth and, not wearing a condom.

"Ryder," she gasped, "condom. Condom. Condom."

"Fuck, sorry," he said, sitting back. He reached into his nightstand and pulled out a foil packet and rolled on the rubber. Then, with the barrier in place he plunged into her, sending a fresh wave of pleasure down her spine. It was too much. She was in the throes of her first orgasm and there he was pushing her towards her second. "Relax, Kitty Cat," he murmured, pushing her hair off her forehead. "I'm going to take care of you." His pace was slow as she came down. Her body spent, but as promised Ryder took his time giving her everything she wanted, and even a few things she didn't know she needed.

After a while her breathing evened out and she started to regain use of her limbs. Jamie wrapped her arms around his neck, pulling him closer. "Please," she begged, but for what she wasn't sure. This was the closest to making love she'd ever been, and the emotion coursing through her was overwhelming. "Ry, fuck me," she moaned.

"No, I want this slow. I want to savor you. Last time I had to share," he whispered, as he continued to thrust in and out lazily. Every time he pulled back she could feel the little silver ball grazing her g-spot. Every movement inched her back to ecstasy. "No more running, Jamie. I want you and I won't apologize for that, but if I go too far just tell me and I'll back off, okay?"

"No more running," she agreed. Heat ignited her body, another orgasm threatening to explode.

"Good." He grabbed her by the waist and slammed into her roughly, tilting his hips down, thrusting into her so hard it was almost painful—only it wasn't. It was exactly what she needed and somehow, he knew. Being there, in his room, surrounded by him, was the closest she'd ever come to nirvana.

EIGHT

Hands to Myself

RYDER

> Sex God,
> This doesn't count as running because I'm leaving a note. Yesterday was fun, thank you. I'm not entirely sure if that antique you call a cell phone lets you send and receive texts messages, but here's my number just in case.
> -x
> Kitty Cat.

Ryder scanned the note again, smiling at the bubbly script written in green ink on a page torn from his sketch pad. Green. His favorite color for as long as he could remember. The color of her eyes. The color of the cacti sitting on his dresser. The color of life. She more than likely chose it at random, but that was the thing about Jamie;

she fit into his life like she was always meant to be there.

Grabbing his phone, he quickly saved her number, then tapped out a text.

Ryder: U could have woken me up before you left, or better yet, kept ur ass in bed.

Her reply was almost immediate.

Jamie: Don't most guys prefer sleeping alone?

Ryder: I'm not most guys. I like having someone in my bed

Jamie: Someone?

Ryder: U James. I haven't slept so soundly since I was 10.

Ryder was a light sleeper, a side effect of the six months he and his mother spent cot hopping from women's shelter to women's shelter when they first moved to Seattle. It comforted him having someone close, and sleeping next to Jamie was the equivalent of chasing an Ambien with two shots of whiskey.

Jamie: eyeroll I would insert an emoji, but I'm not sure if it would work on your phone.

Ryder: Fuck u I would insert the middle finger emoji but…

Jamie: I don't think you thought that one all the way through. Your phone is still the butt of the joke.

Ryder: ok smart ass. what are you doing today?

Jamie: Kicking ass and taking names.

Ryder: come over when ur done. we have a show tonight.

Jamie: Is that a request or a demand?

Ryder: It's whichever one will get u here.

Jamie: I'll see what I can do.

Ryder sighed, throwing the phone back onto the side of the bed that still smelled like her. In the span of twenty-four hours Kitty Cat impressed his mother, won over his friends, and somehow managed to make him even more pussy whipped than he already was. She was a tornado, a savage, and just when he thought they were starting to get over some of her commitment issues, she goes and runs—again. The note was something, but waking up with her would have been better.

Standing, Ryder lifted his arms over his head, and cringed. No wonder she left, he reeked of sex and stale weed.

As he made his way to the bathroom, images of the night before flooded his brain. Jamie's body on top of his, the way she felt, the way she tasted, it all came rushing back around the same time the blood in his body went south. He was hard as stone, and the one girl he wanted to sink his dick into, couldn't seem to stand his presence for longer than a few hours at a time.

Ryder made a promise to himself as he stepped under the hot spray of the shower. The next time he had her in his bed, he was going to fuck her within an inch of her life. She'd be too exhausted to run, and he wouldn't have to jerk off like a fucking tool. He wrapped his right hand around his shaft and began to stroke himself, thinking of Kitty Cat and the way her green eyes rolled to the back of her head when she came.

The steam rose, thick, almost suffocating as he tugged harder, faster, losing himself in the memory. The melody of Jamie's whimpers served as the instrumental to his solo performance.

Thump.
Thump.
Thump.

The baseline built in his mind as he pictured her riding his face. She tasted sweet, a combination of peaches and musk that was uniquely Jamie. He could survive eating only her for the rest of his life. He pumped up and down squeezing his shaft. The sounds of the snare crescendoed. Desire swelled in his cock as music and moans combined to orchestrate his fantasy. His stomach muscles tensed, and hot white cum shot from the tip of his dick, leaving him utterly sated.

The moaning stopped.

The drumming stopped.

All that was left was the sound of the water beading down on his skin and Jamie's voice, as she chanted.

Sex god.

Sex god.

Sex god.

Ryder's head fell forward, and he gasped. "Fucking Kitty Cat." She inspired him even when she wasn't around. *Sex God* was fucking genius, and it could be a game changer for Lithium Springs.

It was poetry; she was art.

Once he caught his breath he reached for the soap, and quickly washed away the remnants of his morning rub and tug. He needed to be fast. Javi would be leaving for work soon and who the fuck knew if CT was even home. The lyrics were coming to him in a rush and he wanted to get the beat out before he lost it. He finished his shower, threw on a pair of shorts and took the steps two at a time.

Javi and CT were in the kitchen, Javi in his work overalls while CT sported the same clothes as the night before. No doubt he'd just rolled in.

"What's up?" Javi nodded as Ryder took a seat in the empty chair. The fourth chair had disappeared one night after one of their more epic ragers. None of them knew what happened to it. "Where's

Kitty Cat?"

"She left a while ago," Ryder said, trying to conceal his disappointment. They already gave him enough shit. He didn't need them calling him a clinger too.

"You guys should have come out with us last night. It was so much fun. I thought I was going to get alcohol poisoning." CT grinned, looking oddly proud. "Also, I smashed Tiff. That was cool, right?"

Ryder waved his friend off, "I don't give a fuck."

"Just making sure dude." CT narrowed his eyes at Javi. "I don't want to be like some people and stomp all over the boundaries."

"Dude, how many times do I have to tell you, I didn't know Quinn was your cousin." Javi and Quinn had hooked up randomly one night a few months earlier, and CT flipped his shit when he found his little cousin in the kitchen, straddling the bass player. It was all Ryder could do to stop World War III. Family was off limits, but to Javi's credit, Quinn never mentioned being related to CT and he'd ended shit before it went any further.

"Anyway," Ryder said, in an attempt to steer the conversation back to safer waters, "I was trying to catch you before you left for work." Javi was the only one of them with a real job. He worked at his brother's body shop. Carlos was cool. He supported them, and gave Javi a lot of leeway to take time off for band stuff, but he never let his little brother slack off. If anything, he worked Javi harder than the other mechanics, saying their father didn't work his entire life to raise an entitled asshole.

"You know how we were talking about it being spring break and we needed to capitalize on students being home for Easter?"

"Yeah," the drummer and bassist said in unison.

"Well, I've got an idea for a new song, something Jamie said," Ryder smiled.

CT rolled his eyes. "Nobody wants to hear that love-sick shit."

"One," Ryder held up a finger, "suck my dick from the back. Two, it's not a love song. I was thinking of calling it *Sex God*."

His friends looked at him like he was crazy. "Damn, Ry, what the fuck are you doing to that girl and can you teach me?" CT joked.

"It can't be taught," Javi smirked, "you've either got it or you don't."

"Cocky bastard."

"Ask your cousin how cocky I am," Javi quipped, before realizing his mistake.

CT moved to stand but Ryder grabbed him by the shirt, and pulled him back into his chair. "When I was in the shower just now, I could hear it in my head. It was like background music."

"Ew, dude, were you jerking off?" CT asked, forgetting about his anger.

"No, well yes, but that's beside the point. It would be a great song to fuck to. C, man, I have this idea for a wicked drum solo. Hell, the whole song is heavy on percussion. It's a pounding baseline, it's going to change the game."

"It sounds dope and now would be the perfect time to start selling hats, t-shirts, and all that. Ry, you could draw a logo and the cousin-fucker can build the website."

"Dude," Javi groaned.

"I'll look into copyrighting it all," CT continued. He was in charge of the day to day aspects of managing the band, and Grant, his brother helped out with the rest. Their dad was a big shot corporate lawyer with a client list that read like a copy of *Forbes Magazine*. CT never went to college, but his upbringing and fancy prep schools taught him more about business than Javi's technical degree in mechanics, and Ryder's year at community college combined.

"Do you have work today?" Ry asked.

"Not until later," CT said. He worked at a gym, but didn't do much actual work, unless you called scamming pussy and lifting weights work.

"You good to jam for a bit or do you need to knock out?"

"You know my motto, plenty of time to sleep when I'm dead," CT grinned. "Let me just grab some coffee and we can get started."

Javi frowned, standing to take his dirty cereal bowl to the sink. "I wish I didn't have to go. It sucks you fuckers don't have day jobs. I always miss all the good shit."

"At least you have money, man. Since we started at the Rabbit Hole, I had to give up my Saturday nights at Cibo and the little bit we are getting from the door ain't cutting it."

"Just have faith," CT said, slapping him on the back. "This shit, it's going to explode, you just gotta believe."

Faith was something Ryder lost years ago. His entire life was a series of bad days and storms to weather, but even he had to admit, it was all starting to fall into place. His band, his music, his art. He could almost see it, the dream Ryder dreamt since he was old enough to hold a guitar was just within reach.

NINE

All the Small Things

Jamie

When Jamie was younger, she and her brother Chris spent weekends at their grandparents' house. They'd run around the backyard of the massive estate for hours while their grandpa watched from the porch with the newspaper in one hand and a glass of ice tea in the other.

Jamie loved going to her grandparents' house. It was as much an escape for Chris and her as it was for their parents. They would play and play until their breathing was shallow and their limbs were sore.

Then they'd run back to the porch, throw themselves on the ground and huff, *"Grampy James, we're so exhausted."* He would promptly reply with a, *"You kids don't even know what exhausted looks like,"* and chuckle as they stalked into the house to harass their grandma for lemonade. Back then she didn't get what he was trying to say. Now though, she understood his meaning crystal clear.

In the weeks that followed the interview, Jamie settled into a routine of sorts.

Work.

Work.

Work.

And for good measure, a little more work.

Sarah's maternity leave increased Jamie's workload in more ways than she could have ever imagined. In addition to finding talent, preparing interview questions, and hosting *The Local Spotlight*, Jamie maintained her normal roster, and even volunteered for an overnight trip to Portland. The hours were grueling, the assignments were mostly fluff pieces, but she prayed that her willingness to be a team player would force Tina to take notice.

Exhausted didn't even cover it. Twelve hour days at the station and one thing kept her sane. One person kept her motivated. Ryder and his Prince Albert did more to relieve her stress and anxiety than baking and her other slew of vices combined.

Their sex was intense; her orgasms left her breathless. Even on nights when all they could manage was a lazy side fuck, he left her sated. But it wasn't just the sex. It was him. It was the modest house that she somehow became a fixture in. Much like the table with three chairs in the kitchen, and the old sofa in the living room, Jamie's presence in their space was a natural fit.

One night, after a particularly long day, she arrived to the house around midnight. The guys were in the living room, hanging out with a few of the Rabbit Hole staffers, drinking and laughing. Jamie was so drained from the day, she barely had enough energy to say hello, before trudging up the stairs and falling into Ryder's bed. An hour later, she awoke nestled between his strong arms. "*Good night Kitty Cat*," he whispered, his whiskey scented breath an odd comfort as they both drifted off to sleep.

She hated those nights, the ones when she was too exhausted to think. She hated her body for taking her to his house on autopilot. She hated him for being so goddamned perfect. Most of all she hated the feeling of waking up in his arms, knowing that Ry wanted more than she was capable of giving.

Jamie's issues with commitment didn't seem to deter Ryder

any. In the past three weeks, he had taken her on more dates than she'd been on in two years. He was smart, never called them dates. He would say things like, "*I'm sick of takeout, let's go somewhere.*" Or "*Javi and I were supposed to see this movie, but he bailed on me.*" What was worse than his deception was that she fell for it. She blamed her lapse in judgment on the long hours and lack of sleep.

Once she caught on to his little game, Jamie knew she needed to make the boundaries clear.

No more sleeping over.

Ryder didn't fight her on it, not much anyway. He didn't push—he promised he wouldn't—but he did things to make it known he wasn't giving up. He walked her to her car every night, flash an easy smile, and with his dimples on display, he'd ask her to stay. She'd decline and he'd nod, press his lips to her temple and say, "*One day.*"

Those two little words caressed her heart. They made her feel hopeful and that scared her even more than the dates. Hope was a dangerous thing for the hopeless. It was a fallacy Jamie couldn't allow herself to fall victim to. She knew she should put a stop to it, to the entire thing, but he was quickly becoming her new addiction. The way she craved him was unhealthy, but Jamie was nothing if not consistent. She replaced her co-dependence on drinking and partying with Ryder. He wanted her heart and she was selfish enough to let him believe he could have it.

Ryder: u know what sucks?

Jamie rolled onto her back, grinning at the phone. *Stop James*, she scolded herself. It was just a text message, but seeing his name on the screen first thing in the morning made her stomach flutter.

Jamie: What?

Ryder: going to sleep with a hot blonde in my arms and waking up alone.

Jamie: You'll live.

Ryder: but I was really hoping for some morning head.

Jamie: It's Easter Sunday, I'm pretty sure you aren't allowed to talk like that.

Ryder: Jesus died for our sins, don't let his death be in vain.

Jamie: You're going to hell.

Ryder: I'll b sure to get the WiFi password for u when I get there.

"What's got you so smiley?" Kensie asked, pushing her way through Jamie's door and plopping down on the bed.

"Nothing." She still hadn't gotten around to telling her friend about Ryder. Partly because this was the first time they'd seen each other in three weeks, and partly because there was nothing to tell—well, nothing but a few mind-blowing orgasms. "Are you going to mass?" Jamie asked, motioning to the light blue sheath dress her friend wore.

"Yes, I came in here to see if you wanted to ride with me and Trey."

"Wait," Jamie said sitting up, "Trey's going?" Taking a guy to mass on Easter Sunday, was as good as putting a marriage announcement in the paper as far as their small community was concerned. This new development could only mean one thing, Trey dropped the *'I love you'* bomb and it detonated all over Kensington's fairytale princess heart.

Kensie nodded, biting down on her lip. "I figured now was as good a time as any for him to meet my parents."

"Oh." Jamie was still processing Trey going to mass, and Kensie not mentioning the *'I love you's'*. Yes, she was being a hypocrite, but

Jamie never brought guys around and Kensie told Jamie everything. If anything she over-shared.

"Come with us," Kensie said, shooting Jamie her best puppy dog eyes. "I haven't seen you for more than five minutes at a time for almost a month. You're always working, and yes, I spend more time at Trey's than I should, but I miss you."

Jamie missed Kensie too. It was strange being so disconnected from her. Their lives were moving in opposite directions and there wasn't much Jamie could do to stop it. "Trey meeting your parents for the first time, that's like a family thing. I don't want to crash."

"You *are* family, Jam."

"You know what I mean."

"I hate leaving you here alone on Easter."

"It's fine," Jamie scoffed, "I'm practically Buddhist now anyway."

"Are you sure?" Kensie asked, her attention now on her glowing cell phone.

"Is that him?"

She nodded, typing something out on the screen. "We can wait."

"Don't bother. I'm just going to lay here and enjoy the day off. I might even attempt to make macaroons."

Kensie lifted her eyes from her phone, "Please don't burn down our apartment."

"Get out," Jamie smirked, throwing a pillow at Kensie's head. She sidestepped it and wrapped Jamie in a tight hug. Kensie lingered a moment, brushing stray hairs from Jamie's face. It felt less like see you later, and more like don't go. "Happy Easter, Jam," she said, searching Jamie's green eyes for the answer to her unspoken question.

"Happy Easter, Ken," Jamie replied, shifting under her friend's scrutiny. Jamie had a habit of shutting down and shutting people out, but never Kensie. She knew she was doing it, but she couldn't help herself. It was jealousy, but for what Jamie wasn't sure. Maybe for Trey monopolizing her time when Jamie needed a friend, or maybe it was jealousy for Kensie being able to love so freely, while Jamie struggled with letting go enough to go to the fucking movies. Whatever it was, they both felt it. The plates were shifting, and Jamie had to trust that the foundation of their friendship was strong enough to withstand the pending earthquake.

Jamie spent the next two hours lying in bed, binge watching *The Real Housewives*, and sexting Ryder. She pushed her unease about her relationship with Kensie to the back of her mind, sweeping it under the same rug where she kept the rest of her emotions. It was easier to lose herself in the petty drama unfolding in Atlanta than it was to examine her own shortcomings.

A dull buzz reverberated on her chest. Her lips twisted into a smile as she eagerly snatched up the device to see what Ryder wrote, only the buzzing never stopped. It wasn't the text message she had been expecting, but an incoming call, from just about the last person Jamie wanted to talk to on her one day off, *Caroline Manning*.

Against her better judgment, she clicked the green phone icon, answering tersely, "Mother."

"James," her mother replied with an equal amount of venom in her tone. Caroline Manning was like a jellyfish, more beauty than brains, but if you crossed her, she stung. There was nothing maternal about her. "You weren't in mass."

"Nothing gets by you, Mother."

"Are you coming to brunch?"

"No." There was a long pause on the other end, followed by a deep sigh. Jamie hadn't participated in family holidays since she graduated, so why now was her absence a big fucking deal? Inhaling and exhaling, Jamie chanted her affirmations to help calm the fire boiling in her blood.

Be thankful.
Be mindful.
Be kind.

"If Christopher can make it on time from Boston, then you can come in from downtown."

Jamie sat up in bed, "Chris is home?" she asked. Her brother was a junior at MIT, and lived on the East Coast full-time since his freshman year. He rarely came home but when he did, he called.

"It was a surprise, one you would have known about had you come to mass," her mother snipped.

Jamie didn't bother hiding her annoyance. "When's the last time I went to mass?"

"Your father emailed you."

Jamie redirected emails from her parents to her spam folder after her dad wished her a happy twenty-first birthday via his Gmail account. "Did he forget my phone number?"

"I'm calling now, and I expect you, well the television version of you, to be here in an hour."

Rubbing her tattooed finger across her lips, Jamie inhaled, then exhaled, before starting over with the chant. She wanted to tell her mother to go fuck herself, but she refrained. It was Easter and she did miss her little brother.

"Of course, Mother. I'll be there in—" The line went dead before she could finish. "I love you too," she muttered, dragging herself out of bed.

𝄞

Madison Park was a small beach town located to the east of Lake Washington, Seattle's summer getaway. The beach was Jamie's happy place, but going back there was always bittersweet.

Sweet because, as a teenager, she'd spend hours wandering up and down the grassy shoreline. It was where she went to lose herself. The gentle whooshing the lake made as it crashed against the shore comforted her more than her parents ever did.

Bitter because, although Jamie was born into a world of wealth and privilege, her life in Madison Park was anything but happy and the place where she laid her head was never home. A home was a sanctuary filled with love and acceptance; a shelter from the storm of life.

Jamie never had a home there, just a fancy cage. Appearances were everything to Archer and Caroline Manning, and Jamie was never good at fitting in. She was the disappointment, the daughter who wasn't supposed to be. The girl who never did as she was told.

Jamie straightened her lilac dress, and slipped her mask of indifference into place. Holding her head up high, she unlocked the front door of the massive five acre estate, and made her way inside. She wasn't a kid anymore, and she didn't need her parents' validation. Another mantra. Maybe if she said it enough times, it would be true.

Voices billowed out from the dining room. It was the same, year after year, early morning mass, followed by Easter brunch. She'd been able to avoid coming home for every major holiday in the last eighteen months, using her job as an excuse. "*The news never sleeps,*" she'd say. It wasn't a total lie. It didn't, but she was absent by choice.

Jamie wouldn't even have been there now if it weren't for Chris. She missed her little brother, and despite her parents' blatant favoritism and the physical distance between them, they were close. He didn't ask for the attention and she didn't begrudge him for it. Chris never treated her like second best. He defended her, stood up for her, and since their grandparents died, he was the only family she acknowledged.

As Jamie made her way through the house and into the formal dining room she sighed. The motive for her father's email sat to his left in a blue-flannel, button-down and dark khakis. Her presence was demanded, not because of her brother's surprise visit, but because she was being set up. Her father sat at the head of the table, her mother across from him on the other end. Chris sat to the right hand of their father, and his "roommate" Parker, next to him. The mystery man sat to her father's left and she assumed the empty spot beside him was intended for her.

This wasn't the first time her father had played matchmaker with one of his colleagues, but it didn't make it any less annoying. She was expected to be beautiful, charming, and obedient. Her father drilled it into her head. *"Everyone has a role to play in the Manning empire; your brother will take over the family business, your mother is the perfect wife, and you James, are the incentive. One day, when I find you a suitable partner, you'll marry and help grow our legacy."*

All eyes shifted to Jamie. The men stood as she made her way to her seat, catching her brother's gaze as she went. Pinning him with a, *you could have warned me, asshole*, glare. Chris, at least, had the decency to look contrite.

She took her seat, not bothering to acknowledge the sperm and ovaries who created her. "James, dear," her mother eyed her, no doubt dissecting her choice in wardrobe. Nothing Jamie wore was good enough for Caroline Manning.

"Mother," she responded coolly.

"We missed you at mass this morning."

Jamie plastered on a fake smile, internally debating on whether she should play along with the happy family façade. Before she could make up her mind, her father cleared his throat.

"James, I'd like you to meet Jared Foster," he introduced, a warning in his tone.

Archer Manning was an intimidating son of a bitch. He was smart, got in on the internet craze from the beginning and stayed relevant with the ever-changing landscape of the tech industry. If he were anyone else, Jamie would have been impressed by his ability to sustain longevity in a career where there was always some young hotshot with a million-dollar idea looking to knock him off the throne, but she knew better. She knew what a heartless bastard her father truly was.

Jamie bit the inside of her cheek until she tasted blood. She didn't want to be there. She didn't give a fuck about Jared, and suddenly she wished she would have kept her ass in Ryder's bed.

Once she trusted herself to speak she extended her hand, offering the man a smile that didn't reach her eyes. "Hi, Jared. I'm Jamie. Nice to meet you."

"Jamie," he said. His voice was deeper than she expected. His brown eyes shone with curiosity behind his tortoise-shell rimmed glasses, and his shaggy brown hair made him look as if he'd just rolled out of bed. He was handsome, for a tech nerd. "Your dad has told me quite a lot about you."

"Don't believe everything you hear," she quipped.

Jared shot her a lopsided grin. Old Jamie would have totally fucked this guy without giving it a second thought, but new Jamie missed her sensitive rocker. "All good things. He seems quite proud of you."

At that she snorted. Archer Manning had never expressed an interest in anything Jamie did. He only ever called her when he needed her help to close deals. She wondered why she even bothered playing along anymore.

"It seems you have me at a disadvantage. You know about me, but I know nothing about you."

"Well," he began, his gaze dropping from hers, down to her lips then to the swell of her breasts, before quickly returning to her face. "I was at Harvard when my roommate and I created a navigation app that combined satellite GPS with social media. When I graduated, I bought him out and moved the company west. GoTech was born and the rest is history."

Jamie stared, awestruck. "Oh my gosh," she squealed digging in her purse for her phone. She swiped over a page before clicking on the light blue icon. "This one?" Jared grinned and nodded. "I don't even use the navigation in my car anymore."

Jamie was impressed. Most of the guys her father brought around did things in programming that she knew nothing about. At least this one she could relate to. "I'd love to interview you for the station," she said.

"James, it's Easter," her mother interrupted, "Please leave the work talk for Monday."

"Here," Jared took her phone, "I'll save my number in your contacts and you can call me Monday to set it up."

Jamie nodded, biting her cheek yet again. She was going to tear a hole in there before brunch was done.

The food was served and the conversation flowed with the guys engaging in a spirited debate about lithium batteries. Jamie couldn't help the smile twitching at her lips. She wondered how Ryder was spending his Easter. Sneaking a peek at her phone she tapped out a text.

Jamie: I need to be fucked into oblivion

Biting back another smile, she slipped her phone under her thigh, and nearly jumped out of her seat, when his reply came through.

Ryder: I told u to stay in my bed.

Jamie: eyeroll

Ryder: I'm at my mom's, she is just about to start on dinner. Swing by, I'll feed you then fuck you.

"Can you put your phone down for five minutes, James?" Caroline bit.

"Sorry, work," she lied. "It was nice to meet you Jared. I'll be in touch about that interview. Chris, Parker, have a safe flight back to Boston." And without another word, Jamie sprinted out of the dining room.

"Wait, Jam," Chris chased behind her, "where are you going?"

"Work, I told you."

Her brother narrowed his eyes. "I saw you in there grinning like an idiot, spill."

Jamie forgot how inconvenient it was having Christopher around. He could read her like a book. "It's just…I mean," she stuttered.

"What's his name?"

"It doesn't matter."

He assessed her for a moment then changed tactics. "Are you happy?"

"Are you?" Jamie countered.

"This isn't about me," he said rubbing the back of his neck.

"When are you going to tell them?" she asked.

"We were going to do it this weekend, but Jared…"

Jamie nodded her understanding. "Is Parker okay?"

"He isn't happy, but he loves me and he gets it."

The Mannings' were slaves to appearances, and even though Chris was the favorite, Archer Manning would sooner die before he'd accept that the heir to his throne was gay.

TEN

Misery Loves Its Company

RYDER

"It looks like the Easter Bunny took a shit in here," Ryder said entering the kitchen at his mom's house. Pastel garland and plastic eggs were placed strategically throughout the house, and a collection of rabbit and duck figurines stared back at him from the windowsill above the sink.

Easter was a big deal in the Ryder household—scratch that, it was a huge fucking deal. Annette Ryder celebrated Easter the way most people celebrated Christmas, not because she was particularly religious, but because of what it meant for her: an Independence Day of sorts.

"Jesus, Napoleon, watch your mouth," she chastised, whisking brown sugar and pineapple juice into a concoction that turned ordinary ham into crack. It was his one vice—aside from Kitty Cat's pussy.

"Sorry Ma," Ry snorted. It took everything he had not to laugh out loud at the hypocrisy. She could take the Lord's name in vain, but he couldn't say 'shit'. "Where do you want them?" he asked, holding up the bag of potatoes she sent him to the store to buy.

"Get to washing," she replied, tipping her chin toward the sink.

Ryder smiled tightly at her back. Annette forced him to help her cook every year and every year he'd end up fucking up. Yet, every year he was back in the kitchen because as his mother would say, *"Eventually we'll find something even you can't burn."*

The creepy decorations and unlimited supply of chocolate and peanut butter eggs were one thing, but cooking was a tradition Ryder could live without.

"Nice ears," he teased, flicking one of the grey and pink bunny ears sitting atop his mom's head.

"I got you a pair too."

Ryder shook his head from left to right. "Oh, no. Absolutely not."

"Why?" Annette frowned. "I promise I won't tell any of your friends that their fearless leader wore bunny ears."

Ryder watched mesmerized as his mother poured the glaze over the ham. "There won't be anything to tell," he swallowed back the saliva pooling in his mouth, "I'm not wearing them, plus Kitty Cat's coming."

"Who?"

"My girlfriend. How long is that going to take?" he asked, following behind her as she slid the ham into the oven and closed the door.

"A couple hours and I thought Jamie was your girlfriend?"

"I'm still with Jamie, Ma, it's just a nickname."

With hands placed firmly on her hips, his mother continued to pry. "Well, what's the deal with you and Kitty Cat?" Everyone had an opinion on Ryder's love life. His friends seemed to think he moved too fast, and his mother thought he moved too slow.

"Jamie. Just, Jamie, okay?" Ryder set the potatoes on the counter and washed his hands. Then he dumped a few in the sink and went in search of the peeler. He could feel her eyes on his back as she waited for him to speak.

"Are you deliberately avoiding the question?"

"Maybe." Ryder was definitely avoiding the question. How could he explain his relationship with Kitty Cat when he didn't understand it himself? He peeled a potato—mangled—whatever. "I...I think I'm falling in love with her."

"I know, I saw it in your eyes the day you brought her to the diner."

"It isn't easy. She won't let me in." For as much as he learned about Jamie in the last month, there was still so much that was a mystery. He'd never been to her apartment, he only met one of her friends, and he didn't know anything about her family. Ryder was trying not to push, but his growing feelings made it difficult. He was greedy, he wanted all of her, every complicated inch.

"Real life isn't easy. It's messy and unpredictable. Not to mention you're my son and too much like me for your own good," Annette said, looking past the decorative ducks and out the window. It was a breezy spring day.

"Why do you say that?" Ryder asked. Annette was far from a saint, but if there was anyone in the world he would want to emulate, it was her.

"Because son," she said, bumping her shoulder against his in the way she did when she was about to say something important. "We're drawn to wounded animals and in our quest to mend them we tend to break ourselves."

Maybe she was a saint.

Ryder pressed a kiss onto his mother's forehead, "How'd you get so smart, Ma?"

"I've been around the block once or twice," she shrugged, grinning up at her son.

That much was true. Annette was the expert on loving broken things—things that threatened to break her—but somehow, she survived. Somehow, she managed carve out a quiet life for herself and for her son. So much had changed since they left California sixteen years ago. He was no longer the kid running from the shadow his father cast, and she was no longer the meek housewife dependent on an alcoholic asshole.

The doorbell rang and Ryder made his way to the front of the house, pausing at the door. He had fucking butterflies. His hands were drenched in sweat and potato water and his grip on the knob slipped the first time he tried to open it. He was being a pussy and he didn't know why.

It's just Jamie.

Expelling a long breath, Ryder swung the door open and stared, slack jawed, at the woman in front of him. Kitty Cat was holding a bouquet of pink tulips, and she was wearing a dress. He'd seen work Jamie and party girl Jamie. He even had the pleasure of meeting PMS Jamie last week, but Jamie in a dress; that was a first.

"You look like a girl." He grinned. Her legs and shoulders were exposed, and the light purple dress seemed to float on thin air.

"Don't I always look like a girl?" Jamie asked, stepping over the threshold. She looked up at him through her lashes; her face was painted, and her hair curled. She appeared soft and demure but her eyes gave her away. Jamie could dress up in all the fancy clothes in the world but his ferocious Kitty Cat was never far from the surface.

"You always look like *my* girl," Ryder clarified, taking the tulips from her and laying them on the entryway table, "but this isn't you. It's nice, but it's not you." He pulled her inside and shut the door, pushing her back against it. His fingers skated up her legs until he reached her ass.

Jamie laced her fingers through his hair, bringing his head into the crook of her neck, "Your mom is going to walk in here and catch you with your hand up this *nice* dress."

"She's finishing up dinner," he said squeezing her round bottom. "We've got at least an hour before she comes looking for us. I could show you my bedroom."

"Not gonna happen."

"Why not?" he pouted. Her skin clung to his clammy palms, and it felt like he was grasping at the promised land. His tongue found flesh and he sucked on the skin at the base of her throat. They were apart for less than twenty-four hours but it seemed like an eternity. "I missed you."

"I can't believe I'm letting you feel me up in your mother's house," she moaned, dropping her head on his shoulder.

"What do you mean, 'let'?" he asked, hooking her leg around his waist. "You kick ass and take names out there in the world, but when you're with me, I'm in charge." Jamie was his. She could try and deny it, she could fight it, but it was as true then as it was the first night she came apart in his arms.

"You think so?" she challenged.

"I know so. Don't you feel it?"

"Feel what?" She writhed and wiggled and squirmed as he pressed his body into her. The vibrations of their erratic heartbeats flowed between them like a current. She talked a good game but her physical reaction to his touch gave away her true feelings.

"What I do to you. The way your body reacts to me? The way mine reacts to you?" Ryder kissed every inch of skin within reach. She was as nervous and excited as he was and judging by the small tremors that rocked her frame every time he bit into her neck, Jamie was just as intoxicated by him as he was by her.

"Maybe I'm just horny."

"Maybe one day, you'll admit the truth."

"And what truth would that be?"

"That you're here for more than dick."

"One day," she breathed, clinging to him.

※

Surprisingly, Jamie was happy about the, *'everyone helps cook'*, rule. Watching her with his mother, both of them moving around the kitchen with a comfortable ease, was Ryder's idea of heaven. He didn't realize how much alike they were until then. Perhaps it was what drew him to Jamie in the first place, his need to protect her, to erase the sadness in her eyes. To do the things he was too young and too afraid to do for his mom.

"Ma, do you remember our first Easter here?" Ryder asked as they took their seats at the dining room table. Although it was only three of them, Annette prepared enough food to feed a developing country. There was the traditional stuff like crack ham, mac and cheese, green beans and dinner rolls, but thanks to his mother's new found obsession with Pinterest, they also had mini potpies and something that looked like a cross between a taco and a wonton.

Annette raised a brow. "You mean when you and Carlos nearly put a hole through the wall because he made fun of you for wanting to color eggs?"

"I've never seen you so angry in my life," he chuckled.

"I was *livid*," she smirked, putting emphasis on the last word. "We just moved in, I could barely afford the rent, and you two knuckleheads were fighting over Easter eggs."

"Who's Carlos?' Jamie asked, helping herself to more crack ham.

"Javi's older brother."

"Oh, you were friends with him first, right?"

"Yeah. He's still one of my best friends, but he's married with a kid and real responsibilities, so he doesn't hang out like he used to," Ry explained. He chose to ignore the look his mother gave him. He and Carlos were the same age, and his mother had grandchildren, something Annette never let Ryder forget.

"You got into a fight over Easter eggs?"

"Napoleon was sensitive when he was younger."

"He's still sensitive," Jamie mumbled around a glass of water.

Annette threw her head back in laughter, "She knows you well, son."

Ryder also chose to ignore that. He was okay with sensitive, he embraced it. While some men would consider it a flaw, Ryder saw it as one of his greatest attributes. Because the thing he feared most, even more than his father, was becoming him.

"What's next on the agenda?" Annette asked bagging up the leftovers for Jamie and Ryder to take with them.

Ryder looked to Jamie who was mid-yawn. "We were supposed to meet the guys at the bar, but we can just go home if you're not up for it."

Jamie smiled happily at him. "I'm fine with whatever you want."

It was exactly what he wanted to hear after a near perfect day. Jamie was always so guarded, so strong, but whether it was the food coma his mother put them in or something else, seeing her so light gave him hope.

"Maybe we'll swing by for a little bit. I just want to check on CT. He's usually on edge after spending the day with his family," he said, rubbing his nose against hers.

Jamie tugged at the hem of his shirt. "Sounds good, Napoleon."

"Oh. My. Goodness!" Annette yelped. "You two are so stinking adorable. I need a picture."

Ryder rolled his eyes as his mother scurried off into the kitchen. She returned moments later with her phone, and the set of rabbit ears she bought him. "Ma," he groaned, "really with these fucking things?"

Annette narrowed her eyes. "Watch your mouth, and yes really, so put them on," she demanded, pulling her ears off her head. She handed a pair to him and the other pair to Jamie.

"The real issue here," Jamie said, "is that your mom has an iPhone and you don't."

At that, Ryder couldn't help but laugh. He had a hard-enough time telling one of them no, but both?

Impossible.

Annette shuffled them to the entryway where she took no less than seventy-five pictures. She made them stand side by side, back to back, face to face, and every other goddamned combination she could think of. Just when he thought she was done, she pulled out a fucking selfie stick.

"Okay, I think you got it," Ry said eyeing the godforsaken thing like it might bite.

"I need one of the three of us."

"One more, make it count," he grumbled, wrapping one arm around Jamie's shoulder and the other around his mother's. Annette connected her phone to the stick and extended the wand so it hovered three feet in front of them, then angled it until they were all in the picture.

"Ready?" she asked.

"Ma," Ry warned.

"Okay, okay," Annette said, and Jamie giggled.

They were driving him crazy, and he was loving every second of it. His mother clicked the button three times in rapid succession, then the screen went dark, before illuminating with an incoming call. The number wasn't assigned, but the area code was one he'd never forget, *510.*

Oakland.

Annette stilled, grasping at the phone, and quickly ended the call. Her eyes shot to her son, and what he saw behind hazel eyes that were identical to his own, was the one look he hoped he would never see again. "Who was that?" he asked, though he knew the answer deep down in his gut.

"Telemarketer," she replied a little too quickly. Annette cleared her throat and started fiddling with her phone. "Y-you kids wanna see?"

"A telemarketer, on Easter?" He felt like someone hit him over the head with a lead pipe. This couldn't be happening. Not today, of all days. It was Easter. It was *their* day, not *his.*

"Who knows?" his mother shrugged. She inhaled, scrubbing the emotion from her face. "Let's take one more."

Ryder pulled the ears off his head and threw them on the ground. One phone call and his universe was driven into darkness.

It was a beautiful tragedy. His happiest day turned to ash all because his mother couldn't help but look back. "Happy fucking Easter," he growled, snatching open the front door. "Kitty Cat, let's go."

Jamie looked up at him, confused, "But—"

"Now, James," his tone left no room for argument.

"Thank you for a lovely meal," Jamie murmured as she walked out the open door.

"Wait," his mom called after him. A tear slipped past her mask, and her voice cracked, "you're forgetting the leftovers."

"Send them to California," he grunted, slamming the door behind them.

ELEVEN

Ride

RYDER

Ryder steered Jamie's Range Rover out into the Seattle streets. His jaw ticked as he replayed the last ten minutes over in his mind. His mother lied and she didn't even bother to come up with a good one.

A fucking telemarketer? Bullshit.

He recognized the guilt shimmering in her eyes as the lie spilled from her lips. It was a look he knew well. It was the same way she looked at him then, back in the dark ages, when his father ruled them with an iron fist.

For sixteen years, he admired her, worshipped at her feet as if she were a fucking saint. He trusted her to keep them safe. They *were* safe. They'd beaten the odds and escaped. Now, those sixteen years were down the drain, all because his mother decided to invite chaos back into her life.

It was a soul crushing realization, the woman he idolized—his hero—was flawed.

When Ryder was a child, he spoke as a child. He understood

things as a child. His father was a bad man, and they had to run away, but as a man, Ryder understood his father was an alcoholic asshole who got his kicks from beating women and children. He understood the fate they would have suffered had his mother not run. A fate, that after sixteen years, she decided to tempt.

"Fuck!" he yelled, banging his fist on the steering wheel. How could she do this? How could she talk to him after everything he did? She uprooted their lives to get away from him, and now what were they?

Friends?

Lovers?

The thought made him sick.

"Did I miss something?" Jamie asked, speaking for the first time since he stormed out of his mother's house.

"No."

Her reply was so soft he almost didn't hear it, "You can talk to me. I'm here if you need me."

The SUV rolled to a stop. The glow from the traffic light illuminated the dark cabin red. He watched from the corner of his eye as she brought her finger to her mouth and exhaled. *Her tell.* Her mind was racing too. He could only imagine what she was thinking. They were having a good night, laughing, eating, taking cheesy pictures with those goddamned bunny ears and in a split second, everything changed. All because of his fucking father.

"I'm fine, Kitty Cat." Ryder did his best to keep his attitude in check. It wasn't Jamie's fault his father was a leech put on this earth to suck every glimmer of light from his mother.

Jamie turned slowly, unleashing the full force of her gaze onto him. When he stared into those emerald orbs, he swore he could see the past, present, and future. Normally, he loved that shit, but right now, he prayed for the light to turn green, because he wasn't ready for that talk. Jamie didn't need to be dragged into his fucked-up family history—not yet, not ever.

"If you're fine then why are you strangling my steering wheel?"

she asked, pointing to his hand. Ryder's knuckles were white, his fingers numb.

"It's nothing, James, drop it," he snapped, flexing his hand.

The light changed, and his focus returned to the road. He'd hate to wreck her ninety-thousand-dollar graduation present.

"You don't have to be so defensive." Her words were measured, no anger, no pity, just calm, sensible, and annoying as fuck.

"The queen of shutting down is mad at me for not wanting to open up this *one time* about this *one thing*?" he asked. An ugly, bitter noise escaped his throat. "A bit hypocritical, don't you think?"

"I'm trying, Ry. I thought that's what you wanted?"

"Great timing, Kitty Cat," he said giving her a sarcastic thumbs up. Funny how she was so eager to try when it was his bones they were digging up.

"I don't need the gritty details. I'm just saying, don't be an asshole to your mother. You're lucky to have a mom like Annette. We don't all get that."

"What, did Mommy and Daddy buy you the wrong color Range Rover?" He was being a dick. Jamie was a lot of things but a brat wasn't one of them. Guilt flooded Ryder's subconscious, but pride kept him from apologizing. What was the point? The thing with words was that once spoken, they were rarely forgotten.

"Fuck you, Ryder. You don't know shit about me."

"And who's fault is that?" he yelled, speeding down the empty street. He was pissed, at his mother, at his father, at Jamie, at the fucking world. The dam broke and the rage he struggled to maintain, gushed out. "I've been begging you for a fucking month to let me in. *A month.* You won't talk to me! You don't even sleep at the house for fuck's sake!"

She shifted her body, resting her forehead on the glass, and stared out into the dark night. "Just forget I brought it up," she whispered.

Silence swallowed them as they each retreated inside their own heads.

He was a jerk for taking his anger at his mother out on Jamie, but also, fuck her. Why was it okay for her to keep her secrets, but not him?

In a perfect world, there wouldn't be anything between them, but the world they lived in wasn't perfect, and neither were they. Perfection was an illusion perpetuated by insecurity. He didn't want illusions with Kitty Cat, he wanted reality—and sometimes reality was fucked up.

Spotting the burgundy awning of the bar, he could feel his body start to relax. The double shot of fireball he was about to down would help calm his brain and if he was lucky, someone in there would have a blunt.

Ryder parked Jamie's Rover at the end of the dark lot, sandwiching her car between a brick wall and CT's Mustang, and killed the engine. He snuck a peek at his girl, hoping to gauge her mood. Her face was impassive, but he could tell by the way she sat with her back ramrod straight that she was pissed.

"I'm sorry," he sighed. Ry didn't want to fight, not with her too, "I didn't mean to snap at you."

Jamie didn't bother looking at him. She simply held out her hand, palm side up, and said, "Can I have my keys, please?"

"No." He recoiled as if she'd slapped him.

"Give me my keys." Her tone, her face, even her eyes were emotionless. It should have unnerved him, but after the day he had, it only pissed him off.

"I'll break it down for you, so there's no misunderstanding, N-O, No." He was poking the bear. He wanted a reaction. Her wrath would be better than this bullshit act she was putting on. He wanted his Jamie, the girl who always had to have the last word.

"Napoleon," she warned.

Opening the driver side door, he got out and slammed it shut behind him. She could be mad but he wasn't going to let her run. Not tonight. Not when he needed her. He'd rather they be happy, he'd rather they be fucking, but he'd take fighting too. As was always the case with Kitty Cat, he'd take anything she was willing to give.

"Napoleon," she screamed, jumping out of the car, "give me my goddamn keys!"

He ignored the angry grunts and insults she hurled at his back. Slipping the keys in his back pocket, he continued walking towards the entrance. His long legs ate up the distance in no time.

"What's up Tee," Ry greeted the doorman as he approached.

Tee was a tall, burly motherfucker with a sinister grin, but he wouldn't hurt a fly, well, he would if the fly provoked him. "Ry, Kitty Cat," Tee nodded, "you guys good?

"Yeah, man—" Jamie dug into his back pocket and pulled out her keys so quickly, she was halfway back to the parking lot before Ryder had a chance to react. "Give us a second," he shouted over his shoulder, before turning to run after his girl. They looked ridiculous, him chasing her down the dark sidewalk, arguing about keys instead of the things they were afraid to speak into existence. "Jamie, I'm not in the mood for this shit."

"Then go have fun with your friends and leave me alone." She lifted her middle finger in the air, flipping him off as she went.

A low growl ripped from his chest. He grabbed her elbow, and yanked her forward, towards her car. If she wanted a fight, he would give her one. "Let's get one thing straight," Ryder growled, pushing her up against the hood of her Rover, his face inches from hers, "I will never leave you alone. Even when I'm pissed at you, and right now, I'm fucking enraged. There's no running. You mad at me?" he barked. "Then tell me, damn it. Push me. Yell at me, I don't care how you need to deal, but you deal."

"You're such a fucking bastard," Jamie shoved her palms into his chest. The apathy drained from her irises leaving a fiery passion that sent a signal south of his brain. She thrashed around in his arms, but he wasn't letting her go, not now, not later tonight, not ever if he had his way. She quickly realized it, and stopped fighting. Her chest heaved up and down. Her face was flushed, and her body trembled. She was either really pissed off, or really turned on. "I hate you so much." Reaching up her dress, he slid her panties to the side, and just as he suspected, she was drenched. "That means nothing," she growled.

"Tell me how much you hate me," he pressed his body against hers. He needed this, to lose control with her. He spent too much time trying to control his emotions. *Don't be too angry, or too sensitive. Don't care too much.* Well fuck that.

"You're a dick," she moaned as he slipped two fingers inside her wet channel, "and you aren't that great a singer."

Ryder chuckled. "Always so damn feisty. I'm going to enjoy fucking the attitude out of you. Did I mention I love that you're wearing a dress? I should pull my dick out right here, right now."

"I thought you said the dress wasn't me?" Jamie whimpered, clawing at his back.

"And I thought you said this meant nothing," he retorted, adding a third finger. He was also going to enjoy fucking the sarcasm from her tone. His balls ached, he needed to feel her, to sink into her, and fuck every ounce of anger and frustration out of his body.

"It doesn't."

Ryder slid his fingers out, and she mewled in protest. "Am I still a dick?" he smirked as he unzipped his jeans, freeing his erection.

"Yes," she gasped as he rubbed the tip of his cock through her folds. *So. Fucking. Hot.* "What if someone sees?" It wasn't a protest. She was down to fuck. It didn't matter that they were in the parking lot, up against her car. She wanted it as badly as he did.

The bar was the only thing on that side of the street. They were alone in the parking lot, in the world, for that matter. Nothing and no one else existed. She carried the entire universe between her legs and he held the key to unlocking the mysteries of the sun and the stars and the planets between his. "No one will see, but if they do, let's give them one hell of a show."

"Condom," she moaned, laying back against the hood of her shiny white Range Rover. The sight of her propped up on the car with her legs spread wide for him, nearly knocked him on his ass. He lifted the hem of her dress. The tiny swath of fabric only covered half of her pussy. She looked delicious, so good he couldn't stop himself from having a taste. Ryder bent down as far as he could with the building behind him and kissed her there, licking her, swirling his tongue inside her wetness.

"Are you on birth control?" he asked, biting the inside of her thigh.

"Ry," she moaned as he tongued her slit.

All he could think of was penetrating her, bare. It was all he ever thought of. There were so many barriers between them already, he needed to conquer at least one. "Are you on the pill?" he repeated, stroking his shaft.

"Yes."

"Then I'm coming inside you," he grunted, standing upright.

"You think that's a good idea?" Again, not a protest. So, he pushed inside of her warmth, and wrapped her legs around his waist.

"What do you think?" he asked, his voice garbled as he tried to maintain control. Sex with Jamie was addicting with condoms, but without, he was a goner. The way her warm, wet, walls hugged his dick was enough to drive him mad. She called him sex god, but Kitty Cat was nothing less than a goddess. She was made for him. When Ry was inside her, it felt like home.

"Best. Idea. Ever." She gritted her agreement as he thrust in and out of her. Slow at first, trying to adjust to the sensation. He forced himself to breathe in through his nose and out of his mouth. She felt too good. "Fuck me, hard, please," she begged, unabashedly.

He lifted her higher, angling her body so half of her weight was on the hood while he supported the other half. Once she was situated, Ryder pounded into her, setting a punishing pace. He fucked her, and it wasn't nice or sweet or kind. It was brutal, and what they both needed after a day pretending with their families.

Her muscles clenched around him, the telltale sign of her impending orgasm. Her thighs clamped around his waist and she clung to his body, desperate for his arms to hold her together while his cock ripped her apart.

"Shit, Kitty Cat." Ryder's dick twitched and their bodies slapped together under the night sky. He wasn't sure how much longer he'd last inside of her. His grip on her ass tightened and he pushed into her wildly. Her moans increased and her body shook as she fell over the edge.

"Thank God," he growled, spilling his seed inside her.

They huffed and puffed, desperate for air. Their bodies coated in sweat.

"You're still a fucking asshole," she panted.

He smiled, dropping his head in the crook of her neck. "I know. I'm sorry."

"Be nice to your mom," she said quietly.

"It's complicated." It might as well have been Astrophysics.

"Tell me." She laid her head on his shoulder, her legs still wrapped around his waist even as his erection softened inside her. Ryder feared she would regret it, but she seemed content with the new level of intimacy. There were no more barriers between them, no physical ones anyway.

"It was my dad," he whispered. If she could let her guard down enough to ask, he could let his down enough to tell her the truth.

"And that's a bad thing?"

He stared into the night. "When I was seven, I watched him break her arm. The night before my ninth birthday, he got drunk and smashed all my gifts." Ryder's voice wavered. He slipped his penis out of her, and back inside his jeans, zipping up. Talking about this shit was hard enough without the added distraction of being buried inside of Kitty Cat.

"I'm sorry." Jamie tucked a strand of blond curls behind his ear. Her eyes glistened with unshed tears.

"I'm fine," Ry said tipping the corner of his mouth up. "I survived, but him calling her, them talking..." He shook his head, looking for the words.

"I get it. I didn't mean to pry." Intentions were funny, even the best of them could lead a person down a dark path. "I'm a mess,"

Jamie giggled, thankfully changing the subject. The tips of their noses touched. It was the closest thing to a kiss she could offer, and Ryder greedily accepted it.

He looked down, lifting her dress, a ball of milky liquid rolled down her leg. "We should get you cleaned up," he smirked, oddly proud of the fact that his semen dripped down her thighs.

"You're not sorry," she grinned, "fucking, possessive asshole."

"You're right, I'm not."

They walked hand in hand back through the parking lot. Tee, the bouncer stared at them, cocking a brow. "You guys look…relaxed."

Ryder turned to Jamie. Her neck was red from where he bit her, her dress wrinkled, and her hair tangled.

"So, fucking relaxed."

TWELVE

Take Your Time

RYDER

New message.

Those two little words taunted Ryder daily over the last couple of weeks. He stared at the screen as they flashed, then did what he did every other time his mother called; he ignored it. Slamming the phone shut, Ry tossed it back on the nightstand.

He wasn't ready to hear the truth.

"I think you're being a little hard on her." Kitty Cat eyed him from the foot of the bed. She wore nothing but her bra and panties and looked good enough to eat, *again.*

"Me?" he asked incredulously. He watched as she scanned the floor for her slacks. Much to Ryder's disappointment, Jamie reinforced the *no sleeping over rule* shortly after Easter. "My dad can break her bones, but I'm the one over reacting?"

"I didn't mean it like that. It's just, she misses you," Jamie said, bending down to pluck her shirt off the floor. Ryder instantly regretted not ripping the damn thing to shreds when he had the chance.

"I'm sure she's fine," he deadpanned.

"She's sad."

"How would you know?"

Jamie lifted her shoulder unapologetically. "I was on location and the diner was nearby."

"You went to see her?" Ryder asked. He shifted onto his side, propping an arm up to rest his head on his hand. He wasn't sure how he felt about Jamie going to see his mom behind his back. He loved that they had a connection, but he was pissed at his mother. Jamie was supposed to be Team Ryder, not Team Annette.

"Don't be mad. I just wanted to make sure she was okay. She's human, cut her some slack."

In the grand scheme of things his mom talking to his dad wasn't the worst thing in the world. His father was in California and his mother was more than capable of making her own decisions, but she was making the wrong ones and Ryder couldn't condone that, not after everything he'd seen.

"Why don't *you* cut *me* some slack?" he asked changing the subject. This line of questioning could only lead to an argument, and he wasn't in the mood to fight.

Ryder crawled to the end of the bed, his shaggy hair fell over his eyes as he shot Jamie his patented *I'll make it worth your while*, look. He was sick of sleeping alone, and he wasn't above begging. "Stay the night, please."

She shook her head slowly, her gaze traveling from his mouth, down his chest, and didn't stop until she reached his penis. His girl loved his dick, so he did what any desperate man with a nine-inch cock would do—he swiveled his hips and let the monster swing from side to side.

"Stay," he said, giving his hips another wiggle.

"I can't," she giggled, her eyes still on the prize.

Ryder slipped his hand under the elastic band of her panties and pulled her onto her knees. They were chest to chest, him naked, her with her blouse half buttoned. "Why can't you?"

"Because I have a job," she said, lifting a finger, "and I don't have anything here," another finger, "and your mattress sucks."

Three excuses.

Three bad excuses.

Ryder was fully prepared to give her shit for them, but the tips of her fingers grazed his V-shaped hip bone. Placing a kiss on the tip of Jamie's nose, Ryder murmured, "I'll wake you up early so you can go home and change, and my mattress isn't that bad."

It was fucking awful, but her resolve was crumbling. She was starting to open up to him. Just last week she let it slip that her birthday was next month, bringing the grand total of things he knew about her to three: her birthday, where she worked, and the location of her g-spot.

"I don't have pajamas or my toothbrush," she reasoned. Her hair was a mess, blonde waves tumbled over her shoulders as the bullshit tumbled from her lips. Jamie was running out of excuses, and Ryder was running out of patience.

He dug his fingers into her waist, pulling her as close as he could. The sex they had earlier clung to her skin. "Sleep naked," he dropped a kiss on the corner of her mouth, "or wear some of my shit," another kiss on the other corner. "We can go to the drugstore and get you a toothbrush and whatever else you need. You can keep it here so you don't have to carry it back and forth."

"Keep stuff here?" Kitty Cat swallowed, resting her nose on his.

Ryder felt her trembling. He saw the alarm bells ringing behind her eyes as she retreated emotionally. It was the same reaction he got every time the conversation steered towards the forbidden topic of their relationship status. If he were a less confident man he'd be worried, but he was the sex god and Jamie had a fucked-up world view.

"Chill out, James. I'm not asking you to move in. It's just a toothbrush and whatever that fruity shit is you put in your hair."

"Fruity shit?" she asked, her lips tipping into a half smirk.

"Fruity shit," he confirmed.

Buttons flew in every direction as Ryder ripped open Jamie's blouse. He pulled down the cups of her bra, circling her nipple with his tongue. His teeth grazed the hardened nub sending a fresh wave of shivers down her body.

"I thought we were going to the drugstore," she moaned, arching into his mouth.

Ryder was proud of himself. He was getting better at defusing the commitment bombs and he deserved a reward. "We will. After I fuck you."

One hour and two orgasms later, Ryder and Jamie were still naked, their limbs still intertwined, and they were no closer to the drugstore than they were before.

"You know what the best part about having you in my bed is?" Ryder asked, pulling Jamie on top of him.

She pressed her palms into the headboard, and her long hair fell forward creating a curtain around them. "Having your own personal cum receptacle?" Kitty Cat only looked like the all-American girl next door, but she possessed the spirit of a drunken sailor, and a mouth on her as crass as any of his friends. She never stopped surprising him.

"No, but I'm not complaining," he said, gripping her thighs as she grinded on his dick, their combined juices, smearing all over his shaft. At this rate, they'd never fucking leave. He'd be lying if he said he wasn't excited about the possibility of fucking her whenever he wanted, but it wasn't why he wanted her there. "The best part is this," Ryder motioned between them, "you and me without all the bullshit. It's the only time I get the real you."

"As opposed to?" she asked, hovering inches above his face.

"The person you want everyone to see; the party girl, the badass, the savage."

"I hate to break it to you, Sex God, but that is the real me."

"If you say so, Kitty Cat," he replied, flipping their bodies so he was on top. They laid there, mouths and fingers lazily exploring each other. Neither of them in a rush to leave the comfort his shitty mattress provided. Jamie was everything Ryder swore he'd never go for again. She was complicated and broken, a combination that left him with scars, but for her he'd gladly do battle.

"Can I ask you something?"

"Anything," he murmured against her neck.

"What's this mean?" Jamie ran her fingers down his side, across the circles and lines and dots etched in his skin.

"That's a geometric guitar," he grinned. She was a curious little kitten. Reluctantly, Ryder pulled himself up, sitting back on his haunches, so she could get a better look at the ink on his ribcage. "See how the circles overlap?" Jamie nodded her understanding and Ryder continued. "These lines are the strings. My guitar is an extension of me, my rib. It got me through some dark shit. It's geometric because it looks cool as fuck."

"It's sexy as fuck," she said biting down on her bottom lip.

Ryder chuckled, "I'll tell Nic you like it."

"Who's Nic?"

"My artist. He did most of my shit, all of our shit, actually. He has an art exhibit coming up next weekend, I think. Wanna go?"

Panic flashed in Jamie's greens. "Like a date?"

"We can call it whatever you want, Kitty Cat."

She gave him a noncommittal shrug before running her fingers up to his collarbone, over the black *Catch-22* there. "What about this one? I never would have pegged you as a Heller fan."

"I'm not," Ryder said, scratching his stomach. In truth, he didn't know it was a book until after he got the ink and CT asked him the same question. "It's something my mom always said when I asked about why she put up with my dad. *Life is a Catch-22. You're damned if you do and damned if you don't*. I didn't fully grasp what she meant until we moved and I had to watch her struggle. She stayed because she couldn't afford to leave and she thought the abuse was better than us being homeless."

"What made her change her mind?" Jamie asked, looking down at the bed. He couldn't see her eyes, but he could hear the apprehension in her tone. They were getting deep and that made her uncomfortable. The last month taught Ryder that Jamie was okay with discomfort as long as she wasn't the one sharing.

"He hit me," Ryder admitted.

They sat in silence for a moment, letting the weight of his confession cover them like skin over bone. "I was ten. He bashed my head off the dining room table. The next day we were on a bus to Seattle." Up until that point, Ryder's dad had directed all his anger towards Annette. The look on his mother's face when she saw her son cowering with fear from a man who was supposed to protect him, reminded him of the sadness Jamie hid beneath her green eyes.

Kitty Cat kissed the script before her hands trailed over his chest, "and the fish?"

The fish wasn't deep or meaningful, or even good for that matter. "I dated a girl who was apprenticing at a tattoo parlor. I was drunk, she had her gun, and I told her to give me a tattoo. She picked a fish because I'm a fucking Pisces."

Jamie snorted in a vain attempt to control her laughter, but the dam burst and she fell back, erupting into a fit of giggles.

Ryder shook his head and covered her body with his once again, pressing his weight into her. "Okay, that's enough about me, what about you? You want any tattoos?"

"I'd love to get another one, but with my job –"

"Wait, you have a tattoo?" he asked in shock. Ryder had seen every inch of her body and never noticed a tattoo.

"Yeah," she said, rubbing her finger across his bottom lip. "It's my little secret."

He caught her hand, bringing the finger up to eye level. "White ink, no wonder I missed it. A semi-colon?" he asked, and she nodded. "Why? I mean, did you..." he let the sentence trail off, not wanting to say the words out loud.

"We should probably go get that toothbrush."

"Kitty Cat," he begged.

"And the fruity shit," she said, pushing him away from her. And just like that, show and tell was over.

THIRTEEN

Save Rock and Roll

Jamie

"Shit," Jamie grunted, banging her knee off the dresser. She was trying to wiggle her foot into the strappy, Givenchy pump, but the damn things were harder to get on then a straitjacket. Pulling it off, she chucked it across the room in a fit of rage. Jamie was running late, and she hated being late.

Her phone rang and she yanked it off the bedside table, not bothering to check the caller ID. "I'm sorry," Jamie whined, "I got stuck at work, but I'm home now and I'm almost ready." She would have gotten out of there on time if it weren't for fucking Ruben and his obsessive need for b-roll.

"I thought you were coming straight here," Ryder said with barely concealed agitation.

"I didn't want to wear my work clothes," she explained walking into the closet to grab her leather jacket, "and I can't show up to your friend's exhibit in a pair of your sweat pants."

"You've known about this for a fucking week."

Jamie rolled her eyes while thumbing through the rack of

clothes. "Yes, but I only agreed to go last night, remember?"

Last night, when Ry refused to let her come until she said yes. The man could get her to agree to anything when he was fucking her, a tactic he used to his advantage. Jamie needed to get a handle on that shit before he did something crazy like propose marriage while her ass was in the air.

"I was there," he quipped dryly, "and do you realize it was easier to get you to have sex with me without a condom than it was to get you on a date?"

"I can still say no, jackass."

"If you do, I won't let you come for a week."

"Who says I need you to come?" she challenged, tossing a pile of clothes from the hamper over her shoulder, onto the floor. *Where the fuck was her jacket?*

"I'm going to assume you're talking about vibrators," he bit, "and I'll break into your apartment and hide all the batteries."

"But you can't take my fingers," she sang smugly.

"The day your fingers make you come harder than my dick will be the same day I wear a pink tutu and sing I'm a little teapot." His voice was laced with sarcasm, but unfortunately, he had a point.

"Fair," she conceded, "now text me the address so I can order my Uber."

"Fine, but hurry the fuck up."

"Get off the phone and I will."

Ryder grunted a goodbye before disconnecting the call.

Jamie took one last glance around her closet, then headed back out into her room with her hands on her hips. *Think James, think.* Jamie checked every inch of her closet, her jacket wasn't there. She was sure she didn't leave it in her car or at the guys' house, so there was only one other explanation, *Kensie.*

Grabbing her shoes, Jamie slipped them on slowly, careful not to bruise her other knee. Her phone buzzed: the address from Ryder. She put it into the Uber app, shoved her keys into her purse, turned out the lights, and headed across the apartment to Kensie's room.

They lived in a warehouse style building in downtown Seattle. The ceilings were high and tall windows stretched across the back wall. The main living area was open, the kitchen, dining and living rooms all ran together, creating a modern vibe.

Kensie's room was near the kitchen. Light spilled through the crack of the slightly opened door and Jamie pushed her way inside. She froze in wide-eyed horror at the sight of her best friend on her knees in front of her boyfriend. "Holy shit," Jamie squealed. "Kensington Grace Roth, were you about to suck his dick?"

Kensie blushed, scrambling to her feet, chuckling as she buried her head in Trey's chest.

"Jesus, Jamie, ever hear of knocking?" he groaned, buttoning his pants.

"The door was open. Also, I'd rather pour bleach in my eyes than see your *little* friend," she smirked.

"Jam, did you need something?"

"My leather jacket, have you seen it?"

Kensie nodded, disappearing inside her closet. She returned seconds later with Jamie's missing garment. "You look pretty," she said eyeing her friend. "Where are you going?"

"Really babe?" Trey huffed, frustration etched across his face.

"An art exhibit."

"For work?" Kensie arched a brow.

"No," Jamie said, checking her phone. Her car was five minutes away. "I'm going with a friend."

"Lo? How come you guys never invite me to things?" Kensie pouted. Trey stared at his girlfriend, not blinking once, before grunting and stalking off into the living room. Jamie stuck her middle finger up behind his back as he went. She should have felt bad for interrupting them, but Trey was an ass who didn't deserve a blow job.

"Another friend."

"Who?" Kensie pressed.

"You don't know him," she grinned, checking her phone again. *Four minutes.*

"Since when do you have friends I don't know?" Annoyance rolled from Kensington's body in waves.

"Ken, we aren't thirteen." Jamie didn't get why she was so upset. They barely saw each other anymore, and it wasn't like she was leaving the country. She was going to a fucking art show.

"I know, but we *are* drifting. Who is this person you're spending all this time with?"

Three minutes.

Trey popped his head back into the room. "Liam just called. You wanna go have dinner with him and Reagan?"

Jamie couldn't help but chuckle at the hypocrisy. How could Kensie be mad at her for having a friend she didn't know about, when she was hiding a Liam and a Reagan.

Kensie nodded, waving her boyfriend off. "Don't look at me like that, Jam, it's Trey's brother and his girlfriend."

"You're allowed to have friends, Kensington."

Kensie's hands flew to her hips. "That's not what I'm saying and you freaking know it."

"Freaking? Since when don't you say fuck?" Trey was turning her beautiful, self-assured best friend, into a proper lady, and it pissed Jamie the *freak* off.

"I'm not letting you turn this around on me."

Two minutes.

Jamie slid the jacket around her shoulders. "I have to go."

"This isn't over, James."

"I'm leaving, so it kinda is."

𝄞

The car rolled to a stop in front of what appeared to be an abandoned building, located in an up and coming neighborhood. The sidewalk was jam-packed with guys with beards and flannel shirts and girls with multi-colored hair and outfits to match—hipster even by Seattle standards.

Looking down at her all black ensemble, Jamie felt like a fish out of water. She believed in signs, and she couldn't shake the feeling of dread engulfing her. Not only was she late, but her run-in with Kensington left her feeling off kilter. Her night was doomed to fail before it began. She exhaled, fighting the compulsion to rub her tattoo against her cherry red lips, and lifted her head high as she walked into the gallery.

The large room was brightly lit. People milled about, stopping here and there to admire the scrap metal sculptures dotted throughout the space. There were two makeshift bars, one towards the back of the gallery and another near the entrance.

Jamie scanned the crowd, looking for a familiar face. When she came up short, she decided to make a detour to the bar. A drink would calm her nerves and it would give her the chance to text Ry and let him know where she was.

After she fired off the message, Jamie took her place in line. It moved quickly, and much to her disappointment there were only two drinks on the menu, beer or champagne. She kicked herself for forgetting her flask. She'd need something stronger than champagne to quell the anxiety eating away at her insides.

When it was Jamie's turn to order, she grinned at the bartender, a boy who looked like he wasn't even old enough to drink, and said, "Got anything stronger than champagne?"

"Nah," he shook his head. "I think there's some vodka at the other bar, for a toast at the end of the night. We aren't really supposed to give it out before then."

She swiped a plastic champagne flute from the table and tilted it back, swallowing the contents of the glass in two gulps. "Can I have another?"

The kid looked around, running his fingers through his hair. "We aren't really supposed to."

"Please," Jamie pouted, fluttering her lashes. Flirting with bartenders was her specialty.

"You're going to get me fired," he grinned, sliding another her way.

"I won't tell if you don't," she winked. Not that he saw, his eyes were focused on her tits. She would have told him he didn't have a snowball's chance in hell, but that would mean cutting off her alcohol supply and it was going to be a long night.

"What are you doing after this?" the kid asked, more to her boobs than to her face.

"Me," a grunt came from somewhere behind her.

Jamie didn't bother turning around. She knew *that* voice anywhere; it was the same one he used when he was fucking her.

The kid's eyes bulged out of his head as he looked over her shoulder. "You… you…Lithium Springs?" he stuttered.

"You a fan?"

To anyone listening, Ry sounded agreeable, but Jamie knew better. Ryder was an asshole. He may have been nicer than most assholes, but that was like saying Charles Manson wasn't technically a murderer.

"Yeah, dude," the bartender squealed. Jamie fought hard to suppress an eyeroll. "I've been a fan since battle of the bands. Hey, you don't want this shit." He reached under the bar, pulling out a bottle of vodka, and poured two healthy shots.

Asshole.

"Thanks, Bro," Ryder said looking down at Jamie with a self-righteous expression. If she didn't need the damn drink to calm her nerves, she would have thrown it in both of their faces.

"Sure thing, Ry. Whatever you need, I'm your man."

"You hear that Kitty Cat?" Ryder smirked, handing her one of the shots. She knocked it back without flinching, before turning to face the smug bastard. He was dressed in skinny jeans and a white Stone Temple Pilots tee. His skin glowed, tattoos peeked out from under the shirt and his medium length blond hair was pulled up high on his head in a bun. His jaw was set into a rigid line and she fought the urge to trace it with her tongue.

He looked like the serpent in the garden and Jamie was down to bite whatever he had to offer.

"Show me around?" she breathed, trying to shake off the image of his dick sliding in and out of her wetness.

Ryder flexed his hand protectively around Jamie's waist. "I should bend you over the bar and fuck you in full view of the party just so everyone knows who you belong to."

"I don't belong to anyone," she whispered.

He arched his brow, shooting her a look that said, *oh really?* For a split second, she thought he actually might do it, that he actually might fuck her, right then, right there. The really twisted part, she would have let him.

"Wrong answer, James." Ryder took his shot and tossed the empty cup in a nearby trash can. His hands found her ass and squeezed hard, pulling her into him. "This is mine." His mouth hung inches above hers. There was a determination in his gaze that made her want to cower. The way he held onto her was obscene. The people in line at the bar were staring, but Ryder didn't care, nor did he make a move to release her. Their noses touched, his lips parted, and he spoke in a tone laced with so much passion, she struggled to breathe. "You belong to me as much as I belong to you."

Jamie nodded. All the air left her lungs around the same time reason and common-fucking-sense left her brain. For as strong and domineering as she was to the rest of the world, she submitted to Ryder with an ease that made her uncomfortable. He had the irritating ability to make her feel completely sane and utterly insane at the same time, like the two emotions were best friends, not bitter rivals.

"Good girl," he grunted, "now let's go look at some motherfuckin' art."

Jamie stood in front of the massive eagle sculpture constructed from feathers and recycled aluminum, one of the fourteen pieces on display. Each piece, varied in size, shape and texture, working together to tell a story, *Sins and Virtues*.

She couldn't help but feel exposed as they meandered through the physical representations of her vices: *pride, greed, lust, gluttony, anger, envy, sloth;* and waded through her shortcomings: *humility, liberality, chastity, abstinence, patience, kindness, diligence.*

This is my first time seeing these," Ryder commented, wrapping his arms around her. "They're incredible."

"They're really good," she agreed, doing her best to keep her voice neutral. Ryder was always affectionate and normally she went along with it—at times she even enjoyed it—but this felt different, too raw, too real. Jamie circled the statue, using her perusal of it as an excuse to shrug out of his embrace. There was a poem on the shiny metal plaque standing in front of the eagle.

I'm fine,
I repeat for the millionth time.
A lie constructed by pride.
Silly little thing,
always keeping me from breathing.
-pride

"Are you okay, Kitty Cat?" Ryder asked, turning her around to face him. His hazel eyes searched hers, concern etched across his face.

"Why wouldn't I be?" She nodded, her gaze drifting back to the plaque.

"Because you're crying."

Jamie blinked, surprised to find water leaking from her eyes. "It's really, really good," she said, turning away from him, swiping at the hot tears that rolled down her cheek. She was a mess, and in need of more vodka.

Grabbing her hand, Ryder laced his fingers with hers. "You have to let me in," he begged.

"Why?" she asked taking her hand back. She felt the same way about holding hands as she did about kissing, too intimate. It was too much, the date, him claiming her in front of a room full of people, and those damn sculptures. They haunted her. They howled her story into the wind, spilling the secrets of her soul.

"Because I want to kiss you and hold your hand and I don't want to have to beg you to do shit with me. I want this to work."

The devastation on his face almost broke her. "You said you wouldn't push, but this entire night feels like one big fucking shove."

Be thankful
Be mindful.
Be kind.

She chanted, but Jamie couldn't get the self-destructive side of her brain to listen to the rational side. If she wasn't the cold and heartless bitch she pretended to be, then her emotions would consume her. She hated doing this to Ryder, but she needed to protect her heart.

"I'm being patient," Ryder whisper-hissed. "I've *been* patient. What the fuck else do I have to do?"

Shaking her head, Jamie sighed, "This was a bad idea."

Stop talking. Don't self-destruct, not now. Not with him.

Ryder nodded his head, his sleepy eyes scanning the crowd. "Let me say bye to Nic and the guys, then we can go." Unspoken promises hung in the air. Jamie could see his gears turning. His plan to fuck her into submission once and for all was written in the air between them. In truth, she wanted him to, but the ball of self-loathing that knotted in her belly, sparked by the emotions Nic's poetry evoked, had her stomping on the self-destruct button once more.

"Not just the show. This whole thing," she motioned between them, "us." The rational angel on her shoulder screamed for her to shut up but of course, Jamie didn't listen.

She never listened.

"No," Ryder shook his head. "I'm not letting you off that easy, Kitty Cat." Broken, honey-colored eyes bore into her green, searching for answers she wasn't ready to give voice to.

Jamie opened her mouth to speak, whether to fight him or submit to him, she'd never know. Before she had the chance, a man walked up behind Ryder, and dropped a hand on his shoulder. "Ry, dude, you made it." He, like Jamie, was dressed in all black. He wore thick rimmed glasses, but unlike most people in attendance, his looked more practical than fashionable.

Reluctantly tearing his gaze from Jamie, Ryder smiled at the man. It was a smile reserved for those closest to him. "Nic, bro, this is fucking epic. We wouldn't have missed it." Ryder said, grabbing Jamie's hand. "This is Jamie, my girlfriend. Jamie, this is Dominic, the madman behind *Sins and Virtues*."

Jamie swallowed past the dry lump in her throat. *Girlfriend*? The room began to spin, and she did her best to focus on the man in front of her while ignoring the urge to crawl out of her skin. "Nice to meet you," she extended her hand. She hoped to God it wasn't too sweaty. "Ryder is right, your stuff is incredible." She could do this, she could pretend. She was good at pretending: on air, with her family, with her friends. "I work at WSEA-9. I'd love to interview you sometime."

Work.

Yes.

Work was good.

"I saw the one you did with Lithium. Is that how you two met?" Nic asked. He had curious eyes, the eyes of an artist. Not only was he listening to her, but he studied her, collecting data to fuel his muse.

"Kinda," Ry chuckled. He dropped his arm around Jamie's shoulders, oblivious of the anxiety boiling in her belly.

"Excuse me," Jamie smiled. "I'm going to run to the restroom." She didn't have to pee, but she did need a minute. Air, space, whatever. She needed time to process his words. She knew the lines were blurring, but the moniker didn't surprise her as much as the effect it had on her heart did.

Pressing a kiss on her forehead, Ryder released her. "I'll go find the guys so we can go soon."

Jamie turned to Dominic. "Nice to meet you, Nic. I'll get your info from Ry and I'll be in touch."

"Sounds good." He nodded.

Jamie retreated toward the front of the gallery. Her plan was to stand out in the cool air and over analyze why hearing Ryder call her his girlfriend made her want to throw up and swoon at the same damn time. But first, she needed to make another visit to the kid with the hidden bottle of vodka at the bar.

The crowd had died down over the last hour and thankfully, there was no line. "Hey," she said as she approached. "Got any more of that Ketel One?" And for good measure she added, "Ry asked me to get one for him and the guys."

The kid nodded dutifully, reaching under the bar. He filled three plastic cups with the clear liquid, and replaced the cap. "It's so cool that they're here."

"Um-hmm," Jamie mumbled, consolidating the contents of each cup into one extra-large shot. "Thanks," she grinned, making her way towards the exit.

The cool night air kissed Jamie's cheeks and the warmth from the vodka burned her throat. She exhaled for what felt like the first time all night.

Girlfriend.

Would she even be any good at it? What would be expected of her? Normally, when she felt this overwhelmed she'd call Kensie, but lately it was harder and harder to talk to her best friend. It was partly her fault, Jamie knew that, but her pride stopped her.

Silly little thing.

FOURTEEN

Wrecking Ball

RYDER

Being in a relationship with Jamie was like playing *Grand Theft Auto*. It was all fun and blow jobs until there was a gun pointed at your head.

Kitty Cat never hesitated to pull the trigger.

Ryder thought they were past all the, *"I don't do the boyfriend,"* bullshit. He thought they were making progress, slow progress, as slow as Pink Floyd's *Comfortably Numb*, but he was okay with that as long as they were inching forward.

And they *were* inching forward.

He was her boyfriend in every way that mattered. At this point, she was closer to his mother than he was. If she wasn't at work, she was with him. Hell, she spent more time cleaning his cum from between her legs than she did at her apartment. Ryder ignored her little meltdown in front of Nic, but now as he watched the blonde retreat to the bar, anger seared his intestines.

"Everything okay?" Nic asked, eyeing him like he was a live grenade.

Ryder bobbed his head up and down, the skin around his mouth stretched into a grimace. "It's complicated."

Complicated, the fucking understatement of the century. After a week of begging, he was forced to resort to extortion just to get Jamie's ass to go to the show. Now she goes and pulls this shit.

He could forgive that she was late, by an hour. He could forgive her flirting with the dick riding bartender, but he couldn't forgive her denial of him.

"I don't belong to anyone."

Bull-fucking-shit.

She was his. He owned her. Was that unhealthy? Maybe. Misogynistic? Definitely. But she owned him too.

"You really got it bad this time, huh?" Nic chuckled, slapping him on the shoulder. Nic, like Ryder's other friends, subscribed to the notion that he fell in love too easily, but that's who he was, and he wasn't going to apologize for it.

"Why so serious?" Javi asked, doing his signature Joker impersonation as he and CT sauntered over. Was he really that transparent? He thought he was doing a decent job of keeping his temper in check, but so far he was 0-2.

"He's about to go have angry sex with the hot blonde," Nic informed them.

"What are you and Kitty Cat fighting about now?" Javi's tone was as exasperated as Ryder felt.

His eyes drifted back to the bar where little miss *I belong to no one*, was pouring three shots into one cup. "Same shit," Ry grunted, tipping his chin in her direction. "I'm all in and she's afraid of commitment."

"Dude, I'm afraid of commitment. Kitty Cat is a straight fucking savage."

"Yeah, but he's gotta take it easy on her. You're too intense. Not everyone is ready for marriage after two months," CT said, because apparently it was, *give Ryder unsolicited advice* day.

"I said we're good," Ry grunted.

"Do you believe that shit?" CT asked looking to Javi.

"Nope."

CT then turned to Nic, "What about you?"

Dominic's answer, while more diplomatic, was also a negative. "It did seem a bit tense when I walked up."

"Since when do you fuckers give relationship advice?"

"Don't get all pissy, dude," CT said, punching Ryder in the shoulder. "All I'm saying is cut the girl some slack."

"No, she's got to give a little too. Ry's a good guy and she's playing mind games with him."

"Do you assholes just sit around and talk about my love life?"

"Love?" CT raised a brow. "See it's that shit that makes Kitty Cat think you're a fucking psycho."

"Fuck you. And you," he growled pointing at his friends. "Nic, thanks for the invite, but I'm out."

Ryder turned and stomped his way toward the exit. They could kiss his ass. His and Jamie's shit might be messy and imperfect, but it was theirs and no one else's. He'd take real and complicated with Kitty Cat over superficial and easy with anyone else.

Shouldering his way out the door and into the Seattle night, Ryder closed his eyes. The wind felt good against his face and the cool air calmed the fire in his belly.

Jamie evoked emotions he spent his life burying under the easy-going, sensitive façade. It was easier to be that Ryder than the Ryder he was born to be. Erratic. Volatile. Angry.

She was a wild cat, one who couldn't be tamed. It wasn't that he wanted to change her. He liked her fucked up, because even with the sadness, she persisted.

"Hey," he heard the familiar voice calling from the distance. Turning in the direction of the sound he spotted Kitty Cat standing there, a plastic cup clutched in her palm and a frown etched on her beautiful face. Her sad, droopy, eyes were like a healing balm to his rage. "Why the long face, Kitty Cat?" he asked as he approached.

Jamie studied him for a beat, searching, for what, he didn't know.

"Why did you tell Nic I was your girlfriend?" Accusation pierced her tone.

"Because you are," he answered simply. It was a truth she needed to accept. They weren't casual. This wasn't for fun. It was difficult. Jamie was a pain in Ryder's ass most days, but she was also the other half of him. The ice to his fire. It was the stuff of tragedies. A soul burning, slightly toxic, and totally unhealthy kind of obsession. It was the exact thing he swore off, but with Kitty Cat, Ryder found himself grasping at whatever scraps she threw his way.

"When did that happen?" she asked. It wasn't her usual brand of smartassness. She was being sincere. She was falling just as hard as he was. The fundamental difference was that Jamie wanted to catch herself.

"Does it matter?" he asked, pulling her to him by the lapels of her leather jacket.

"Yes, it matters. I never wanted this." Her voice was haunted. Like he did this to her. Like he was the monster.

"Why can't you just let me in. This could be easy, and fun. We could be happy, but you won't let me in." His grip on her tightened. The wrath bubbling and fizzling in his stomach.

A thousand emotions played out on Jamie's features: fear, self-loathing, and frustration, chief among them. For a brief moment, he could see the broken bits of her soul. They were jagged, sharp little pieces that stabbed at something deep inside his brain. *His compulsive need to protect.* But they vanished just as quickly as they came. Her mask was back in place. She was shutting down and shutting him out.

"Why do you do that?"

"Do what?

"Why do you shut down every time I start talking about anything deeper than the fucking weather?" he spit. Rage colored his vision, and his world went red. The beast that laid dormant inside him was rearing its ugly head. This was what Ryder was afraid of, this reaction. It was his worst nightmare, but beneath the anger was shame. Shame that took the form of his ten-year-old self. It screamed for him to stop, to breathe, but he couldn't. Leaning in, inches from her face, Ryder seethed, "Do you like this? Seeing me like this? Is it a game? How far can I push him until he snaps? Well, guess what? You're fucking winning. I give up, okay?"

Pushing him back, Jamie sneered, "I don't know what you want from me. The first night we met you fucked me and another girl in the back of a bar. What did you think this was?"

She brushed past him, but he caught her elbow before she could get far. "Fuck that Jamie. You can't throw that shit in my face now. I didn't ask for that. I didn't want that! You did!"

"I didn't hold a gun to your head."

"That's not fair."

"But it is life."

The two of them stood, toe-to-toe, nose-to-nose. "You don't always have to be a bitch. You know that, don't you?"

Jamie stiffened at the harshness of his words. "And you don't always have to be a possessive asshole."

"You know what James, I'm not doing this with you," Ry grunted. He took a step back, and then another before turning and heading back into the gallery. It was a lie. Ryder was willing to love her through anything. She was dancing with demons, but he was powerless to help if she refused to tell him what he was up against.

FIFTEEN

20 Something

Jamie

Cinnamon filled the air, rousing Jamie from a merlot induced slumber. The unmistakable whizzing and whirling of her KitchenAid Stand Mixer forced her out of bed for the first time in two days. She stood, then instantly regretted it. "Too fast," she groaned, plopping back down on the bed. Empty wine bottles were strewn on her night table, and her leather jacket laid discarded on the floor. It had been there since the art show, her *pièce de résistance* in self-destruction.

There were times when Jamie doubted she was a normal person. One with a heart, feelings, and emotions. She wasn't a sociopath, she felt remorse, *after the fact,* but in the moment, she couldn't help herself. Her brain was wired wrong. She couldn't accept that Ryder liked her, not just having sex with her, or the idea of her, but the real, broken, spiral mode Jamie.

The last month with Ryder was nice. She grew to enjoy the time she spent with him in his world. She knew she would fuck it up. Jamie always fucked it up, but a tiny piece of her hoped it would last longer, maybe even forever.

Jamie tried standing again, this time slowly. She pulled the hood up on her green footless onesie, not bothering to look in the mirror. No need to confirm what she already knew. She hadn't showered or left the bed for anything, other than to pee or open the door for the Postmates delivery person, in the last couple of days. She even called in sick to work, something she only ever did once, last fall.

Jamie stumbled into the kitchen to find Kensie with her face buried in one of their cookbooks. "Good morning," Jamie grunted. She opened the cabinet and pulled down a coffee mug, filling it with the remains of the half-drunken bottle of wine abandoned on the counter.

"There's coffee," Kensie said, pointing to the pot.

Coffee was for people with plans and goals and motivation. Jamie had none of those things. So instead, she ignored the inference and steered the subject to safer waters. "Where's Trey?" she asked, sipping from the mug of wine.

Kensie eyed her friend, her lips puckered like she was dying to protest, but knew to tread lightly. "At his place."

Jamie's eyebrows shot up. "And you're here?" Since the beginning of their relationship Kensie and Trey had spent every night together. An unwanted pang ran through her chest. She had that with Ryder. She used to think it was obsessive, his need to be in almost constant contact with her, but now after forty-eight hours of radio silence, she missed it. The phone calls and text messages were what got her through those long hours at the station. As much as it killed her to admit it, she finally understood why Ken was always with her boyfriend.

Trey was still a dick though.

Kensie looked up from the cookbook, giving Jamie her best, don't *be a smartass* look. "I thought we could hang out today, just you and me."

"Rain check," Jamie snorted. She topped her coffee mug off with the rest of the wine in the bottle and turned to leave. She loved

Kensie, but she was giving herself one more day to mope. Whatever little intervention her friend had planned would have to wait until Jamie was less hungover and more drunk.

"Jamie," Kensie whispered, "are we okay?"

Jamie, not Jam.

Shit.

Jamie wasn't emotionally stable enough for this conversation. "Why wouldn't we be?" she asked cautiously, her back to her friend.

"I know I've been pretty shitty in the best friend department lately—"

"You think."

"—but so have you," Ken added coming around to face her.

"How would you know? You're never here." Jamie was deflecting. It was a bitch move but she was on a roll this weekend. Why stop now?

"I didn't realize how bad it got until the other day. I'm sorry, but I'm here now." Everything in her brown eyes read sincere. Kensington Grace Roth could be clueless and at times, immature, but she was a loyal friend, and the only person who was there when *it* happened.

"Ken, I've had a tough few days and I just want to wallow." Jamie wasn't ready to talk about her latest fuck-up in the string of near constant fuck-ups that was her life. She wanted to drink wine, binge watch *Friends,* and gorge herself on whatever it was Kensie was baking.

"I'll let you wallow, for now," Kensie said, switching off the mixer. There was flour everywhere, and broken egg shells and apple peels discarded in the sink. Kensington was a decent cook, but baking wasn't her thing. If she was home, and awake, *and baking,* Jamie didn't stand a chance. "But look at you. You're a mess, and you smell bad—like really bad." She sniffed Jamie's blonde hair, lifting a greasy, matted strand with her finger. "When's the last time you washed this?"

Jamie swatted Kensie's hand away. Months of being ignored for her douchebag boyfriend, and she chooses now to pay attention?

"I just…work is kicking my ass."

"Work?"

"Yes, Sarah's going to be out for another month and my workload has doubled," Jamie rambled around her mug.

"So, we lie to each other now?"

Jamie sighed, nibbling on her tattooed finger. "What do you want from me Kensington?"

"The truth, for starters. Did something happen with your parents?" She was doubling down. Nothing good could come from this.

"No."

Kensie stopped, her too big brown eyes widened. "Jam," she gasped, her voice barely a whisper, "Is it about last fall?"

"No, Jesus," Jamie shrieked. It was time to come clean. She was a bitch, but she wasn't a big enough bitch to let her best friend think she'd fallen back into the depth of depression just to keep the Ryder secret. "It's a guy, okay. Just a guy. I've turned into a cliché, moping around in pj's and pining over a fucking guy."

Kensie's lips twitched, "All this angst is over a guy?"

"I hate you," Jamie groaned.

"James Michele Manning is sad about a penis? I never thought I'd see the day."

Jamie narrowed her eyes at her friend, doing her best to suppress her grin. "He's…different. Amazing, and gorgeous, and kind, and talented."

Holy shit she belonged in a Kate Hudson movie.

"JAM!" Kensie screamed, jumping up and down. "This needs something stronger than wine." She ran to the freezer and pulled out a bottle of tequila, grabbed two shot glasses from the cabinet and practically dragged Jamie to the couch, forgetting all about whatever it was she was mixing in the mixer.

"Okay, tell me everything." Kensie said after they each took a shot.

"There's nothing to tell. We met and had sex. I Jamie'd it up, and now he hates me."

"Did he say he hates you or did you assume he hates you so that you had an out?" Kensie asked.

Sometimes Jamie loved having a friend like Kensie, one who knew her well enough to know her quirks. One that wasn't afraid to call her on her bullshit. This was not one of those times.

"He called me a bitch and walked away. I haven't heard from him since."

"He called you a bitch? Do you want me to kick his ass?"

Jamie laughed, then frowned, then shook her head. "No, I deserved it. I was being a bitch." Bitch wasn't even the right word. She was like the angel of death, roaming the earth, snuffing out joy and happiness wherever she went.

"Did you apologize?" Jamie took a large drink of her wine, avoiding Kensington's gaze. "Jam, no wonder he hasn't called you. Here." Kensie jumped up from her spot on the couch. She jogged the distance to Jamie's room and was back within seconds. "Text him," she demanded, thrusting her cell in her face.

"And say what?" Jamie held the phone like it might explode. Would he even respond? He shouldn't. If he knew what was good for him, he'd have blocked her number. Then again, can you block numbers on a flip phone?

"Uh, how about I'm sorry?" Kensie snarked.

Jamie rolled her eyes, wondering where the sweet, demure, little Kensington she pretended to be around Trey went. "It's better this way. I'm sure I'll just do something else irrational. Why bring him into my shit?"

Kensie looked at Jamie with sadness in her eyes. Pity wasn't what Jamie was going for, but the angel of death had struck again. Their eyes met, green to brown. Words weren't needed when the bond was as deep as theirs.

It's not your fault.

I deserve this suffering.

You deserve to be happy and if this guy makes you happy, then fuck your pride and say sorry.

Jamie's phone rang, interrupting the unspoken conversation. "Hello," she answered cautiously, the number unrecognizable.

"Jamie, hi, it's Jared, from Easter."

"Oh, Jared, hi," Jamie said, looking at Kensie. She deleted his number after Ryder fucked her on the hood of her Rover, figuring it best to leave well enough alone. Jared was the last person she was expecting to hear from, but he was probably the best thing that could happen. She'd caused enough destruction in Ryder's life.

"Is that him?" Kensie mouthed.

"I was wondering if you wanted to join me for dinner? I know a great Italian place downtown."

"Dinner?" she asked, looking to her roommate.

"Say yes. Say yes. Say yes." The giddy brunette chanted, raising to her knees. It was ridiculous, seeing her all worked up over a phone call. Her excitement was beginning to permeate Jamie's two-day layer of grime and sadness.

"Sure," Jamie agreed. A reluctant smile tugging at her lips. She was a complete asshole for lying to her friend, but honesty was an illusion. Kensie was happy to be able to help her and Jamie had a reason to shower.

"Should I pick you up or would you like to meet there?"

This night would require lots of alcohol, so she opted for the former. "Pick me up at seven. I'll text you my address."

"Sounds great, see you then," he said, before ending the call.

Biting down on her tattooed finger, Jamie silently recited her affirmation.

Be thankful.

Be mindful.

Be kind.

"OMG," Kensie squealed, grabbing Jamie by the hand and pulling her up off the couch. "Let's go. We only have eight hours to make you presentable."

"Now who's the bitch?" Jamie grumbled, following behind her friend.

Jamie made her way downstairs at seven sharp. Kensie had ensured she was showered, shaved, and that her hair no longer reeked. She even forced her into a dress, an emerald green off the shoulder number that stopped just below her knees. Kensie said it was Gucci and perfect for a romantic Italian dinner.

Ignoring the dull ache in her chest, Jamie stepped off the elevator and out into the lobby. Her legs pushed her forward, powered by her brain and its eagerness to erase the memory of Ryder. Mere seconds after passing the reception desk, Jamie spotted the black on black Tesla parked in front of her building. Jared was standing there, leaning against his pretentious car, smiling at her with a predatory gaze.

Each step felt less like freedom and more like captivity, but she brushed off the ominous feeling, nodding her head at the doorman as she passed.

"Hey," she greeted. Her voice was soft, breathy. She was fucking flirting with the guy because when the going got tough, Jamie pulled on her party girl mask and pretended like nothing affected her.

In reality, she hated herself, for two hours ago, and for two days ago. What was she doing getting into this man's car while the man she really wanted to be with was probably home, burning the stuff he insisted she keep at his place?

"You look gorgeous, although you always do," Jared said, his hand at the small of her back. Opening the door, he guided her into the passenger's seat. Jamie acknowledged the gesture with a plastic smile as he trotted around to the driver's side.

Breathe James, just breathe.

She didn't get out of bed and wash her hair to continue her pity party. Jamie was determined to have a good time, even if it killed her. "This is only the second time you've ever seen me."

"In person, maybe," Jared said putting the Tesla in drive, "but I watch you most nights on the six o'clock news."

Jamie narrowed her eyes at Jared, a real smile threatening to break free. He was good, she'd give him that. He had this aura about him. He was this confident, self-assured man, undoubtedly the most charismatic tech nerd she had ever met. A tech nerd who didn't act, talk, or look like one. One who would most likely con her out of her panties if she wasn't careful.

"So, remind me, what is it that you do?" she asked as he navigated the hundred-thousand-dollar electric car through the Seattle streets.

Jared chuckled. It was a deep, rich sound that sent a shiver down her spine, but not the good kind. Not the kind she got when Ryder would sing in her ear as he fucked her, but the kind that made alarm bells ring out in her mind.

"I made my fortune off the GPS app you're so fond of," he explained. "Then once I graduated, I moved back to Washington and opened up my company in Seattle. Palo Alto is a rat race and I wanted to be home."

"You're from Seattle?"

"No, Tacoma, but with Amazon, Microsoft and Expedia here, I figured the market was ripe for the picking, so to speak." He smirked. "I was right. GoTech is thriving. We've got the tech side with development and programming, but more recently, we've been looking at expanding," he explained as the car rolled to a stop. He studied her face for a moment, an easy smirk tugging at his lips. His eyes glinted with something dark, sinister.

Jared was a complete mystery to Jamie. If she were honest, something about him made her uncomfortable, but in her haste to forget the hazel-eyed sex god, she ignored her gut and settled back into her seat. "That sounds fascinating."

"You have no idea," he chuckled again, and again she shivered. After the bizarre exchange, the two fell into an easy conversation about nothing and before she knew it, Jared was handing his keys to the valet and leading her into the restaurant.

"I feel like I've heard of this place, but I've never eaten here," Jamie commented as they followed the pretty hostess to a table in the back. The lights were low and pink seemed to be the theme. The color was everywhere, from the large floral displays set throughout the dining room, to the accents on the chairs, and the lettering on the staff's otherwise black uniforms. The women wore tight dresses with the words *Cibo* embossed across their chest, and the men donned equally tight t-shirts, with equally pink lettering. It was all so familiar, yet so foreign, but that was her life these days, existing in a world unknown to her; a world where she cared about a boy, a world where she lied to her best friend.

Jamie was taking the self-destructive thing to a new level.

"It's been here for about a year. The couple who owns it also owns a few others. They were initial investors in my app, and are big contributors in my upcoming endeavors."

The dining room was bustling with activity, every table was occupied, and if the smells coming from the kitchen were any indication, at the very least she'd have a good meal.

"Should we get a bottle?" Jared suggested, pointing at the wine list. She nodded mechanically. Being here was wrong. Something about this place grated on her conscience. There was no way she was getting through this date without a little liquid courage. "You pick, just nothing too sweet."

Jamie's face turned up in disgust. "Nothing about me is sweet."

"I don't know," he mused, "you don't seem too bad."

"Give it time. My sour side will rear its ugly head eventually."

"Like a Sour Patch kid?"

She grinned, nodding as their server appeared. Jamie ordered a bottle of dry white wine because it was her favorite and since she planned on drinking most of it, she figured she might as well get what she liked.

"Tell me something about yourself," Jared asked.

Something about myself, she thought, looking around the room like the answer would magically manifest. The couple to their left looked to be in their thirties, married, judging by the huge diamond on her finger and the shiny gold band around his. He was on his phone, and had been since the moment Jamie and Jared arrived, while the wife, belly swollen with child, played with her dessert.

Jamie wondered if she should tell Jared that she was basically the Antichrist and that she'd undoubtedly ruin his life, or if she should just keep it light?

"I am a terrible cook, but an excellent baker," she said opting for light. It went better with the wine.

"I have a live-in cook and an incurable sweet tooth. It's a match made in heaven," he laughed, just as their server, Steven, returned with the wine. Jared tasted it, a smile on his lips, and nodded his approval. Steven poured them each a glass, then explained the specials for the night. Jamie went with the fish and Jared, the chicken.

It was all so normal, but no matter what she did, that nagging feeling, caused by the Ryder shaped hole in her chest, wouldn't go away. Lifting her glass, Jamie said, "It's your turn. Tell me something, something good," then took a sip of wine.

"I was born with six toes on my left foot."

A lady must never spit.

It was a lesson her mother drilled into her brain as a child, and one the first guy she ever gave a blow job to, reinforced. A lady never spits, but the six toes thing had her breaking that rule. "No way," she said, dabbing her chin with the cloth napkin, "let me see."

"I don't have it anymore," Jared laughed. "My parents had it removed shortly after I was born. There are pictures, at my place."

Swiping her finger across her lip, Jamie inhaled, and exhaled slowly. "Will you show me?" she breathed, deciding in that moment to use Jared to fuck away any residual sadness she had over Ryder. But then Karma did that thing it does; it bit her right in the ass, because no sooner did she think about sleeping with another man, the one she wanted appeared.

Jamie's face paled as she locked eyes with Ryder from across the room. His expression was indecipherable, but there was no mistaking his anger. She felt it in her bone marrow. His skin emanated a radioactive glow as he stalked over to their table. The black t-shirt she'd stepped over many a night on her way to the bathroom stretched across his chest. That was it, the reason this place gave her a sense of dread. This was *the* Italian restaurant. The one that put pineapples on pizza all the time.

"Who the fuck is this?" The words seeped from his teeth like a poisonous gas.

"Hi," Jamie said slowly, trying not to choke on the fumes. Ryder's anger confused her. He didn't want her. He made that clear when he walked away and didn't call for two days.

"Who. The. Fuck. Is. This. James?" Ryder growled, ignoring the other man all together. "What the fuck are you doing here?"

"I'm having dinner, Napoleon." If he wanted to use first names, she could do it too.

"You're on a fucking date?" His voice was low, but his presence screamed so loudly she was sure the angels heard.

Jared cleared his throat. Jamie almost forgot he was there. Ryder's appearance eclipsed everything in his path. "Do you know this guy, Jamie?"

"I... he's..."

"Her fucking boyfriend. Who the fuck are you?"

Jared snorted, "You're not her boyfriend. You're a bus boy. Now run along and leave us to enjoy our meal." His tone was harsh. It was like he transformed into her father before her eyes.

"Us?" Ryder seethed.

"Jamie and I."

"Ryder, relax, it's only dinner."

That time he roared, "ONLY DINNER?" His voice was so loud, the man to her left put his phone down. "Get the fuck up." He grabbed Jamie by the arm and pulled her to her feet.

Jared stood, "Take your hands off her."

"Or else what?" Ryder asked, taking a step towards Jared. Jared in turn, took a step towards Ryder.

"Ry, why are you doing this?" Jamie did her best to keep her voice steady, but it came out all cracked and broken. When it came to Ryder, everything was always cracked and broken. Her brain, her decision-making capabilities. He'd torn her apart from the inside, and insisted on piecing her back together.

"Get. Your. Shit," he gritted. His fists clenched and she obeyed because even though he didn't want her, she knew she needed to end this. For once, she had to be responsible. For once, she needed to latch on to the good and not cling to the bad.

"Okay," she said grabbing her purse, "now can we go?"

"You're leaving with this guy?" Jared's face fell in disbelief. Jamie could tell he wasn't a man who was used to losing.

"I'm sorry. I just," *Miss him. Need him. Want him.* "I'm just sorry."

Ryder grabbed her by the hand and led her through the dining room, and into the kitchen. Every eye was trained on them. His long legs moved swiftly. At that pace, in those shoes, Jamie nearly slipped on the greasy kitchen floor.

Shoving his way out a side door, Ryder paused, turning back into the kitchen. "Wait here," he demanded. Minutes passed before Ryder returned, pushing a helmet into her chest. "Put this on."

"You don't have to be such a dick," she said snatching the helmet.

"And you don't have to be such a slut." The sun was settling over the horizon. The sky darkened and they hurled insults back and forth like a tennis ball. The alley behind the restaurant was dirty and damp, a stark contrast to the inside. It was fitting. This fight was gritty, their pain, real.

"Fuck you!" she yelled and tossed the helmet back to him. "You pulled me from a date with a nice guy so you could yell at me some more? I think I'd rather drink my wine and eat my dinner." If she was lucky, Jared would still be there, or at least their table would be.

Jamie made it all of two steps before Ryder was on her, the helmet falling to the ground with a loud crash. "What if I brought a girl to the news station? How the fuck would you feel?" he asked gripping Jamie's waist. Ryder spun her around, forcing her to meet his gaze.

"I wouldn't feel anything, because we broke up. Hell, we weren't even really together."

He looked at her like she'd sucker punched him. Her words hit their mark, and she was glad for it. Glad to inflict a little of the anguish he'd caused her in the last forty-eight hours. "When did we break up?" His words, were more accusatory than questioning.

"Don't play dumb."

"Dumb? Jamie, we had a fucking fight." His grip on her waist tightened. His mouth, inching closer to hers. "We will have a lot of fucking fights, but that doesn't mean we aren't together."

"You didn't call me for two days," she whispered, because she didn't trust herself to speak any louder.

"I was pissed at you. I *am* pissed. You fucked up, and you're still fucking up. You told that asshole you were sorry, and you have yet to tell me? That's messed up."

Jamie looked down, unsure of what to say. It was easy apologizing to Jared, but hard to say the words to Ryder. "I told you I wouldn't be good at this."

"I'm in love with you, James." He said it with so much passion, so much conviction, she couldn't help but believe him.

"You can't love me." Pulling his hand from her hip, she placed it over her heart. "There's nothing in here but broken pieces."

"I love you, James," he repeated, his mouth hovering over hers. "I'm not going to let you push me away. I'm not going to let you keep yourself from me anymore. You can put on a brave face for the rest of the world, but not with me, not anymore."

"You can't love me."

"Kitty Cat."

"No, Ry, you can't."

"I love you." His tongue slipped out, tracing her bottom lip. His mouth closed in on hers, his soft lips begging for entrance.

Jamie froze, letting the gravity of the situation wash over her. Her first kiss was in the same damp and dirty alley, and it was just as fitting. She exhaled, and flung her arms around his neck, submitting to him. Ryder grinned against her lips, before licking his way into her mouth triumphantly. Jamie could taste the cinnamon whiskey on his tongue.

He tasted like home.

SIXTEEN

By Your Side

Jamie

Promises, like hearts, were made to be broken; a lesson Jamie learned the hard way. Her heart went first, when it was ripped from her body last fall. That's when she promised herself to never let love destroy her again. Then along came Ryder, and there went that. He was her very own Saint Peter, clutching the keys to the Kingdom in his palm, but was she worthy? He told her he loved her, which after her behavior was inexplicable. A part of her held out hope that he meant it. They were three little words that never held much weight before, but felt like a boulder coming from Ryder's lips.

Jamie's thighs clenched around Ryder as he steered the older model Harley Davidson down the quiet residential street. He pulled to a stop in front of the small home he shared with his friends and killed the engine, submerging them in silence.

"Are you okay?" he asked, helping her to her feet. Ryder bent into a squatting position to inspect her legs. Physically, Jamie was fine. Riding on the back of his bike in a dress wasn't the worst thing to happen that night, but mentally, she was fucked.

Was she okay?

Probably not.

Were they okay?

She hoped so, because as scary as the thought of letting him in was, the thought of never again feeling his mouth against hers was worse. Jamie didn't do the kissing thing, blame Julia Roberts and *Pretty Woman,* but when Ryder's lips crashed down onto hers, it was heaven.

It was nirvana.

It was everything.

Jamie wasn't sure what would happen next, but in typical Jamie fashion, she opted for deflection. It was always easier than saying what was on her heart. "I'm okay," she said pulling the helmet off her head and running her fingers through her blonde locks. "But I think my hair has seen better days."

Ryder snatched the helmet from her, searching her eyes for answers she didn't have. "Fuck your hair. Jamie—" he began. The front door burst open and a giggling Tiff walked out with CT behind her.

Jamie exhaled in relief, rubbing her tattoo across her bottom lip. They couldn't save her from his wrath or her guilt, but they could buy her a few extra moments to figure out how to make things right. CT nodded in their direction. Jamie expected judgement from the drummer, but much to her surprise, there was understanding in his blue eyes." You're home early. I thought you worked until eleven?"

Shit.

Another thing to add to the long list of reasons why Ryder should tell her to fuck off. He had caused a scene at his job, *because of her*, and he'd probably be fired, *because of her*. Ryder grunted a string of expletives under his breath, grabbed Jamie by the hand, and pulled her up the stairs.

"Hey," Jamie greeted meekly as the two passed the drummer and their ex-threesome partner.

"Somebodies in trouble," CT said in a singsong voice. Oh, how Jamie longed to wipe the shit-eating grin off his face, but it wouldn't win her any points with the angry blond stomping into the house ahead of her. And, the bastard was right, though it didn't stop her from flipping him the middle finger as she followed dutifully behind her boyfriend.

Boyfriend.

Her poor heart never stood a chance. What was worse, she wanted to give it to him. Jamie longed to give him everything he wanted, she just wasn't sure how. She was so out of her depth she couldn't see the bottom of the pool anymore.

Why did she agree to dinner with Jared?

Why didn't she listen when Kensie said to call?

Tension spilled from Ryder's pores as he pushed open the door to his bedroom. "I want you to take this shit off," he growled, tugging at her dress. "All of it, the make-up, the clothes, the shoes, everything. I don't want to see you dressed up for another man."

Jamie did as she was told, peeling away layer after layer until she was bared to him. "Ry, I—"

"No," his fingers brushed gently over her lips, "first we shower, then we can talk."

She nodded and watched as he pulled the black t-shirt over his head. Once he undressed, he grabbed the pink, terrycloth towel that hung on his closet door and wrapped it around her body. Then he retrieved her toiletry bag from his dresser and led her to the bathroom.

Shutting the door behind them, Ryder shuffled through her bag, pulling out the makeup wipes. His brow furrowed in concentration as he gently wiped her face, taking special care around her eyes. A few minutes and two wipes later, the mask she donned for her date with Jared was gone. In fact, this was the first time she'd ever really shown herself to Ryder. The first time she let her guard down enough for him to see. "Ry, I—"

"*Shh,*" he murmured, pulling back the curtain. "Let's just get you clean, Kitty Cat."

Jamie followed Ryder into the shower. It felt like she was following him over a cliff, and in a lot of ways, she was. This was uncharted territory for her, but she trusted him to be her guide. Ryder wrapped his arms around Jamie. Her bottom lip quivered. It was too much, too intimate and she fought with everything she had not to do what she did best, run.

"I'm sorry," she sobbed. She couldn't hold back the tears any longer. The ache in her chest was too great a burden to bear alone and for the first time, she didn't have to. For the first time, it was okay for her to let go. Jamie once thought showing emotion made her weak, but she was wrong.

There was strength in vulnerability.

In that shower, she wasn't Jamie, the big sister who used herself and her own shortcomings to shield her brother from their parents. She wasn't Jamie, the friend who protected her naive bestie against men who only sought to take. She was just Jamie, and that was enough.

It was okay for her to be sad and unsure.

It was okay to need someone.

Time slipped away, or maybe no time passed at all. She wasn't sure how long they stood under the hot spray, her crying, him brooding, both trying to figure out where to go from there.

It wasn't until Ryder reached for her shampoo that she remembered where they were, not physically, but emotionally. They were at an impasse. She had to give if she wanted to keep him, she knew that, and she was willing.

Ryder got to work on washing her hair, then moved on to her body. Sudsy hands skated over every inch of her flesh. He took care of her in a way no man ever had before. He worshipped her shoulders, her arms, her back and her stomach, paying special attention to her scar.

His touch paralyzed her. Reciting her mantra in her head, she willed herself to relax.

Be thankful.
Be mindful.
Be kind.

It was difficult, standing there while his fingers explored her greatest sin, but she didn't push him away. She was done pretending she didn't care.

"There she is," he said, the words a prayer on his tongue. His fingers tangled into her wet hair and his mouth crashed against hers.

His lips were everything she never knew she needed. Gentle, firm, consuming. She clung to him, molding her body to his. They kissed under the shower until the water ran cold and her teeth chattered.

"Come on, Kitty Cat, time to get out." Ryder lifted her out of the tub, setting her feet on the old towel thrown across the floor. He wrapped the pink towel around her body, kissed her nose, her lips, then gathered their stuff, and led her back to his room.

"Thank you," she muttered as they went.

"For what?" he asked, locking them behind his door once more.

"Not hating me." She never really appreciated the calm vibes his space created until then. It was comforting, although she knew whatever came next would be hard.

"I could never hate you."

"You should though."

"Why? Did you fuck that guy?" He exhaled the words in a rush. There was bitterness there, like tea that had been left to steep too long. They hurt—his words—but she couldn't say she didn't deserve them.

"No," Jamie shook her head vehemently. Water flew from the tips of her hair with each swing of her neck. "I would have though. I thought you didn't want me, and I just needed to forget you." She couldn't look him in the eyes. The reality of her existence was gut-wrenching. She was more willing to give her body to a stranger than she was to give her heart to the man it belonged to.

"I know this relationship shit is new to you, so let me just make this clear. If we ever break up, you will know. Until that happens just assume you're mine."

"I can do that." She shivered. *His*. She could be his, she wanted that, she craved it.

"Who was that guy, anyway?" Ryder threw over his shoulder as he got to work digging through his drawers for clothes. He tossed her a pair of his boxers before slipping on a pair himself.

"He's one of my dad's business partners," she explained. "He came to our house for Easter."

Ryder turned, glaring at her. His legs ate the distance between them and in an instant, he was on her, his face inches from hers. He radiated heat. "You've been talking to that motherfucker since Easter?"

"No!" Jamie exclaimed, running her fingers through his damp blond hair. Her touch soothed him a little, but there was only one way for them to move past this. She needed to put herself out there, full disclosure. "Yes, he came over for Easter, but I was late. I spent the morning lying in bed talking to you," she reminded him.

"Then when I got there and saw him sitting at the table, I regretted even making the drive to my parents' house. I just wanted to be with *you*, so I left and went to *your* mom's house." Jamie lifted on the tips of her toes and pressed a soft kiss to his bottom lip. "I didn't see, or hear, or even think of him again until this afternoon when he called me. I agreed to have dinner with him because I'd been pining over you for the last two days and I thought you hated me."

"Why would your dad's business partner think it was okay to take you to dinner?" Ryder asked, walking her backwards to the bed. "Wouldn't your dad be pissed, or was it like a two birds, one stone type of thing? Piss me and Daddy off at the same time?"

Jamie deserved that too.

"I wasn't trying to piss you off, and my dad would be elated. The entire reason he was invited over for Easter was so he could meet me."

"And you didn't think of mentioning it until now?" he grumbled, pushing her onto the bed. She fell back with a bounce. Ryder crawled up her body, settling between her legs.

"It wasn't a big deal. It happens," Jamie explained more to his mouth than to his eyes.

"How often?"

Full disclosure, she reminded herself. It was that messy bitch karma again, she pushed him about his dad, now he was pushing her about Archer. "Let's just say it's not the first time I've had to entertain business partners or their children."

"*Entertain?*"

"Like a sweetener," she shifted under him as a million questions played out on his features. He didn't come from the same world she came from. He didn't understand how these things worked.

"What's a sweetener?"

"An incentive," her voice was barely above a whisper. She didn't know why this was so hard to talk about. This was normal. Just another part of her life.

"But what do you have to offer these rich assholes?"

It was a loaded question, one that had her gnawing on her finger. Ryder stared at her, his hazel's penetrated her green in that way they did when he looked inside of her and pulled the truth out. "My wit and charm," she quipped.

Ryder stared at her, eyes unblinking. She could hear the sound of the door opening and closing downstairs. Sirens blared in the distance. Her heart beat erratically in her chest. If he didn't say something soon she was going to lose it.

"Are you fucking kidding me, James?"

"Why are you making this such a big deal?" she huffed, pushing him off her. The weight of his body was stifling. "That's how deals are made. It's the part no one likes to talk about, but it's not uncommon."

"You're his fucking daughter, not a whore, or stripper, or sugar baby."

Jamie rose to her feet. How could she make him understand it wasn't like that? Her dad was awful, but he loved her, deep down... *right*? "It's not about sex. Sometimes they need someone to go to events with them and stuff and I come from pedigree. I'm not some random unknown. These are important men. They can't just show up with anyone," she rambled, pacing the length of his room. This wasn't how this was supposed to go. She was supposed to be apologizing and begging for his forgiveness, and somehow, she ended up talking about this shit.

"But you have had sex with these men." Ryder wasn't letting it go. *Why couldn't he let it go?*

Jamie stopped pacing, and glared at him. "It's not like my dad says, *go give this a guy a blow job*."

"He might as well."

That stung. She wasn't his whore. She was his daughter. She was playing her part. "You just don't understand." She put her palms on the dresser, silently chanting her mantra.

Be thankful.
Be mindful.
Be kind.

She didn't know when Ryder got off the bed, but she felt his presence at her back before she heard his words. "How long?" he asked.

She didn't answer. Her mind was going a hundred miles a minute.

This was normal.
This was how things worked.

"James, tell me how long your dad has been pimping you out to the highest bidder?"

"Fuck you, Ryder," she scoffed. "I don't need this shit. I'm done sharing."

"Kitty Cat," he said pulling her back to his front, "tell me how long."

"I don't know."

"Bullshit. Talk to me."

Her eyes burned with unshed tears. Her first reaction was to push him away, shut down, self-destruct, but last time she did that, she nearly lost him. "I was sixteen the first time."

"Jesus, Jamie," Ryder exhaled as his strong, tattooed arms enveloped her. His hold was solid, unyielding. Ryder was her anchor. He kept her from floating away. "I'm sorry."

"Don't. It wasn't like that," Jamie insisted for what felt like the tenth time. "I went to prom with some guy's loser kid. I told you it isn't always sex or romance. Once, I had to let this girl hang out with me and my friends for a while, shopping and football games, that kind of stuff. They'd just moved to Seattle and she didn't have any friends."

"That guy tonight didn't want you to take him shopping, Kitty Cat."

"I could have said no." Jamie did her best to pull out of Ryder's grasp, but his arms flexed possessively around her midsection.

"But you didn't."

"Because I wanted to forget you," she whimpered, clawing at his forearms. She needed a minute.

"No, that's not it," he loosened his grip enough to turn her around in his arms, his eyes glistened with tears as he spoke. "You said yes because he conditioned you to say yes since you were sixteen years old."

Jamie shook her head. "My dad isn't perfect, but he wouldn't—" Her voice trailed off. "He wouldn't," she cried, dropping her head into Ryder's chest. Her body was sore from holding all the tension. "He wouldn't," her nails dug into his collarbone as she clung to him, the tears flowing freely. Unlike the cathartic ones from their shower, these were sour. "He wouldn't, would he?" Her words were swallowed by sobs as Ryder lifted her off her feet and carried her to his bed.

The world was burning around her. The demons Jamie suppressed floated freely. Everyone could see.

SEVENTEEN

Intro

RYDER

"Hey, Kitty Cat," Ryder whispered. "I gotta take a leak." He shifted, gently rolling Jamie onto her back. Even with matted hair and a blotchy face, she was breathtaking.

"No," she moaned, pulling him down on top of her. "You're warm and I was comfortable."

"Would you rather I piss on you?"

"It wouldn't be the first time," she muttered sleepily.

He chuckled at her teasing, but she had a point. He could be a possessive bastard. It never bothered him before, but with last night's revelations, Ryder knew he needed to get a handle on that shit. Every man in Jamie's life treated her like property and there he was doing the same thing. He'd practically dragged her back to his house, caveman style, and threw her into the shower. He'd even considered ripping that damn dress to shreds.

"I'm sorry I was an asshole," he said, brushing her nose with his.

"I'm sorry I was a bitch." Wrapping her legs around his waist, Jamie tilted her head back, her mouth finding Ryder's. "And sorry for the morning breath." Jamie's kiss, unlike the woman herself, was timid. The way she brushed her lips against his, and the small, unsure strokes of her tongue made him happier than it should have.

Ryder was the only man to have this part of her, the only one to see her like this. That alone was enough to give him a semi hard-on.

Yeah, he needed to get a grip on the possessive shit, but first he had to pee. "As much as I love your morning breath, I'm about to piss myself."

"Fine," she groaned, untangling her legs from around his body, "if you must."

Ryder hopped off the bed, feeling lighter than he had the last few days.

Life with Kitty Cat was never boring. In the short time they'd been together, he'd experienced the highest highs and the lowest lows. Her pieces were jagged, but together they would make magic. Jamie'd probably call that philosophical bullshit, and that only made him love her more.

Once he finished in the bathroom, Ryder ran downstairs to make coffee. Jamie would be leaving for work soon and as much as it sucked, he was going to have to tuck his dick between his legs and go see if he still had a job. The list of reasons to go find Jamie's dad and beat his ass was getting longer and longer. Ryder grew up with a failing musician father who took his shortcomings out on his mother, but he had his mother. Jamie didn't have anyone, and that killed him. She was good, and she deserved better than the shitty hand she was dealt.

Guilt speared in Ryder's gut as he poured two mugs full of coffee. He was being a dick to his mom. He knew that, but he couldn't help but feel betrayed. His dad was the enemy and it felt like his mom had switched teams. Ignoring that problem wasn't going to make it go away, but Ryder could only deal with one thing at a time, and today his job took priority.

Grabbing the coffee, he headed back upstairs. Jamie's muffled voice spilled out from the crack in the door. He felt like a perv for eavesdropping, but he couldn't help himself.

"Daddy, why are you yelling? It's seven in the morning, can't this wait until after coffee? Calm down...he's my boyfriend."

Her boyfriend. Those words—on her lips—made him feel invincible.

"I will apologize to Jared, but I'm with Ryder...I'm not...no...this is my life, Daddy. It isn't up for debate." Her voice was devoid of emotion, she'd shed all the tears she was going to for her father last night, and Ryder would be goddamned if he ever let that cocksucker make her cry again.

Pushing through the door, he set the coffee on the night stand and took the phone from Jamie. "Go fuck yourself, Mr. Manning," he barked, before ending the call. Hanging up on people was a lot more satisfying on his flip phone. He wanted to punch something, to break things. Ryder paced back and forth, willing himself to calm down. The urge to break every bone in that man's body grew with each lap around his bedroom.

"Mr. Manning?" Jamie asked, an amused smirk stretched across her sleepy face. The corner of her lip twitched before she broke out into a full on laughing fit. She was laughing so hard she snorted, which caused her to laugh even harder.

Ryder stopped his pacing and looked at her. His girl was stretched out across his bed, wearing his clothes, but most importantly, she was happy. "It sounded better in my head," he grinned.

He made it to the bed in three quick strides and fell on top of her, covering her with the weight of his body.

The old mattress whined in protest. "You're going to break this piece of shit," Jamie giggled.

"Then let's have fun doing it," he suggested, pressing his mouth to hers. The feel of her soft, pouty lips could make a grown man cry. How the fuck did he last so long without kissing her? Ryder licked his way into her mouth with long, slow strokes. "I love you," he murmured, "morning breath and all."

Jamie's eyelids fluttered shut. Long lashes tickled the tops of her cheeks as she pulled his head into her neck. "I'd like nothing more than to break this damn thing with you, but I've got to go to work."

"I'm not stopping you," he said, swiveling his pelvis into her. His dick was so hard it was probably stabbing her in the stomach. Jamie sighed contently as he bit into her neck. Ryder sucked on the skin until it turned a satisfying shade of pink, then worked his way down, kissing and licking and biting her collarbone. His hands slid up her soft skin, his fingers lingering at the raised scar before they made their way up her body, finding a home on her perky little tit.

Arching into him Jamie moaned, "You're not making it easy either."

He kept up his assault on her breast, pulling and pinching her hardened nipple; the little noises escaping her mouth egging him on. This was the one area in their relationship that they got right, the physical stuff. They may fuck up everything else but their attraction to one another was pure. It was as if she was made for him, *made of him*. He was Adam and she was born of his rib.

Buzz.

Buzz.

Buzz.

The incessant vibration of Jamie's phone interrupted the melody of her moans. "I'm going to have to deal with you hanging up on him all day," she sighed.

"I got this," Ryder assured, reaching for the goddamn device. Despite his massive hard-on, he managed to pull himself together enough to answer. "Jamie's phone, Ryder speaking, how may I help you?"

"Put my daughter on the phone this instant," her dad growled. The motherfucker actually growled. He sounded like a mix between Burt Reynolds and Clint Eastwood. Jamie's dad was a man who perfected the art of intimidation, but Ry wasn't fazed.

"Sorry, she's busy right now. Can I take a message?"

"You think you're funny?" Burt Eastwood sneered.

Jamie bit down on her lip, amusement dancing in her eyes. Ryder would give his life to keep it there, to keep the sadness at bay. Trailing his hand up her leg, he tickled the back of her knee.

"Stop it," she giggled, thrashing underneath him.

"Your daughter seems to think so," he said, ducking a pillow Jamie threw at his head.

"I hate to break it to you, son, but a girl like James will never end up with a piece of shit like you. This isn't some fairytale where you'll ride off into the sunset with my daughter. Jared *will* get the girl, and there isn't a damn thing you can do about it."

Ignoring him, Ryder turned his attention to Jamie. "I love you and I promise to always protect you from this asshole. Also, you're going to be late for work."

"I will destroy—" *Gran Torino* began, but Ryder let the phone fall. He needed both his hands to drag the boxers down Jamie's thighs and toss them over his shoulder. Kitty Cat's legs fell open and Ryder licked his lips at the sight of her glistening pussy. It was as pretty as a picture. Her arousal perfumed his room.

Jamie was his, no matter what her dad thought.

Around noon Ryder made his way to Cibo to beg for his job. Not only did he walk out during the middle of his shift, but he caused a scene in the dining room. A part of him knew he would be out on his ass, but a bigger part, the part that liked to eat and pay rent, sent him into town with his tail between his legs.

If he was fired, he was fired. He'd accept it. He deserved it, but if there was a chance he still had a job, even if it came with consequences, he was in no position to pass it up.

Ryder pulled his bike into the employee parking lot. Oscar, the dishwasher, stood by the side door smoking.

"What's up, bro?"

"Same shit," Oscar said taking a swig from his flask.

"Is Liz here?" Ryder asked, running his fingers through his blond hair. The gravity of the situation was beginning to hit him. He'd spent the morning in heaven with Kitty Cat. Now that his feet were back on earth, Ryder realized how badly he'd fucked up. Lithium was doing okay, their fan base was growing more and more with each show, but it wasn't enough.

"Yup," he said handing Ry the flask. A commiserating gesture.

"Did she hear about what happened last night?"

"Yup."

"Fuck," Ryder hissed, knocking back Oscar's homemade moonshine. The shit was awful, but if he was going to go in and beg to keep his job, he needed the boost.

"Yes, and she's pissed my friend. You might have to fuck her."

"So Ben can kick my ass?" Ben was Liz's husband and business partner. He was in his late sixties but he was a mean bastard. Ryder could probably take him, but the only senior citizen whose hip he was interested in breaking was Archer Manning's. Lifting the flask to his lips once more, Ryder took another deep pull before screwing on the lid and handing it back to Oscar. "Wish me luck."

The kitchen was bustling with activity. The cooks were busy preparing for the Monday lunch rush while the wait staff tucked silver into cloth napkins. Ryder slipped by them all with his head down, avoiding the questioning glances. Working in a restaurant was like high school, and he'd just been called to the principal's office.

Liz was seated in the private dining area in the back. She was sipping from a teacup, looking over some paperwork. Her eyes met his and she sighed, throwing the pages down on the table. "Sit," she ordered.

He did as he was told, slumping down in the chair. His arms were relaxed at his sides, his outward demeanor cool, though inside he was seconds away from falling to his knees and begging.

"Tell me why I shouldn't toss you out on your ass right now?"

"Because I'm sorry," Ry said in earnest. He was sorry, not for taking his girl back, but for leaving the way he did. He let his wrath get the best of him. He was, after all, his father's son.

"You're sorry?" Liz scoffed. "Tell me why you're sorry."

"For causing a scene in the middle of the dinner rush, for leaving before my shift was over, and for threatening to punch a customer," Ryder droned, listing his transgressions. It sounded even worse out loud.

He was so fucked.

"Not just any customer," Liz added. "Jared Foster is like a son to me and you embarrassed him in my restaurant."

Ryder inhaled, taking a page from Kitty Cat. Jared, of course he was friends with Liz, because that was the way his luck was set up. "He was on a date with my girlfriend," Ryder gritted. "What was I supposed to do? Ask if I could get them clean silverware?"

"You're supposed to keep your personal life out of my restaurant." Ryder sat there, staring at her. She was right and there wasn't much else he could say. "Is this girl really worth risking your job?"

"Yes." *Without doubt.*

Liz arched her perfectly sculpted brow. "She was on a date with another man. How can you say that?"

"I know how it sounds, but we had a fight and shit—"

"Language, Ryder. I'm still your boss."

"Are you?" he asked hopefully, pressing his tattooed hands onto the white linens for support. He went there to beg, but he never actually thought he had a snowballs chance in hell.

"I should kick your ass out the door and not think twice about it—"

"Liz, I promise—"

"But I like you," Liz sighed, picking up her teacup. Her pink, button-down blouse was pressed within an inch of its life. She was the definition of sophistication. He imagined it was what Jamie's mother was like. Theirs was a world he never understood, never wanted to understand. Ryder always existed on the fringe, and that was fine with him, but for the first time since he'd met Kitty Cat, he was beginning to realize that might change.

"I'm not fired?" Ryder asked. A slow grin crept across his face.

"No. It took a lot of balls to come and face me. I respect that, but if anything like this ever happens again you're out. Don't even bother showing up. This is your only chance."

"It won't, I swear."

"If Jared comes in for lunch or dinner, or to say hello, you are to stay out of sight until he's gone."

"That's fine with me."

"And," she paused, before adding, "you're suspended for four weeks."

"Four weeks?" Ry groaned, dragging his hands down his face. What the fuck was he supposed to do for money for the next four weeks?

"I can make it permanent," Liz warned. "I should make it permanent."

"No. Don't. Thank you." Ryder stood so fast the chair screeched across the hardwood. "Four weeks. I'll take it. Thanks Liz."

At least he still had a job.

Jamie

Jamie allowed herself three days to dwell on the fact that she was nothing more than a high-end prostitute. She cried, got angry, broke things, but now she was done. She couldn't live in the suffering of her past any longer. She needed to move on. She needed to be mindful and focus on the things that mattered.

Sarah was due back from maternity leave in another week and Jamie was determined to take on more serious projects. Hosting *The Local Spotlight* had been a great opportunity. It garnered Jamie more recognition at the station and helped pad her reel, but her heart was in investigative reporting. It was why she had gotten into journalism in the first place. Jamie had dreams of going to war-torn countries and exposing political scandals. She longed to report from the White House or the front lines, uncovering the ugly truths of the world.

Who more qualified to talk about the ugliness of men than Jamie?

After the morning meeting, Jamie found herself outside the door to Tina's office. She inhaled, standing there, hand raised, poised to knock, but something held her back. *All she can say is no*, Jamie thought. That was literally the worst outcome and even it wasn't so bad.

So, why couldn't she bring herself to knock?

They say it's best to never meet your idol because they would inevitably let you down, but Tina, quiet, reserved, and sharp as a tack, was everything Jamie hoped she would be. If anything, it was Jamie who felt inadequate.

"Are you looking for me?" Tina asked from behind.

Jamie jumped, her face red with embarrassment. Turning to face her boss, she stuttered, "Uh…yeah. D…do you have a minute?"

"Yeah," Tina said lifting her paper coffee cup, "I've got five."

Swallowing back her anxiety, Jamie followed Tina into the office. It, much like the woman herself, was utilitarian. No plants or fancy paper weights, just a large steel desk, and a set of chairs. Four TV's were mounted on the wall to the left, each playing a different twenty-four-hour news channel. Everything was clean, sleek and served a purpose.

"What's on your mind?" Tina asked taking a seat.

Jamie sat in the chair across from her and smiled nervously. She was being ridiculous. This was Tina, the woman who had been her mentor for the last year and a half. She could talk to Tina.

"Sarah's coming back next week," she blurted out. So much for the thoughtful speech she practiced that morning with Javi.

"I'm aware," Tina nodded, taking a sip of her coffee. Her eyes stayed trained on Jamie, like she was expecting what was coming next.

"Right," Jamie tucked a strand of hair behind her ear. *Get it together James.* "Were you also aware of the town hall meeting next Thursday?"

"Vaguely, but Frank does the political reporting for WSEA-9. That's his assignment."

"But what if I tagged along?" she asked. Frank was old. Not in the distinguished, Dan Rather kind of way, but more like your senile grandfather who confuses you with your cousins.

Tina set her coffee down and steepled her fingers in front of her lips. "How old are you Jamie?" Tina asked, giving Jamie her patented, *I'm about to crush your dreams*, look.

"Twenty-four."

"Do you know what I was doing at twenty-four?"

"No." Jamie settled back into her chair, preparing for the lecture that was sure to come.

"I was covering school closings and newborn baby pandas. Grunt reporting. The stuff no one else wanted to do. I did it. All of it."

"I know I need to pay my dues, but I was just hoping—"

"That's your problem," Tina said cutting her off, "you hope. In this business, there's only hard work and connections. Do you know why Frank has the political beat? Why David reports on crime? How I got to where I am?"

"By paying your dues?" Jamie groaned. She rarely got in trouble as a child. Her parents mostly ignored her, but on the few occasions they did bother with parenting, she never felt a shred of remorse. Being reprimanded by Tina, however, made her feel like the biggest disappointment in the world.

"Because we paid our dues," Tina repeated. "But not *just* that. While we were out there doing the work, we talked to people, built relationships, created a rapport with locals, networked. And you know what happened?"

"No," Jamie muttered.

"People started calling *me* with story ideas. Suddenly, I got the scoops. That's when my producers took notice. That's when my career took off."

Jamie sank down in her chair, her shoulders sagging in defeat. The only thing that sucked worse than being told no, was being given a valid reason for the rejection. Tina wasn't being unreasonable or unfair, she was being honest. Jamie, for all her affirmations and claims of hard work, was still just a spoiled little rich girl.

"Thanks, Tina."

"Don't thank me Jamie, just do the work."

"I will. I promise."

Don't cry. Don't cry, she chanted as she made a beeline for the door.

"Wait," Tina drawled.

"It's fine, I'm fine." Her voice cracked. Stupid feelings. This was Ryder's fault, she wasn't always this… emotional.

"Go with Frank, but remember Jamie, nothing in this business will be handed to you. You've got to earn it."

EIGHTEEN

L.A. Love

RYDER

Ryder was the romantic.

He found inspiration in the little things. His art was fluid. It was both his escape and his cage. Beauty was everywhere and nowhere, but it wasn't until he crossed paths with the sad, green-eyed girl that he truly understood what it meant to be inspired. Every move Jamie made fueled his soul. From the way she rubbed her tattoo across her lip when she was anxious, to the way she called everyone on their bullshit, and especially the way she melted under his gaze.

Ryder never realized how dull the world was until Kitty Cat made it shine. His love for her was dangerous, reckless, and because of it, he was suspended without pay for four weeks. If he had the chance to go back and do it again he would, because Jamie was worth fighting for. The only problem was he was suspended without pay for *four fucking weeks.*

Crowds at the band's shows were steadily increasing, and thanks to social media, the Lithium Springs fan base was also. The first shipment of t-shirts had arrived and they were selling faster than any of them expected. Even with things going well with the music, Ryder didn't have a savings and not getting a steady paycheck made it hard to eat, let alone afford studio time.

He couldn't deny his happiness, though. Standing under the blinding stage lights, sweat dripping down his chest, he was in his element. They were gods among men.

"Okay Rabbit Hole, before we continue, I want to take a minute to introduce you to my boys, my brothers." Ryder leaned into the mic as he stared out into the audience. It wasn't a packed house by any means, but everyone in attendance was there to see Lithium Springs.

Ryder looked to his right and the crowd erupted in cheers. "This pretty motherfucker with the badass bass guitar is Javi. Behind me, on drums, that's my boy, CT." Ryder paused, allowing his patented rock star gaze to wash over everyone in attendance. "I'm Ryder, but after tonight, you can call me *Sex God*."

Javi plucked out the opening chords to the song on his bass. CT came in on drums, then Ryder joined in with his guitar. It was the first time they played it for an audience. The collective pulse of the room thumped in time with the beat as he growled into the mic. By the second verse, the crowd went crazy.

Sex God was a hit.

Grant stood in the center of Dave's office shooting the shit with a mystery man in a black Mad Season t-shirt. The guy was probably twice their age, his gray hair was pulled into a ponytail and he looked like he hadn't missed a meal in years.

Javi eyed the guy, giving him a once over, before asking, "*River of Deceit* or *Long Gone Day*?" It was a test, one that would determine if they were going to take this dude seriously or if they needed to jump Grant's ass for wasting their time.

"Both are amazing," Pony Tail smirked, "but, *Artificial Red* is next fucking level."

Ryder, CT, and Javi exchanged impressed glances before plopping their asses down on the sofa. They still didn't know who the fuck the bastard was, but if he was a Mad Season fan, they'd at least listen to what he had to say.

"One more question," CT said, his voice gruff. Ryder rolled his eyes. Whatever his drummer was about to say was going to be completely unfiltered. His prep school background, coupled with his *I don't give a fuck attitude,* made him a loose cannon.

"Shoot."

"Where the fuck did you get that shirt?" CT asked. His collection of vintage t-shirts was unmatched.

"Layne Staley sent it to me as a thank you."

Holy.

Shit.

The room was so quiet you could hear a pin drop. Layne Staley was a hero to every kid in Seattle with a bad attitude and a problem with authority. For them, Layne was the alpha and the omega. Ryder was twelve when he died. He spent that whole day in his room, listening to Alice in Chains and breaking shit.

"Who are you?" they asked in unison.

"Oh, right." Pony Tail extended his hand, "Creed Jackson, nice to meet you." The band took turns introducing themselves before Creed continued. "I got my start working A&R for Columbia and climbed my way up the chain. Recently, I left to start my own company. My daughter is a huge fan and had been bugging me to check you out for the last month. She finally cornered me and forced me to watch a video from Battle of the Bands, and here we are."

"Guys," Grant interjected, "Creed thinks it would be a good idea for you to go to LA for a few weeks, get a feel for the Hollywood music scene, see his setup. I can make some calls and maybe book you a few gigs while you're there."

"And I've got connections at *Rolling Rock Magazine*. Maybe we can do something with them," Creed added.

"What's in it for you?" Ryder asked. The guys went back and forth with the idea of signing to a label. They heard countless horror stories about labels screwing over artists or forcing them to make a certain kind of music. They'd been offered a few contracts in the past, but nothing that was worth selling out for.

"Right now, nothing. I left Columbia because I was sick of *'the machine.'*

It isn't like it used to be, when we took the time to nurture artists. Nowadays, people care more about how many followers you have over talent and musicianship. Then I see you guys, and while you're a little rough around the edges, there's no denying you've got something special here. I'd like to be a part of that. I get that I don't have the power of a major label behind me and I don't expect you to sign your lives away to me, but come to LA. I think we can help each other do great things."

Ryder's head spun as he made his way back out into the bar. It was near closing time and most of the crowd from the show had already dispersed, leaving only a handful of groupies who were waiting to see who Javi and CT would choose, and the barflies who didn't leave until they were told to go.

"Everything okay?" Jamie asked, wrapping her arms around his neck. He tucked his hands under her knees, lifted her off the barstool, and carried her towards the back of the bar.

"Never better," he said, nodding to Grant and Creed as they passed. "Is it bad that even though Grant has been fucking amazing, I still want to knock his teeth out for asking you to dinner?"

Once locked inside the office Ryder sat Jamie on her feet. "Try irrational and pig headed," she said, her lips jutting out in annoyance. They were pink and pouty and begging to be kissed.

So he did.

Kissing Jamie was Ryder's new favorite thing. He devoted hours to exploring her mouth. The added layer of intimacy to their already explosive chemistry ensured they didn't do much sleeping at night.

"But you love me anyway," he whispered, walking her backwards towards the old couch.

Jamie still hadn't returned the sentiment, a fact that only slightly annoyed Ryder. She didn't express her love like most people, but he felt it every day. He felt it in the way her body gravitated towards him without her brain's consent. He felt it in her honesty, and in her kiss.

Their tongues danced, slow and lazy. They were in no rush. Jamie's hands trailed down his ribcage and across his abdomen. Her touch made his fucking heart flutter. He was so pussy whipped, it wasn't even funny. His boys could wade through the sea of groupies for the rest of forever, but no amount of one-nighters and fuck buddies could replace the feelings he felt when Kitty Cat touched him like that. Lacing his fingers in her hair, Ryder tilted Jamie's head so their eyes met.

"Why'd you stop?" she panted. Her fingers dug into his back, a not so subtle hint she wanted him.

He groaned against her lips, "Because the things I want to do to you require a bed." Dave's office was more of a bend her over the desk and smack her ass kind of fuck. Ryder wanted to take his time and worship her body. He wanted to run his tongue over every inch of her flesh. He wanted to bury his cock inside her pussy deep enough for his Prince Albert to graze her cervix. He wanted her screaming his name, but first, he needed to tell her his news.

Jamie's fingers traced one of his nipple piercings through the thin fabric of his tank. Leaning over, she pressed a soft kiss to it before gently tugging at it with her teeth. "You can't improvise?" she purred.

"I promise, I'll take care of you when we get home," he said. Jamie bit him hard that time. "Ouch," he yelped. His hands found her ass and he squeezed it, hard, causing her too-short denim shorts to ride up.

"That's what you get for teasing me," she admonished, grinding against his cock.

There were two things to know about Ryder. One, music was his life. Two, when Jamie grinded on his dick, he lost all brain function. "Kitty Cat," he warned.

"If we aren't going to fuck then why'd you bring me back here?" she pouted.

"Because I've got good news."

"What?" Jamie scowled, but he could tell her curiosity was penetrating her sexual frustration.

"That guy with Grant was a big shot at a major label, but quit to start his own. He wants us to come down to LA for a couple of weeks to take meetings and record and shit. Can you believe it, Kitty Cat? It's all happening."

"That's…really great," she said, looking past his right ear. Ryder couldn't decipher the expression on Jamie's face, but the sound her heart made as it beat wildly in her chest was unmistakable. She was shutting down. He could smell it on her. The stench permeated the air like rotting flesh.

"What the fuck, Jamie?" His voice was like lava, hot and violent. She was driving him insane.

"I'm not Jamie'ing this up. I swear. I'm just…processing," she whispered, resting her forehead against his.

"What is there to process? I'm going to be a fucking rock star." That was the plan, his dream. He needed her to get on board.

"I just don't want you to feel burdened. I get it, you guys are on the cusp of greatness, and you should enjoy that. Girls are going to be throwing themselves at you. You aren't going to want me around, cock blocking."

"Bitches throw pussy at me all day."

"Thanks for that visual—" she said with a grimace.

"No," he interrupted, tugging on her ponytail. Her head tilted back and he stared into her eyes, "I love you and there's only one place, well three places, I want to stick my cock, and they are all located on your body."

"Sure, now, but what happens in a year or two or three when you guys are famous?"

"The only thing that's going to change is my mattress, and maybe your last name," he smirked, tugging her hair again. "It's you and me kid, understood?"

Jamie ran her tattooed finger across his bottom lip. He caught the tip between his teeth and bit down slightly. "You're going to be a fucking rock star." Although her voice cracked on the last word, there was pride in her tone. Not the kind of pride that kept you stagnate, but the kind that helped you fly.

Ryder ran his hands down the length of her body, his nose nuzzled against hers. "I need to fuck you."

"Wait," Jamie pushed him back. "What will you do for money? I could loan you some. It's my fault you got suspended."

"No, James, I'm not taking your money."

"It's fine. I'll be twenty-five soon and I'll gain access to my trust, so, if you need something, I can help. I want to help."

"You don't have it now?" he asked, because he didn't have a clue how any of that shit worked. CT had one, but it wasn't like they talked about it.

"Limited, I get a monthly allowance, but when I hit twenty-five, I'll have full access. We can blow it all in Vegas if we wanted to."

Ryder thought for a minute, debating if he should ask the question searing his tongue. Curiosity won out in the end. "How much?"

Guilt flashed in Jamie's eyes. Her next words took Ryder's breath away.

"Five million dollars."

NINETEEN

Girl

Jamie

Jamie pushed open the heavy, glass doors of the Seventh Street Diner and slipped inside. The rain fell from the sky in buckets, crashing to the ground with unceremonious splats. It had rained every day since Lithium Springs loaded up their old, white van and left for California, taking the sunshine with them. Mother Nature understood Jamie's longing and as much as she tried to convince herself that two weeks would come and go in no time, every day Jamie woke up to gray clouds was another day in misery.

Work was her saving grace. She spent more time with Frank, learning which secretaries in the city building to befriend, and about the janitor with whom the Mayor confides in. She was networking, making connections, and doing work that mattered.

"Hey, Kitty Cat," Annette greeted her with tired eyes as Jamie weaved through tables on her way to the counter. Ryder made his feelings about her visiting his mother clear, but Jamie couldn't stay away from Annette any more than she could stay away from Ryder. Though she had only known Annette a short time, she'd come to rely on their talks. She craved the maternal guidance her boyfriend's mother gave, guidance Caroline couldn't be bothered with.

The greasy smell of deep-fried food assaulted Jamie's senses as she took a seat. "Hey," she smiled brightly. Just being on Ryder's turf calmed her. His presence surrounded her. It was as if his essence was ingrained in the brick and mortar.

"What would you like today?" Annette asked, setting down a Shirley Temple.

"I need carbs," Jamie sighed. Technically, she needed a salad. Since Jamie started going to the diner, she'd gained ten pounds. Her mother would have a fit if she saw the slight pudge in her stomach. Annette assured her that she wore the extra weight well and Ryder was obsessed with her newly found ass—so no complaints there.

"Long day?"

"They're all long lately," Jamie confessed. It was selfish, complaining about missing Ryder to his mother, but it was also cathartic. She was the only other person who knew what it felt like to be absent from him. While Jamie's loss was temporary, Annette's exile had no end in sight.

"It sounds like you need lasagna," Annette offered. "I get off soon. We can eat together."

"I'd love that," Jamie nodded in earnest.

Annette went to place the order, and Jamie claimed Ryder's favorite booth. Her phone pinged, a new message.

Ryder: I miss u so fucking bad Kitty Cat.

Jamie: I miss you more.

Jamie: Having dinner with your mom.

Ryder: Of course u r. eyeroll emoji

Jamie: Don't be mean.

Ryder: I'm never mean.

Jamie: I'll call you when I get home.

Ryder: Can we have phone sex? My dick misses u 2.

Jamie: Phone sex is prehistoric. Borrow one of the guys' phones so we can video chat.

Ryder: We r close, but Idk if we r that close.

Jamie: This is why you need a smartphone.

Jamie stuck her tongue out at the screen. She was determined to drag Ry into the twenty-first century, whether he liked it or not.

"Napoleon, giving you a hard time?" Annette asked, appearing with two huge plates of lasagna and a basket of garlic toast.

"Oh no," she blushed, hoping like hell she hadn't seen the R-rated sexts, "I just miss him like crazy."

"Why?" his mother asked, three little wrinkles forming across her forehead; a look she saw on Ryder's face countless times.

"Oh, he didn't—" Jamie began. "Of course, he didn't." Ryder had ceased all communication with his mother, but not telling her he was going out of town for two weeks was a dick move. "I'm sorry I didn't think to mention it sooner. The guys met this ex-label big shot or whatever, and he invited them to California. They've been there for the past week."

"Oh? How's it going? I mean, are they killin' it?" Annette asked, doing her best impersonation of a millennial. Jamie could tell she was trying to mask the hurt in her tone. For the last ten years, it was Annette and Ryder against the world, but with one phone call everything changed.

She'd lost her best friend.

"They're good. It isn't glamorous or anything but they are getting their name out there and making connections. They'll be gone for another week."

Annette forced a smile. "Well, that's great. We should eat before it gets cold."

Jamie nodded digging into the plate of lasagna. It tasted just like her grandmother used to make, but also a little like guilt. Here she was moping over missing Ryder for two weeks, when it had been over a month since Annette last spoke to him.

"Can I ask you something?" Jamie asked after a few minutes of weighted silence.

"You want to know why?"

"If I'm overstepping—"

"It's fine, Sweetheart." Annette sighed but held Jamie's gaze. "Love is strange, Kitty Cat. It causes you to do all sorts of crazy things, things that don't make sense to anyone else."

"You're in love with him?" Jamie asked incredulously. Ryder was terrified of his dad. As unaffected as he tried to act, Jamie could see it in his eyes whenever he talked about him. He transformed into the sad little boy who hid in closets because he'd rather face the boogeyman than his father.

"I never stopped loving him. He wasn't always a monster, and I am not a saint. Before Napoleon, we would drink and party all night long. Then I got pregnant and I grew up. He didn't. He was a musician too, but unlike Ry, his future wasn't promising. The constant rejection took a toll. It was hard for him to give up his dream to support his family. The drinking got worse and he became unrecognizable. He wasn't the same working a nine-to-five."

Her admission floored Jamie. It was quite possibly the last thing she expected to hear, and the way she said it, so casually, like they were talking about the lasagna.

Jamie opened her mouth to speak, but Annette stopped her. "I'm not justifying what he did or who he became. If we didn't leave, he would have killed me, and I don't even want to think of what could have happened to my son. He is my reason for being. He's my air. My lungs pump for him. It's my job to keep him happy and safe, so I left."

"And now what?"

"Nothing. Arrow is clean—"

"Arrow?" Jamie asked? *Archer and Arrow, the world's worst dads.*

"We grew up in the sixties," Annette chuckled. "Anyway, he's been in treatment for a year. He got in touch just before Easter and wanted to apologize. He wants to see Napoleon and I didn't know how to bring it up."

"You did a pretty great job just then."

"It's different with Napoleon. He knew a very different man than the one I married. His memories are only the painful ones."

"Do you still talk to him?"

Annette looked away for the first time since the conversation began. "Every day," she whispered. It was like a punch to the gut. The woman who she looked up to let the man who, by her account, would have murdered her, the same man who was responsible for her being estranged from her son, back into her life.

That wasn't love.

It was insanity.

Love was strange.

Jamie spent the entire drive home thinking about love, and what it meant. It was something that plagued her still, hours later as she sorted and organized piles of clothes into boxes. *Keep. Toss. Donate.* Spring cleaning, though it was nearly summer, but with Ryder's departure and Kensie spending most of her time at Trey's, Jamie suddenly found an abundance of time on her hands.

Love.

It was an emotion Jamie was uncomfortable with. She loved her brother, her best friend, and even though she had a hard time expressing her feelings for Ryder, they were there. But when were feelings illusions? If Buddhism taught Jamie anything, it was to be mindful of emotions. Was this need for Ryder her subconscious mind latching onto a savior, or were her feelings true?

Love was scary.

Annette fell in love with a man who terrorized her. Jamie wondered if she had the capacity to love someone so intensely.

As a child, Jamie thought parents were supposed to be these perfect beings, angels, but once she got a little older, a little wiser, she realized they were only human. People like Ryder, and like Jamie, the ones who were saddled with the most flawed, never really stood a chance.

Love was disappointing.

It wasn't this sacred thing movies and books portrayed. Sometimes love wasn't enough. Sometimes love was the thing that destroyed. Jamie had caused enough destruction for one lifetime.

The loud buzz of the doorbell reverberated through the apartment, breaking her from her thoughts, and sent the laundry she was carrying crashing to the floor. *Who could that be?* She wondered as she side-stepped the mess and jogged towards the door. It was one o'clock on a Sunday afternoon. Kensie was at her parents, and since Annette loaded her up with enough food to feed a small army she didn't bother ordering takeout.

Lifting onto the tips of her toes, Jamie looked through the peephole finding just about the last person on earth she was expecting to see. Making quick work of the locks, she swung the door open and threw herself at her little brother.

Chris stumbled back, laughing as Jamie nearly tackled him to the ground. "I take it you like your surprise?"

"What are you doing here?" Jamie squealed, looking around the deserted hallway. "And where's Parker?"

"He's in Boston. He had a make-up exam and a few other loose ends to tie up. He'll be here in a few days. We're spending the summer in Seattle interning at Manning Solutions. Dad made an offer I couldn't refuse," he said, doing the worst *Godfather* impersonation she'd ever heard.

Jamie groaned, rolling her eyes at the mention of her father. She hadn't spoken to him since *that* morning and thankfully, he'd stopped calling.

"So, it *is* true," Chris accused, following her into the apartment.

"What's true?" she asked, eyeing the younger Manning.

"You're not talking to Dad because of some biker."

Jamie spun around on her heels, her eyebrows knit in confusion. "A biker?"

"Yeah, Dad said, and I quote, '*Your sister is back to her old tricks again, riding around with some tattooed menace on the back of a Harley.*'"

A noise that was part growl and part snort escaped Jamie's throat. "Ryder isn't a biker," she sighed, pinching the bridge of her nose.

"If you say so Jam." Chris shouldered past his sister and went straight to the kitchen, his first stop whenever he visited. Her brother could sniff out baked goods like a bloodhound, and Jamie was convinced he had two stomachs.

"When did you get into town?" she asked, sliding onto one of the bar stools.

Chris rifled through the fridge, grabbing the Styrofoam container of lasagna. "A little over an hour ago. I went home, only to find out the prodigal daughter had taken up with the local MC, so I'm here to talk some sense into you." He scooped the remainder of the pasta onto a plate and popped it into the microwave. "Is it working?"

"What do you think?" She deadpanned.

"I think I want to know more about this Ryder," he said, crossing his arms over his chest. Chris was every bit the frat boy you'd expect from the spawn of Archer and Caroline Manning. Chris was the golden child. While Jamie had to pretend to fit into the Seattle social scene, her brother excelled.

"You want to meet him?" she asked and Christopher nearly choked on his garlic bread. It was the first-time Jamie ever brought up the prospect of him meeting a guy she was dating. Mostly because she didn't really date outside of the men her father introduced to her, and the few who did last longer than a night or two weren't really *meet the family* material.

"You want *me*," Chris jabbed a thumb into his chest, then pointed to his sister, "to meet a guy *you're* dating?"

Jamie tipped up a shoulder. "If you want. He's out of town for another week, but he should be back in time for my birthday."

Grabbing a bottle of water out of the refrigerator, Chris came around to sit next to Jamie at the breakfast bar. Green eyes identical to her own assessed her. "This guy makes you happy." It was a statement, one that made her blush. "Oh, my God, Jam."

"What?"

"You're blushing."

"I am not. I was just doing some spring cleaning and it's hot in here," she rambled on as heat spread from the top of her head to the tips of her toes.

"Sure, Jam."

"Anyway, focus please. My birthday?"

"The big one," Chris mused. "What are we doing to celebrate?"

"I'm not sure, yet. Ken and I have been like two ships passing in the night, but I'll talk to her when she gets home."

"Good. Also, was that pie I saw in there?"

Jamie giggled, hopping off the bar stool to retrieve the pie and two forks.

Love was sharing your dessert.

After Chris ate his way through the kitchen, he and Jamie migrated to the living room, where he told her all about his plan to come out to their parents; a dinner that he guilted her into attending. Then he forced her to watch her very first episode of *Game of Thrones*, which led to her second and then her third. She was finally beginning to understand the hype.

"Why am I so attracted to this man?" Jamie asked reaching for the bowl of popcorn. It sat next to a half-finished bottle of white and a bag of all red Starbursts.

"Because you have eyes," Chris said, tipping his glass to his lips, "and because Jason Momoa as Khal Drogo is as hot as it gets."

Jamie scrunched her nose. "But he's kind of a douche and a little rapey. Don't get me wrong, I'd totally fuck him, but does that make me a bad feminist?"

"Kind of an oxymoron don't you think?"

Just as Jamie was about to respond, the front door slammed, followed by the jingling of keys. "Chris!" Kensie squealed, dropping her bag down and running to the sofa. "What are you doing here?"

The three of them had been inseparable growing up, and even though life seemed to be taking them in different directions, whenever they got together it was as if they were kids again.

"I'm here for the summer, interning at Manning Solutions," he smiled.

Kensie toed off her flats, and folded herself onto the couch, tucking her feet underneath her body. "Where's Parker?"

"I'm starting to feel like you two like Parker more than me."

"We do—" both girls replied at the same time.

"JINX!" they yelled in unison, again.

"Oh, God," Chris groaned. "I forgot how annoying you guys are together.

"You love us," Kensie said, her eyes floating towards the screen. She sighed, the sound light and dreamy. "That man is gorgeous. I cried like a baby when they killed him."

Jamie turned to her friend, mouth agape, "They what?"

"Oops," Ken squeaked, her hand flying over her mouth.

"They kill Jason Momoa?"

"Yes," Chris confirmed, "but to be fair, you should have known that. This show is like six years old."

"I'm done. Fuck this show, forever," Jamie huffed. She was going to kill her brother for making her watch this bullshit. Whoever thought it was a good idea to kill Khal Drogo should be fired.

"So," Kensie began. "I'm guessing now isn't the best time to bring up the biker?"

Wine.

Jamie needed wine.

First Khal Drogo now this. Reaching for the bottle in front of her she refilled her glass. Her father was a pain in her ass. Why couldn't he just let her live her life? Jared was nice enough, and maybe old-new Jamie would have entertained him just to keep the peace, but new-new Jamie had more self-respect than that.

"My dad said, and I quote, *James is throwing her life away, running around with some felon. You've got to talk some sense into that girl, maybe introduce her to one of Trey's friends.*"

"He's not a biker," Chris chirped up.

Kensington's eyes widened, "Wait, you know about Jared too?"

"Jared?"

"Jam's biker... or not biker? I guess."

"Jared isn't a biker, and he isn't Jam's boyfriend, much to our dad's displeasure. Which, by the way, is a little weird. Why is he pushing that so hard?"

"I don't know," Jamie shrugged.

"Then who's the biker?"

Kensie and Chris turned to Jamie as she did her best to meld her body into the sofa. This was karma in its purest form.

"Ryder," she mumbled, then drained her glass.

"And where did you meet this Ryder?" Kensie pressed. Jamie looked from her brother to her friend. The thought of telling her little brother about her threesome made her physically ill so she opted for the safe version of their meet cute. "You remember my first *Local Spotlight*?"

Guilt flashed in Kensington's eyes. "I'm a little behind," she mumbled. There was once a time when Kensie watched everything

Jamie did, even her college stuff.

"It doesn't matter," Jamie said with a wave of her hand. She was as much to blame as Kensie was for their disconnect, and Jamie was determined to atone for her sins against their friendship. "Anyways, I interviewed him and he asked me out, and then he wouldn't go away." She shrugged. "Now, I'm kind of attached, or whatever."

"Attached," Kensie said slowly.

"She blushed earlier," Chris added.

"Fuck you both."

"When do I get to meet him?" Kensie grinned.

"My birthday. What's the plan, anyway?"

"Uh," Kensie's face turned beet red as she wrung her fingers together. "I've been meaning to talk to you about that."

"It's okay if you don't have anything elaborate planned. I know we've been kind of off lately. I'm good with dinner or whatever. Maybe we can go check out that new driving range?"

"Sounds great," she nodded, biting down on her lip. "I can't believe you have a boyfriend."

"It's so trippy," Jamie giggled. She giggled a lot lately, a side effect of the pure joy that had spread through her body.

Joy. Another unfamiliar emotion; one she never thought she'd experience again, not after last fall, but there she sat, a joyous bitch.

TWENTY

Papa Don't Preach

Jamie

A few days later, Jamie found herself making the familiar drive to her childhood home. The sight of the stone and stucco mansion, looming eerily under the dark sky, triggered something in her brain. This was going to be a disaster, but Parker's presence at the end of the long driveway called to her like a beacon. His hands were stuffed in the pockets of his dark blue Chino's, a scowl etched on his handsome face.

Parker was an East Coaster through and through. He had a no-nonsense personality and came out to his family when he was seventeen years old. Parker had always known who he was and he resented Chris for forcing him back into the closet. This dinner was as important to him as it was to her brother.

"Hey stranger," Jamie said, shutting the door to her Rover.

Parker shot her a pained expression. "Thanks for being here. It means a lot to Chris and to me."

"Don't mention it," she waved off his undue gratitude with a flick of her wrist. "Let's get this show on the road."

With arms linked, the two of them walked into the house to find the rest of the Mannings seated in the parlor. It was one of the more pretentious rooms in the house. The walls were painted hunter-green and a large crystal chandelier hung from the ceiling. A wide bay window spanned the distance of the right wall and cream furniture surrounded a mahogany coffee table. Everything was neatly arranged and perfectly in place, even the Vermeer her father bought at Sotheby's was hung to precise measurements.

Archer and Chris discussed work—no surprise there—while Caroline sipped on a martini—again, shocker.

"James, dear," her mother greeted leering at her from the sofa, "you look… fat."

"Mother!" Chris admonished.

Closing her eyes, Jamie recited her affirmations. It took her a solid minute of deep breathing before she trusted herself to speak. She knew it was coming, but that didn't lessen the urge to turn around and walk out the door.

"What?" Caroline chirped. "I caught the live broadcast the other afternoon. I assumed it was the camera adding the extra weight, but now I understand why they say what they do about assumptions."

"I think you look beautiful," Parker added. "You were too skinny before."

"There's no such thing as too skinny," Caroline scoffed. "James, are you still seeing your trainer?"

"It's fine, Park," Jamie gritted, biting the inside of her cheek. "It's how my mother expresses her love. Hugs and kisses might wrinkle her Balenciaga." Jamie turned to her mother. "And yes, I am still seeing him, but unlike you, I work for a living. I don't have the time nor the desire to spend hours in the gym."

"You wouldn't have to work if you stopped being so goddamned stubborn," her father growled, striding over to the bar cart. He lifted one of the crystal decanters and poured himself a finger of scotch. "Jared's company went public fourth quarter. They cleared ninety million in profit last year alone, and that's only the beginning. We are working on a deal that could double that, and all he wants in return is you."

And there it was, bones spilled out of the closet and tumbled onto the floor of the parlor. "Daddy," she warned, taking the scotch from him and pouring herself a glass.

"James, have the vodka, fewer calories," her mother advised from her spot on the sofa.

Jamie rolled her eyes and brought the glass to her lips. It burned going down, both the booze and her parents' words.

"The man seems infatuated with you. Why, I'll never understand, but he's willing to forgive the little incident with your biker friend and try again." Her father's severe gaze latched onto her. "You're beautiful, obviously, but your attitude…" Archer sighed, tipping his glass towards her. "We're lucky he's willing to overlook that."

"Jam's a catch dad. Any guy would be lucky to have her, not the other way around," Chris said, shuffling from one foot to the other. He was nervous, a first. Her brother was usually so sure of himself, a side effect of growing up with parents who worshiped the ground he walked on.

"You called us here for a reason, right baby brother?" Jamie encouraged. Chris was sweet for trying to defuse the atomic bomb her presence caused, but this day wasn't about Jamie.

"Yes," Chris said, clearing his throat. "I, well, we wanted—"

Ignoring his son, Archer bit, "James, your little rebellious streak is getting old. Don't you think?" For the first time in her entire life, it was Jamie, not Chris, who was the center of attention. It was one of those catch twenty-two's Annette was always going on about. Jamie put herself in the line of fire so her brother would have an ally when he came out to his parents, but her metaphorical execution ended up stealing the spotlight.

"Daddy," Jamie said, her tone measured, "I have done everything you've ever asked of me. I'm almost twenty-five years old. It's time for me to make my own decisions. Chris, please continue."

Her brother laughed uncomfortably. "Right, uh, we just wanted—"

"You think you know everything, don't you?" Archer seethed, turning his back on his son, not a strand of his salt and pepper hair out of place. "Twenty-five means nothing when you behave like the same spoiled little brat you've always been."

Jamie squared her shoulders, thankful for the extra three inches her heels afforded her. "Well, Daddy, twenty-five is old enough to know I don't want to be your whore anymore, and it's old enough for me to access my trust, so with all due respect, you can go fuck yourself." Jamie had to fight to keep the smile off her face. She wished Ryder were there to see. He'd be proud.

"You're not twenty-five, yet. That money isn't guaranteed and with the way you're behaving, I don't think you're ready for it."

Jamie scoffed. Her eyes bore into her father's. His threats meant nothing to her, the money meant less. She'd grown up with more than most, and it hadn't saved her from misery. Neither had her parents.

"Jam, Dad," Chris pleaded stepping between them. His face was broken. He'd spent his life in a bubble, and peeling back the layers of their dysfunction shattered his reality. Chris was the good kid, and as such, he'd been spared the ugliness of his parents.

"Quiet, Christopher," Archer boomed, pointing the highball glass at his son, but his eyes, dark, menacing, never left Jamie. Gray clouds rolled in the sky, darkening the parlor, casting an ominous shadow over the older man's face. He looked like Lucifer after the fall. "Everyone has a role to play in the Manning Empire, James, never forget that."

Taking a step forward, Jamie answered with an equal measure of venom in her words. "I know that better than anyone. It's a lesson I learned on my back."

"James, this isn't a discussion. You will give Jared a chance or you can kiss your trust goodbye."

A bitter laugh escaped her throat as she chugged the dregs of her scotch. Slamming the glass down on the pretentious mahogany bar, she smirked, "Keep it," before stalking out of the room and out of the Manning Empire.

They'd have to make do without her.

Thunder boomed in the sky as Jamie steered her Range Rover into the garage of her apartment building. Her phone rang. Sleepy hazel eyes stared back at her from the screen, and a calmness washed over her. She wasn't sad or angry about what happened at her parents' house. Oddly enough, she was relieved. Archer could keep his blood money and she would keep her sunshine.

"Hey," she sighed, shifting the car into park.

"Hey, Kitty Cat," Ryder breathed, his voice thick with exhaustion.

"You sound tired."

"I am. We've been going nonstop. Today was our first morning off."

"That's good, though, right?"

"Yeah, it is. We've met a lot of cool people, and hey guess what?" he exclaimed. Excitement cracked through the fatigue. There was a ruffling noise on the other end and Jamie pictured Ryder turning to lay on his side. She imagined his muscles bunching, causing his tattoos to dance, while his unruly blond mane scattered across the pillow behind him. She'd give anything to be lying in bed with him.

"What?"

"We recorded *Sex God*."

"That's amazing," she said, unable to help the smile quirking on her lips. His excitement was infectious. Ryder had a way of chasing out all the bad in her life and replacing it with good.

"Do you know it's rained every day since you guys left?" she asked.

Ryder gasped dramatically, "Rain? In Seattle? You're kidding."

"Fuck you, Napoleon."

"Depends. What are you wearing?"

Looking down at the pleated white material flowing over her legs, Jamie groaned, "A dress."

"Another dress, James?"

"I know, but I was trying to be diplomatic."

"For the dinner, right?" She'd told him about it in passing one night. It was late, and the band was just getting off stage. She didn't think he would even remember.

Nodding, even though he couldn't see her, she recounted the events of the last hour. "The first thing my mother said to me was *'James, dear, you look fat,'* and it ended with me telling my dad to go fuck himself." She left the part about her trust fund out. Jamie knew she'd have to tell him eventually, but she didn't want to burden him with the whole truth, not while he was in California living his dreams.

"Way to go, Kitty Cat." Pride laced Ryder's tone. "How does it feel?"

"Odd. Terrifying. Badass," Jamie offered as she pushed the car door open. In truth, she was on top of the world, so high up that Trey's car, which was parked next to Kensie's, almost didn't annoy her. *Almost.* "Great," she muttered, making her way to the elevator bank.

"What's wrong?"

"My roommate's boyfriend is here."

"And why don't we like him again?"

We.

God, he was so cheesy, and so perfect, and so worth every penny she'd given up. "He's basically Jared with less money and more ego," she explained pressing the arrow-up button. The number ten illuminated above, signaling the car's descent.

"Then why is she with him?"

"Kensie wants the fairytale. She tries to turn every frog that hops her way into *Prince Charming*. She's actually a lot like you."

"Does that make you my frog princess?"

"I've been called worse," she laughed, then sighed, glancing up at the numbers. The nine blinked to life, then the eight. "I should go. I don't get service in this damn elevator."

"I miss you, Kitty Cat."

"I miss you more, baby," she said without thinking.

"Baby?" he asked. It was the first time she ever heard a smile. Jamie thought that particular euphemism was reserved for bad romance novels, but standing in front of the shiny metal elevator, she heard Ryder's smile crystal clear.

"Yes, asshole," she grinned, her cheeks flushed, her heart full.

"There's my girl."

They were quiet for a moment. Jamie watched the six, five, and then the four flash above her, counting down to the end of their conversation. She had half a mind to get back in her car just so she could squeeze out a few more minutes.

"I should probably find food and a shower," Ryder said sadly.

"Probably."

"Good luck with the douche bag."

More silence. It was as if her lungs stopped pumping, her heart stopped beating, and the world stopped spinning.

"This is so cheesy."

"What?" Ryder chuckled.

"You know what."

"Then hang up."

Jamie groaned, "I can't believe I've been reduced to this."

"You love it."

"I hate it. I like my soul like I like my coffee, black and bitter."

"Then *hang up*," he challenged.

The elevator was on the second floor. She'd given up five million dollars for him, she could give up a little of her cynicism too. Taking a deep, cleansing breath, Jamie steeled herself before uttering those three little words, "You hang up."

"On the count of three," he offered as the doors slid open and she stepped inside. "One."

"Two," she exhaled.

The doors closed and the last thing she heard just before the call dropped was Ryder's sleepy voice telling her he loved her.

Trey was sitting on the barstool when Jamie entered the apartment. Ignoring him, she grabbed an unopened bottle of wine from the rack, then rummaged through the drawer for the opener. She was determined to hold onto the sun Ryder gave her a little while longer.

"How's the biker?" Trey asked and she froze. *Fucking asshole.* It was the shit cherry on top of the shit sundae that was her day.

Jamie inhaled, and exhaled.

Be thankful.

Be mindful.

Be kind.

She had already told Archer to fuck off.

Trey didn't matter.

Trey didn't matter.

Trey didn't matter.

It was a new chant. A new affirmation born out of necessity. Jamie could handle him one of two ways; she could go all old Jamie and attack or she could do what new, Zen Jamie would do and continue to ignore him. With a roll of her eyes, she took the path of least resistance and walked over to the cabinet, retrieving a wine glass. New Jamie wasn't going to feed into Trey's bullshit.

Nope.

She was rising above.

Popping the cork on the wine, she poured herself a very large glass and sat the bottle on the counter. It was red, she preferred white, but she'd take what she could get.

"I could set you up with one of my friends," Trey said, taking her silence as permission to continue speaking. He folded the corner of his newspaper back and looked up at her. "You're pretty, even though you drink like a fish and seem to think you own a pair of balls. Some guys like that. You don't have to go scraping the bottom of the barrel to get a date."

New Jamie backed away slowly, throwing her hands up in

exasperation, while old Jamie pulled out her earrings and cracked her knuckles.

Fuck the high road.

She was going to crucify him.

"First, my balls are internal, they're called ovaries and trust me, they're bigger than yours. Second, I wouldn't date, sleep with, or even talk to anyone who counts you as a friend." Rounding the corner of the breakfast bar, she added. "And my *biker* is a better man than you'll ever be."

"I'm sure," he grunted as she brushed past him, nearly spilling her wine in the process.

Kensie walked out of her room dressed like a Stepford Barbie. She smiled at Jamie but before she could open her mouth to speak, Jamie hissed, "Keep him the fuck away from me." She'd had enough. The day was supposed to be about love and acceptance, but it turned into a fucking shit show.

"What did I miss?" Ken asked grabbing Jamie's arm.

"He's. A. Dick," she said emphasizing each word.

"Baby," Trey hopped off the barstool and sauntered over to the two women, "talk some sense into your friend, she's being belligerent."

"Can someone please explain to me what the heck is happening?" Kensie asked looking between them.

"I simply said she doesn't need to entertain these… leeches. She comes from a great family. If she had a real boyfriend, they could be in Tahiti with us, but instead she's spending her birthday in the slums."

"Wait," Jamie said, nearly dropping her wine glass, "Tahiti? When are you going to Tahiti?"

"You didn't tell her?" Trey admonished. "I told you to tell her."

"I was going to but…I just… and then… I mean…" Kensie stuttered.

"When are you leaving?"

Kensie looked to Trey, but he shook his head, giving her a, *that's all you*, look. "On the twelfth," she muttered weakly.

"My fucking birthday?" Jamie screamed. It felt good to scream. After the day she had, screaming was mild. She wanted to break something. She wanted to throw things. Turning to Trey, she asked, "When did you book this trip?"

"A month ago. I didn't know it was your birthday when I did it, but I don't see what the big deal is. You two are adults, I think it's time to cut the cord."

"You lied to me?" Jamie asked looking back to her friend.

"Jamie." *Jamie not Jam.* Kensie fucked up. It wasn't a misunderstanding, it was a lie and with one word, she all but confessed. "You were so happy about your birthday and me meeting your guy, and we haven't been on the best terms lately. I just didn't know how to tell you."

"So, you lied?" Jamie shrieked.

"Look, Jamie, don't blame Kensington. She didn't know I was booking the trip until after it was done. It was a surprise."

"I asked her last week about my birthday and she lied to my face."

"I'm sure you misunderstood," Trey offered.

"Did I Ken?"

"No," Kensie shook her head, "I knew then and I'm sorry for not saying anything. We were having fun and I didn't know how to tell you."

"How about my boyfriend booked us a surprise trip to Tahiti, Bitch, I'll meet your biker some other time. Did you really think I'd be mad? I'm not the selfish one, *you are,*" Jamie added because she was hurt.

Kensie bristled at Jamie's accusation. "That right there is why I didn't want to tell you. You've been living a secret life for months. I told one white lie to protect your feelings and now I'm the bad guy?"

"So, this is my fault? Of course, everything always is."

"That's not what I mean."

"Whatever, I'm not in the mood for this," Jamie said, retreating to her bedroom. She'd had enough disappointment for one day. Hell, she had enough for a lifetime.

TWENTY-ONE

Crush

RYDER

The van rolled to a stop in front of the small blue house and the guys breathed a collective sigh of relief. After spending fourteen days crisscrossing the state of California, Lithium Springs was finally home. It was good to be back. The air was different in Los Angeles, not because of all the sunshine and smog, but the people there were different. Everyone was a star, but only a fraction of the population was famous; even less were talented. It made them jaded, and jealousy permeated the air.

Ryder and his band spent most of their time in LA recording songs in Creed's home studio. The audio quality wasn't the best, but the music was next fucking level. At the end of the first week, they had finished their official EP, four songs in total, *Sex God* being the title track. They then worked in shifts, burning their music onto the blank CD's they'd purchased from Walmart by the cart full.

The second week was when the real hustle began, a grunge boot camp of sorts. The guys had traveled up and down the coast, playing in dive bars across the state. Nights were spent at dingy motels in questionable neighborhoods. During the day, the guys passed out the homemade CD's in mall parking lots and played impromptu sidewalk performances. It was hardcore guerrilla marketing shit. The days were grueling, but it was an experience they would never forget.

"Are we unloading this shit now or in the morning?" Javi asked. Their street was quiet, the sun long since set.

"I vote for the morning," CT yawned.

"Me too," Ryder said, fishing his phone from his pocket. Fourteen days since he'd touched his girl and he didn't want to waste another minute.

"You're so fucking pussy whipped," CT chuckled.

Ryder shook his head, "You'll understand one day, Son."

"Not fucking likely," CT grinned, pushing open the door. "Come on Javi, let's light up some of this good Cali bud while I kick your ass in *Madden*."

"Not fucking likely," Javi grunted, jumping out of the van. Before shutting the door, he peeked his head back inside, "Tell Kitty Cat we missed her."

"Will do," Ryder said, dialing the number he knew by heart. Resting his head against the headrest, he listened as the phone rang, and rang and rang. "Come on, Jamie, pick up." It was late. They were supposed to be back hours ago, but Creed's connection at *Rolling Rock* wanted to do a last-minute photo shoot. He thought about hanging up, about joining his friends on the couch, and letting her sleep, but he missed her.

"You're home?" she breathed, answering on the last ring. Her voice was low and thick with sleep.

Ryder frowned, "Yeah, and you're asleep."

"I tried to stay awake, but the wine wouldn't let me be great."

He chuckled sadly, squeezing his eyes shut. He wanted his girl, in his bed, but he couldn't ask her to get up in the middle of the night because he was five hours late. "Go back to sleep, Kitty Cat. I waited two weeks, a few more hours won't kill me."

"It might kill me," she yawned.

"I don't want you driving right now."

"Then come to me."

"Huh?" he asked, caught off guard. He'd never been to Jamie's place. He often wondered if she was embarrassed by him, but he didn't push. Jamie did things on her own time, in her own way, and that was just one of those things. He hoped it would come, but now that it had, those four words rendered him speechless.

"You heard me, Napoleon. Get your ass over here."

"What about Mackenzie?"

"Who the fuck is Mackenzie?"

"Kenzie, your roommate."

"Oh, no, her name is Kensington. We aren't speaking to each other at the moment, so she's hiding out at her boyfriend's place."

"Okay, well I guess I'm on my way," he whispered into the receiver.

"Okay, well I guess I'll see you soon."

Ryder ended the call and climbed out of the van. It took him fifteen minutes to get to Jamie's building. She called ahead to the front desk to put him on the list and before he knew it, he was taking the elevator up to the fourth floor.

"Hey, Kitty Cat," he smirked, taking her in. Her blonde hair was matted to the side of her face and she was wearing the tiniest pair of sleep shorts he'd ever seen.

"Hey, Napoleon," she cooed. "Do you plan on standing there all night or are you going to come inside?"

"At least two times," he smirked.

"God, I missed you." She jumped into his arms, and wrapped her legs around his waist. Ryder walked them into the house, kicking the door shut behind them. He wanted to savor the moment, wanted to take in every inch of her space, but the throbbing between his legs had other ideas.

"Where's your room?"

"Over there," she panted, pointing to a door off the living room. Ryder made his way through the large industrial style apartment, soaking in what details he could in the dark. He spotted Jamie's hand in the decor, specifically the clean lines and neutral colors. The art on the wall was eclectic, a jumbled mix of pieces, varying in color, size, and texture working together to create a playful atmosphere.

Her room was one hundred percent Kitty Cat. Black and white furniture with light blue accents. Easy going on the surface, but nothing out of place. She created the order in her physical space that she craved mentally.

Dropping her on the bed with a bounce, he peeled off his shirt. "I've been in the car for thirteen hours," he warned.

"I haven't been fucked in fourteen days," she countered, lifting her ass and yanking down the tiny shorts. She was bare underneath, no panties, and freshly waxed.

"Did you do that for me?" he asked, bending down to place a kiss on her sex. Fuck, he missed tasting her. His tongue darted out and he licked up one side of her pussy and down the other before dipping inside.

"Yes, God," she moaned, her fingers fisting in his hair.

"But we're good for sex, right?"

"Yeah, I had it done the other day."

"Good. So, are you going to tell me what happened?" he asked, sucking on her clit.

"What? When?" she whimpered, her thighs shaking under his assault.

"With your roommate, *Kensington*."

"You really want to talk about that now?"

"Better now than before my dick is inside you and I can't think."

"It's a long story, but the abridged version is we got into an argument. She's a selfish bitch and I'm an asshole who can't express how I feel without going on the offensive—which you already know—keep licking," she mewled, pushing his head back between her legs.

He kissed and licked and sucked on the damp flesh, worshiping every inch of her. "Is there a chance you're being a little hard on her?" he asked as he inserted two fingers into her core.

"A small chance," she muttered, grinding up against his face, "but she lied to me and hurt my feelings. She is my best friend and birthdays are a big deal for us."

"This is about your birthday?"

"No…I mean…kind of… don't stop," she moaned. "It's just we've known each other our whole lives and it sucks growing apart."

"Sometimes people change and grow. You gotta give them space to explore themselves." As soon as the words left his lips, Annette's face flashed in his mind, his subconscious calling him a hypocrite. Ryder sat back on his haunches. Jamie flashed him a murderous look. "Sorry. I was just thinking about my mom and it…got…weird."

Jamie threw her head back in laughter as Ryder fell on top of her. He relished the feel of her soft skin against his. "I get that," she said, "I do, but some things are supposed to be forever."

"I'm forever," he promised. His mouth found hers and he coaxed her lips open with his tongue, letting her taste herself, taste his vow.

A week later, Ryder found himself sauntering through the dining room at Cibo in his too tight black t-shirt. His temporary exile was complete.

"Look what the cat dragged in," Liz smirked, looking up at Ryder from behind the rim of her teacup.

Ryder pulled out a chair, and plopped down across from Liz. "I'm back."

"I see that."

"Did you miss me?"

Liz set the teacup down on the matching saucer, and regarded him closely, a mask of indifference painted on her face. "Like I miss a headache. How's that girlfriend of yours?" Skepticism laced her tone and Ryder couldn't blame her. The first and only time she'd heard of Jamie was when he nearly started a fist fight in the dining room because she was on a date with another man. It sounded as fucked up as it was, but that was Jamie, a little fucked up on the surface, but beautifully complex underneath.

"We're good," he assured her.

Liz narrowed her eyes as if she wanted to call bullshit, or whatever the fancy, rich lady equivalent of bullshit was, but she held her tongue. "And that little band of yours? I hear you're making quite the name for yourselves. I had to ban cell phones on the restaurant floor because everyone was sharing some video of you dry humping a microphone stand."

Ryder rubbed the back of his neck, cocky grin firmly in place. "Oakland," he stated simply, reverently. That night had been epic; some sort of bizarre-o world prodigal son tale, only instead of going home to repent, Ryder brought the fucking house down. Footage from the show had gone viral. They got so many hits the Lithium Springs website crashed.

"I'm glad to see you used your time off wisely."

"I did," he nodded.

"Well, welcome back. Now get to work. I'm not paying you to sit here and look good." Despite the boredom in her tone, her eyes twinkled with pride.

"Aren't you?" he asked, raising a brow.

Liz chuckled, "*Sit,* was the operative word. Your good looks and charm won't work on me, so save it for the customers."

The chair screeched on the hardwood as he stood. "We could've had something great."

"Yeah, well, your loss," she winked. When she wasn't being scary, Liz was actually kind of a cool boss.

𝄞

The rest of the day flew by with relative ease. Ryder spent the first hour of his shift telling and retelling the story of his Californian adventure to his co-workers. At noon, when the lunch rush hit, no one cared that he was a rock star, they only cared about having their tables cleaned. It was strange, this life he was creating for himself. He was internet famous, but broke as fuck.

Being back at Cibo was humbling to say the least. The highlights of Ryder's day included turning up the charm on a couple of bored housewives and getting felt up by a man wearing a suit that probably cost more than his Harley. It was worth it though. While the guys' hands were on his ass, he slid two hundred dollar bills into Ryder's back pocket. Later, Trav, the bartender, bet him twenty bucks he couldn't chug a jarful of olive juice.

Easiest twenty he'd ever made.

That, combined with the show money they made in Cali, was enough for him to cover his third of rent next month and buy his girl something for her birthday. It wouldn't be the most extravagant gift his five-million-dollar baby would receive, but he knew Kitty Cat. He knew what made her rub her tattoo against her lips, what turned her on, what made her happy, and none of it had anything to do with money.

"Ry," one of the hostesses called as he loaded his tub with dirty dishes.

"What's up?" he asked, placing a half-eaten plate of fried calamari into his bin.

"There's a guy at the door asking for you."

"What does he look like?" Ryder questioned, furrowing his brow. Everyone at the restaurant knew his bandmates by name, some of them biblically, so that ruled out CT and Javi.

"A rich asshole," the hostess replied with a tick of her jaw.

Realization washed over Ryder. It was probably the handsy prick with the fancy suit. Ryder knew the money was too good to be true. "Alright, let me take this to the kitchen," he said. He'd listen to the proposition. Ryder was keeping the money, the least he could do was let the tool down gently.

After dropping the dirty dishes off, Ry made his way to the

hostess stand. The front of the restaurant was bright, a stark contrast from the dimly lit dining room. The sun shined through the large windows, and pink flowers—which were shoved in every corner—perfumed the air.

The hostess nodded towards a man sitting on the plush pink sofa. Ryder's voice dropped an octave and he puffed out his chest. "Jared," he bit.

The sinister motherfucker didn't fool him. He was evil and his intentions regarding Jamie were so far from pure, they might as well have been that murky olive juice he drank earlier.

"Busboy," Jared said by way of greeting. His arms were stretched out wide behind him, and his legs were crossed at the ankles like he owned the place.

"Why are you here?" Ryder chewed out. He silently reminded himself that he was already on thin ice, and knocking this fuckers teeth down his throat would surely result in his termination.

Jared picked at imaginary lint on his black slacks. "Why do you think?"

"Jamie is an adult and fully capable of making her own decisions. So, again, why are you *here* bothering *me*, instead of somewhere trying to convince *her* to choose *you*? Or did she already tell you to fuck off?"

Anger flashed in Jared's eyes, his cool guy façade cracking for the first time since their little encounter began. "I came here first, to address you like a man. James is mine. She's as good as bought and paid for. Her father froze her trust, so it's only a matter of time before she realizes how cruel the real world can be and comes running into my arms." Jared uncrossed his legs, licking his lips like the goddamned predator that he was. "And between me and you, I'm looking forward to breaking her."

Ryder was so stunned he couldn't even process Jared's comment about breaking Jamie. He was too busy trying to process the fact that Jamie gave up her trust. Jamie never mentioned it to him. On top of it being crazy and impulsive, she was keeping things from him, big, life altering things. Regardless of her reasoning, it stung.

The smug bastard leaned forward, resting his elbows on his knees. "Judging by the look on your face, I'd say she didn't tell you."

Ryder's jaw ticked but he stayed quiet. He wouldn't give that ballbag the satisfaction of his words.

"I'll make it easy for you. Walk away from her and I'll give you ten thousand dollars right now."

"Shove it up your ass," Ryder said. He was a ticking time bomb. If this motherfucker didn't leave soon, he'd without a doubt be in jail.

"Twenty thousand," Jared countered with a grin. He was haggling over a human being, getting off on flexing his power. Twenty grand was nothing for a rich dick like Jared, but that kind of money would turn Ryder's life around. Jared wasn't a man, he was a monster in a pretty suit. "Thirty," he said with a yawn.

Unfortunately for him, Ryder didn't bend and his soul wasn't for sale.

Jamie was absolutely his fucking soul.

"You've got about one minute to get the fuck out of my face before I start breaking your bones."

Jared stood, chuckling. He fastened a button on his suit jacket, then added, "If you change your mind, call me."

A small black square hit Ryder in the chest, a business card. Wrath colored Ryder's world. He took two steps towards the door but halted when he felt a hand tugging at his elbow. Turning, Ry spotted Liz, her face solemn. "Get back to work, Son. He isn't worth it."

TWENTY-TWO

Party In The USA

Jamie

Kensie: I know you aren't talking to me and I know I deserve it, but I couldn't let the day pass without saying something. I swear I'll make this right when I get home. I love you, Jam. Happy 25th birthday.

Twenty-five.

There was a time when Jamie thought she'd never see the day. She was running full-speed down the path of self-destruction, hiding from love, and from the truth. She always considered herself a seeker of knowledge, it's why she did what she did for a living. Last fall, she'd learned honesty and self-awareness was like being sliced in the stomach and having your light pulled from the gash. It was ugly and painful, but accepting those truths and releasing her demons into the atmosphere had saved her life.

Be thankful.
Be mindful.
Be kind.

She chanted silently, staring at her phone screen. She was at a loss for words. Things with Kensie had gotten so messed up, Jamie couldn't think of anything to say to her best friend.

"Who died?" Chris asked coming up to the table. They were at The Upper Deck, a driving range and bar that had just opened in Seattle. Her twenty-fifth birthday party was in full swing. All her friends were there, well, all but the one she needed most; the one who knew her deepest darkest secrets and loved her anyway.

Turning her phone to her brother, Jamie showed him the message. Chris' eyes scanned the screen before he took the phone from her and tapped out a response. When he was done, he handed it back.

Jamie: I love you too, Ken.

"I knew you couldn't write it," he shrugged, "but I also know it's how you feel."

She nodded, and her lip quivered with sadness. He was right, she loved Kensington. Neither of them were perfect, but that was part of why they got along so well. Kensie was just better at covering up her flaws.

"This place is great," Chris said, steering the conversation away from the heavy shit. They still hadn't unpacked everything from his failed attempt at coming out, but following Manning tradition, they swept it under the rug. It was easier to pretend everything was fine, even when the world was burning around them.

"It's new," Jamie said. If he was going to ignore the elephant in the room, she would too. "I've wanted to come check it out for a while. I did a piece on it for WSEA-9."

Twenty rows of putting greens lined the rooftop. Their motley crew took up three of those stations. The guys from the band, Parker, Lo, a few of her friends from the station, and some of the Rabbit Hole staff all showed up to help her celebrate. Drinks flowed freely, and everyone was having a good time.

"I know we are avoiding the subject, but how are you and he

doing?" Jamie asked tipping her chin in Parker's direction. It was his turn to tee off, and he and CT made a bet on who would score the most points.

Chris's gaze dropped to his Jack and Coke. "We're good. He's been more understanding than I deserve," he sighed, before finally lifting his eyes to meet hers. "We're worried about you, Jam. Dad freezing your trust, that was—"

"I'm fine baby brother. I'm better than fine. I make enough at the station to live comfortably. I might have to give these up," she said, wiggling her Gucci clad foot, "but I can eat and pay rent and not have to feel like I'm indebted to him for anything."

"What about the other thing?" he asked.

"What other thing?" She knew *what other* thing, but she was hoping he'd drop it.

"James," he pushed. This wasn't how Jamie wanted to spend her birthday. "Why is dad so hell bent on the two of you?"

"I suppose I'm collateral in this deal their working? I don't know. You're guess is as good as mine. You work there."

Chris scanned the room. Everyone was oblivious to their whispered conversation. "Things are rough at Manning Solutions. I'm not sure exactly what's going on yet, but I know Dad has a lot riding on this deal with Jared's company."

Jamie rubbed her tattoo across her bottom lip. Her father was a rich bastard; he came from money, her mother too. Even if the company was in trouble, they'd still be richer than most. This wasn't about money, it was about power. The power that came from being the CEO of a Fortune 500 company. That was the thing that made Archer tick.

"Enough with the sad shit," Jamie said clapping her hands. Her voice dropped even lower, "What do you think of my biker?"

"I'd give up my trust for him too," Chris chuckled before draining his glass.

"I'm telling Parker," she grinned.

"I think he's in love with the drummer." They both turned to look, and sure enough, Parker was laughing a little too hard at whatever it was CT was saying. "He's not gay, is he?" Chris asked.

"You're safe," Ryder smirked, coming up behind Jamie. He tugged on her ponytail, forcing her head backwards. His lips grazed hers. "Happy birthday, Kitty Cat," he whispered before slipping his tongue into her mouth. Their kiss was slow, lazy, and all consuming. He tasted like cinnamon and spice and everything that was right in her life. Jamie lost herself in Ryder, in his kiss and in his touch. It was desperate, the way she clung to him and him to her. Then he was gone.

"There are children here," CT teased, pulling Ryder back playfully. He and Parker joined them at the table. Ryder pulled Jamie to her feet, then slipped into her chair, dragging her onto his lap. She could feel her brother's eyes on her, but she refused to make contact. He'd just witnessed her making out with a guy, *in public,* something old Jamie was firmly against, but this wasn't just any guy, this was *her* guy. This was Ryder.

"Who won?" Ry asked, pulling a silver flask from his pocket. He took a long swig before shaking it and frowning. He was drinking more than usual, but it was a party, and Jamie was in no position to call anyone out for drinking.

Reaching for the flask, she brought it to her lips. "Is that why you taste like Christmas?" she grinned, the cinnamon flavored whiskey heated her cheeks even more than their make-out session.

"It's been a shitty week, Kitty Cat," he replied, rubbing his nose against hers.

"Wanna talk about it?" He'd been a little distant, but he had been pulling doubles at Cibo, trying to make up for the four weeks of work he'd missed, so she assumed it was exhaustion.

"Nope," he said, taking the flask back. "It's your birthday. I want to get shit-faced with my girl and have fun."

He was keeping something from her, but she wasn't sure what. Inhaling, she ran her tattoo over his bottom lip, silently imploring him to let her in. Their eyes met and for a second, the sounds of metal crashing against plastic faded and it was just the two of them.

Ryder caught her finger with his teeth and bit down gently.

"Tell me," she breathed.

"You first," he countered.

Confusion marred her face, but before she could vocalize her thoughts, her brother spoke, tearing her and Ryder from the moment. "I almost forgot," Chris said, pulling an envelope out of his pocket. The corners were wrinkled and there was a coffee stain on the back. Jamie quirked a brow at the mangled card. "Sorry," he added, handing it over.

It was light blue, her favorite color, and the faint scent of sandalwood clung to the cardstock, a scent she'd know in her sleep. "Mom?" she asked.

Chris bobbed his head up and down.

The server came by, replacing empty glasses with full ones. Jamie reached for the icy Jack and Coke and took a sip to calm her nerves. This was her night. Twenty-five was her year and she wasn't going to let her family bring her down, especially not on day one.

"Open it," her brother encouraged. She and Chris were close but they didn't talk often about the stark contrast in their upbringings. His was loving and nurturing, well, about as nurturing as Caroline could be. Jamie, on the other hand, was just there, looking in, doing whatever she could to get their parents attention.

With a roll of her eyes, Jamie slid her finger under the flap and ripped it open. Inside was a card made from heavy stock paper, with an intricate flower design on the front. The message was a generic happy birthday, but it was what was inside that took her breath away. A slim, black credit card fell to the table. Her eyes flew to her brother's before scanning the card again. Written in her mother's flowy script were three little words,

Just in case.

"Why would she do this?" Jamie's voice cracked and Ryder

instinctively tightened his arms around her.

"She loves you, Jam," Chris insisted.

"Hardly," Jamie snorted.

"Dad's an asshole and mom has grown bitter being married to him for so long, but deep down, in her own fucked up way, she loves you. Plus," he added with a grin, "I think she knows I'm queer and is hedging her bets since dad will probably disown me too," he laughed.

"What's that about?" Ryder whispered in her ear.

Shit.

She was going to kill her brother. Jamie still hadn't gotten around to telling Ryder about her trust, or lack thereof, but it wasn't something she could just bring up over dinner.

"I don't know, my brother's drunk," she said, kicking Chris in the shin.

"Hey, that hurt," Christopher yelped.

"Are you sure everything's okay?" Ryder asked.

"I'm sure."

Ryder's jaw ticked and he stood abruptly, nearly sending Jamie crashing to the ground. "I'm going to get a refill," he snapped.

"Dude, there are a million drinks on the table," CT said, pointing to the glasses the server just left.

Ryder kept walking, ignoring the strange looks from their friends. Something was wrong, but in true Manning fashion, Jamie swept that shit under the rug too.

An hour and an ungodly amount of Jack Daniels later, everyone seemed to forget Ryder's little temper tantrum. They also seemed to forget how to play golf. The competition between Parker and CT devolved from how many points they could score, to how far they could throw the golf balls.

The Upper Deck staff didn't appreciate their game.

"You guys get home safe," Jamie said, wrapping her brother and Parker into a group hug.

"You too, and Ry, nice meeting you man." Chris extended his hand to Ryder, pulling him into one of those weird, dude-bro type hugs. They exchanged hushed words, but Jamie couldn't make out what they were saying. Initially, she dismissed it as some sort of drunken bonding experience, but the look on Ryder's face told her it was deeper than that. It was a look that twisted her insides into knots.

Did Chris tell him about her trust?

Worry ate at Jamie as everyone finished saying their goodbyes and climbed into their respective cars. Ryder led Jamie to the back of the UberXL while CT and Javi settled in the middle row.

The car took off into the night and Jamie couldn't help but notice the distance she felt from Ryder. Not physically. Physically, he hovered, like always. One of his arms was draped around her shoulder, casually groping her breast. Emotionally, though, he long since checked out. His head rested on the tinted glass and that damn flask was never far from his lips. He was taking the brooding, bad boy thing a little far.

"What was that thing with my brother?" Jamie blurted out, too drunk for subtlety.

"Nothing I didn't already know," he slurred. His focus remained on the passing scenery.

"Are you mad at me?" she whispered. Her eyes darted to the backs of CT and Javi's head. They were debating who threw the golf ball furthest, oblivious to the tension in the back seat.

"I don't know, should I be?"

Jamie huffed, tired of the cryptic bullshit. "It's my fucking birthday. We are supposed to be happy. You're supposed to be fingering me and whispering for me to be quiet, not pouting like a child." Snorting, Ry unscrewed the top to his flask and brought it to his lips. Jamie yanked it from him, and recapped it. "No. No more drinking. We are having sex."

"Have *I* ever let *you* down before?" The question was as loaded as Ryder was. She heard his implication loud and clear, she was the fuck up in their relationship, not him.

Brushing off the slight, she retorted, "There's a first time for everything, and the way you're throwing back the Fireball, I'd say there's a good chance I won't be getting my birthday wish."

The driver made a sharp turn causing Ryder to fall over onto Jamie. He pushed her on her back, and his body hung inches above hers. He reeked of whiskey and radiated heat. "I can give it to you now." His voice was gruff. She couldn't see his face in the darkness but she could hear his intention. Their sex that night wouldn't be sweet or loving or have any of the normal soul searing intensity. It was going to be angry and raw. He was going to fuck her like she was the enemy, like he hated her.

"Please," she moaned, writhing underneath him. It didn't matter that they were in the back of an Uber. It didn't matter that CT and Javi were right there, she wanted it. She wanted him, anyway she could get him.

"Kitty Cat," he growled, shifting so their pelvises aligned. "Do you feel that?" he asked, referring to the rock-hard erection desperately trying to escape the confines of his jeans. "Do you feel what you do to me? Even when you piss me off, you turn me on."

"You *are* mad," she accused. Her hands fisted in his hair and she pulled him down, tasting his lips. Ryder popped the button on her shorts, and did his best to drag them down her legs. He only made it about half way. The limited space in the back seat hindered him. It was the one time she wished she wore a damn dress.

Ryder pulled her upright, her shorts and underwear around her thighs. He reached for the flask, drained the remaining contents, then wrapped one arm around her. "Be quiet," he warned. His fingers swirled around her opening. Jamie tried to pull her legs further apart but her shorts restricted her movements.

The car drove on, speeding down the empty streets. CT and Javi's voices muffled the moans she desperately tried to swallow as Ryder's fingers pumped in and out of her body. He kept a steady pace, just enough to drive her crazy, but not enough to push her over the edge. "Please, it's my birthday," she begged.

"You're too loud when you come, Kitty Cat. No one gets to hear you but me."

"They aren't paying any attention to us." She lifted her ass, desperate to push her shorts down further. In that lust fueled moment, Jamie didn't give a fuck who heard her.

Sliding his fingers out of her core, he brought them to her lips. Jamie made a show of sucking off her juices, her tongue darting between his fingers, as she licked them clean. "Please," she said again. She wasn't above begging.

"You want to sit on my dick?" he asked.

Jamie nodded, not trusting herself to speak.

"Please don't. That would just make things awkward," Javi said. He didn't turn around, but Jamie could hear the smile in his voice.

Ryder laughed, it sounded like a dog barking. CT and Javi quickly followed suit and Jamie tugged her shorts up in annoyance. "I'm glad you all think this is funny," she pouted. She was horny and surrounded by drunk idiots.

"We're almost there," Kitty Cat. Ryder whispered, his warm breath sent a chill down her spine. An erotic promise hidden beneath his words.

𝄞

"What are you doing down here?" CT asked around a fork full of pie. "I thought I'd need ear plugs after all the foreplay in the car."

Jamie rolled her eyes, and stomped across the kitchen. She pulled open the drawer and grabbed a fork of her own. "Your friend is a drunk idiot," she grumbled, plopping her ass down in the seat next to the drummer.

"Don't tell me he caught a case of whiskey dick?"

"No, I wish, because at least then, he could finger me or I could ride his face or something, but nooooo, he had to get sick." She sounded like a brat, but it was her birthday and she asked him to slow down on the drinking. Now, instead of birthday sex with Ryder, she was having pie with CT.

Stabbing her fork into the dessert, she brought it to her mouth. Diner pie was the only thing that could salvage her night. "What the fuck is this?" she mumbled, unsure of weather to spit or swallow.

"Oh, I know. Shit's trash but your dickhead boyfriend put a moratorium on the diner. It's from a bakery in Bellevue, double the price and not half as good," CT shrugged.

"Bellevue?" Jamie asked, dropping her fork. Bellevue pie wasn't worth the calories.

"I was visiting my folks, so I was high."

"Naturally," she nodded.

"I saw it and stopped. I spent a hundred and fifty dollars on baked goods. Never go to a bakery loaded," he warned.

Sage stoner advice aside, she asked, "You grew up in Bellevue?" Jamie knew CT came from a different neighborhood than Javi and Ryder, but she didn't know his parents were wealthy.

CT brought his finger to his lips. "*Shh*, our little secret," he grinned.

"Where did you go to high school?" Jamie was genuinely curious. Javi was the joker, he even had the Batman obsession to prove it. Ryder was brooding and artsy, he had the emotions to prove it. But CT was a mystery.

"Jefferson Prep."

"No way?!" she shrieked. "I went to St. Andrew's. We killed you guys in basketball. My roommate dated a guy on the team. We were at all the games. Did you play?"

CT bristled. "No. Organized sports weren't my thing, unless you count bagging cheerleaders?"

"No," Jamie rolled her eyes. She went in for another bite of pie. Maybe it wasn't horrible, now that the disappointment of it not being from the diner waned.

"You gonna tell me what you two were fighting about?"

"I would if I could," she sighed. "I thought we were in a good place, then tonight he was so up and down. I don't know what happened."

"Huh," he grunted, taking another bite of pie.

"What, huh?"

"He's been a little bitch all week, more so than usual. I just assumed it was you."

"Nope," she said popping her lips on the 'P', "and fuck you for saying that."

"Can you blame me?" he asked earnestly. "You guys either make love or war, there's no in between."

"You think it could have something to do with his mom?" Jamie asked, choosing to ignore the accurate assessment of her relationship.

CT shrugged, "I don't know. He pretends he's okay with the way they left things, but Ry and Annette are close. It's gotta be fucking with him."

"It's fucking with her," Jamie said absently.

"How do you know?"

"I go to the diner sometimes," she confessed. Ryder hated it, but she didn't agree with his *"cut Annette out"* philosophy and she was never good with rules.

"Why won't you let him in?" CT asked out of nowhere. They were talking about Ryder and Annette's issues, not hers.

Stunned, Jamie answered, "He's as *in* as anyone has ever been, even more than my little brother and my best friend. It's just hard for me. In my world, relationships are contracts and marriages are business deals."

"I get that. I do, but Kitty Cat, he's in love with you." CT's eyes bled sincerity.

"I know. I told him to stop, but he won't listen."

"Do you love him?" he asked, bluntly.

"I don't know," she whispered.

"That's bullshit," CT said. He let the fork drop onto the table with a loud clatter. "I see you two together. It's written in the air surrounding you."

"I can't be what he needs. I should have ended this a long time ago, but I'm selfish and lonely." It was cathartic, speaking these truths to Ryder's best friend, words she'd been too afraid to speak to the man who needed to hear them.

"Why don't you tell him that?"

"Because he'll want to fix me."

"Is that such a bad thing?"

Was it?

Jamie wasn't sure. She spent so much time in the darkness, would she even know how to behave in the light?

"What if he destroys me?" she muttered, running her tattoo along her lip. Last fall had nearly ruined her. She didn't think she could survive another loss.

"What if he doesn't?" CT challenged.

"What if I'm not strong enough to take that risk?"

"But that's just it, Kitty Cat, you're stronger than all of us combined. Let go, give in to the chaos. You might get burned, you might even lose a piece of your heart, but then, something kind of amazing happens. You pull yourself together, and take that first breath towards healing and I swear to God, it's the most freeing feeling in the world."

"How'd you get so fucking smart?" she asked, blinking back the tears. Jamie would have never guessed the drummer from Bellevue would be so insightful.

"I've been where you are," he smirked, "and will you look at that, I'm still standing.

TWENTY-THREE

Heavy

RYDER

Ryder groaned, pressing his eyelids shut. His body contorted, one foot was draped over the tub, and the other jammed against the toilet, while his cheek stuck to the hard tile of the bathroom wall.

He was cold, naked, and felt like shit.

Like dog shit.

Like dog shit that had been left on the sidewalk under the sun on a 100-degree day.

Another fucking hangover all because he let his anger and jealousy get the best of him. The grown-up thing to do would have been to call Jamie the minute Jared had left Cibo, but his pride stopped him. Ryder wanted Kitty Cat to tell him about her trust. He wanted her to finally open up to him. He wanted them to be able to work through shit together like a real couple, but instead of telling her what he wanted, he pouted for a fucking week.

Prying his cheek off the tile, Ryder managed to push his way to his feet. As he stumbled down the hall towards his bedroom, images of the night before flashed in his mind. As soon as they stepped out of the Uber, Jamie and Ryder sprinted to his room. Clothes went flying in every direction and he had her pinned to the bed within minutes. That's when the room started to spin and everything went foggy.

Ryder tip-toed into his room. Jamie was lying diagonally across his bed, wearing one of his t-shirts and a bright green thong. He placed a kiss on her ass before slipping into a pair of boxers and snagging the half-full bottle of water off the nightstand, chugging it down in two gulps.

Ryder stared at the bed, trying to figure out the best way to lie down without waking up Kitty Cat. After a few failed attempts, Jamie grimaced, "You almost threw up on me," and rolled onto her side of the bed.

"I'm sorry," Ryder chuckled. He climbed into bed and pulled her flush against him.

"Why were you drinking so much anyway?" she yawned.

Ryder debated whether he was going to tell her, but decided he couldn't keep behaving like a drunken lunatic. "I think we should talk."

"Me too," she whispered, stilling beneath him.

"Jared came to Cibo and offered me thirty thousand dollars to break up with you. He said you were being stubborn and you needed a little push, that your dad freezing your trust wasn't enough."

"He what?" she shrieked, turning so she could look at him. "When?"

Ryder tucked a strand of hair behind her ear. "Last week. I didn't say anything because I didn't take the money and I didn't want you to feel like you were property."

"You didn't take the money?" Jamie gawked at him like he was certifiable.

"Fuck no, Kitty Cat. You're worth more than that."

"I know I am," she said, pushing up into a seated position. "You know, I am. Jared and my dad know too, but you still should have taken the jackasses money."

Ryder looked at her incredulously. "I wouldn't take a cent from him."

"You are too good," Jamie laughed. "If it were me, I'd have taken it, then sent him a video of us fucking on top of it."

"That's probably the most savage thing I've ever heard you say." Ryder pulled her back into his arms and kissed the top of her head. "Why didn't you tell me about your trust?"

Jamie shrugged. "Because it doesn't matter and I didn't want you to feel like it was your fault."

"It kind of is, though, Kitty Cat. I might never be able to buy you the things Jared can."

"I'm not with you because of money," she insisted. "I grew up with money and I'm *way* more fucked up than most people."

"I grew up without money and let me tell you, problems are exponentially more difficult when you're too broke to solve them." Money couldn't buy happiness but it did buy stability. Ryder didn't have a job and struggled to provide for himself. Jamie deserved the life someone like Jared could give her, but no one would ever love her as much as he did.

"What is it with you guys acting like I'm going to be homeless?" she huffed. "I have a good job."

"But still."

Jamie shifted to straddle him. "Ry, I've been through the worst year of my life. Losing my trust is like number ten on the list of bad things that happened to me."

"What's number one?" Ry whispered. His hazel eyes searched her greens for clues, yet he found nothing but total and utter devastation.

Jamie stared at the brown water spot staining the ceiling, studying it as if there would be a test later.

"What's bigger than five million?" he asked, squeezing her tighter, hoping his arms provided comfort.

"My scar," she whispered softly. Ryder felt her body go rigid. They were getting deep—finally. Jamie was exposing her heart.

"You don't have to tell me if you aren't ready." Ryder wanted this, their relationship needed it, but as always, he wouldn't push.

Jamie inhaled and exhaled. Her fingers trembled as she fought the urge to chew on her tattoo. "I went downstairs after you got sick. CT was in the kitchen eating pie, so naturally, I joined him."

"Naturally," he smirked.

"Anyway, we talked for a while, then he told me something that stuck with me. He said if I just let go, let you love me, I could be free." She sighed, brushing her nose against his. "So, you see, I have to tell you, because I don't want my stubbornness to ruin us."

Jamie leaned back, lifting her t-shirt over her head. She brought his hand to her abdomen and pressed it onto her scar. "I was a mess last year," she began. "I was drinking, partying, doing drugs, hooking up with random people, you name it. Full on spiral. I don't know why I was going so hard. I think I was just lonely, and partying filled that void. But the problem with self-medicating is that it's temporary. Once the high wore off, I was back to being this sad, lonely thing, so I did it again and again and again."

Ryder didn't speak, he simply rested his forehead onto hers. He wanted her to feel his presence, to feel his love.

"Then, one day I got sick. I mean, *really sick*. I assumed it was a hangover. I threw up everything. I couldn't keep down water. My hands shook so bad, I couldn't even Google," she chuckled sadly. "It felt like someone was ripping me open from the inside out. The pain was so intense I couldn't move. I laid on the floor of the bathroom crying. I thought I was dying. Ken was freaking out. She called 911 and I was rushed to the hospital."

Silent tears rolled down Jamie's cheeks as she continued. "I got there and they didn't know what was wrong. They ran a few tests, the basic stuff. My heart stopped when they told me I was pregnant."

"What?" Ryder gasped. He'd wondered about her scar for months. He assumed it was from a childhood trauma, or an illness, but a baby?

"I was pregnant. They tried to do an ultrasound, but there was so much internal bleeding. They said it was ectopic, that's when the fetus develops outside the fallopian tube. They said the fetus ruptured. They had to take my baby or it would kill both of us. They had to work fast. There was already so much blood. I was rushed into emergency surgery. I lost my child that day."

"How does that happen?" he asked, rubbing her back, hoping to provide some comfort.

"They said it happens sometimes and they don't know exactly how or why. Every woman is different. There's nothing I could have done to prevent it, but I know the truth. I'd poisoned my body so much that even my unborn child didn't want to live there." Her body crumpled on top of his and she broke down.

Ryder placed his hands on her face, forcing Jamie to look him in the eyes. "Kitty Cat, that's not true."

"It is. God was punishing me. I didn't know I was pregnant. I didn't know who the father was, but I didn't care. I was in no position to raise a child, but you can't understand how much love I had for my baby. I wanted her," she smiled weakly. "I'd like to think she was a girl. Even if it was only for a few hours, I was a mom. Losing her destroyed me. I didn't want to live in a world with so much pain and suffering. So, yeah," she said rubbing the semi-colon inked on her finger across Ryder's bottom lip.

"Look at me, Kitty Cat," Ryder demanded, and reluctant green eyes pierced his soul. "You are good and smart and kind. Bad stuff happens and it changes us. You can't let your grief keep you from being happy, from living."

"I know that now." She nodded. "I'm sorry I was such an asshole." Her blonde mane was wild, her eyes red-rimmed, and though there was dried slobber on the side of her mouth, Jamie never looked more beautiful. Ryder preferred the unplugged, acoustic version. It was a rare, deep cut that she only shared with a select few. He felt blessed to be in the number.

"You have nothing to be sorry about, James," Ryder assured her, placing a kiss on her tearstained cheek. She tasted salty. They were two imperfect peas in a pod, both lost until they found each other.

"I love you, Napoleon," she breathed.

Ryder's heart nearly stopped beating. He gripped her shoulders, applying more pressure than he intended, but the gravity of her words knocked him down to earth. "What did you say?"

"I love you," she repeated, her gaze locked on his. She didn't waver. There wasn't a shred of doubt or uncertainty. She didn't say it to fill a void. She meant every word.

Water leaked from his eyes. "Say it again," he insisted, pulling her on top of him. His hands fisted in her hair.

"I love you so fucking much."

Ryder's lips crashed onto hers and with a single kiss, he broke through the last of her walls.

He was crying.

She was crying.

The air between them changed. It was no longer sad, but hopeful. Hopeful for a future. Hopeful for a family of their own. Jamie didn't need saving, she needed to be loved, and he swore right then and there to love her forever.

TWENTY-FOUR

Fix You

Jamie

Stillness was a foreign concept to Jamie. To be still. She couldn't remember the last time she felt so utterly calm. She wasn't even a calm child. She was chaos, she'd always been chaos, but in the weeks since her birthday, she was peace.

Spring morphed into summer and life went on. Kensie returned home from the South Pacific with bronzed skin and stars in her eyes. They talked, each woman apologized for the part they played in their argument, each eager to move on. Fighting over white lies and missed birthday parties seemed childish in the grand scheme of things.

Everything wasn't rainbows and sunshine, though. Ryder was right. Sometimes people needed space to grow, and Jamie would give Kensie space. Ryder was Jamie's soul, but Kensington was her heart. Deep down, both women wanted the same things. Each wanted to be happy, each wanted the same happiness for the other, and if Trey was that for her bestie, then she'd back off, for now.

For Jamie, happiness was never Chanel bags or fancy trips to romantic vacation destinations. Happiness was falling asleep staring into sleepy, hazel eyes, and waking up with a kink in her back from sleeping on the old mattress. It was in the way he loved her, the way he protected her, and even in the way he possessed her. Happiness was kissing the *Catch-22* tattoo on his collarbone before gently rolling out of bed. It was in the sound of her heels *click-clacking* on the pavement as she walked up the long staircase of the glass and stone building.

Jamie had an early start that morning. She was off to meet Ruben and Frank at the Board of Education to speak with the superintendent of schools about a controversial budget cut to King County. She stopped for coffee on the way, figuring it was the least she could do for her mentors. "I think we should set up shop at the top of the steps," Ruben suggested, taking a sip from his venti cup.

"That sounds good." Frank dipped his hand casually into the pocket of his slacks. "What do you think, Jamie?" he asked. Frank taught her more in a few short months than four years of journalism ever had. Frank was ready to pass the baton. He was at the end of his run and looked forward to retirement. He didn't treat her like a rookie, but as an equal. The older man let her make decisions and often deferred to her judgment.

"Yeah, sounds good," she nodded as her phone rang. It was too early for Ryder to be awake. The guys played a show in Portland the night before and he hadn't rolled into bed until well after three in the morning. Fishing the cell from her pocket, she groaned, peering at the display. "Sorry, it's my mother. Just give me five minutes."

Jamie turned, taking a deep breath before hitting the green answer button. It was the first time she'd spoken to Caroline since Chris' failed coming out party. Jamie sent an email thanking her for the credit card, but got no response.

"Hello?" Jamie sighed, with a roll of her eyes. Her mother giving her the black card was sweet, but she wasn't entirely sure there wasn't some ulterior motive behind it. Something in her gut told her this was merely a collection call.

"James, dear, it's been a while," her mother said, in that waspy tone she spent her life perfecting.

"It has, Mother. Listen, now isn't a good time. I'm on location."

"I won't keep you. I was simply calling to see if you wanted to do lunch?"

"Like you and me?" Jamie asked. She'd never gone into shock before, but she figured this was basically the same thing. It was like she entered the twilight zone. Never once in her twenty-five years, had Jamie and Caroline *done* lunch, ever.

Never.

Ever.

Ever.

"Of course, with me. Don't be so obtuse, James."

"Umm… is everything okay? You aren't sick or anything, are you?"

"Can't a mother meet her daughter for lunch without having a terminal illness?"

"A *mother* can," she said, leaving the, *but you've never been a mother,* hanging in the air between them.

Ruben cleared his throat, shooting Jamie an exasperated look. He jammed a finger into the face of his watch. They were running out of time. The plan was to catch the superintendent on his way into the building. If they missed him, they would have to scramble to put together an alternative piece for the noon broadcast.

"I'll let you choose the restaurant," Caroline added with a deceptively sweet edge to her tone.

"There's a diner on Seventh Street. I'll text you the address." There was no point in delaying the inevitable. The weighty black AmEx in her wallet solidified Jamie's fate. At least this way, she would have home field advantage.

𝄞

One o'clock rolled around and despite a successful ambush of the school board director, Jamie felt as if she was the one being exposed for taking money from underprivileged children. White strips of paper laid discarded in a heap on the table, the result of her nervously twisting and untwisting a stack of napkins into shreds.

It was lunch time; the diner was overrun with blue collar workers looking for a quick and hearty meal before heading back out to reality. The bell chimed and Jamie's eyes flew to the door. Caroline blew in like a tornado, turning heads with each swing of her Chanel clad legs. She walked with the determination of a runway model, a side effect of being told she was perfect her entire life. She oozed confidence and wealth, sticking out amongst the working-class crowd like a sore thumb.

Annette wrinkled her nose, dropping a Shirley Temple on the table. "I take it that's her?" she asked out the side of her mouth.

"Unfortunately," Jamie said, shrinking down into the booth. As much as she dreaded this little family reunion, she was most nervous about Annette meeting Caroline. She was even more terrified of how her mother would react to Annette.

"There you are, James. When I suggested you pick the restaurant, I wasn't expecting something so, *quaint*." Pulling the designer sunglasses from her face, Caroline turned her head from left to right, taking in the black and white checkered linoleum walls covered with yellowing photographs in glossy black frames. Her nose was turned up so high her head might as well have been in the clouds.

"They have good food." Jamie flashed Annette an apologetic glance, before smiling tightly at her mother.

"But do they have vodka?" Ah yes, vodka, Caroline's main source of sustenance, but Jamie understood her mother's semi-alcoholic tendencies. If she were married to a man like her father, she'd be a day drinker too.

Annette shifted, placing her body between Caroline and Jamie in a protective stance. "I'm afraid not," she supplied, her back ramrod straight.

"Of course, not." Caroline narrowed her eyes. Jamie could see the wheels spinning in her mother's mostly empty brain as she tried to figure out who the imposing force shielding her from her daughter was. "I'll have water then, flat, as I supposed sparkling isn't an option either."

"I can drop an Alka Seltzer in it if you'd like," Annette shrugged.

Jamie choked back a laugh as Caroline shot Annette an unamused look. This was why she insisted on meeting here. Annette was a momma bear through and through. Her presence confirmed that Jamie made the right choice. Money wasn't everything. It didn't help her when she'd lost her baby. It didn't save her when she wanted to kill herself, and it didn't teach her how to love and be loved.

Caroline couldn't intimidate her or make her feel less than, not at the diner, not with her guardian angel standing watch.

"You wanted to see me, Mother?" Jamie asked as her mother slid cautiously into the booth.

"Yes, James." Caroline folded her hands on the table. A look that could only be described as sheer and unadulterated panic flashed through her eyes before she quickly lifted her palms, grimacing at the ever-present layer of syrup that now coated her delicate skin. Jamie should have warned her, then again, this was more fun. "This place is disgusting," her mother shuddered.

"They have great pie."

Jamie's mother tilted her head to the side in that way she sometimes did when she was biting her tongue. It was for show. Caroline didn't have a filter and Jamie knew it was a matter of time before whatever awful thing she was thinking came out of her mouth. Fortunately, or unfortunately, Jamie didn't have to wait long.

"Do you think pie is the best idea, James?" Caroline held her hands up in surrender. "Look, I know curvy is trendy, but you need to be careful. Remember Grandma Manning? The women on your father's side of the family are a little more on the round side, which means you have to work twice as hard to stay fit. It's genetics."

Leave it to Jamie's mom to find a way to use science to call her fat. It was like she had a PhD in *how to chip away at Jamie's self-esteem*. "Mother, I am perfectly healthy and fit. I refuse to starve myself because then, I'd be as unhappy as you." The ridiculousness of the situation hit her in that moment. She was worried this entire thing was some grand ploy to lure her into Jared's arms, when in reality, it was just another way for Caroline to dig her claws into her daughter. Jamie stood to leave.

"It's not so bad," Caroline said with a shrug, "you get use to it."

Her words momentarily stunned Jamie, causing her to plop back down into the booth. Absently, she wondered if her mother was talking about the being hungry part or the unhappy part.

"Both," Caroline said, answering her unspoken thought.

Annette came back with the water and somehow, Jamie managed to pick her jaw up off the sticky table.

Do not pity her.

Do not pity her.

Do not pity her.

She chanted. Caroline wasn't a victim of circumstance. She chose Archer just as much as he'd chosen her. They were a match made in elitist heaven.

"Have you ladies decided what you want to eat?" Annette asked.

Jamie ordered a salad, to keep the peace, and Caroline wrinkled her nose, informing everyone within earshot of her plan to go to a *real restaurant* when they were finished there. Ryder's mom rolled her eyes and walked away. It was probably best Caroline didn't order anything. Annette, while generally agreeable, would have without a doubt fucked with her food.

"Why are we here?" Jamie asked, cutting to the chase. She needed to get back to the station, and back to her life post Manning Empire.

"I want you to talk to your father," Caroline stated flatly.

Jamie blinked slowly, deliberately. Talking to Archer wasn't the problem. Archer was the problem. Nothing was ever simple with her father. Everything was a negotiation and he didn't have anything she wanted.

"James, be reasonable. Everyone has a—"

"—role to play in the Manning Empire," Jamie finished. She

knew the company song by heart at this point. "I've played my part. I'm done, and tell Daddy to stay out of my personal life."

"But what about your trust?" Caroline huffed, slapping the table in frustration. She didn't even flinch at the stickiness this time.

"I don't want it."

"I don't like the idea of you being out in the world alone. Unhappy is better than alone, believe me." It was the nicest thing Caroline ever said to Jamie. Completely backwards and flawed, but for Caroline, it was almost sweet.

"Mother, I'm not alone. I have Kensie, and Chris, and Parker, and a man who loves me."

"Kensington is on the fast track to becoming Mrs. Knight. Christopher, well, this isn't about him. That boy of yours is nothing. Jared is handsome, and smart, and well off. You could do worse."

"Ryder is smart, sensitive, and talented."

"I.e. he's broke," Caroline scoffed.

"Everything isn't about money," Jamie countered.

"Oh, but James, it is, and the sooner you grow up and realize this boy, as fun as he may be, isn't what's best for you, the better." The two women stared at each other, a standoff of sorts, neither willing to concede. While Jamie appreciated her mother's dysfunctional attempt at compassion, this conversation was over.

Annette returned with a plate of lasagna and dropped it down in front of Jamie before turning to glare at Caroline. "My son is the only thing she needs," she growled.

Jamie was shocked by the ferocity in her tone, but also something inside her felt warm, cherished, a feeling her mother never once evoked. Caroline's eyes darted between Jamie and Annette and back again before understanding wrinkled her brow—rather, should have wrinkled, but Botox.

"Now I get it." A bitter laugh escaped Caroline's throat, the sound both high pitched and incredulous. "Did you know *my* daughter gave up five million dollars to be with your son?" Jamie didn't miss the possessive tilt to the word "my".

"You did what?" Annette shrieked, looking down at Jamie. Grasping at her chest, she scooted her way into the booth. The bell above the door rang again. Pots and pans clanked and clacked in the kitchen. The lunch rush was in full swing, but Annette just sat there, staring at Jamie as if she'd grown a second head.

"Not you too," Jamie groaned.

"Listen, Kitty Cat," Annette began, wrapping an arm around Jamie, "my son is a catch, and you two are perfect for each other, but five million dollars is a lot to walk away from without some serious thought."

"Exactly, James," Caroline cooed, awkwardly grabbing her hand. Caroline didn't do the doting mother, but she was a competitive bitch. The sight of another woman comforting Jamie was enough to make her pretend.

Jamie slipped her hand from her mother's grasp. "I don't want Jared. If Ry and I broke up tomorrow I still wouldn't be with Jared, not for money or for the Manning Empire, or because I don't want to be alone, but because that money comes with strings. I'm done being Daddy's little puppet."

"You feel that way now. I get it. I was you. You think I was in love with your father when we married?"

"I guess." Jamie never really thought about it. Her parents weren't the lovey-dovey type. They weren't affectionate unless it was for show. She'd never run into them in an embrace, never caught them kissing, never heard sex noises from outside their door. In Jamie's head, they only ever had sex twice, once when she was conceived and once when her brother was.

"Of course, not. He's ten years older than me and I had a beau, but I knew my place, and the boy from the wrong side of the tracks who gave me mind-blowing orgasms wasn't my future."

"Mother," Jamie cringed, dropping her forehead on the sticky table.

"What? That's what you see in this Ryder, isn't it?"

"What they have is more than sex," Annette said, rubbing

Jamie's back.

"Kill me now, please God, just kill me."

"James, stop being dramatic. You're twenty-five years old. This is life. Think of it as a TED talk." Jamie lifted her head and let it drop back on the table over and over. The thought of her mother giving anyone a TED talk was laughable. "Jared can take care of you. You can quit your little job and make time to do the things you love, like shop, and travel. This life isn't all bad."

Annette snorted at that. "Kitty Cat loves her job." She knew Jamie better than her own mother did.

Her mother's lips pursed like she smelled something sour. "Kitty Cat? Really? A stripper name, James?"

"Kitty Cat," Annette confirmed, with a raise of her chin. "She's happy. She's telling you she's happy. Why wouldn't you want that for her?"

"Happiness is overrated. Look at me, I haven't been happy in twenty-eight years and I'm doing just fine."

Goddamn it, Jamie thought to herself. She promised she wouldn't let her mother weaken her resolve, but that was the saddest thing she'd ever heard her say. "I am not you, mother. I'll never be you, and I know that's disappointing, but I have to live for me."

Caroline regarded her for a beat, then slipped her Chanel sunglasses into place. "I guess we're done here. If you change your mind, you know where to find me." She rose, straightening her tweed blazer, also Chanel. "Annette, I would say it was a pleasure, but that would be a lie." With that she was gone.

Annette rolled her eyes. "Never leave my grandchildren alone with that woman."

TWENTY-FIVE

1+1

RYDER

"Honey, I'm home," Ryder called. The front door slammed shut behind him. Shuffling the takeout bags to one hand, he used the other to lift his guitar over his shoulder and set it on the stairs. The house was quiet.

The guys had been at the bar revamping their set for their upcoming show at the University of Oregon. Afterwards, Javi left for his nephew's first birthday and CT made one of his rare pilgrimages home.

Ryder and Jamie had the house to themselves for the first time and he planned to take advantage of every second.

"Kitty Cat?" he tried again. The smell of baked goods wafted through the air, tipping Ryder off as to the whereabouts of his girlfriend. They hadn't spoken much that day. She left before he woke up and the only communication he'd received was a text saying she was meeting her mother for lunch, which he guessed was why she was baking.

"In the kitchen," Jamie answered and Ryder couldn't help the grin glued on his face. The sound of her voice made his heart do back flips. Yes, he realized that made him a complete, fucking pussy and no, he didn't care.

Jamie stood at the counter, hunched over a mixing bowl that she must have brought over from her place. The only bowls the guys owned were good for cereal and not much else. Ryder sat the food on the kitchen island and wrapped his arms around Jamie's waist. Her hair was piled high onto her head. She wore one of his t-shirts and a pair of his boxers were rolled onto her hips.

"That smells good," he said into her hair. The scent of her fruity shampoo was the best welcome home he'd ever received.

"Thank you. It's the base for my cheesecake. Basically, a thin brownie," she explained, still distracted by whatever it was she was doing with the bowl.

"I love cheesecake." Ryder's hands traveled up her ribcage and he was pleasantly surprised to find that she wasn't wearing a bra. He rolled her nipples as his tongue glided down the shell of her ear.

"Ry," she half-moaned, half-whined. "Do you realize how hard it is to beat cheesecake batter with a hand mixer? You feeling me up is making it exponentially more difficult."

"I've got faith in you, Kitty Cat," he grinned, continuing his assault on her tits.

"You're a dick."

"And you're making *my* dick very hard." He pushed his hips into her ass to drive the point home.

At that, she chuckled, powering the little whirling torture device down and turning in his arms. "How was your day Dear?"

"It was kind of epic," he said, because it kind of was. "We spent the day working on new shit and smoking some of the dankest weed we've had since Cali." *Acapulco Gold.* Javi got it because he said it was Mexican, like him.

"This all sounds *so* epic," Jamie teased.

"Let me finish." His voice was garbled. He wanted to tell her about his day, but he also wanted to fuck her into next week. His dick was stealing the blood from his brain and they had about a ten-minute window before Jamie was face down, ass up. Cheesecake, be damned. "Anyway, you know when you're high and you just talk about random, fake-deep shit?"

"Yes. You guys are the kings of it," she said adding a splash of vanilla into the bowl.

"Well, yeah, true. Javi was going off about the *Saved by the Bell* episode, when Jessie was addicted to caffeine pills."

"The *'I'm so excited... I'm so... I'm so...'*"

Ryder chuckled at her surprisingly accurate impersonation. "Yeah, that one. Javi was going on and on about how he felt like Jessie, between working at his brother's shop and band shit. Like he got why she resorted to such extreme measures—"

"It was caffeine, not crack," Jamie deadpanned.

"Will you let me finish?" Ryder admonished, yanking hard on her messy bun. Her head snapped back, leaving her neck exposed. He licked, then bit her flesh, sucking until it turned a bright shade of pink.

"Okay, I'm sorry," she giggled.

"Promise?" he said, biting her again. The sound of her giggle made his dick ache. He wanted to spin her around and fuck her over the counter, but he still hadn't managed to tell her his good fucking news.

Jamie ran her thumb and index finger across her lips, zipping them. "I promise."

"Anyway," he paused dramatically, "that's when CT came up with the idea of us quitting our jobs and doing music full-time."

"Wait, what?" she asked, pushing him back. "You're what?"

"I'm quitting my job to play rock stars with my friends," he smirked.

Jamie's mouth popped open, her lips made a little "O" shape, that he couldn't help but kiss. "Is that... smart?"

"Who the fuck knows?" he shrugged. "But we are tired of turning down gigs because we can't get time off. We're selling a shit ton of t-shirts and *Sex God* is doing okay on iTunes. CT said he'd cover rent and bills here for a year so we can give this a real shot."

Ry and Javi asked the same questions themselves when CT first brought it up, but the more he talked, the more they were convinced. CT was loaded. He didn't flaunt his wealth. He'd driven the same old school Mustang for as long as Ryder had known him. He lived off his wages from the gym, only dipping into his trust when they weren't enough to cover overhead expenses. The drummer was impulsive, sure, but he was also smart as fuck. He made his own way in this world so the fact that he was willing to use Carter Thayer's fortune, to further CT and Lithium Springs' dream, gave Ryder the motivation he needed to call Liz and tell her he wouldn't be back.

"Holy shit," Jamie gasped.

"I know and that's not all. I stopped at that place you like, the Indian Fusion restaurant, whatever that means, and got your overpriced Tandoori Chicken, because I'm responsible." He laughed, but there wasn't anything funny about how much that shit cost. He knew a little place around the corner that gave twice the food at half the price. "My roommates are gone and I figured we can celebrate my unemployment and you being five million dollars poorer by fucking in as many rooms as we can before they get back."

"God, we're such losers." Jamie giggled, and again his heart did that thing it did whenever he heard the sound.

Ryder dipped his thumbs into the waistband of Jamie's boxers, letting them fall down her legs. "Happy losers," he said with a grin, then with a kiss.

Jamie and Ryder fucked on the kitchen counter. He ate her out on the couch, then she came on his fingers in the shower.

Two-hours later, Ryder woke up to find Jamie sitting crossed-legged on the floor with her computer in her lap and newspaper clippings scattered everywhere.

He watched in amusement as she worked in silence. She was beautiful when she went into work mode, slightly scary, but gorgeous. Watching her was like watching a chase scene in the *Fast and Furious*. Every move was choreographed to the second. Her fingers would glide over the keys, stilling every so often. Her bright greens would focused on the words, then there was the scowl, his favorite part. With her lips turned down, she'd scribble frantically in her notebook, then her fingers would hit the keys again.

Wash.

Rinse.

Repeat.

Ryder climbed out of bed, his mattress squeaked under the pressure, but Jamie's fingers never stopped moving. He toed over to the dresser and swiped his sketch pad. Between Lithium Springs and spending time with Kitty Cat, he rarely sketched anymore. He leaned against the cheap wood, studying her angles for a minute, maybe longer. The curve of her jaw, the arch of her back, the pucker of her lips. She was poetry. She was art. She was the cutest little hunchback he'd ever seen. His hand moved on autopilot as he pressed the charcoal to the page, quickly sketching her form.

"What are you doing?" she asked, not bothering to look up from her work.

"Drawing you," he muttered, also not bothering to look up.

"Now?" she shrieked. "I look like shit." Jamie freed her hair from the messy bun and quickly ran her fingers through.

Ryder didn't have the heart to tell her that only made it worse. What he did say wasn't much better. "Since when do you care?"

"Okay, one—fuck you. Two—I don't want to be immortalized in your sketch pad looking like I haven't showered in days," she huffed, climbing up to her feet. She stretched, tugging up the too big shorts hanging from her body. The thrill of seeing her in his clothes never went away. It probably never would.

Ryder rolled his eyes and dropped the notebook before taking her in his arms. "You. Are. Beautiful," he said, punctuating each word with a kiss.

Leaning up on her tiptoes, Jamie returned the gesture. "I. Am. Hungry."

He chuckled. "I think there's more of that chicken we can't afford downstairs."

"That sounds amazing," she moaned. The sound quickly drowned out by the frantic ringing of her phone. Jamie padded over to the nightstand to retrieve it. *It's Chris,* she mouthed, before answering. "Hey little brother... Oh, Parker, hi, what's wrong?" Her eyes flew to Ryder's and the amusement drained from her face. Gripping the edge of the nightstand for support, she choked, "which hospital?"

A low buzz emitted from the fluorescent lights overhead as Jamie and Ryder rushed through the emergency room doors. The stench of bleach filled the air, causing Ryder's stomach to roll. The urge to turn around and walk back out the sliding glass was strong, but his desire to protect the woman beside him, manically gnawing on her knuckle, was stronger.

Ryder had spent his fair share of time in hospital waiting rooms, clinging to his mother's battered form. Once, while she waited to have her broken nose set after running into a door (*his father's fist*), and another time, when she fractured her ankle tripping over a shoe, (*his dad pushed her down the stairs*). Those moments were burned in his memories. They were what he saw every time he thought about making amends with his mother. How could she talk to him after all that? His brain wouldn't accept it.

The small waiting room was quiet and eerily still. A slight Asian woman, with a child draped across her lap, sat in the corner. Her face was stoic but her eyes betrayed her. *Worry.* No doubt about the sleeping little boy snuggled into her waist. An older man with a gruff exterior stood against the opposite wall, his white-gray head rested against a poster spouting the importance of washing your hands. Then there was Parker. He sat on the floor with his knees pulled into his chest. His eyes were puffy, and he rocked back and forth methodically.

Jamie's hand tightened around Ryder's. It was the first sign of life he'd seen since they'd hastily thrown on clothes and made the drive to the hospital. He feared she was shutting down, shutting him out again, but that tiny squeeze of his hand reassured him that his Jamie was still there.

"Parker," she said. Her tone was soft, but echoed in the soundless space. Dropping to her knees she asked, "What happened?"

Parker met Jamie's gaze, his voice broken. "We got home from a late dinner. I was in the shower and the next thing I know, Chris was stumbling into the bathroom, doubled over, saying his stomach hurt. He'd been complaining about it for the last couple of days. I told him he should see a doctor, I swear, but he insisted it was nothing. It was his appendix. People can die from that."

"It's okay," Jamie murmured, rubbing soothing strokes up and down his arm. "He's going to be okay. Where is he now?"

Parker sucked in a breath, doing his best to compose himself. "They took him back for emergency surgery, and told me to wait here. Since I'm not family they can't tell me anything. Can you believe that? I love that man, and I know him better than anyone else, but none of it matters. I can't be there for him when he needs me most."

"Park, you're here. It matters," Jamie assured, but her voice was drowned out by the ominous sound of high heels slamming into linoleum.

Click-clack.
Click-clack.
Click-clack.

Everyone in the waiting room turned to see the older, blonde woman sashaying through the entrance. Watching her was trippy.

It was like Ryder was looking into a funhouse mirror version of his girlfriend. Her blonde hair was pulled back into a low bun, and despite the hour and the gravity of the situation, she looked like she'd been professionally styled for the occasion. Not a single hair out of place.

"James, Parker, boy for whom James gave up her trust," the woman shrilled.

"You know his name, Mother," Jamie drawled in annoyance. She and Parker rose to their feet. Parker placed a kiss on her cheek, then she and Jamie did this awkward hug, shuffle thing.

"Parker, dear, Archer is under a lot of stress right now thanks to these two," she said flicking her wrist at Kitty Cat. "I understand your feelings for my son, but please try to keep it together when my husband gets here."

Parker and Jamie looked at each other, stunned. "Did Chris tell you?" they asked in unison.

"I'm not blind," Caroline huffed in annoyance. "My husband is a busy man. He doesn't always pay attention to what's going on at home, but I do. I know my children. Christopher looks at you the way the felon is looking at James."

Jamie stared at her mother with wide-eyed shock. Silence descended on the waiting room while everyone tried to process what was happening. Ryder didn't know much about Jamie's family dynamic, but he did know Chris and Parker's official relationship status was kept secret from their parents. Apparently, Jamie's mother wasn't as clueless as she pretended to be.

The doors swooshed open again, and though Ryder had never met the man, he knew it was Jamie's dad without a doubt.

Burt. Fucking. Eastwood.

He wore a black turtleneck, gray slacks, and the face of the fucking devil. Instinctively, Ryder tightened his grip on Jamie, pulling her away from her mother. Caroline, as Parker called her, clicked her tongue disapprovingly, shooting him a look that said, *knock it off.*

Jamie's dad looked every bit the part of imposing CEO. He stood tall, but not as tall as Ryder. His dark hair was gray at the temples, and his gait was sure, like he owned the place and everyone in it. His brow creased as he glanced around the waiting room. He spotted them and relief washed across his face as his eyes met his wife's, but it was short lived. Ryder could see the steam coming from his ears as he walked towards them. Ryder's hand slid around Jamie's mid-section and he pulled her closer, flush against his chest, partly to stake his claim and partly to keep himself from lunging at the bastard.

"Archer, you made it," Caroline greeted her husband. The two had an odd dynamic. They were husband and wife, but the way they interacted was more like a business partnership, and less like a relationship. It was all so professional, not one ounce of passion or love; comfortable, but not entirely familiar.

Archer's gaze stayed on Ryder as he spoke. "Parker, what happened?"

"They think it's his appendix."

Jamie's dad nodded tersely. "Well, we want to thank you for bringing him in. You look exhausted and I'm sure you have more important things to do with your Saturday than wait around the emergency room. Go, enjoy the rest of your night, and take James' friend with you."

"I'm not leaving him."

"I'm not leaving her."

Both men spoke in unison.

"Well then," Caroline sighed, pinching the bridge of her nose, "let's have a seat."

The group went and sat along the left wall. A television was mounted in the corner, WSEA-9 played silently in the background. Caroline sat between Parker and her husband, while Ryder pulled Jamie onto his lap across from them.

"James," her mother said tightly, "don't you think it would be more appropriate to take your own seat?"

Jamie sighed, rolling her green eyes as she moved to stand, but Ryder held her into place. "She's fine," he bit. He knew he was pushing his luck, but these people were done controlling her.

"James, will you tell your friend—" Archer began.

"I'm not her friend." There was a challenge buried just beneath Ryder's words. His hate for Archer blurred his vision. This man was the reason Jamie was so broken. He placed expectations on her body, and set limitations on her heart. Ry fought like hell, wading through all the muck inside Kitty Cat's head and he'd be damned if he'd let her backslide now.

"You're not her boyfriend either," Archer stated matter-of-factly.

"Archer," Caroline warned, "this isn't the time nor is it the place."

Archer ignored his wife. He ignored the devastation on his daughter and Parker's faces. His focus wasn't on his son being in surgery. It was on Ryder's hand on Jamie's thigh. He was under his skin. Ry presented a threat to his precious empire. "You aren't half the man Jared is. She will never choose you over her family."

"You aren't her family. I am." Ryder's lips twisted into a condescending smirk. "She calls me Daddy more than she does you."

"Enough," Parker yelled. The woman in the corner holding the little boy looked over at them with a pointed glare. "Chris is in there fighting for his life and you two are having some weird dick measuring contest."

"It's his appendix Park, you're being a little dramatic," Archer chided.

"No, you're being an asshole. Your son is in surgery and your daughter and wife are upset and all you can think of is your failing, fucking company."

"Watch yourself, son."

"No, this is sick. You can't control them anymore. I've never seen Jamie smile as much as she does when she's with him," he said pointing to Ryder.

Archer's jaw ticked. "I think it's time for you to go, Parker."

"I'm not going anywhere. You are the one who isn't wanted here, not by Jamie and not by Chris."

"How would you know what my children want? They don't even

know what they want. They're young and rebellious but they'll fall in line."

"Jamie gave up five million dollars to get away from you, and Chris—"

"—is none of your concern," Archer said, his brow raised in challenge.

Parker chuckled, but there was no humor in the sound. "Chris calls me daddy more than he does you," he hissed before storming towards the nurse's station.

Ryder laughed, a deep, belly laugh and Jamie elbowed him in the rib. "Stop," she gritted, standing. "I'm going to check on Park."

A fuming Archer grabbed his daughter by the elbow and yanked her back. Ryder saw red. He moved without thinking. Before he could stop himself, he was on his feet. Rearing back, he swung so hard he felt the crunch of cartilage breaking under his fist. The impact sent Archer backwards into the chair.

"If you ever touch her again, I will fucking kill you."

TWENTY-SIX

Soldier's Poem

Jamie

"You shouldn't have hit him," Jamie sighed, walking Ryder out to her car. A million possible outcomes ran through her mind and none of them were good. "Did you see his face? It was exactly what he wanted." There was no masking Archer's twisted pleasure. It was his *gotcha face*. Her father was a calculating son of a bitch, and Jamie could see the wheels spinning the minute he spotted Ryder in the waiting room. Archer's eyes never strayed far from him. It was more than intimidation, he studied him.

This was her fault. She knew better than to bring Ryder with her, but she had been so shaken when she got off the phone with Parker, he'd refused to let her drive.

"He shouldn't have put his hands on you," Ryder grunted, his hazels darkening to chocolate pools of wrath.

Her steps faltered and her eyes burned as she looked at him. The bright LED lights dotted throughout the parking lot made everything shine with a startling clarity. "Baby," she said, wrapping her arms around his neck. "I love that you protect me, but he's my dad, he wouldn't—"

"Stop with that shit. He pimped you out at sixteen, he's still trying to pimp you out. Don't fucking defend him to me."

"I'm not. I'm just worried about my brother and I don't need to worry about you, too." It wasn't entirely the truth, she was *already* worried about Ryder. He was her true north, her sex god. The bright and shiny star in her otherwise gray existence.

"Kitty Cat, I'm not afraid of your father. I want to go back in there and kick his ass."

"Please, just go home," she begged. She'd get on her knees if she had too. "I'll be there once I find out what's going on with Chris."

Ryder's jaw ticked and his grip on her waist tightened. She could tell he wanted to argue, but was holding back. "Text me when you're ready and I'll come pick you up."

"No, I don't want you to come back here," she implored. Jamie didn't want Ryder, her angel, anywhere near the devil.

"I'll get an Uber. I want you to be able to bail if you need to." He fished her car keys out of his pocket and handed them to her. He had a point. It was always a good idea to have an escape plan when dealing with her family.

Six minutes later, a burgundy Corolla pulled to a stop in front of them. The pit in Jamie's stomach grew. She wished he could stay, but it was too risky. "I love you, Napoleon."

"I love you, James." Ryder pressed a kiss on her temple, and she watched as he slid into the backseat. "Call me as soon as you find out about your brother."

"I promise." Jamie stayed rooted in place, watching as the car drove off. She brought her tattooed finger to her lips and exhaled. The feel of warm breath against her skin reminded her to keep going, to keep fighting, so that's exactly what she did.

Her keys jingled with each step towards the ER, the rattle of discord. Her father looked deranged, gauze shoved in his nose, a smirk etched on his face. This was bad, she knew, but she held her head high because in her family, appearances meant more than feelings.

If Archer sensed her worry he'd attack, nipping at her flesh until it was stripped to the bone. The Devil, her father, was a vulture, and nothing, not even his own seed, would stand in the way of him and his next meal.

"Are you okay?" she asked despite herself. She didn't care one way or the other, but she didn't know what else to say.

"I'm better than I've been in a long while, James."

A security guard approached, clipboard in hand. "Sir, would you like me to call the police?"

The police. Jamie hadn't thought of it, but now that the words were out there floating in the atmosphere, she couldn't think of anything else. Images of Ryder flashed in her brain. Him with his hands cuffed behind his back, standing shoulder to shoulder in a line up, his crumpled face behind a thick wall of bullet proof glass, every awful thing she knew about prison from television assaulted her.

Archer's eyes lit up with dubious intent. "What do you think, James? Your little felon attacked me. Should he be punished?"

"No," Jamie cried, her gaze darting from her father to the security officer, "It was a family squabble. My brother is in surgery, things got a little heated, but it's fine. Everything is going to be fine."

"Is it?" Archer's voice was low, menacing.

She knew, in that moment, she fucking knew, he had her. Jamie's heart stopped. The world stopped. A catch twenty-two. Her shoulders slumped in defeat as she whispered, "It is."

The security officer looked again to Archer. "Would you prefer coming with me to give your official version of events?" he asked, clicking the top of his pen.

"It's like my daughter said, just a family squabble, best to handle it amongst ourselves, but thank you," he said, his eyes locked on Jamie.

The officer pulled a card from the clipboard and handed it to Archer. "Call if anything should change."

"Will do." Archer nodded, pocketing the card.

Jamie returned to her seat. Her mother watched her, but didn't speak. The Asian woman and her child were gone. The old man was gone. Parker was gone. The Manning's were left alone to resume their negotiations.

"Your brother is a faggot," Archer stated, coolly. The Manning children thought their parents were so wrapped up in their own lives, their own wants, that they didn't have time to pay attention to them. Jamie should have known better.

Caroline let out a huff of annoyance, "don't say that word. It isn't PC."

"I don't give a damn about politically correct. James has attempted to throw away her future for a goddamn busboy, and Christopher, well, he and Parker will *never* happen."

"What about James?" Caroline asked.

"Jared still wants her."

"But, Daddy—"

"No," Archer boomed, "you will end things with that boy or I will unleash the full force of my legal team on him. He will go to jail, and I will use every penny in your trust to ensure he rots. He has a record of violent crimes. Did you know that?"

"He was a teenager, it's sealed." Jamie croaked, fighting back the sob threatening to tear from her throat.

"That doesn't mean it disappears, James, it only means it won't show up on a background check. But make no mistake, the courts will know. And I'm sure there is video of his latest vicious attack," Archer said, pointing to the camera mounted in the corner behind them.

"He hit you, once, and you deserved it."

"He also threatened to kill me. I'm afraid for my life."

Jamie dug her fingers into the side of her leg. She itched to pull out her phone and Google the possible ramifications.

"Four months minimum," her father grinned a bloody grin, "but I've got good lawyers. They'll push for a year, and with the death threat," he whistled, grimacing from the pain the action caused, "it may even be longer."

Jamie fought hard to swallow back the sob. Ryder was on the edge of the abyss, looking to dive head first into a life he and the guys fought for. They were going to be rock stars. She couldn't let him go to jail.

"What's it going to be, James? Break up with him and he goes free, or sign up for a life of bus trips and conjugal visits."

"Leave him alone and I'll do whatever you want." She would do anything for Ryder, even if that meant setting him free.

Archer laughed, the sound dripped with contention. "Not what, James, but who."

"Is that him again?" Chris asked, as Jamie silenced her phone.

"Yeah," she muttered sadly, before turning it off altogether. It'd been three days since she last spoke to Ryder. Three days since he rode an Uber off into the sunset, off to his destiny, a destiny that no longer included her. It hurt, cutting him off without warning, but it was what Archer demanded.

She cried for twenty-four hours straight. They were ugly, brutal tears of heartache. The tears of love and of loss. It was a pain she knew. It was the same pain she felt when they took her baby.

Love was selfless.

Jamie gave up her happiness so that Ryder could live his dreams. He'd move on, find someone worthy of him. Although the thought hurt, it gave her strength. Her suffering didn't have to be his. She'd do it, just like her mother, she'd live a life without joy. Without Ryder, there was no reason to fight, no reason to rebel. Archer would find any flicker of happiness and snuff it out too.

"You should answer," Chris said from his spot on the bed. "At least tell him why you stopped taking his calls."

"Daddy said no more contact." She said mechanically, robotically.

"Since when do you listen to Dad?" he argued.

"Since he threatened to take away the only man I ever loved."
Silence.

Her words struck a chord. Jamie didn't mention Parker's absence. She didn't need to. It engulfed them like a wool blanket, heating the room to an uncomfortable temperature.

"Manning Solutions isn't doing well," Chris whispered, "that's why he's pushing Jared on to you. It was a hostile takeover, or rather it was supposed to be. Dad's a good negotiator. He always says, *everyone has a weakness, and once you figure it out, you can make the impossible, possible.* Dad noticed the way Jared's eyes never strayed far from the family picture hanging in his office. He would have given him mom if that's what he wanted, but it was you."

Jamie stared out the window of her brother's hospital room. He was being discharged today, finally strong enough to go home. Chris would finish his internship in a few short weeks and head back to the east coast for his senior year. What was to come after was still a mystery. Archer held that card close to his chest, but Jamie knew her brother's time would come.

Everyone had a role to play in the Manning Empire.

"Dad negotiated a merger, citing the mutual benefits his older more established company could have on Jared's fledgling one. The business made sense but Jared's a hunter. He wanted to hang Manning Solutions on his trophy wall, but Dad wasn't going down without a fight. That's when he threw in the sweetener."

"His pretty blonde daughter," Jamie grunted bitterly.

"I swear I didn't know until after you gave up your trust," Chris said. "Jam, you don't have to do this. Fuck Dad and his arbitrary spot on some board."

"No," she shook her head. "I will do anything for Ryder. Just like you put Park on a plane back to Boston to keep him away from that monster, I'll break Ryder's heart to give him a chance at his dream."

"Then what, you go play house with Jared?"

What would happen next? Jamie thought about that a lot over the last three days. She could fight, but deep down she knew that's what he wanted. *Jared's a hunter*, and Jamie was big game. The only way to win this battle was with her surrender. "He'll get bored. I'll let him have me. I'll let him break me and then he'll throw me away."

"That's dark shit, Jam," Chris said. He stood, too fast. Pain twisted his features as he clutched at his right side.

"Are you okay?" she asked, rushing to help him.

"Yeah, I just forgot about these damn staples," he said, lifting his t-shirt to reveal the three-inch incision on his lower abdomen.

The wound would soon heal and a scar would form. A scar similar to her own. The Manning children were casualties of war. Some of their scars were physical—ones you could see. The others, the ones that ran the deepest, the ones that hurt the most, were invisible.

TWENTY-SEVEN

Too Good at Goodbyes

RYDER

Ryder walked up to the front desk, his palms were coated with sweat. He'd only been to Jamie's apartment a handful of times and never without Jamie, but he didn't know what else to do. She'd been dodging him all week. He went to her job, waited outside the gym, he even tried the hospital. Nothing. He hadn't had a full night's sleep since he left in the Uber. His emotions ran the gamut from worried, to sad, to angry, to hopeless. Going to her apartment only solidified his stalker status.

The woman behind the desk was young, a college student maybe. The shiny metal name tag on her mint-green vest read *Jenni*. He smiled his lopsided grin, the one he flashed Kitty Cat that night at the Rabbit Hole, and prayed to God this worked. "Hey, Jenni. I was hoping to surprise my friend. You think you can let me in?"

"Umm, are you on the list?" Jenni blushed.

Ryder pushed out his lips in an exaggerated pout. "Not sure, I'm usually with her."

"Her," Jenni noted, an air of disappointment in her tone.

"Yeah, Jamie Manning in apartment 405."

Jenni's fingers floated over the keyboard. Ryder's heart pounded in beat with each *peck, peck, peck*. "Found her. What's your name?" she asked.

He was tempted to lie, to say Chris or Parker, but something inside of him, his masochistic side, wanted to know if she still cared, even on a subconscious level, or did she cross him off this list like she had crossed him out of her life.

"Napoleon Ryder."

Jenni grinned, "Seriously?"

"My parents were…different," he shrugged. Ryder leaned forward, resting his forearms on the desk. The muscles in his biceps bulged. He lost his shame, when he lost his girl, not that he had much to begin with.

Jenni's stared at his body, slack-jawed, for nearly ten seconds longer than was socially acceptable, before returning her attention to screen. "There you are. Looks like you're good to go," she sighed wistfully.

"Thanks Jenni," he said tipping an imaginary hat towards her.

"Anytime, Napoleon," she chuckled.

The smile on Ryder's face as he sauntered over to the bank of elevators was genuine, brilliant, hopeful. Step one was complete, but step two was where things got tricky. What if she wasn't home, or worse, what if she was, but refused to see him? He had no clue what happened. She ghosted on him without so much as a fuck you, but Ryder fought tooth and nail for Jamie to let him in and wasn't giving up.

The elevator pinged and he stepped inside. No matter what the outcome, he would see this through. The ride up to the fourth floor was quick, the walk to her door even quicker. Ryder built this moment up in his mind all week. He'd rehearsed what he was going to say when he saw her over and over again, but his thoughtfully crafted speech went out the window the moment his knuckles touched the wood.

He needed to feel her, to kiss her, to smell her fruit scented hair. They could fight later, they could fight forever, he just needed her. He knocked again. His hopes diminished more and more with each second that passed. Just as he was about to turn to leave the door swung open, revealing a petite, brown-haired girl in a fluffy white robe. *Kensington not Mackenzie.*

"Are you the Postmate's guy?" she asked. Looking from his face down to his empty hands. Her brow knit in confusion as she stepped behind the door, closing it slightly. Panic flashed in her big, brown eyes.

"Oh, no, sorry," Ryder held his hands up. "I'm actually looking for Kitty... uh, James...Jamie," he stuttered.

"Oh, umm, Jam's not here, but I can tell her you stopped by? What's your name?"

"I'll just catch her later. Uh, sorry again for bothering you," he said, rubbing the back of his neck. He didn't know why he was apologizing. Perhaps he could blame sleep deprivation, depression, or any of the other emotions coursing through his body.

"Wait," Kensie said stepping out into the hall, "are you... you're Ryder, right?"

"Umm, I think I am. I don't feel much like me, though," he muttered, taking the awkwardness to a new level. This was Jamie's best friend and roommate. He had imagined meeting her under different circumstances. He would have been charming and funny, not some sad loser who showed up unannounced to beg her friend to take him back.

Kensie smiled. "I'm glad I finally get to meet the man that turned my bestie into a romantic."

"I take it she didn't tell you she dropped my ass?"

"Jam isn't what you'd call a sharer, but I do know she's in love with you, and in all the years I've known her, she was the happiest she's ever been when she was with you. She was like a flower in full bloom, she brightened up the room with her presence. Your effect on her, how happy you made her, it was a beautiful thing to witness. "

"Then why won't she talk to me? What did I do?" He ran his fingers threw his hair to keep from putting his fist through the wall. Probably not a good idea to scare off his one connection to Jamie.

"It's complicated."

"That's not an excuse to disappear without a fucking goodbye," he snapped.

Kensie took a cautious step toward him. Like he was a cornered animal that she was trying to coax back into its cage. "I know."

"Then why?" he asked pacing the empty hall. "Did I do something?"

"It isn't my place to say."

"Did something happen to her brother?" he asked, halting. He'd been so busy drowning in his own sorrow he didn't think about Chris. Was that the reason? Did she shut down because she couldn't handle another loss?

"God, no. He's fine. I promise," Kensie assured.

"Then it's her dad, right? He's making her do this?"

"You should really talk to her."

"That's what I'm trying to do," he yelled. He couldn't help it. The only thing worse than losing Jamie was not knowing why. The why was important. The why determined how he should fight for her. "Help me?" Ry pleaded.

"She's my best friend. I have to respect her wishes."

Tears burned in his eyes. "I miss her so fucking much. Every time I close my eyes, I see her face. Every time I hear someone with an obnoxious laugh I hope it's Jamie. She's my soul. I just need to see her."

"God, she's going to be so pissed at me," Kensie huffed, pushing a strand of brown hair out of her face.

Ryder's head snapped up. He felt hope for the first time in a week. "Fine. Blame me. Tell her I forced you to help."

"She's at work. She's been taking my car and parking in the lot across the street. It's a black convertible."

"Thank you so much," he said wrapping her in a bear hug and

spinning around. "I owe you one." He was going to talk to Jamie even if he had to sit outside all fucking day.

The sun gleamed off the shiny paint of the black luxury car. Ryder stared, studying it as if it had the answer. Last week he was on top of the world. He quit his job and decided to pursue his dream. He had his girl and his friends, everything was starting to fall into place. But now he was the fucking creeper who waited in a parking lot for two hours, stalking a woman who'd made it clear she wanted nothing to do with him.

He was a fool for thinking his luck could change, that he'd get everything he wished for. That only happened in books and movies. Real life was struggle. Real life was suffering, and the current cause of Ryder's distress was trotting across the street with her phone to her ear.

In the last seven days, Ryder had called Jamie no less than one hundred times. At one point, he thought her phone was broken or lost, and that's why she wasn't calling him back. Then on day two, he feared something was wrong with her, that she was hurt or in an accident. It wasn't until day four that he realized she was just blowing him off. Seeing her living her life as if his absence had no effect made him angry. She was every bit the beautiful fucked up girl he remembered. It looked like she was sleeping soundly at night, like she hadn't miss any meals. Like she was fucking happy. How could that be? Jamie was a savage, he'd always known that, but she was in love with him. How could she be happy without him?

"I just need to run to my apartment first, then I'll meet you there," Jamie said, leaning over to fish her keys from her purse. Her steps faltered as she pointed the key fob towards the car. "I gotta go," she whispered into the phone. Whatever the other person on the other end said made her roll her eyes. "Sure, I can't wait."

"Who's that?" Ry asked. Anger and uncertainty seared his intestines. He knew. He fucking knew, but he needed to hear the words on her lips.

"My boyfriend," she answered. Her words were like a punch to Ryder's gut, but somehow not a surprise.

"Jared," Ryder spat the name out like a curse. Of course, it was Jared. It was always going to be Jared, the rich dick with the thousand percent IQ. Archer told him, Jared told him, but Ryder didn't listen. He's the kind of guy who gets a girl like Kitty Cat. It didn't matter what her heart wanted. All that mattered was pedigree and net worth.

"Yup," she said, the 'P' sound popping on her lips. She turned her head, left and then right, surveying the empty parking lot behind her dark aviators. There was no help, no easy out, it was just Jamie and Ryder and a fleet of news vans. She was going to talk to him. They were going to have this out.

Ryder waited for her to continue. Waited for an explanation. Waited for the bullshit to spill from her mouth. Waited to hear she was doing her father's bidding. Or that she'd second guessed giving up the money. Anything really. But nothing came.

"So, you gave up?" he asked, when he couldn't wait any longer.

"Ry, this was never forever," she said, but he heard the crack in her voice. He was willing to bet sad, green eyes stared back at him from behind her mirrored sunglasses.

"They only win if you let them, Kitty Cat."

"Just let it go. This was fun while it lasted, but it's over now."

"No. I know you love me. I'm not letting you do this to us."

"I don't love you," she said. It was a lie. Ryder felt her love, even now when her words stung, he could bathe in it.

"Take off your sunglasses. Look me in the eye and tell me you don't love me." Her lip quivered, but she remained silent. Ryder took a step towards her and she took a step back. "Don't do this, Kitty Cat. Whatever he threatened you with, whatever it is, we'll get through it." He took another step forward, then another, until they stood toe to toe. She smelled fruity, like his Jamie. It gave him hope. Everything would be okay if she just talked to him.

Jamie waved a shaky finger between them. "I don't want this anymore. It has nothing to do with my dad," she whispered.

"What? James, stop this bullshit right now." Ryder grabbed her face, pushing the sunglasses up over her head. Just as he suspected her eyes were broken, even under the layers of studio make-up he could tell she was wrecked. "You love me," he said, firmly, because she did and because he'd scaled the walls of her heart to earn that love, and he wasn't letting it go without a fight.

"I'm afraid of you." Tears spilled down Jamie's cheeks and mascara stained her perfectly painted face.

Ryder cocked his head to the side, his thumbs swiping at the black tears rolling down her cheeks. "I don't understand."

"Please let me go." She tried to shake out of his hold but he couldn't let her walk away. She was his muse. His reason.

"Jamie, please don't do this," he begged.

"Or what, are you going to hit me too? Break my nose like you did my dad?" She was burning him alive; a sacrifice to some god or devil he couldn't defeat.

"I would never fucking hurt you." Ryder wasn't perfect. He was a slave to his emotions, and sometimes wrath, and pride, and lust, and envy won out over patience, and humility, and chastity, and kindness, but he'd sooner die before causing her an ounce of suffering.

"I'm sure your dad said the same things to your mom, and look how that ended."

Ryder's arms dropped to his sides. The anger flowing through his tendons eased, as total and utter devastation took its place. "That's low, Kitty Cat, even for you."

Guilt twisted on Jamie's face, but she continued driving the knife into his heart. "It's the truth. You were just something I did because it felt good, because I wanted to fill the void of losing my baby, but I won't trade in one devil for another."

"Fuck you, Jamie," he said, because, what else was left to say? Ryder told Jamie that day in the back alley at Cibo that if they ever broke up, there would be no doubts, no gray area.

Jamie promised Ryder she'd destroy them, he just never wanted to believe her.

"Goodbye, Ryder." She hit the button on her key. The locks clicked, and it was the most heart-breaking sound he'd ever heard.

"If you leave now, I swear I'm done. I can't keep chasing you." The show was over. There wouldn't be an encore.

Jamie shook her head, and got into the car without another word.

TWENTY-EIGHT

Snuff

Jamie

Three Months Later.

Jamie stared at her reflection in the mirror, careful not to make eye contact with the blonde bimbo staring back at her. She hated that she was getting ready to go out to dinner with a man who bought her. She hated that they were being joined by the man who sold her, and most importantly, she hated herself.

Pressing a kiss onto her new tattoo, a pale pink *NR* located on the inside of her right wrist, she inhaled and exhaled. The tattoo was a new source of strength. Whenever she felt like giving up, she'd look at it and remember why she was putting on this show.

Lithium Springs spent the last three months making headlines. They were touted in *Rolling Rock Magazine* as Seattle's best kept secret, and were booking gigs up and down the west coast: information she'd gathered over obsessively stalking them online. She'd even set up a Google Alert, with both Ryder and the band's name. Logically, she knew reading about them, looking at pictures and watching videos of them perform, was unhealthy, but she couldn't stop. Just an hour earlier, she was treated to an Instagram Live video on the Lithium Springs page of the guys hanging out after a show in Toronto. She didn't miss the bottle blonde whose hands seemed to be glued to Ryder's torso.

Jamie didn't have the right to be jealous. Hell, she had a boyfriend, but it hurt to see him moving on. Her heart belonged to Ryder regardless of who her body belonged to. It was the one thing Jared didn't own.

The merger had been a success. Jared's company absorbed her father's and as promised, Archer kept his seat on the board. Tonight's dinner was in celebration of the news going public, taking the tech world by storm. As a result, stocks in GoTech rose to a historic high. The men were going to drink to their victory, and the women, well, she'd been instructed by her mother to wear something *nice*. The tailored romper would have to do. She wasn't in the mood to be the millionaire's plaything tonight.

With a deep sigh, Jamie turned her back on the girl in the mirror and grabbed the Chanel clutch, a gift from Jared, off her bed. He was waiting in the living room, sitting on the sofa with Trey, discussing some motherboards that he intended to sell on his upcoming trip to Tokyo. She couldn't help but roll her eyes at how pretentious they sounded.

Two peas in a rich, prick pod.

"Don't look so happy, he might start to think you actually like him," Kensie teased, coming up behind her. She was wearing one of her signature shift dresses and smelled of lavender.

"Trust me," she replied under her breath, "he knows exactly how I feel. Unfortunately, he also knows I'm not going anywhere until he sends me away." Something she hoped would have happened by now. She was dutiful, well mannered, and only occasionally an asshole to him. They weren't having sex—ever if she could help it. Jamie *"wasn't ready"* and Jared *"didn't want to rush"*.

"Everyone isn't as cynical as you are, Jam," Kensie retorted.

"Maybe he actually likes you. Maybe you should give him a chance."

Jamie bit her tongue. Kensington wanted to see the good in everyone. She wasn't naïve, but she was blinded by her incessant need for everything to end with happily ever after. Some endings weren't happy. Not every guy was *Prince Charming*, but Jamie didn't want to spoil the fairytale for Kensie. Instead, she shrugged. "Maybe."

Jared's eyes met Jamie's. There was something dark in the way he looked at her, like she was a shiny new Barbie and he couldn't wait to tear her legs off. It made her skin crawl. "We should get going. We wouldn't want to keep your parents waiting."

"No, we wouldn't want that," she said, doing her best not to flinch.

In the beginning, they pretended this was a normal courtship. He picked her up, took her on dates, lavished her with gifts, but slowly, as the lights died in her eyes, they stopped pretending and started treating this as what it really was. He bought her. He was no Richard Gere and she certainly wasn't Julia Roberts. The only person she needed saving from was him. Jared led her out the door, down the elevator and into the waiting black, luxury car idling in front of her building.

"Am I really that bad?" Jared asked.

His profile was illuminated by the setting sun. He was handsome, chocolate waves set atop his head, and a light smattering of hair dotted his normally clean shaven chin. He was rich, smart, and ambitious. Any girl would have been lucky to have him—anyone but Jamie.

"No, you're amazing. I'm just preoccupied with work. I'm sorry," she whispered low so he wouldn't hear the lie.

"Come here," he commanded and she obliged. Unbuckling her seatbelt, she slid over to him and let him pull her into his lap. He kissed her neck and she shuddered, willing her body to relax. "I could make you happy," he murmured, twirling a strand of her hair around his fingers, "if you let me. I'll give you whatever you want. Cars, clothes, a big house, a family."

"What if what I want is for you to let me go?"

"James," he *tsked*, "you're already bought and paid for. You aren't going anywhere, but that doesn't mean I want to be your nightmare."

"You can have anyone you want, someone who loves and cares for you, a real relationship, not some deal brokered in a boardroom."

"This isn't about pussy, James. This is about finding a suitable wife. I've got big dreams, political aspirations, and you graduated summa cum laude from USC. Your blood is blue. You're beautiful, you know how to behave, although you drink too much, and despite the fact that you still won't let me touch you," he whispered, his hand running up her thigh, "I know deep down you're a little slut. We can have a lot of fun. You can help me, be my willing partner, and I'll give you the world, or I can keep you locked away in a gilded cage and roll you out when I need to show you off. The choice is yours, but you are mine. So, forget about the busboy. It will make this easier for both of us."

Jamie swallowed hard and scuttled off his lap. A part of her, a small part, held out hope that Jared would tire of her and then her father would back off and she and Ryder would find their way back to each other. But now…now she knew the truth. She was stupid for thinking this was about sex. Who would go through all the trouble Jared went through just to fuck a few times?

Political aspirations.

He was never going to let her go. She lived her entire life ruled by appearance, and now, she'd die doing it.

Dinner went as well as could be expected. Jamie ordered wine, a bottle, and spent most of the night pouting. She was settling into her bored housewife role beautifully. Caroline only insulted her once, and Archer pretty much ignored her. Jamie and her father never had a close relationship, but since the hospital incident, they hadn't spoken more than five words to each other.

Somewhere around Jamie's fourth glass, Jared leaned into her side. His warm breath tickled the back of her neck causing the hair there to stand on end. He dropped an arm around her shoulders and with his free hand he swiped her glass, taking a small sip before setting it down on the linen tablecloth.

"You're drinking a lot," he murmured. His mouth was hot on her ear, and she had to fight the urge to push him away.

Jamie's eyes met Caroline's from across the table. She couldn't read her mother's expression, but she could tell she was scrutinizing her every move. Jamie's gaze dropped and sand colored lashes coated with thick clumps of black mascara fanned the tops of her cheeks. "Am I not allowed to drink?"

Jared tugged on her chin, forcing her to look at him. It was the same hand he used to steal her wine, and probably the same one he used to sign the ink on the deal that stole her happiness. He pressed his lips to hers, not forcefully, but not welcomed either. It wasn't the first kiss they'd shared. He'd kissed her cheek, her neck, her shoulder, but never her mouth. That was something she'd only ever given to Ryder.

"You're allowed to drink, but you aren't allowed to embarrass me, understand?" he asked, sucking her bottom lip into his mouth. He bit her, a gentle warning to behave. From an outsider, it looked sweet, almost loving, but his tone held darker intentions.

Jamie nodded slowly, running the back of her hand down his cheek, nibbling on his earlobe. "I'm here. I'm all in, but if you ever threaten me again, I will stab you in your sleep, understand?"

A dangerous chuckle rumbled from Jared's chest as he fingered lazy circles around her bare shoulder. "I like you, James."

"I loathe you, Jared," she growled. He was evil, a monster in Armani. Jamie wouldn't let a few kind words thrown to her like scraps to a pig, delude her thinking. He was a dragon, a fire-breather, a destroyer.

Their server returned to the table to refill water goblets and inquire about dessert. Jamie took it as an opportunity to excuse herself. Her head was spinning, mostly because of the wine, but also due to her little encounter with Jared. She weaved in and out of tables, teetering on the burgundy shoes Kensington insisted she buy because, '*Kendall Jenner wore them in Milan last week.*' They were overpriced, but Jamie had five-million dollars to burn.

The restroom was small, intimate. Soft, yellow bulbs glowed from circular lighting. Faucets floated above basin style sinks and spa soaps and lotions were nestled into wire holders. Jamie inhaled, and exhaled.

Be thankful.
Be mindful.
Be kind.

She snorted at the last part. *Kind.* The world had been everything but kind to her. The world was cruel. Life was suffering. It was drowning in a pool of inadequacy, praying for someone to save you. Praying for the strength to save yourself. Jamie stroked the *NR* on her wrist to remind herself that she was the life raft.

The door blew open and with it Caroline and the scent of sandalwood and wealth.

"Mother."

"James, are you well?"

"Why wouldn't I be?" Jamie asked cautiously.

"Because you've been putting the wine back like it has no calories, and you've barely touched your fish, which I suppose is understandable, but you shouldn't drink so much—so quickly—on an empty stomach."

Words of WASP wisdom. Jamie had no doubt her mother used her Vassar degree to calculate how little food a person needed to eat in order to sustain a mostly *liquid* diet.

"I'm fine," she lied waving off her mother. Jamie turned the water on and pumped the floral scented soap into her palms. The image of Ryder and the Instagram slut flashed through her mind. He was off having the time of his life while she was in the ladies room discussing the finer nuances of being a Stepford wife. In truth, she was miserable.

"You don't look fine."

"I'm seeing the trainer you recommended. I'm following the prescribed food plan. I've lost fifteen pounds even though I only gained ten. Give me a fucking break," she whisper-hissed.

"Language, dear. Ladies—future First Ladies—don't say fuck," Caroline reprimanded. "I didn't mean physically. Physically you've never looked better, although it wouldn't have killed you to wear a dress," she added. Caroline always made sure to punctuate any compliment with an insult, just to keep the scales balanced.

"Are you going to arrive at a point anytime soon?" Jamie asked, snatching a towel from the holder.

"I just notice a difference in the way you are with Jared, and the way you were with…that boy. It's startling."

"His name is Ryder, not *that boy*, and thank you for your concern, but please stop. You're really bad with these maternal speeches, like, the worst."

Caroline shrugged, and shot her daughter a look that said, *we all have our strong suits*. "I've been preparing you for this your entire life, James. You are destined for great things and Jared can help make it happen."

Jamie conjured up the most unladylike snort she could muster. "You've spent my entire life ignoring me and telling me I'm not good enough."

"Do you think men like Jared are going to hold your hand and tell you how pretty you are?" Caroline asked, turning to her daughter. Her face was sincere for the first time, ever. Gone was the brainless housewife Jamie grew up with and in her place was someone new, someone calculating. "Do you think this life is easy, James?"

"I didn't ask for this life. I don't want Jared or to be the first lady of anything. And since we're being honest, I would have preferred for you to have hugged me and told me you were proud," Jamie choked. Tears stung in her eyes but she held them back. Caroline would undoubtedly chastise her for ruining her make-up.

"I may never be the mother you want, but I'm the one you have, and believe it or not I only want the best for you," Caroline pulled Jamie into a hug. It was their first, at least the first Jamie ever remembered receiving from her mother. The dam broke and fat tears spilled down Jamie's face as she cried in her mother's arms. The moment was monumental, but also super-fucking-weird. "This is so awkward."

"It is," her mother agreed, but neither woman broke the connection. After another stretch of silence, Caroline asked, "Do you have any make-up in that Chanel? It's going to take a miracle to salvage your face."

Jamie chuckled. That was the mother she knew, and maybe even loved a little.

TWENTY-NINE

Party Monster

RYDER

The Guinness clock mounted on the wall behind the bar at the Rabbit Hole was broken. Ryder knew this because he spent ten minutes staring at the damn thing, willing it to move. That was the first sign he'd crossed the threshold from wasted to blackout drunk. It was a fine line—he toed it daily. One minute he was laughing with his friends and the next minute, he was staring at a broken clock. The little hand was permanently stuck on the six, the big hand on the eleven. Time stood still in the small bar. It stood still outside of the bar too. It was Monday, the Rabbit Hole was closed to the public, but they were there for a private party, a celebration.

It had been three months since he quit his job, two months and three weeks since the day Kitty Cat reached inside his chest and pulled his heart out with her bare hands, and one month since he realized she wasn't coming back. That was a particularly dark day. He stopped at the liquor store to get a handle of Jim Beam, then home to purge his place of her. The fruity shit—gone. Her clothes—gone. The fucking mattress cover she insisted they buy—gone. Everything that reminded him of Jamie—gone, just like her.

Ryder thought they were forever. He thought she was his truth, his way, his light, but he was wrong. Some people were only meant to be in your life for a moment. It was okay, that was life. Jamie was temporary, his band, his brothers and their music, that was permanent. That was what he needed to focus on.

Music was his future.

Not Jamie.

Ryder tipped his beer back and shook his head, blond curls tumbling into his eyes. The room started to spin. Yeah, a blackout was in his future.

"Hey, easy there, Ry. You okay?" Tiff asked, wrapping her arm around his waist to steady him.

"I'm good," he slurred, pivoting to wrap her in a hug. His hands slid down her back and didn't stop until they felt ass. "Are *you* okay?" he said suggestively, scanning her body. Tiff was hot. Her green and black hair hung down her back, and her tits were on display.

"You're drunk," she giggled.

"What's the deal with you and C?" Ryder needed to get laid. As much as he told himself he was over Jamie, he still hadn't had sex with anyone else. He'd come close last weekend. There was a party, a hot blonde, and lots of dank weed. She did her best to try to convince him to let her suck his dick, but after forty-five minutes of begging, Ryder sent her packing.

"I don't know. He's your friend, why don't you ask him." Ryder could hear the sadness in Tiffany's voice. CT was across the bar chatting with a girl with smooth, dark skin and long braids. Ryder recognized the look in his eyes, and apparently, Tiff did too.

"Oh, he's about to fuck the shit out of her," he said on a whistle.

Tiff bristled at his comment. Her and the drummer weren't exclusive, they both hooked up with other people, but she was falling for CT, and everyone could see it but him.

"Yeah, well, what about Kitty Cat?"

"Do you see her around here?" Ry snapped. He didn't mean to, but it still hurt to hear her name.

"No, but—"

"Have you seen her once in the last three months?"

"No." Tiff shook her head.

"Then don't worry about her." Even saying the words aloud felt foreign, but he needed this. He needed help forgetting. The drinking and the weed only dulled the hurt. He wanted it gone, permanently. He wanted to feel the way he felt before Jamie turned his fucking world upside down.

"Look, I like Jamie, and when you two get back together, I don't want to have this weirdness between us, or between you and CT."

"Jamie and I aren't getting back together, and CT looks like he's about to throw that girl against the wall and fuck her until she can't walk. I'm alone, you're alone, let's go be alone together." He gave her ass another squeeze to emphasize his point. "C," Ryder yelled across the room. The drummer looked up from the girl's tits and over to where they stood. Ry's gaze shifted from his friend, to Tiff, then back again, silently asking permission. CT nodded his head towards the back of the bar, the gesture saying, *'Go for it,'* before he returned his attention back to the girl with the braids. "See, it's settled," he said, lifting Tiff up and wrapping her legs around his waist.

Her mouth found his as he carried her through the empty bar and to the back room. Ryder walked the familiar path by memory. His tongue licking lazily inside of her mouth. It felt wrong, kissing someone other than Jamie, but he kept going. Eventually he wouldn't feel anything.

The old couch wasn't as comfortable as it usually was, but none of that stopped Ryder from lying down and crawling his way up Tiff's body. His hand slipped down the front of her shorts. Pushing aside the thin swath of fabric, Ry sunk two fingers inside her damp pussy, and swirled them around and around. The squishing noises the wetness made woke the sleeping giant in his pants. It was the first time he'd gotten it up for anything other than his right hand.

"God," she moaned into his mouth. Her back arched into him as he bit down on her collarbone. The sounds she made spurred him on. Her moans drowned out the agonized sobs screaming in his head. Tiff was familiar. Ryder was comfortable with her. She didn't have any expectation other than sex and that was just fine with him. He had lived the last three months of his life in a drunken stupor. To have a beautiful woman writhing under him, to feel soft skin against his lips, made him feel like himself, like *Sex God*.

Sitting back on his haunches, Ryder pulled the gray tank over his head. Tiff's eyes glazed over with lust. Her chest heaved up and down and her lipstick was smeared from his kiss. Any reservations she had were gone. She sat up, pulling her shirt off too. Her large breasts spilled out from under the racerback. Her tits were creamy and soft. Ryder's teeth grazed her nipple. She had perfect tits.

Jamie used to stare at them for hours.

Jamie.

Jamie.

Jamie.

He had a beautiful woman underneath him and all he could think about was her. She was like a fucking ghost, haunting his every waking moment. Hell, Ryder even saw her in his dreams. "Fuck," he hissed, shaking his head, desperately trying to focus but her scent was all wrong. She was warm and spicy, not light and fruity like his Kitty Cat.

His dick was softening by the second.

"What's wrong?" Tiff panted, grabbing both sides of his face. She tried to pull him back in for another kiss but he turned his head.

"I'm sorry. I can't," he choked. "Fuck, I'm a little bitch." His eyes were awash with unshed tears. God, he fucking missed that girl.

"No. No, it's okay," Tiff cooed, brushing a stray tear away with her thumb. "We can just talk if you want. Tell me what happened? I've never heard why you two broke up. No one talks about her, even when you're not around."

"It's hard for them, too," he whispered. His friends loved Jamie like a sister. Her absence affected everyone in his life.

"Look, I know I'm just a girl you guys fuck every once in a while—"

"It's not like that," he said, suddenly feeling like the world's biggest asshole. Tiff was a nice girl—too desperate for attention—but then again, weren't they all?

"It's fine," she said with a wave of her hand. "I like sex and I like you guys. I know what I signed up for. This isn't about that."

"Okay?"

"What you and Kitty Cat had was real, and when it's real, it's worth fighting for."

Ryder groaned, sitting back on the cushion. "I've fought for us our entire relationship. I love her more than life itself, but I can't be the only one fighting. I'm tired of doing it alone. If she wants me, she knows where to find me, but obviously, her money and her last name mean more to her than I did."

"That's not true."

"Then where is she?" he asked. It sounded like he had a mouth full of marbles. It was pathetic. He was crying to the girl he was supposed to be rebounding with, about the girl who broke his heart.

"Life is beautiful, Ry. You can't change the past, but you can learn from it and grow. That way you don't have to spend the present steeped in anger or resentment. And the future, that's the beautiful part, the future is *yours* to mold into whatever you want it to be. You just gotta let go of the grudges and stop feeling sorry for yourself."

"That sounds like some of Kitty Cat's Buddhist shit."

Tiff shrugged, "She rubbed off on me, too."

"I bet." Ryder chuckled sadly. He took one last peek at her rack before tossing her, her tee. They really were great boobs, they were just on the wrong girl.

The next morning Ryder woke up feeling lighter. He got out of bed, showered off the remains of last night's party and made the familiar drive down to Seventh Street. The most humanizing realization was that the world didn't stop spinning just because Ryder did.

Humanity was humbling.

Ryder spent the last six months on a self-righteous pedestal, judging everyone around him for being too human. His parents, Jamie, they all made mistakes. He could live his life in a cloud of anger and hate, or he could stop holding grudges and learn to forgive. Forgiveness wasn't weak. There was freedom in it, a freedom Ryder never knew.

The silver bell above the door chimed and Ryder pushed his way inside his sanctuary. The breakfast crowd was thinning. A table of construction workers gulped the dregs of their coffee, enjoying their last few moments before their work day began.

It was strange. For months Ryder avoided the diner, but now it was like he had never left. Hazel eyes scanned the room. He knew she was there, her schedule hadn't changed in the last ten years. Ryder checked every blonde with the red uniform he could see, to no avail.

Maybe she was running late?

Ryder made his way to the counter. His plan was to ask Terry, one of the line cooks, where his mother was, and grab a bite to eat while he waited. He missed the food almost as much as he missed his mom. Sliding onto the stool, Ryder surveyed the dining room once more. In the back, sitting at his favorite booth was a blonde head he'd know anywhere.

His legs ate the distance. He didn't know Jamie kept in touch with his mom, but then again, how would he? He hadn't seen either of them in months. "Kitty Cat?" The woman turned around and his heart sank. "Are you lost?" he growled at the older, stuck-up version of Jamie.

Was she there too?

He did another quick scan of the crowd, his heart beating wildly in his chest. *Please. Please. Please.*

As if reading his mind, Caroline sighed. "She isn't here."

"Then, why are you?" He couldn't help himself. This was a direct connection to Jamie, and though he was pissed at her, he couldn't deny he missed her.

"I had breakfast with your mother. Well, she ate. I had more of a liquid meal," she grinned, unscrewing the top of a small, rose-gold flask and tipped its contents into the glass of ice in front of her.

"How do you even know my mother?" Ryder asked, taking a seat. The Manning's had caused him enough harm, but fucking with his mother was crossing the line.

"We met the last time I was here. I had lunch with James. Your mother's quite protective of her," she said bitterly.

"Someone needs to be."

Caroline narrowed her eyes at Ryder. "I may never win parent of the year, but James is my daughter, and everything I've ever done, right or wrong, has been to protect her. It's just taken me longer than I'd like to admit to realize who she needed protecting from." Lifting the glass, she took a sip of what he assumed was vodka. Her face remained passive but her voice gave her away. She was worried, and that made him worry.

"What changed?" he asked. Why now, after months of being 'Team Jared', was she here talking to his mother?

"You changed everything," Caroline said with a scowl.

Ryder stared at her in confusion. "I haven't spoken to your daughter in months."

"I know."

"Then why are you here?"

"Because she's unhappy."

"She's been unhappy her entire life." Ryder was done with this conversation. If Jamie wasn't there, they had nothing to talk about. The shiny, red plastic seat squeaked as he stood. This was going nowhere and he needed to find his mom.

"That's where you're wrong, Napoleon." Caroline wrapped a manicured finger around his wrist and gestured for him to have a seat. Ryder wasn't sure why he did it; morbid curiosity maybe, but he sat his ass down.

"She was happy for a spell. There was a spark in her eyes, one I never noticed before. And you can imagine my horror when I discovered you were responsible for it. I swear James lives to test me, but that's not the point."

"Oh, so there is one?" he asked. No wonder Jamie was so fucked up. Ryder was going crazy after only five minutes in her presence. He couldn't imagine a lifetime.

"It's gone now—no, not the point," she added sardonically, taking another sip of her lunch. "The spark. It's like that thing your mind does when you see something for the first time, like a book or a certain kind of car. Once you know a thing exists, you begin to seek it out. But the problem is the spark is gone. I check for it every time I see my daughter, but it hasn't returned. I don't like it. It makes me sad, and frowning causes wrinkles. Do you see my dilemma?"

Ryder nodded. Caroline was like some sort of vapid Yoda. She made no sense, but perfect sense. It was trippy.

"On the one hand, you're poor, and while Archer has finally released her trust, I don't love the idea of my daughter being someone's sugar mama."

"I've never asked Jamie for a cent."

"On the other hand, Jared, who is perfect on paper, looks at her like she's a piece of meat. The way he handles her…" She bristled in disgust. "I don't care about love. It's useless, but I will not hand my daughter over to a predator either." She took another drink. The bell over the door chimed and Ryder craned his neck, hoping to spot his mother. For all he knew, one breakfast with Caroline was enough to make her run for the fucking border.

"Jamie broke up with me. I don't think I have as much influence over her decision-making as you think."

"My God, you're an idiot," Caroline groaned. "For the life of me, I can't understand what she sees in you. I mean, you're handsome, in a tattooed, ex-felon who will ruin your credit kind of way, but a complete imbecile."

Vapid Yoda strikes again.

"You're not nice," Ryder said. It wasn't a question but a statement of fact. Caroline Manning was a fucking bitch, and she didn't make any apologies for it.

"Nice. What's nice? I'm honest, and it's gotten me a lot further than nice ever will. Now, would you like to know the reason for my lunch with your mother?"

Ryder inhaled, taking a page from Jamie's book. "I'm sure you're going to tell me."

"You need to win James back."

"She doesn't want me." Three months. Jamie had three-fucking-months to apologize, to figure her shit out, but instead of making amends, she'd been traipsing around town on Jared-fucking-Foster's arm. It sucked, but she'd made her choice.

"If you think that, then you really are an idiot. Why do you think she broke up with you?"

Ryder narrowed his eyes at Jamie's mother. She wore a white button down blouse and dress pants. Business casual, though Ryder knew she wouldn't be punching anyone's clock, ever. "She said it was because she was afraid of me, but deep down I think she changed her mind about giving up all that money."

"James doesn't care about money. She has never cared about pleasing me or her father. In fact, there are very few things in this world she cares about. Her brother, Kensington, and now you."

"Me?" he snorted. "She ripped my heart out."

"You think she did that because she stopped..." she paused, wrinkling her nose like her next words were unfathomable, "loving you? No. Archer forced her hand."

"What could be worse than taking away her trust fund?"

"My daughter cares about three things." Caroline repeated, emphasizing her earlier point. "Christopher is the heir. Kensington is American royalty. You are nothing. Who do you think Archer could use to scare James into submission?"

"I'm not afraid of Archer and I can take care of myself."

"Like you did the day at the hospital? You assaulted my husband, in front of a security camera. Did you know James had to beg Archer not to press charges? Do you have any idea what the penalty is for aggravated assault? No? Let me clue you in; a year, *minimum*."

Ryder was quiet as he took in her words. A fucking year. That rat bastard would have had him locked up for a fucking year. It would have ruined everything with the band. You don't get second chances in music. Most don't get a chance at all. Suddenly, everything made sense.

"He gets it! Hallelujah."

"That's enough, Barbie." Ryder turned to see his mother approach. "Hey, baby boy," she smiled.

God, he had missed his mother. Fifteen minutes with Caroline and he quickly realized what a fucking asshole he'd been. "I'm sorry, Ma."

"Well," Caroline sighed, polished off the rest of her drink, and stood. "This has all been great fun, but I have a ball to shop for. Your mother will fill you in on the particulars." Caroline shouldered her expensive looking bag, and sauntered out of the dinner.

"She. Is. Awful," Ryder grunted once she was out of earshot.

"The worst," Annette chuckled, dropping a Shirley Temple in front of her son. "I wasn't expecting to see you here this morning."

Ryder took his mother in, her hair a mix of blonde and gray, her eyes, tired. Years of serving coffee and working doubles had done a number on her, but she did it, all of it, alone. She never once complained. Never blamed him or treated him with an ounce of malice. Who was he to judge her for wanting closure?

"I'm a terrible son," he whispered.

"You're not so bad," she said, tucking a strand of blond hair behind his ear. Ryder placed a kiss on each of her knuckles. He was wrong about his mother. She wasn't weak, she had the type of silent strength that endured.

"I was wrong for judging you. I should have trusted you. I just don't want to see you get hurt."

"I promise. I'll never let that happen again."

"I believe you, Ma."

"Okay, good. Now, let me tell you how that witch plans to get your girl back."

THIRTY

I Miss You

Jamie

Even the most expensive chiffon was miserable. There was something about the way the fabric brushed up against the skin, something in the way it moved, it was all wrong. Jamie was never a fan of dresses, but the pink, pleated Gucci number she wore was her own personal torture chamber.

Tonight, was the night; the Christmas party at the Governor's Mansion in Olympia. Jared planned to announce his candidacy in the upcoming election. He had his sights set on Representative Hudson seat in the House. Rep. Hudson was due to retire and per Jared, *"People are sick of career politicians."* He believed with the changing political climate, his inexperience would be viewed as a good thing. A true man of the people. Jamie only cared about how his ambition would affect her. He'd be on the campaign trail most of next year, and had already dropped hints about them marrying before he left.

"Stop fidgeting," Jared reprimanded as their car pulled to a stop. Thousands of tiny white bulbs twinkled and strings of white lights highlighted the beautiful mansion. A row of cars lined up out front as politicians, local businessmen, and dignitaries waited for their turn to be shuffled through security and escorted inside.

"I hate this dress," Jamie sneered, looking out the tinted glass. In the middle of the sea of people, a tall blond man caught her eye and she forced herself to blink back the tears. Jamie saw Ryder everywhere and in everyone. Last week, while on location, she nearly tackled a man who wore a pair of Doc Martens. He didn't even look like Ryder, but the shoes triggered something in her brain. Napoleon Ryder was seared onto Jamie's soul and no matter how hard she scrubbed, she couldn't wash him away.

The valet, a young woman in a bright red vest, opened the door and Jamie and Jared exited the limo. Camera's flashed and reporters fired off questions in rapid succession.

"Mr. Foster, congratulations on the deal with Tokyo Gijutsu."

"Mr. Foster, is it true you're planning to run for Hudson's seat, next year?"

"Jamie, Jared, pose for a picture?"

Jared paused, dropping his hand to the small of her back. "You are the most beautiful woman in attendance tonight," he whispered in her ear. "I know that bitch mother of yours did a number on your self-esteem, but you're perfect." He leaned in, pressing a soft kiss to her mouth, causing a flurry of flashbulbs and a new onslaught of questions.

"Are there wedding bells in your future?"

"Did your affair with his daughter affect your decision regarding the takeover of Manning Solutions?"

"Is this why Archer retained a spot on the board?"

Jamie was grateful to security for shuffling them forward. It wasn't the first-time Jared had stolen a kiss, but the urge to vomit never went away. She only hoped her face didn't reveal her true feelings. Since local media caught wind of their "romance", the papers had been obsessed. The shrewd businessman falling for his opponent's daughter was the stuff of fairytales. According to them, Jamie captured Jared's heart, and saved her father's business in the process.

The society pages loved her. She'd done more for Jared's reputation in a few months than all his accomplishments combined.

The inside of the mansion was just as beautifully decorated as the outside. The large ballroom looked like a winter wonderland. Crystal snowflakes hung from the ceiling. The tables were set with pale blues, silvers, and whites. Servers passed hors d'oeuvres, and champagne flowed freely, while a man in a white tux played soft music from behind a grand piano.

Jamie followed dutifully behind as Jared worked the room. It was a who's who of Seattle government. Jamie's hours of research had paid off. She recognized most of the men and women in attendance. She was witty, charming, and able to keep up conversation with ease. On more than one occasion, Jared flashed her a proud smile, an action that should have comforted her, but didn't. Jamie never wanted to be a good housewife, but with Jared making things official tonight, her fate was sealed.

Jamie spotted Kensie across the room. She looked gorgeous in a floor-length satin gown. Kensington was built for this kind of thing; it was in her DNA. Her family was Washington State's equivalent to the Kennedys.

"Excuse me," she whispered.

Jared nodded at Senator Wallace, before turning to Jamie.

"Kensie," she said by way of explanation. Jared scanned the crowd and spotted Kensie standing next to her grandfather.

"Go ahead, sweetheart." Jared's eyes ran the length of her body. His perusal made her skin crawl. She'd avoided his advances for months, but something in his posture told her tonight that would change. "You really are the most beautiful woman in the room," he added darkly.

Senator Wallace grinned, and Jamie realized she wasn't going to be able to skate through the ball as easily as she'd hoped. "And you're the most handsome man," she said, returning the compliment with a kiss. She felt their eyes on her back as she retreated and a shiver ran through her veins.

"Jam!" Kensie squealed, barreling towards her. "Oh. My. Gosh. You look amazing."

"I feel like an imposter," Jamie confessed, scanning the crowd. Everyone else seemed to be having a good time, yet Jamie was ready to peel off her skin. "Come to the ladies' room with me?"

Kensie nodded and the women linked arms, making their way through the maze of tables. Once inside the restroom, Jamie checked each stall, one by one, to ensure they were truly alone. She needed a minute to be candid with her best friend and didn't want to have to worry about any fallout.

"I hate this dress," Jamie moaned.

"It's gorgeous and you look amazing in it," Kensie smiled.

It was comforting to have her friend there. Kensie and her family had been coming to these things for as long as Jamie could remember. Her plan was to latch onto her best friend for the rest of the night, and let Kensie's quirky charm do the work for her.

"Jared says pink makes me look innocent, and that I need all the help I can get," Jamie said, rolling her eyes.

"It does," Ken giggled, "and you do." Kensie dug into her clutch and presented a baby-pink lip gloss to Jamie. "Gloss?"

"Please." She took it happily. Jared tended to keep his lips to himself when she wore the stuff. She planned on buying a year's supply.

"How are things with Jared? Ken asked, fixing her mascara.

"I think I'm going to have to have sex with him soon," Jamie shuddered. "When he came home from Tokyo he tried, but I told him I had my period. I don't think he'll buy that tonight."

"I'm sorry, Jam," Kensie said, finding Jamie's eyes in the mirror. All primping ceased and the two women stared at each other. Their relationship over the last few months had been strained, but tonight that all disappeared. When one of them hurt, the other hurt.

"It's fine. I'm fine," she lied. It was pointless. Kensington knew her better than anyone else, but the only way she was going to make it through this was by donning the mask. "Anyway, where's Trey tonight?"

"He's back in Seattle. It's his parents' wedding anniversary. They're having a party."

"But you guys are good, right?" Jamie asked.

"We're great. He's so much like my daddy, and you know all I've ever wanted was to marry a man like him." Kensie was lucky enough to have parents who didn't subscribe to the whole arranged marriage thing. She could marry whoever she wanted and her folks would accept it, so it blew Jamie's mind that her best friend chose Trey. He was fundamentally wrong for her. Kensie was a free-bird, but Trey wanted to clip her wings.

"Are you happy?" Jamie pressed.

"Yes," Kensie said, smiling a smile that didn't reach her eyes. It was a lie. One Jamie didn't call her on.

The party wore on. Archer and Caroline arrived and pretended to be the proud parents of a daughter so beloved by Seattle. It was maddening. Archer took from Jamie's body, he placed unfair expectations on her shoulders, expectations that Jamie carried in stride. His burdens became hers to bear, and yet he treated her like a chore, doling out bits of love and acceptance when it suited him.

"You're doing great, sweetheart," Jared whispered in her ear. His hand rested firmly, possessively, on her ass.

"Thank you," Jamie's cheeks were sore from all the fake smiling.

The party congregated towards the stage as Governor Johnson thanked everyone for attending. They had entered the posturing portion of the evening. The politicians were looking for donations to upcoming campaigns, while the lobbyists sought to further their interests. At the end of it all, Jared would announce his bid with a special introduction from Representative Hudson himself; a blessing that would have the entire party rallying behind the young tech entrepreneur.

"We'll leave after my speech."

"I'd like that," she said as the governor made a toast to good health and a prosperous new year.

"You'll stay at my place tonight," he added pointedly. Jamie eyed the exit, wondering if she ran now, would he let her. "I think I've waited long enough." The hand on her ass flexed, letting her know it wasn't a request. He was a man who took what he wanted, and he wanted Jamie, officially and in every capacity. Jared got off on exerting his power. Money afforded him a lot of it and tonight, he'd have his first taste of political power, a high he'd planned on taking out on Jamie's body.

As the governor droned on, a familiar figure hovered near the west stairwell. *Ryder. Could it be?* She thought. Craning her neck, Jamie looked again. *Nothing.* He was gone, or more likely, he was never there. Disappointment racked her body. She imagined it, just as she'd imagined it many times over the last three months, hopeful for a hero that would never come.

"I thought we were waiting for marriage," she said, clearing her throat, and her mind.

Jared pulled her to him, her back to his front, facing the stage. The governor introduced Rep. Hudson. Jared would be speaking soon, and then everything would change.

With his erection grinding into her ass, he snorted, "Try again, James." Jared's breath was hot on her neck. "I like you. I didn't think I would, but I do. I did my research when I chose you. Perfect on paper, a party girl, but that stuff is easy to bury. I was expecting a spoiled, little brat, vain and vapid, like your mother. Imagine my surprise when you showed up on Easter Sunday, smart, and confident, and witty. When you told your dad to shove that trust fund up his ass, I think I fell in love."

"I can't say the same," she gritted, resting her head on his shoulder, always aware of appearances.

"It's a good thing I don't give a fuck," Jared flicked her earlobe with his tongue, sending a shiver down her spine. Ominous goosebumps erupted across her flesh like a volcano, hot, violent, and devastating. Her heart pounded.

A blond flash caught Jamie's attention, this time by the ice sculpture. It couldn't be him. They were an hour away from Seattle and the place was crawling with security. Even if he'd managed to track her down, they'd never let him through the front door. Jamie was losing her mind, and after tonight she'd lose what was left of her freedom. "I need to freshen up a bit," she said, wiggling out of Jared's arms. She needed a break. The Ryder hallucinations were making her head hurt, making her heart hurt.

Caroline and Kensington turned in her direction. "You want me to come with?" Ken mouthed. Jamie shook her head and held up five fingers, indicating she'd be back in as many minutes.

Jared gripped her elbow in warning. "I'd hate for you to miss my speech."

Jamie pressed her lips to his gently, "Five minutes," she reiterated before slipping through the crowd. She scurried towards the ice sculpture, where a few of the caterers stood, laughing and sipping on half empty bottles of champagne. The hallways were quiet now. Everyone was gathered in the ballroom, listening to Hudson wax poetically about his time in office. After spending the last couple of hours with all eyes on her, Jamie relished the isolation.

"Can I have one of those?" she asked the caterers. They grinned and handed her a bottle. Jamie nodded her thanks and turned, making a beeline for the west stairwell. She sat on the concrete stairs and lifted the bottle to her lips. She didn't have much time. Jared would be speaking soon, but she needed a minute away from everyone to sort out her shit. She was losing her damn mind. Ryder hated her, she made sure of it. He wasn't there. She was only hallucinating. The trauma of what was to come was affecting her brain.

Somewhere in the distance, she heard Hudson introduce Jared. Her alone time was up. Her place was at the front of the stage, watching adoringly as Jared pledged to bring change to Seattle. Steeling herself, she pushed through the doors and slammed right into a wall of muscle. Strong, tattooed hands encircled her, pushing her back into the stairwell, and up against the wall. Ryder's mouth crashed onto hers as he lifted her, hitching her legs around his waist. "Mine," he growled, as he tore through the delicate fabric of her pantyhose.

"Ry," she panted, pushing him back. "Why? How are you here?"

"Why was his mouth on you?" Ryder's gruff voice echoed throughout the quiet space. He trailed hot, wet kisses up her neck.

"What are you doing here?" she repeated. If anyone found them like this, while Jared was on stage, it would ruin everything, but fuck, she missed him.

"I'm here to take you home, wash all that ridiculous make-up off, then fuck you until you can't walk straight," he seethed. "I can't believe you let him kiss you." Ryder bit into her neck, hard, marking her.

"He's my boyfriend," she mewled, clawing at him. She missed the out of control feeling Ryder inspired. This was stupid and reckless and throwing away everything she spent the last three months creating, but it was Ryder. He was there, claiming her. If they only had one last stolen moment, she would bask in it. He could hate fuck her in the empty stairwell for all she cared. She needed him, one last time.

"I'm your boyfriend," he declared. "I bet if I pushed these panties aside your pussy would be wet and throbbing and it ain't because of that tool on stage."

"But nothing's changed."

Ryder stabbed two fingers inside of her, causing her to yelp at the intrusion. "No," he said, waving the wet digits in her face, "it seems it hasn't."

"Fuck yo—" she started but was cut off by his fingers returning to her core.

"I know you still love me. I know you're only with him because you think you're protecting me. I know why you said what you said and I'm pissed at you for not telling me the truth, but I fucking love you, James. You put me through three months of agony, but I need you like I need air. Like I need music."

"I need you too, but my dad. I won't let you throw your life away," she panted as he pumped in and out of her.

Ryder kissed her, hard. "Your mom is as big an asshole as you are, but like you, she protects the people she loves. And like you, her methods are ass fucking backwards, but effective."

Jamie's breath caught. *Caroline did this?* "Are you sure you trust her?"

"I'm sure. She's on our side. How do you think I got past security?" he asked.

Jamie took him in, his hair was pulled back into a low bun. He wore a sleek black tux and shoes so shiny she could see her reflection in them. If he was handsome in skinny jeans and loose fitting tanks, he was downright sinful in a tuxedo.

"If you keep eye-fucking me, I will be forced to pull out my dick, right here in this stairwell."

Jamie wanted nothing more, but it was too risky. Jared's speech would be done soon and she wasn't foolish enough to think her absence would go unnoticed. "If you say we can trust my mother, then I believe you, but what about Archer? He won't stop until you're in jail."

"I've got that covered too."

"How?" she asked as he set her on her feet. She felt like she'd just been hit by a train. The Ryder Express.

"I'll explain everything later, let's just get out of here before someone sees my broke ass leaving with Seattle's Princess."

Jamie nodded, and they bounded down the stairs two at a time, busting out of the door and sprinting across the empty hall to the kitchen. The backdoor was open. The staff, who were outside smoking, barely gave Jamie and Ryder a second glance.

The cold December air assaulted Jamie's senses. "Please, don't tell me I have to ride all the way back to Seattle on your bike," she asked through chattering teeth.

Ryder pulled off his jacket and slipped it around her shoulders. "No, I've got CT's Mustang."

"Thank God," she said, clutching the jacket closed. They walked through the courtyard, past the fountain, and made their way to the parking lot. Rows and rows of cars were lined up neatly. The ground was cold, and hard, and near impossible to walk on in heels, but she trudged on, wanting to put as much distance between her and Jared as possible.

"Not so fast, James," a dark voice called from behind.

A chill ran down her spine as they turned to spot a seething Archer hot on their trail. There would be fallout, of that she was sure, but she trusted Ryder. If he said he took care of it, she believed him. Whatever the future brought, they'd face it together. It was them against the world.

THIRTY-ONE

The Reason

RYDER

"James, get your ass back inside right now," Archer boomed as the wind howled.

Ryder took a step forward. "No, we're leaving."

Archer had interfered enough in his life and it took every ounce of self-control he possessed not to knock his fucking teeth out. Ryder was patient. After living in hell for three months, he waited another two weeks in purgatory while he and Caroline gathered enough information to bury the motherfucker. Now that he had it, he wasn't backing down.

"Like hell you are," Archer said, rising to the challenge. "I'm calling the police."

"No!" Panic laced Jamie's tone as she sidestepped Ryder. "Baby, I love you too much to let him send you away."

"It's okay, Kitty Cat," Ryder promised, resting his hand on her cheek. "He can't hurt us anymore."

"Can't I?" Archer pulled a cell phone from the inside pocket of his jacket, leveling his gaze towards his daughter. "One last chance, James."

Jamie's eyes darted back and forth between Ryder and her father. There was fear there, fear of the unknown, fear of releasing control and finally letting go, but there was also trust. She turned to Ryder, green eyes wide-open for the first time. "I trust you. Whatever you say, I'll do."

"Your dad can go fuck himself." Ryder grinned triumphantly.

Jamie was his, totally and fully. He fought for this, for her. He scaled the walls of her heart, and though he came out on the other side bloody and battered, he made it. He wouldn't trade a second of their journey, because it was theirs. Their love was imperfect, but it was pure.

"They're going to love you in prison," Archer seethed. His salt and pepper hair blew in the wind. His eyes were so dark they looked like coal. He was a demon in the flesh, but Ryder was fully prepared to vanquish him.

"Not as much as they're going to love you."

"Sure," Archer chuckled. His phone glowed in the dark night. His fingers stabbed the screen in rapid succession.

"Irony is a funny thing," Ryder said. "Here you are, this solutions mogul with access to the most advanced technology in the world, and yet, a housewife and guitarist hacked into your private email, and from a Starbucks, no less."

Jamie's head swung around. "You and my mom hacked his email?"

"Yup," Ryder arched a brow. "I spent two weeks with your mom. If that ain't love, I don't know what is."

"I don't believe you," Archer said, lowering his phone.

Ryder took a step forward. The urge to throw a punch was strong, but he was more calculating now. Instead of fists, he'd throw facts. "On April twenty-fifth, you received an email from the head of your development team, saying the motherboards your company was working weren't ready for market. They were hazardous to users, even resulting in a minor injury to one of the developers. He told you they needed at least six more months to perfect the technology. Two hours later, you replied saying they didn't have six months, and if he couldn't workout the glitches, you'd hire someone who could."

"Daddy is this true?" Jamie asked.

Archer didn't respond, but Ryder didn't miss him slipping his phone back inside his pocket. "May sixth, that same developer resigned, citing ethical misconduct from management as his reasoning. He refused to have his name on a faulty product. June eighteenth, Jared was no longer interested in dismantling the company and instead, was looking to merge. You sent him an email telling him the motherboards your team created would change the landscape of cellphone technology. The motherboards, along with your daughter, is what saved your ass, but you failed to mention they weren't ready for market."

"Daddy," Jamie said, stomping towards him. "Jared just got back from Japan. He sold those things to Tokyo Gijutsu. Their new model is going into production next month."

"And you wanted me to get a smart phone," Ryder snorted.

"Do you have any idea who you're dealing with, boy? I have gone the distance. I've been up against the likes of Apple and Microsoft and GoTech and I always come out on top. Emails can be altered. No one would believe the word of a felon over me," Archer growled.

"There's an ex-senator in New York who would disagree with you," Jamie chided.

"There's also an ex-Manning Solutions developer who would corroborate everything. And I happen to have a connection at WSEA-9. Look inside my jacket, Kitty Cat," Ryder instructed.

Jamie did as she was told and with shaky hands, she pulled out the smoking gun. Printouts of the emails along with an SD card where Ryder backed up everything, including a detailed report from the developer. It was enough information to ruin both Archer and GoTech's reputation.

"Appearances are everything," Jamie whispered.

"What do you want?" Archer bit. He didn't have a fucking leg to stand on. He knew it. Ryder knew it. Jamie knew it. It was over.

Ryder closed the distance between them. The two men, nose to nose, once again. "Leave us the fuck alone or I swear to God, I will move heaven and hell to destroy you."

Archer swallowed, dipping his chin down, accepting his defeat.

Jared stormed up behind Archer. He eyed Ryder with distain. The smug bastard, thought he'd won. "What the fuck, Jamie? Why is the busboy here? Archer I thought you took care of this?"

"I…um…" Archer stuttered. He wasn't so scary anymore, just a sad, old man who'd lost everything; his family, his company, and what little power he had left.

"Jamie is mine now," Ryder smirked, linking hands with his girl. She melted into his side, her body's natural reaction to his nearness. Jared noticed too, and his eyes flashed with anger. If looks could kill, Ryder would be as cold as the ground beneath them.

"Like hell she is. James, I don't have time for this shit." Jared waved his hand, beckoning her forward.

Jamie let go of Ryder and walked over to Jared, shoving the papers into his chest. "Find someone else to take to the White House. I quit. Come on, baby," she said, giving Ryder back the SD card. "Let's get the fuck out of here."

<hr />

"Are you okay?" Ryder asked as he climbed into the bed next to Jamie.

He still wore his tux, only managing to remove his shoes and bowtie before saying to hell with it. The tension between them was so thick he could barely breathe. Jamie was quiet the entire drive from Olympia to Seattle, quiet as they climbed the stairs to his room, and quiet when his mattress creaked as she sat on the bed. That scared him most. Jamie never missed a chance to give him shit about the damn thing, but tonight, she was different, almost withdrawn. There was so much to say, but neither of them knew where to begin.

"Are you okay?" he asked again, once the silence became too

much to bear.

"I think I'm in shock," she confessed. Her gaze dropped to her lap, and she fingered the fluffy pink trim of her dress. "How? I mean, you and my mom aren't exactly master hackers," she chuckled sadly.

"No, but your dad *is* an idiot. Did you know the password to his email is your grandfather's birthday? It might as well have been one, two, three, four."

"How did you and Caroline even…" she mused. Her big, green eyes shimmered with curiosity.

"Your mom came to the diner and spent twenty-minutes insulting me."

Jamie grimaced. "I'm sorry."

"I'm not. It was the kick in the ass I needed. A few days later, we met at a coffee shop and she said, and I quote, '*Archer is an asshole who has pissed a lot of people off. All we have to do is find someone who hates him as much as we do*'."

"We?" Jamie interrupted.

"I hate to be the one to break it to you, but your mom fucking hates your dad. She only stays with him for—"

"—appearances," Jamie finished for him.

"Yeah," he nodded. "Anyway, the first few days were dead ends. Your dad keeps everything, literally, every-fucking-thing and your mom was no help. She mostly left me to go shopping and would return hours later, annoyed that I hadn't found anything useful."

"That sounds like Caroline," she giggled.

Ryder pressed a soft kiss on her lips. "I missed your giggle."

"I missed it too," she confessed. A million unspoken words passed between them in those few seconds, yet there was still much to say.

"I scrolled through pages and pages of expense reports, meeting notes, and business proposals. Most of it I didn't understand, then I saw the resignation email. Corporate misconduct and unethical practices sounded like a smoking gun to me, so I searched for every email sent by that user and hit the motherload."

"You conquered your aversion to technology for me?"

"I mean, I may or may not have had to pay the kid behind the counter to show me how to search through the emails, but, yes, I'd do anything for you, James."

A strangled noise escaped Jamie's throat and tears flooded her eyes. "I'm sorry," she sobbed. "I'm so, so sorry. I don't deserve you. I was such a bitch. I should have never said what I said, but I just thought it would be easier for you if you hated me. You should hate me."

Ryder pulled Jamie onto his lap. "Are you afraid of me?" he asked. He understood why she had said what she said, but he needed to know if there was any shred of truth to it. It was the only way he could get past it.

"No," she choked. "No, Ryder. I know what's in here," she pointed to his heart. "I know you would never hurt me. Hell, I've done all the hurting in this relationship. I swear, I will never hurt you again. I love you more than I love myself. I will do anything for you, too."

It felt as if Ryder had waited forever to hear those words, and even with all the waiting, he wasn't prepared for how fucking elated they made him feel. Jamie was hard on the outside. A lifetime of having to protect yourself would harden anyone, but the woman beneath the savage was beautiful, kind, and so damn good, Ryder couldn't help but fall in love with her all over again.

"You just have to talk to me, Kitty Cat. From now on, when shit gets hard, you talk to me. We do this together or not at all, understand?"

"I get it. I do." Jamie nodded emphatically as a fresh wave of tears streamed down her face. "I can't believe it," she said, her voice barely a whisper.

"Believe what?"

"I'm free. Thank you for setting me free." Jamie wrapped her arms around his neck. God, he missed her scent, fruity and light.

Ryder turned, shifting her onto her back. He flipped her dress up, sending layers and layers of pink fluff flying. "You're mother still hates me," he murmured, dragging the tattered remains of her stockings down her legs. "She'll probably try to kick my ass to the curb as soon as she finds a suitable replacement."

"The only man for me has a flip phone and likes pineapples on his pizza," Jamie exhaled, pressing a kiss on the inside of her wrist.

"What was that?" he asked, tossing the mangled fabric over his shoulder.

"I got a new tattoo," she blushed, extending her wrist.

A pale pink *NR,* stared back at him. A slow smile spread across his face as he examined it. "What's *NR* stand for?"

"News Reporter," she offered with a grin.

Ryder laughed, shaking his head slowly. "I don't think so."

"Nice Rack?" she giggled as he plopped on top of her. His mouth found hers and he relished the taste of her lips.

"You want to know what I think?" he sighed, finally content.

"I'm sure you're going to tell me."

"I think you got my initials tattooed on your body," he said as he slid inside her warmth.

She moaned, "Napoleon Ryder," his name, a prayer on her lips.

EPILOGUE

Jamie

The Following Easter.

The fallout continues for solutions giant, GoTech, as the biggest recall in telecommunications history grows by an additional hundred thousand units. This comes after the company CEO, Jared Foster, negotiated an exclusive deal with Japanese retailer, Tokyo Gijutsu, to provide the motherboards for the companies MotoBlaze 8. Weeks after the Blaze 8 hit the market, customers complained of phones catching on fire.

Photos of the flaming phones went viral on social media, prompting both GoTech and Gijutsu to launch a full investigation. The result, GoTech board member Archer Manning was fired for mishandling information regarding the new technology, which promised faster performance and an elongated battery life. Manning pushed for the release of the product while head developer, Topher Lee, insisted it wasn't ready for market. Lee ultimately resigned and Manning pushed the product through to manufacturing.

In an official statement, Foster claims to have been completely unaware of the misconduct and has resigned his bid for Representative Hudson's seat in The House, stating the need to focus on rebuilding the integrity of his company. When asked about his relationship with Manning's daughter, he simply said, there will always be a place in his heart for Jamie, and one day, hopefully soon, they will find their way back to each other.

"Turn that shit off," Ryder scoffed, exiting the kitchen, holding a platter full of crack ham. He was flanked by his bunny-ear-wearing band mates, CT and Javi.

Jamie rolled her eyes, but did as she was told. Last year had been a rollercoaster of emotions. First, her baby, then the distance between her and Kensie, meeting Ryder, Chris' surgery, and all the stuff with her dad; she was just happy to be watching the fallout—not living it.

"Language, Napoleon," Annette chastised, swatting her son on the shoulder. "Dinner's ready. Everyone come and sit down."

Jamie stood, along with her brother, and Parker and they each took a seat around the Easter table. Pastel blues, and pinks, and purples dotted the eight-seater. Annette was elated to be able to use the table extension. Normally, Easter was just her and Ryder, but this year they had a full house.

"Mother," Jamie scolded, "don't be rude."

Caroline sighed dramatically and stood. "I refuse to eat anything that woman cooks, but I guess it wouldn't kill me to sit at the monstrosity she calls a dinner table."

"No, but I might," Annette muttered.

Life was beautiful. The eggs were dyed, the garland was hung, and Jamie was surrounded by her family.

"Mom, can you pass the ham please?" Ryder asked. He was drooling.

"Baby, you've got a little something right there." Jamie leaned in for a kiss, and her tongue swiped at the saliva on the corner of his mouth. He loved his mother's ham, and she loved him.

"You two are gross," Javi teased.

Jamie grinned at Ryder. They were totally *that couple*, it was so fucking cheesy.

"Caroline, dear, can you put the flask down long enough to thank the Lord for allowing us to see another Easter?" Annette arched a brow at Jamie's mother. Those two still didn't get along, but deep down, they were kindred spirits. Women who didn't always make the best choices, but did what they had to do for their children.

"It won't kill you Mom," Chris said, from across the table. Chris and Parker were back on the East Coast full-time and planned to get married after graduation.

"Fine," Caroline huffed, putting the vodka down. She stood, clasping hands with her son to her right and Jamie to her left. "Not too much ham for you though, dear," she added eyeing her daughter. Jamie rolled her eyes.

Some things never changed, but some things did.

Caroline had filed for divorce shortly after the Christmas party. Unfortunately, Jamie's father was a petty bastard, fighting her tooth and nail on every aspect of their combined estate. Caroline pretended to be unaffected, but sometimes, when they were alone, Jamie could spot the cracks in her mother's armor.

Annette said grace, thanking God for everything he'd done, for everything he'd given. Then they took their seats. Jamie helped herself to a double portion of ham, and Caroline nearly had a heart attack when she piled a big glob of mac and cheese onto her plate.

Dinner was a success. Everyone, except Caroline, ate until they were stuffed. "Who wants pie?" Annette asked, chuckling at the answering chorus of groans. Everyone balked at the idea of another bite, everyone but the drummer and bass player; they were high, so it didn't count. "Thank you, boys. One slice won't kill the rest of you."

The phone rang. Annette and Ryder locked eyes. "It's probably for you, Napoleon."

Jamie gave Ryder's thigh a reassuring squeeze and he stood and stalked over to the rotary phone hanging on the wall. The spiral cord tangled into a ball as he grabbed the phone from the receiver. "Hello?" he said, his voice hesitant. The whole table watched Ryder's back as the conversation wore on. "Happy Easter to you too… yeah, she made the ham…No, we're just finishing up…We have a show in Oakland at the end of the month if you wanna come…Okay…I'll tell her…bye Dad."

Ryder's relationship with his father was strained, but they were working on it. His dad had been sober for a little over two years, and he worked every day to prove to his son that he was a changed man. Jamie suggested they try therapy, but Ry said he wasn't ready and she didn't push. For now, they talked occasionally. Sometimes the talks were good and other times they weren't. There was so much to forgive, but Ryder's heart was big enough to contain multitudes.

"Are you okay, baby?" Jamie asked as Ryder returned to the table.

He rested his forehead against hers, and their noses touched. "Never better, and you?"

"I'm the happiest girl in the world," she said, because it was true.

Life was suffering; at least that's what the Buddhists believed. James Michele Manning knew a thing or two about suffering. She'd spent her life craving the conditional love of her father, but what she really craved was to have someone to catch her when she fell. Ryder wasn't perfect, neither was their love, but he showed up, every single day. He loved Jamie, even when she didn't love herself.

Love was patient.

Love was kind.

Love endured.

Ryder was love, and his love was divine.

THE END

AUTHOR'S NOTE

If you've been a fan of my work for a while now, you'll know I started my creative writing career with fanfiction. I'm a reader first and foremost. I fell in love (became obsessed) with someone else's characters. They moved me to the point where I wanted to create more stories with them. Then in October of last year (2016 for anyone in the future) tragedy struck my family and I realized life was short, and I needed to follow my dreams while I was still around to chase them. Enter in Jamie and Ryder. In April, 2017 I began their journey. I went through the highest highs and the lowest lows writing them. I didn't think I was good enough to tell a story of my own, but here we are. They are my babies, my first, and I hope you enjoyed reading about them as much as I enjoyed writing them. CT is up next. His story inspired this whole universe. For those of you who are new to my work, I can't wait for you to read it. For those who know what to expect, I hope the new version lives up to the original.

Thank you for reading.
As always, Unedited & Slightly Inebriated,
Carmel.

Waves Spoiler Group:
www.facebook.com/groups/1957704077844712

Playlist:
open.spotify.com/user/author.carmelrhodes
playlist/72nAMuAtpliKVaRfnhCVhD?si=KHQQWkdZ

Pinterest Board:
www.pinterest.com/authorcarmelrhodes/lithium-waves

Reader Group:
www.facebook.com/groups/299310880471688/?source_id=412662795801262

Website:
authorcarmelrhodes.wordpress.com

Amazon:
www.amazon.com/Carmel-Rhodes/e/B074R6BC53/ref=ntt_dp_epwbk_0

Goodreads:
www.goodreads.com/author/show/17070667.Carmel_Rhodes

LITHIUM TIDES

A Lithium Springs Novel: Book Two
By: Carmel Rhodes

CHAPTER ONE

Girls Just Wanna Have Fun

Kensington couldn't help the small smile playing at her lips. She wasn't used to seeing herself like this. She wasn't a prude by any stretch of the imagination, but she'd never worn something so revealing—at least not in public.

Jamie Manning was the only person who could convince her to buy the red, mid-length, off the shoulder, cutout dress that did little to contain her breasts. "Under boob is the latest wave, Kensie. Kylie Jenner wore something similar last weekend," Jam said condescendingly. It was payback for Kensie making her friend buy the burgundy Zanotti's a few months back, when she used the other Jenner sister as a selling point.

"Great, because that's the look I'm going for," Kensie quipped, rolling her eyes at the blonde bombshell applying a final coat of bright red gloss to her pouty lips.

On the outside, Kensie played it cool, but inside, she'd never felt so hot. Too bad this hair and makeup would go to waste. "I just wish Trey were here to see me."

Now it was Jam's turn to roll her eyes. She never liked Kensie's boyfriend and she never missed the opportunity to tell her. "Well, he's not so you're stuck with me."

Kensie's smile quickly turned into a frown. Trey was in Nevada for his brother's bachelor party. Although he'd never given her a reason to distrust him, she couldn't help the pit that formed in her stomach when she thought about what could be *staying in Vegas.*

"Hey, no frowning," Jam scolded. "This night is supposed to be fun."

"Fun for you," Kensie reminded her friend. "Slumming it at some dive bar with you and your boyfriend isn't my idea of fun." She sounded like a snob, but Kensie didn't want to waste this dress on a grunge party in downtown Seattle. She's not even sure how she let her friend talk her into going in the first place. Kensie was more champagne and caviar than beer and chicken wings.

"Excuse me for trying to get my two favorite people in the world in the same room. It's weird that you guys haven't met."

"We met last year," Kensie corrected. When he showed up unannounced at their apartment after he and Jamie broke up. "Remind me again how you met this guy?"

Jam always had a thing for bad boys. The privileged guys they grew up with were never quite interesting enough for Ms. Manning. Kensie always assumed she would grow out of it. Sure, it was fun to sneak around with undesirables when they were in high school, but they were adults now.

Jam grinned, fluffing her tousled curls. She looked stunning as always. "Okay, so remember how I told you and my brother we met when I interviewed them for WSEA-9? Jamie said.

"Yeah," Kensie nodded, shoving her foot into a pair of strappy Louboutin's.

"That wasn't exactly the truth. We actually met at the Rabbit Hole, the bar we're going to tonight. I was with Lo—"

"—so you were drunk," Kensie supplied. She wasn't jealous of Lorena. Okay, maybe just a little.

"Yes, smart ass. Anyway, I was trying to fight the attraction to him all night, but I couldn't take my eyes off him," Jamie explained. "His stage presence was electric, he had the entire crowd captivated, hanging on his every word, his every note. I had to have him, scratch lead singer off my fuck-him list, ya know," she winked.

"I knew every girl in the bar was thinking the same thing and I was kind of a bitch to him when he approached me earlier in the night, so I needed to do something big. I wasn't leaving that bar without feeling him inside me."

Kensie bit down on her bottom lip. She didn't realize how tightly her thighs were pressed together. She'd never admit it, but she loved hearing all about Jam's conquests. Of course, she had Trey and their lovemaking was great, but Kensie always wondered what it would feel like to be fucked.

"So, how'd you do it?" Kensie breathed, heat rising from her core. She didn't know if it was the skimpy dress or the details of Jam's latest conquest that made her so flush, but she did know the only man who could extinguish the flame burning inside her was doing God knows what in Las Vegas.

"I walked up to the stage and flashed him," Jam said proudly.

"WHAT?" Kensie shrieked. She knew her best friend was a go-getter but she had no idea she was that brazen.

"Yep. It was insane. We didn't even make it out of the bar, we fucked in the back office."

"You had sex in a dirty office?" Kensie blushed.

"With the bartender."

Oh my god. Kensie, thought. What was she getting herself into?

A pang of fear poured through Kensie's veins as the Uber driver pulled up in front of the small brick building. Had it not been for the line outside the door, she would have sworn the place was abandoned. "Are you sure this is safe?" Kensie questioned, tempted to have the car take her back to their apartment.

"Yes, Kensie. Do you really think I would bring you somewhere that wasn't safe?"

Kensie thought about it for a moment; as wild and carefree as Jamie was, she'd always been fiercely protective of her best friend.

"Alright Manning, let's just go before I change my mind."

A chill ran down Kensie's spine as they exited the Uber. She couldn't tell if it was caused by the cool breeze that greeted them as they stepped onto the street or if it was how uncomfortable she felt in the red dress riding dangerously high up her thighs.

"They must be pretty good," she commented, noting the growing line. "I wonder how long we'll have to wait?"

"Hmf," Jam snorted. "Fuck waiting, we're VIP, babe." Jamie walked right up to the bouncer, bypassing the line entirely. He was the largest man Kensington had ever seen, six foot six and all muscle.

His grim face lit up with amusement upon seeing Jamie. "Hey, Kitty Cat," he smiled, waving them forward, despite the groans from the crowd. "Who's your friend?" He eyed Kensie up and down, pausing at the strappy, black Louboutins on her feet. Apparently, he missed the *don't eye fuck the patrons,* class in bouncer school.

"Kensie, this is Tee," Jam introduced, trying and failing to stifle her laugh. "Tee, this is my best friend, Kensington. I'm popping her Rabbit Hole cherry."

Kensie shot her best friend a look that said, *please don't encourage him. After all, she has a boyfriend.*

"Hurry the fuck up," someone yelled angrily from the line.

Heat crept up her neck. She was sure her face was now as red as the dress currently painted on her body.

Taking her by the hand, Jamie led Kensie inside. The bar was much bigger than she thought. It was dark and the wooden panels covering the walls were painted blood red and plastered with various posters for live shows and upcoming events. The Rabbit Hole's claim to fame was a skee-ball tournament held every Tuesday night.

There was no wait at the bar. The show was in full swing, and most people were already down by the stage. "I need a drink!" Kensie yelled over the music.

"What would you like, princess?" Jam asked, snagging two empty barstools."

Kensie thought for a moment. She hadn't been to a place like this since college, she was wearing a tight red dress that left little to the imagination, and she missed her boyfriend desperately. There was only one thing that could salvage this night. "Tequila."

"Tequila it is." Jamie smirked.

An hour and four shots later, Kensie was relaxed and curious to learn more about the men on stage. "The band is decent. What's their name?"

"Lithium Springs," Jamie said, wistfully. Kensie could practically see hearts in her eyes. Jamie was normally the love 'em and leave type of girl, but this was new. Nice. Strange, but if anyone deserved love, it was Jamie. Seeing her so in love with this Ryder was strange-- nice-- but strange.

"Wanna dance?" she asked, pointing toward the stage.

"Hell yes." Jam jumped off her stool and dragged Kensie through the crowd until they reached the front. There was no room to move, forget dancing, Kensie was just trying to stay on her feet.

The music was intense. Kensie understood what Jam had been trying to explain earlier. The way they commanded the stage, she couldn't keep her eyes off them. It didn't hurt that they were all gorgeous.

The lead singer, Jam's Ryder, was tall and slim and covered in tattoos. He was shirtless, revealing the two shiny metal bars that pierced each of his nipples, and his black skinny jeans hung dangerously low on his hips.

The bassist was equally as handsome and equally as tatted. His light brown skin glistened with sweat as his fingers deftly plucked at the strings on his bass guitar.

Behind them, partially hidden behind a drum kit, was the most beautiful man Kensington had ever laid eyes on. If the other two men were kings, this man was a god. His face was perfection. The light brown hair covering his jaw matched the curly, brown tendrils peeking out from under his black baseball cap. His strong arms were covered with brightly colored tattoos, intricately interwoven together to tell a story, his story.

But as good as all that was, the best part of him, the part that had Kensie weak-kneed and breathless, was his eyes. Those mysterious blue orbs bore straight into her soul and left her feeling more exposed than the red fuck'em dress ever could.

She stood there, statue stiff, as the sounds of the final guitar riff crescendoed. The crowd swayed, a sea of sweaty bodies propelled her forward until she was pinned against the stage.

She couldn't move.

She couldn't breathe.

She couldn't help the moisture pooling between her legs.

The skimpy thong she wore under her dress was drenched. The tiny swath of fabric was no match for her wetness.

"Kensie. Kensington! Let's go," Jam screamed, shaking her out of her daze. The music stopped and Ryder thanked the crowd for coming out, reminding everyone to download their latest EP. She took a moment to regain her composure before turning to look at her friend.

Go?

Just as Kensie was preparing to protest, Trey's face flashed in her mind. Yes, she needed to get the fuck out of there. She needed air. She needed to put some distance between her and her blue-eyed tormentor. She needed new panties.

Kensie followed Jam to the back of the bar. Her head was spinning. She was so preoccupied with trying to figure out what the fuck that was back there, she didn't notice Jam following the large bouncer from before. She didn't question him leading them out the side door, and she didn't question climbing into the waiting van. She didn't know when Jam called the Uber but she was glad to see it.

"That was intense," Kensie breathed.

"I know, right?" Jam agreed distractedly. Her eyes locked on the door.

"Why aren't we moving?" Kensie questioned, realizing for the first time that no one was in the driver's seat. Her heart was pounding. She looked to her friend, the friend who came here with every intention of introducing her to the lead singer of the band they just watched perform. "Jam?"

Even in the dark alley, Kensie saw Jamie's eyes light up. Her breath caught in her throat as the side door swung open once again. She felt his presence long before she ever saw his face. Ryde exited the club first, then the bassist, and then him, the drummer with the eyes that caused her soul to shake.

"Jam?" she repeated. The van door opened and Ryder pulled Jamie up from her place next to Kensie and redirected her to the back row, winking at her as he gave her friend a firm smack on the ass.

The bassist was at the door next, looking at her like she was something to eat. "I'm Javi," he extended his hand, his voice dripped with sex.

Before she could reply, she heard him, his deep voice just as intoxicating as the rest of him. "Back off, homie," he growled, grabbing Javi by the shoulders. "She's mine."

Kensie knew she should protest. They were fighting over who gets dibs, like she wasn't even there, like she wasn't a person, just a snack to be devoured.

Javi looked at Kensie longingly and sighed, "you're lucky it's your birthday, mother fucker."

His birthday.

She committed the date to memory and instantly hated herself for it. She hated the way her traitorous body reacted when he'd called her his, hated the rush she felt as he climbed in the van and sat next to her, completely invading her personal space. Their legs touched and he draped his arm lazily around her small frame and pulled her into his side.

She fit perfectly, like she was made for him.

Jam giggled behind her. Javi jumped in the front passenger seat and the bouncer, Tee, got in the driver's side.

She knew she needed to break the contact. She knew she needed to get the hell out of there before she did something she would regret, but instead, she looked up at the man absently rubbing circles on her knee and whispered, "I'm Kensie."

"CT," he grinned.

Her poor thong never stood a chance.

Kensie should have liberated herself from CT's arms, but his touch paralyzed her. His strong body made her feel safe, his bright tattoos were mesmerizing. He was like a Calla Lily, gorgeous, but toxic, and 100% likely to cause a rash. She'd always been the careless one, and she couldn't deny the affect he had on her.

God, she was an awful person. Trey was loving, and kind, and he trusted her. Yet, there she was having illicit thoughts about a complete stranger.

"Everything ok?" CT asked, noticing the shift.

"I have a boyfriend." Kensie admitted, biting down on her lip. She hated herself for saying it, then hated herself for wishing she hadn't. She loved Trey.

She was in love Trey.

"I'm not trying to be your boyfriend," he smirked, bringing his thumb to her mouth, gently wiggling her bottom lip free. His words stung, although she wasn't sure why. She was in love with Trey.

"Good." Kensie shifted, trying to put as much distance between them as the cramped space would allow.

"Not so fast." CT hauled her back under his arm. His hand ghosted up the hem of her dress, higher and higher. "This is short," he said, more to himself than to her. His face burrowed into the side of her neck, while his beard tickled the soft skin there.

"I have a boyfriend," she gasped as his teeth grazed her ear. The move sent her heart into convulsions.

"Tonight, I'll be the one fucking you."

Kensie pressed her lips into a thin line. She couldn't let the small moan forming in her throat escape; she couldn't encourage him. "Listen," she whispered once she'd forced the moan back to where it came from. "I know you're probably used to girls throwing themselves at you but you're barking up the wrong tree. I have a boyfriend and he's the only one who gets to fuck me."

A smile danced on CT's lips, amusement twinkled in his eyes. He was trying not to laugh and he was failing miserably. The cocky bastard had the audacity to laugh in her face and it pissed Kensington off.

Anger was good. The anger coursing through her veins helped suppress the lust that nearly consumed her seconds ago. Kensie wiggled out from under his long arm and gave him a hard shove. CT fell onto the seat, laughing hysterically on his way down.

"Care to tell us what's so funny?" Javi inquired from the front seat.

"Nothing," he croaked, regaining composure. He righted himself and returned his arm to its home around Kensie's neck. "You're funny," he whispered, his mouth on her ear. His warm breath sent a chill down her spine.

"And you're a pig," she huffed, crossing her arms over her chest. She was going for incensed, but feared she came off as insolent.

"So, where is this boyfriend of yours tonight, and why was he stupid enough to let you out of the house in this?" he asked, slipping his hand back up her thigh.

Kensie should have moved it, but they were trapped in a moving vehicle, so it was pointless. He just kept coming back, that's what she told herself anyway.

"His brother is getting married; they're in Vegas for his bachelor party."

"I should send his brother a thank you gift then." CT gently massaged her leg.

Back and forth.

Back and forth.

His hand crept up, centimeter by centimeter, until it reached the edge of her thong. The arm around Kensie's shoulder pulled her closer until their foreheads met. "These are drenched."

There it was again, the moan threatening to break free. She bit down on her bottom lip, hoping to keep it at bay. This man was more intoxicating than the tequila she guzzled earlier.

She didn't mean to part her legs; it was her body reacting to the sensual torment. CT's fingers tugged at the useless material covering her, twisting and turning before releasing it with a soft thud. She was his instrument and he played her masterfully.

"I have a boyfriend." It was a plea and thankfully her prayers were answered. The car lurch to a stop and Kensie released a breath she didn't realize she was holding. The overhead lights sprang to life, illuminating the cabin of the van. Slowly, so deliriously slow, CT withdrew his hand from between her legs. "Do you get this wet for him?" he asked, his voice low, garbled.

Don't encourage him Kensington.

Don't encourage him.

Don't.

"No," she breathed.

Coming Spring 2018

Made in the USA
San Bernardino, CA
14 November 2017